NEAR THE RUINS OF PENHARROW

NEAR THE RUINS OF PENHARROW

A CORNISH ROMANCE, BOOK THREE

DEBORAH M. HATHAWAY

DRAFT HORSE
PUBLISHING

BOOKS BY DEBORAH M. HATHAWAY

A Cornish Romance Series

On the Shores of Tregalwen, a Prequel Novella

Behind the Light of Golowduyn, Book One

For the Lady of Lowena, Book Two

Near the Ruins of Penharrow, Book Three

In the Waves of Tristwick, Book Four (Pre-Order)

Book Five (Poppy Honeysett's Story), Coming Soon

Belles of Christmas Multi-Author Series

Nine Ladies Dancing, Book Four

On the Second Day of Christmas, Book Four

Seasons of Change Multi-Author Series

The Cottage by Coniston, Book Five

Sons of Somerset Multi-Author Series

Carving for Miss Coventry, Book One

Timeless Regency Collection

The Inns of Devonshire—The Coachman's Choice

For my Grandma Cox—
Your support and love for my books
was incomparable.

May you still read in Heaven.

PRONUNCIATION GUIDE

Gwynna – GWIN-uh
Trevethan – treh-VEH-thin
Penharrow – pehn-HAIR-oh
Coffrow – COFF-row
Fynwary – fin-WARE-ee
Golowduyn – goal-oh-DEW-in
Tregalwen – treh-GAWL-when
Kerensa – keh-REN-zuh
Jago – JAY-go
ye – ee

CHAPTER ONE

Cornwall, 1815

The soothing sound of the sea's waves coasted toward the shoreline, creeping over the cliff's edge where stood the soaring Wheal Favour Engine House.

The mine's main building pressed up against the upper cliff behind it, as if its grey stone walls kept the land from falling forth onto the pathway before it, or farther into the sea three hundred feet below. The burnt red chimney released wispy smoke into the blue skies, and arched windows spotted the tall, rectangular walls.

As striking as the image was, Gwynna Merrick was captured instead by the sea. She couldn't remember the last time the water rested so calm and clear. The sun flashed against the slight swells, shifting from light blue to dark with each tepid wave, like the fabric she'd seen last market day displayed in the windows of the modiste's shop—rich, blue silk as soft as a flower's petal.

Of course Gwynna hadn't touched the fabric herself. She could never afford such a thing. She couldn't even afford a few extra hairpins, of which, incidentally, she was in great need. She told Mama the wind had stolen them, but they both knew Gwynna removed them herself, consequentially losing them one by one.

She couldn't help it. Where was the joy in walking along the cliffside if she couldn't allow the wind to run its fingers through her hair?

Even now, with her brown locks held back by a frayed, scanty cloth, the wind pulled stray strands out, curving them round her face and across the bottom of her nose.

She pursed her lips and wrinkled her nose to scratch the tickle. The ocean responded with a deep, rumbling laugh.

No, Gwynna couldn't afford fabric, pins, or even a new ribbon for her hair. But the sea was hers for the taking.

A metal bell clanged behind her, sharp and jarring against the lull of the ocean, but Gwynna didn't flinch a muscle.

After nearly ten years of the disruptive chime, she'd begun to expect it, as well as the subsequent sounds that always followed. The miners singing as they ascended from the nearby shaft. The creaking of the mine's whim slowly ceasing, wheeling up the last of the kibbles filled to the brim with damp ore.

Elderly maidens would soon shoo children away from the whirling gears now slowing, and barrows, spades, and hammers would drop to the ground, clanging loudly against each other or with dull thuds on the ore.

The bal maidens and children working on the surface would then stretch out their aching backs and tightened arms before gathering together in groups of family or friends, situating themselves on patches of grass or heather or simply the dirt beneath their feet.

Gwynna had done the very same with her father and brother, once the men had made it to the surface. They'd eat pasties Mama had made earlier and swap stories about their day, hoping to feel refreshed before the bell signaled the end of crib, their midday meal—their only break.

That was before, though. Now, with the new mine owner, Mr. Peter Trevethan, and a new captain to oversee the running of Wheal Favour, they were allotted two breaks per day. Papa said things were different. Better.

Gwynna would have to take his word for it. She hadn't worked at the mine in months.

"Gwynna!"

Papa. He'd finally come up. Gwynna turned, meeting his eyes with a smile. He waited on the incline beside the engine house. His hands cupped his mouth then waved her toward him.

Gwynna swept one last glance across the sea then pulled herself up the short, steep hill.

"Are ye ready?" Papa asked when she reached him.

His chin-length hair slid out from his tattered, brown cap. The stubble growing on his jaw was darker than usual, made black by the dust and soot from the shaft. He squinted heavily, still adjusting to the bright sunshine, though the hesitation churning in his green eyes was evident.

Gwynna had always loved her father's eyes. Hers were more amber-colored. "I am, Papa."

"Ye don't 'ave to do this. We be managin' just fine without ye workin' here."

That wasn't true, and they both knew it. No matter the help she was to her mother at home, and no matter the odd work Gwynna had found in and around St. Just mending clothing or helping with others' harvests, her family still struggled for money—as did most miners.

She eased her arm through his and led the way to the upper cliff. "I know, Papa. And I know ye want me safe. 'Tis time, though."

Her gentle tone did nothing to raise his sunken shoulders, but then, they'd appeared such a way since June last. If her staying safe at home hadn't raised his spirits by now, it never would.

Two bal maidens sat together on a patch of grass, neither of them looking up as Gwynna and Papa passed by. A group of children ran alongside them, their laughter lifting the air. Papa maintained his somber look, but Gwynna smiled back at them, refusing to lose her resolve.

Stubborn rocks, half-buried in the earth, dappled the dusty pathway they ambled up—a pathway created by hundreds of footsteps coming and going to and from the mine. Those footsteps belonged to many in her family. Her father, her brother, even at one time her mother.

And now, Gwynna was proud to have them belong to her once more.

Before long, the counthouse rose before them, a small, three-room hut with nearly slatted walls and a roof constructed of buckling, faded wood. The structure had been there since she was a child, though small improvements had been made over the last few months, including the expansion of a spare room and kitchen.

Papa tapped on the door, and a loud voice bade them enter.

A resounding creak echoed as Papa opened the door, his boots thudding on the wooden floor. Gwynna quickly followed.

A small hearth to the right of the room carried a few blackened logs, the fire having no doubt been left to wane as the late August sun warmed the room instead. The walls were bare but clean, the floor had been freshly swept, and two chairs were neatly tucked in beneath a small table pressed up against a side wall. It wasn't much to look at, but the room certainly was a great deal tidier than the last time she was there. Was this due to Mr. Trevethan, as well?

A single window at the far side of the room spilled light onto a small, wooden desk. A gentleman sat behind it, leaning over a paper, scratching madly with his quill.

Another middle-aged man spoke to him, standing in front of the desk with a fisted hand on his waist. "Of course I'm happy to support Mr. Trevethan with my finances, but I cannot agree to attend any further meetings here. My jacket is littered with dust each time I step foot in this dingy room, and the people, well..." He glanced over his shoulder at Gwynna and her father, continuing in a softer tone. "As much as one might attempt, one cannot improve the state of a miner, nor his family. In manner *or* cleanliness."

Gwynna bristled. How she despised those who thought themselves above miners.

The man still seated continued to write, though he nodded his head distractedly. He must be the new mine captain, Mr. Harvey. Gwynna had never met him, but Father said he was a just man, like Mr. Trevethan. "I understand your frustrations, Mr. Pinnick," Mr. Harvey said, "but the counthouse is where we have all agreed to convene. If it displeases you, you are always welcome to forgo the next investor's meeting."

"Perhaps I will," Mr. Pinnick said. "Do tell Mr. Trevethan when you see him today."

"Of course, sir."

Mr. Pinnick made for the door where Gwynna and Papa still stood. A dismissive wave from the man signaled them to move without so much of a glance in their direction, but Father lingered with a raised chin before stepping aside.

The gentleman sniffed, muttering as he departed from the room. "Miners. All the same. Disdainful, filthy..."

His words were silenced as the door closed.

Gwynna and Papa exchanged glances. They'd grown accustomed to such opinions from the upper class, but hearing the words still set them on edge.

"Merrick."

Mr. Harvey beckoned them forward with a flick of his finger. He had yet to look up from his paper.

The floor groaned as the father and daughter approached the desk. A clang from the side room—a small kitchen—drew

Gwynna's attention to an older woman juggling pans in her arms. She placed them on a small shelf near a window then turned sharp eyes on Gwynna.

That was why the rooms were tidier. Mr. Trevethan had hired a counthouse woman to oversee its cleanliness.

When her nod to the woman wasn't reciprocated, Gwynna returned her attention to Mr. Harvey, who wiped his quill free of ink and replaced the cap on the bottle.

"So," he began, lacing his fingers together and leaning one elbow on his armrest, "you said you wanted to meet with me?"

Papa removed his cap, his stringy hair falling over his eyes before he raked it back with his fingers. "Yes, sir. 'Tis me daugh'er, Gwynna. She be wantin' her job back as a maiden."

"I see." Mr. Harvey leaned forward in his chair once more, holding his unfinished correspondence by its corners to set it aside. He then plunked a large, leather-bound book before him. "How long did you work here before you left, Gwynna?"

"Ten years or so, sir."

His eyes met hers under a raised brow. "Might I ask why you left? Did the work environment not suit?"

"No, sir. But I..." She glanced to Papa with a parted mouth.

What could she say? The work environment certainly had *not* suited, but that wasn't why she'd left.

"She be needed at 'ome," Papa responded instead.

Mr. Harvey's scrutinizing gaze shifted between them both, but he allowed them their secrets as he opened his book. "Have you any other children working here, Merrick?"

"No, sir. She be all we 'ave...now."

CHAPTER TWO

A hollowness expanded in Gwynna's chest, as if her heart had stopped its beating. She'd grown accustomed to such emptiness. It had been there since June, just like the constant presence of Papa's sunken shoulders.

Mr. Harvey glanced up. "Casualty in an accident?" His words were brief, but his tone had softened.

Papa raised his head in a sort of nod. "Yes, me son, Jago." He cleared his throat. "We lost 'im a few months back."

She hung her head. Jago. Her parents' only son, and Gwynna's only sibling. He had been one of her closest friends, killed because…

But she wouldn't allow herself to dwell on the accident, or how greatly she missed her brother. Not when she needed her courage fortified, preserved, for the work ahead.

"You have my condolences, Merrick," Mr. Harvey said.

"Thank ye, sir."

The mine captain paused, clearly wishing to say something more, but he redirected his attention to his book. He must have been as uncomfortable as Papa with the compassion he'd shown. "We've had a few bal maidens leave us recently, so you've come at the right time. I have a place in bucking that I think will suit you just fine."

Gwynna dipped her head. Bucking. That was the last thing she wished to do, crushing rocks into powder, damaging her fingers, inhaling and tasting the dust of the copper ore. The task had to be one of the most grueling assignments at the mine, and she had suffered through it for nearly four years before advancing elsewhere.

Fortunately, Papa was not unaware of her feelings for the chore. He wrung his cap in his soot-covered fingers. "Sir, mightn't there be a place here, in the count'ouse? Me Gwynna be a fine cook and a hard worker."

A barely discernible huff came from the kitchen. The count-house woman stared at Gwynna with beaded eyes, as if Gwynna had tracked horse manure across her clean floors.

Gwynna sniffed. She couldn't smell anything beyond wet wood and smoke.

"We haven't the need for more than one, I'm afraid," Mr. Harvey said, his head still bowed as he uncapped his bottle of ink.

The woman raised her chin and walked triumphantly away, fiddling once more with the pans.

Thank goodness there wasn't a place for Gwynna here. What a prison the counthouse would be, remaining inside, cooking, cleaning, and washing day in and day out, all with that woman lording over her. She'd almost prefer bucking.

Almost.

With a sidelong glance, she caught Papa's eye. He was already staring down at her, shaking his head.

"Please?" she mouthed out.

He added a lowered brow to reaffirm his refusal.

They had discussed this the night before. Papa would push for the safest task for Gwynna, and *she* would not speak unless Mr. Harvey addressed her.

She didn't blame Papa for his desire to acquire her a safe placement, especially after what happened to Jago. But this was a mine, and the duties where she could be out of harm's way were few and far between.

She just couldn't go back to bucking.

"Sir?"

"Gwynna," Papa warned under his breath.

Mr. Harvey glanced up with a quirked brow. "Yes?"

Well, there it was. The mine captain was asking her a question. It would be rude not to answer him.

Sorry, Papa.

"I don't mean to speak out o' turn, sir. But I...I be better at spallin'."

"Spalling?"

"Yes, sir. 'Tis what I did 'fore I left."

Spalling wasn't any easier than bucking, in her opinion, what with a larger hammer and more forceful hitting. But at least then she'd be out in the open air with a view of the sea. That was always a fine distraction, and a distraction was necessary during hard labor.

"Spalling," Mr. Harvey repeated under his breath, mulling the word over.

Gwynna stood still as he eyed her from her boots to her head.

The previous mine captain had attempted to coerce many a maiden to, well, to engage in activities befitting a woman of ill repute. Fortunately, with Papa and Jago at the mine, he'd kept his distance from Gwynna. But that didn't mean the mine captain didn't leer at her from afar, discomfiting her in the worst way.

Mr. Harvey, however, was simply judging her capabilities— as was evident by the way his eyes skimmed away from where they ought not linger.

Rather than bestowing comfort, however, that realization

cinched a knot around her hope, nearly severing it. She was taller than the average woman, it was true, but nearly half the width of the other bal maidens—a fact that was not in her favor.

She took a step forward. "I know I ain't be as stuggy as the other maidens who be spallin', but I can do the work, sir. I can."

Mr. Harvey rubbed his jaw. He needed further convincing. Gwynna peered up at Papa with silent pleading.

His jaw twitched. Gwynna wouldn't blame him if he dragged her right out of the counthouse with a severe scolding. In truth, she probably deserved it.

Fortunately, Papa blew out a heavy breath and faced Mr. Harvey. "'Tis true, sir. Gwynna be stronger than she looks. She be the finest at spallin' you'll ever see. A keen eye for breakin' the ore down, and she be determined. As ye can see now."

Gwynna bounced up on the tips of her toes at Papa's hidden smile. He didn't want her working at the mine, that much was clear. But Papa had never been able to hide his pride in his daughter's strength, even if it went against his wishes.

Finally, Mr. Harvey leaned toward his book again. "Very well. Mary Hocking has left us, so we *are* in need of a replacement in spalling."

Gwynna bit the inside of her cheek. She knew full well her friend Mary had recently married and quit the mine to live in St. Ives with her new husband—leaving a vacancy at Wheal Favour perfect for Gwynna. But Papa didn't need to know that.

She avoided his suspicious gaze and focused hard on the words Mr. Harvey scrawled in his book. She could only slightly recognize a few of the letters.

G, w, y...

He continued to write as he spoke. "I suspect you won't have a problem working hard, being your father's daughter. But if you struggle or can't keep up with the ore given you, know that we will have to move you to bucking."

If that wasn't motivation to prove her work ethic, nothing was.

"Will you be ready to start next Tuesday?"

A vein of disappointment cut through her excitement, but she nodded anyway. She dared not test her father or push the mine captain further by telling them that date conflicted with plans she'd made weeks before. Mr. Harvey wouldn't care, and Papa, well, this was another piece of information he didn't need to know. Ever. She would simply adjust her plans and continue in silence.

After Mr. Harvey finished instructing her about the certain rules of the mine she'd been abiding by since she was a child, they bade farewell to the mine captain and made to quit the counthouse.

No sooner than they reached the door, however, did it swing wide open, causing them both to take a quick step back.

Two gentlemen entered the room. Gwynna recognized the first as Mr. Trevethan. She'd never spoken with him before but had often seen him from afar as she'd visited with Papa during his breaks.

"Merrick, my apologies," Mr. Trevethan said after noting he'd nearly hit them with the door. "I didn't know you'd be in here."

"Not a problem, sir."

The second gentleman, no doubt a new investor, moved out from behind Mr. Trevethan.

At first glance, Gwynna was rather struck. Not dumb, by any means. She was not the sort of woman to fall down at a man's feet. But to say she didn't admire a handsome face would be an obvious lie—and he certainly had a handsome face. Straight nose, firm jaw, distinguished cheekbones. Dark eyes below even darker brows.

No doubt the bal maidens outside stopped their chatting when *he* walked by.

"Did you have business with Mr. Harvey?" Mr. Trevethan asked, glancing between the mine captain and Papa.

"Yes, sir. We be askin' for me daugh'er Gwynna to return as a maiden."

Mr. Trevethan shifted his attention to Gwynna. "Excellent news. We'll be happy to have another Merrick with us."

Mr. Rosewall—the previous owner—very rarely came to the mine, and he *never* spoke with the miners, let alone the bal maidens. Now Gwynna knew why Papa spoke so highly of Mr. Trevethan.

"I thank ye, sir," she responded.

Her attention wavered for the smallest moment toward the younger gentleman again—she pegged him to be in his mid-twenties—and found his eyes on her.

One side of his mouth turned down but not in a frown. It appeared more as if he were attempting to hide a smile. What did he find so humorous, the raggedy fabric in her hair? Had she dirt on her face? She'd almost prefer him to blatantly ignore her, as Mr. Pinnick had done.

Papa inched toward the door. "Excuse us, sir. Break's nearly over." He'd never been comfortable around members of the upper class. Whether he thought he wasn't deserving of their company or vice versa, Gwynna wasn't entirely certain.

"Of course, of course," Mr. Trevethan said. "Only, allow me first to introduce to you my son."

Son? Gwynna glanced between the two gentlemen. There was hardly any resemblance, unless she counted the darkness of their eyes.

"He's finally come home after all these years in Bath," Mr. Trevethan continued. "Jack, Merrick is one of the finest workers we have here at Favour." He clapped his hand on his son's shoulder. "And I'm sure his daughter will be now, too."

Jack Trevethan shifted away from his father, causing Mr.

Trevethan's arm to fall to his side. Gwynna caught a quick, uncertain glance pass between them before she dipped her head.

"Good to meet ye, sir," Papa said, his hand on the latch of the door.

The younger Mr. Trevethan didn't respond. His brown eyes traced the scant walls, the grim stretch of his lips replacing the shadow of a smile he'd nearly revealed before.

He was clearly finding fault in the room she had just admired for its cleanliness. By the sight of his silk green waistcoat and spotless cravat, he was no doubt used to extravagant ballrooms and lavish furnishings—something Gwynna had only admired from afar.

That, of course, would change for an evening not too far from now.

The click of the door Papa had finally opened drew her attention away from the gentlemen once and for all. Papa excused himself swiftly then slipped through the doorway with a nod of his head.

Gwynna promptly followed without a glance back. She didn't have time to dwell on the mine owner's son, nor his disapproval of anything less than lofty in nature. She had far more important things on which to focus—providing for her family, doing well with her upcoming work at the mine.

And soon, attending a private ball, somehow, without her true identity being discovered.

Heaven help her.

CHAPTER THREE

The door closed behind the miner and his daughter, but Jack Trevethan was still too preoccupied with the state of the room to really notice. Father had said they'd made vast improvements to the counthouse. If that was the case, how must it have appeared before? The walls hardly kept out the wind, and the roof no doubt leaked fiercely during storms.

"Come, son. Meet our mine captain, Mr. Harvey."

Jack followed Father across the creaking floor as the mine captain stood and allowed Father to take his place behind the desk. Could they only afford one for the both of them? Perhaps they should've made *that* improvement, instead of the minute bedroom Father had boasted of as they'd approached the counthouse earlier.

"I trust you are enjoying your time in Cornwall, sir," Mr. Harvey said after they'd been introduced.

"I am, thank you." Was Jack's indifference apparent? He'd always preferred Cornwall and its views to Bath and its crowds, but the bustling city had two clear advantages—it was far away from Father, and the women there were plenty.

Although, some of these bal maidens weren't half so bad to

look at. He blinked away a pair of amber eyes and placed a polite smile on his lips. "It is good to be back for a time."

Father straightened in his chair. He obviously hadn't seen through Jack's lies, still buzzing after their walk around Wheal Favour. Jack shouldn't be surprised at Father's joy in the mine. He hadn't stopped going on about it since Jack had arrived in Cornwall the day before. Father clearly had a great deal of pride in his new endeavor. He spoke of his love for it as if it were a second child.

Or his only child.

Jack, however, most certainly was *not* enjoying himself. He never would have agreed to quit Bath for Cornwall and this forsaken mine had not his conscience spoken to him—his conscience that sounded suspiciously like Mama.

Go to him, son. He wishes to see you.

Jack had started ignoring this voice more than twelve years ago—the last time he'd heard it aloud, the last time he'd seen his mother alive. But three years had gone by now without any interaction with his father. It was probably time to see to his duty for a week or two.

"This here is the logbook," Father said. "It's where we make record of all the happenings at the mine."

Jack stared mutely at the pages of the book through which Father flipped. He'd decided to remain apathetic to the mine so Father wouldn't attempt to bore him with even more details. Thus far, it hadn't worked. Why he thought Jack would be interested in a logbook was beyond him. But then, Father didn't really know Jack at all.

Sending a son away at the age of twelve to live with distant cousins and only visiting him once a year tended to have that effect.

"The new hires are recorded, as well as those who have left us," Father continued. "I think it extremely beneficial to have thorough records. Not only for us, but for those who come after. I hope when you take over Favour, you will do the very same."

He watched Jack expectantly, but Jack hesitated. He didn't want the mine, nor the responsibilities that came with it. Father was the one to make the foolhardy decision to add this to his other ventures—purchasing a second estate in Suffolk and investing in one scheme after another, anything to keep his mind busy. Why should Jack have to take all of this over because it was Father's dream?

Heavens, you could curdle milk with that scowl, Jacky.

Mama's voice echoed in the recesses of his mind once again. He *was* scowling. Mother had always said he had too fierce a frown. When he was angry, she would stroke a gentle thumb into the crease between his eyebrows until it faded away.

He was old enough to be rid of his scowls himself now. "Just so, Father."

Apparently pleased with Jack's change in demeanor, Father returned his attention to his book.

It was just as well. There wasn't any need at the moment for Jack to admit he had no desire to accept anything but monetary gains from his father. When Jack was given control of all financial matters, he'd simply sell Father's shares and businesses. His family estate, though, he'd keep. Mother loved Coffrow Place too much for Jack to ever consider selling it. He'd simply lease the house and use the money to fund the life of leisure he'd planned for his future—a life away from Cornwall, single and free to do whatever he pleased.

"Mr. Pinnick was here earlier, sir," Mr. Harvey said as Jack took to staring out the narrow window. "He once again complained about holding our meetings here."

Father sighed, rubbing his fingers against his eyes. "I wish I had never accepted his investment. He's done nothing but complain from the beginning."

"Indeed, sir."

"Have the Yeomans agreed to the use of their horse for the whim?" Father asked.

How long would they continue in this regard? Perhaps Jack should excuse himself and return to Coffrow Place alone. That would be more entertaining than listening to matters of business.

"Yes, and Mrs. Yeoman has agreed to allow her daughter to take the job."

"Excellent. And Merrick's girl. Gwynna was it?"

Jack's attention slipped back to Father. The bal maiden? She had to be more entertaining than a logbook.

"Yes, sir."

"Did you hire her for bucking?"

"No, sir. She..." Mr. Harvey paused, sliding his fingers along his jaw with an amused expression. "She was determined to do spalling instead."

Father leaned back in his chair, amused. "Indeed?"

Despite his attempt to remain indifferent, Jack's intrigue grew. Why was the girl's choice so comical?

"She was very insistent," Mr. Harvey continued, "and Merrick defended her capabilities. She worked in that position for a few years before she left, so I have hope she will do a fine job. Either way, if she does not succeed, we can move her elsewhere."

Silence followed, Father deep in thought as he tapped his finger on his lips.

Jack had seen bal maidens from afar on walks with his mother around the Cornish countryside when her health had permitted it, but he admittedly knew very little about them or mining in general.

"Why is it strange she would do...sprawling, was it?" he asked.

Father's eyes lit with excitement, but he spoke slowly, as if to prove he wasn't overtly thrilled with Jack's interest in his work.

"Spalling, actually," he corrected. "It's certainly not the most difficult job a maiden does, though they're all quite laborious. But it's essential to the economy of the mine. It requires the girls to wield a long-handled hammer to break down the ore."

"Hence why we typically reserve the spalling to the larger of the maidens. Stout, if you will," Mr. Harvey added.

"And it takes a great deal of skill to hit the ore in its proper shattering sphere."

"I see," Jack said.

He tried to imagine the slight bal maiden, Gwynna, brandishing such a tool. She was tall, as tall as the regal women he'd known in Bath, and even thinner than they were. It would be a marvel if she didn't fall over.

A smile played on his lips. No wonder Father and Mr. Harvey had been amused. Such a thing would be humorous to see. Perhaps Jack would return to the mine after all, if only to see if the maiden could, in actuality, do such a task.

He had very little faith that she could.

CHAPTER FOUR

*G*wynna flung her cloak around her shoulders as she made for the door, the depleting heels of her boots thumping across the scratched, wooden floor of her home.

"Where ye be off to then?" Mama's voice came from behind.

Gwynna adjusted the threadbare cloak until the worn fabric fell more comfortably around her. Dinner had been eaten and cleared from the small table in the corner of the room, and her parents had just sat down across from each other before the fire, Mama with a needle, thread, and a worn pair of stockings, and Papa with his pipe.

"Fynwary Hall," Gwynna replied with a skirted gaze. "I promised Sophia I'd visit."

Her parents swapped glances. "Ye have work at the mine tomorrow," Mama reminded.

As if Gwynna could have forgotten. Wheal Favour had been at the forefront of her mind nearly as often as the ball she would attend that evening.

She hoped her carefree nod was convincing enough. She disliked lying to her parents, but they simply wouldn't understand her desire to attend a high-society gathering. It was better to keep that a secret from everyone. Everyone but her upper-class friend, Mrs. Sophia Hawkins, who'd helped Gwynna's idea come to fruition.

Mama drew the frayed sides of her grey stockings together with her needle and a small piece of string. "I suppose t'wouldn't hurt if ye go. So long as ye come back 'fore dark."

Gwynna focused on the lint clinging to her faded cloak. "Oh, I-I mightn't be back 'til later. After dark, likely."

Long past dark, if she had her way.

Mama's eyebrows curved. "Why so late?"

"Ye know how Sophia and I can get to speakin'. This might be our last night to do so."

"And how do ye expect to work with so little sleep?" Mama asked next.

Gwynna dropped her eyes. For once, she didn't have to lie. "I hardly sleep now as it is."

Her parents shared another look. "Are the nightmares still occurin'?" Mama asked.

"Not as bad as they were," Gwynna lied again.

The nightmares *were* worse, more than they'd ever been before. Now, instead of simply hearing or seeing visions of Jago's death that she did not in actuality witness, she was expe-riencing in her dreams the same horrifying demise for herself.

She shook the frightful images from her mind. "So ye be all right then, with me not returnin' 'til later? Past midnight, per'aps?"

Past midnight would allot her an hour or two at the ball. Plenty of time to enjoy herself, though not anywhere long enough to be recognized or remembered.

"I suppose ye be old enough to make the decision for your-self. If Papa agrees, 'course."

Papa remained silent. Mama had always been more lenient than him.

"Father?" Gwynna pressed.

He blew out a breath from his pipe, white smoke curling in the air. "Why are ye goin'?"

Gwynna swallowed. She'd rehearsed this conversation countless times in her head. She knew the answers like she knew the frayed holes in her hem, but would her parents believe her lies? And would they ever forgive her for speaking such falsehoods?

"I be friends with Sophia. Ye know that."

Papa's expression didn't change. "Are ye certain ye still are?"

"Yes, Father," Gwynna answered carefully.

Papa had always been wary of Gwynna's friendship with Sophia. After all, it was unusual for a lady to befriend a miner's daughter. But Sophia wasn't like most members of the upper class. Not after she'd lost her fortune and most contact with her family. She'd married the Merricks' landlord and had converted to a kind, thoughtful individual, but Father still found her difficult to accept.

"I thought she'd leave ye alone," Papa continued in a steely tone, "now that she be married and wealthy again, in her fitty house with clothes and servants."

"Travers," Mama warned under her breath. Her fingers continued to stitch, though her eyes were on Papa's. "Ye know Mrs. Hawkins be a better person than her father. Ye said so yourself."

Gwynna remained silent. She knew better than to speak when Sophia's father, Mr. Rosewall, was mentioned. Mr. Rosewall had once owned Wheal Favour and was responsible for the early hardships of the mine, including Jago's death and many others. Sophia wasn't responsible for her father's reckless decisions, and Gwynna wouldn't hold that against her. But Papa did.

He pulled his pipe from his mouth, the wood clicking against his teeth. "I know she ain't be terrible, only..."

He lifted his gaze, the same fear reflected in his eyes that Gwynna had witnessed days ago at Wheal Favour.

"I don't want ye hurt, Gwynna. Many folk o' the upper class think they be better than we. I don't want ye unhappy with what ye 'ave here." He turned away, facing the fire. "Or what ye don't 'ave."

Guilt swarmed her insides like a flock of seagulls to a dead pilchard washed up on shore. Father had worked all his life for his family and had prevented them from starvation countless times. How ungrateful would Gwynna appear to him, should he learn of her attending the ball. This would be an experience she'd dreamt of her whole life, but he would only see it as what he couldn't give her.

She knelt down beside him, her knees pressing hard against the crooked floorboards. "Sophia don't believe she be better than I, not anymore. And I have everythin' I need here. Ye and Mama. A warm fire. A full stomach. How could I not be happy, Papa?"

His brow softened, and he smoothed his thumb against her cheek. "What would us do without ye, Gwynny?"

"Ye never will 'ave to answer such a question." She stood, placing a kiss against his temple. "I'll be back after midnight."

Papa nodded, sucking on his pipe before the smoke drifted once more around him. "Fine. Only promise to not allow that woman to coerce ye into doin' things ye ought not be doin'."

"Heavens, Papa. What do ye imagine us to be doin'?" Her nervous chuckle sounded far too strained. "She be a lady. She ain't be bein' up to no good, ye know."

But Gwynna was. *She* was the one to have suggested attending a ball. Sophia had merely taken the reins and galloped ahead.

"Worry not, Father," Gwynna finished with a resolute nod. "I know me own will. I be strong."

His eyes creased at the corners. "Nobody stronger than a

miner's daugh'er."

"Or a miner's wife?" Mama asked with a teasing smile.

Papa took her hand from the stocking and placed a kiss to the top of her rough skin. "That be the very truth."

Gwynna watched them for a moment. She was fortunate to have the parents she did. Not even Sophia had that.

So why was Gwynna dressing up in a fine gown and pretending to be someone she wasn't? Was she truly that selfish, so ungrateful for what she *did* have?

"Gwynna?"

She blinked, looking to her parents, who watched her expectantly.

"Are ye goin'?"

"Oh, yes."

She forced aside her feelings and opened the door, pausing as Papa called after her. "If ye be comin' home late, be sure to 'ave her bring ye home in one o' them carriages she has."

"Yes, Father."

"And do try not to stay out too late," Mama added.

"'Course."

With a small wave and a shared smile, she slipped from the house and closed the door behind her, pausing on the dirt path to draw a steadying breath.

She'd done it. She'd convinced her parents to believe her. Now she simply needed to do the same with those at the ball, as well as herself.

As she began her journey, however, no matter how she tried, she couldn't remove the worry that she was betraying her parents' trust, the work they'd done for her, and her heritage as a miner's daughter. Surely wishing to be someone else for just one evening was not so distasteful.

But then, should she not be grateful for what she had, instead of chasing after a dream of the upper class?

This was going to be more difficult than she thought.

CHAPTER FIVE

*G*wynna curled her fingers around the golden fringe of the curtain she hid behind. Slowly, she pulled the heavy, blue velvet to the side, just enough to peer through the opening, though the rest of her body remained hidden.

For the past quarter of an hour, she'd been tucked away in an alcove off of the ballroom, watching the guests trickling in like waves seeping through the cavity of a rock. With their fine dresses and jackets, their happy chatter and sparkling eyes, Gwynna wasn't sure she could face them all.

She recognized ladies she'd seen in town before, and a few investors from the mine. Mr. Pinnick, the gentleman who'd left the counthouse in a sneering huff days before, wandered through the crowds with a haughty smile. His jacket wouldn't get dirty in *this* room.

Gwynna had expected to see people she knew, but no one who might possibly know *her*, apart from the Hawkinses. Those of the upper class didn't take much notice of miners and their families, and Sophia had done her best with fulfilling a smaller guestlist. She'd also reassured Gwynna countless times that she was unrecognizable.

But was it worth the risk, walking around amidst those who might discover Gwynna's true identity?

A heaviness nestled at the bottom of her stomach. She rubbed a hand against her abdomen, attempting to settle the lead weight of her nerves, but nothing worked.

She withdrew back into the dim light of her hiding place, staring at the smooth floor beneath her dance slippers. Sophia wouldn't be happy with Gwynna expelling her morning's meager breakfast of pillas porridge onto the polished wood, or onto Sophia's pink footwear Gwynna had borrowed.

Although, if becoming sick would provide an excuse for her to return home early and abandon this ridiculous scheme...

Gwynna flattened her hands out to the side of her, steadying her body as well as her straying thoughts. She'd worked too hard getting to this point to give up now.

After hours of primping, pulling, curling, and securing, she'd finally been made presentable for that evening. The oil and dirt had been washed clean from her hair that morning, and now, the brunette ringlets at her temples shone nearly copper colored in the candlelight. Her brown dress and greyed underpinnings had long since been replaced by a soft pink gown with ribbons and lace to match.

She fit the part of a proper lady. The only problem was, she wasn't.

Music drifted toward her, the musicians tuning their instruments as the crowds brimmed. She leaned closer to the curtains, eying the splendor once again.

The ballroom had been breathtaking during the day when she'd practiced her dances with Sophia. Now, with the candles aglow and reflecting off of the crystal chandeliers and gilded mirrors, the sight was stunning. Paintings of the seaside were depicted in the highest parts of the ceiling, and the same blue curtains she hid behind adorned the tops of every large window and alcove.

Fynwary Hall's previous owner—Mr. Rosewall—had clearly used his wealth to create the opulent ballroom, instead of improving Wheal Favour when he'd owned the mine. He clearly cared very little for the state of his workers and focused more on the state of his pride.

A thread of guilt slivered round Gwynna's heart at the thought, and she withdrew into the alcove once more. As much as she liked to point out Father's dislike for Mr. Rosewall, Gwynna held just as much disdain for the gentleman who had since moved away from St. Just—disdain that she consistently and consciously had to let go.

But was Gwynna not adding to the problem he'd started? Was she not now participating in all this affluence, while her lower class friends were at home in their brown dresses, dirty aprons, and worn boots?

She couldn't deny the pride she'd felt, admiring her appearance in the mirror beforehand. Now, that pride made her conscience squirm.

"Gwynna?"

A hushed whisper passed through the curtain nearby, and Sophia's face followed, poking past the fabric. "Ah, here you are." She slipped into the alcove, closing the curtain behind her. "I thought you'd be out already."

Gwynna remained silent, tugging her gloves more securely above her elbows. She was glad for them, if only because they covered her callused fingers and her childhood scar at the back of her arm.

"Are you well?" Sophia pressed when Gwynna remained silent. She tipped her head to the side, her coal-black curls falling against her brow.

With her dark hair and blue eyes, Sophia was an incomparable beauty. Although they shared the same height and thin build, Gwynna always felt dowdy around her friend, even now, after the hours of primping she'd just undergone. Sophia was a true lady. Gwynna was just a bal maiden.

"I can't do this, Sophia," Gwynna said, her courage escaping her drop by drop.

Sophia nodded her head straightaway, though disappointment and worry shaded her bright eyes. "Is that what you really wish for, Gwynna?"

Gwynna groaned, rubbing her fingers to her temples. Sophia had worked just as hard as Gwynna to ensure they were both ready for the evening, but Sophia would never push to continue the charade if Gwynna didn't wish to.

Before, Gwynna had wanted to attend this ball so badly, but now that the consequences were laid out before her eyes, real and tangible, she wasn't sure she could continue.

"I don't know," she answered truthfully. "I just keep thinkin' 'bout someone discoverin' me dressin' above me station. I'll be tormented by the upper classes and lose me place at Wheal Favour for certain. And Mr. Hawkins and ye will be ridiculed for allowin' me under your roof. I can't do it. I can't."

She stopped, shaking her head adamantly until Sophia walked forward with outstretched hands, clasping Gwynna's fingers in her own. "My dear friend, we were both aware of the consequences from the beginning. You must remember, we have discussed every possible outcome and have taken every measure to ensure you remain unnoticed this evening."

Gwynna closed her eyes, drawing in recurrent, steady breaths. Sophia was right. They *had* taken every precaution, from ensuring the smaller guestlist included no one who might *truly* recognize Gwynna to having her learn the ins and outs of proper behavior at the ball. She'd spent weeks learning dance steps and how to dine properly. Gwynna had curtsied until her calves were sore and practiced the calculated stroll of a lady until she never wished to walk again.

They'd even taken measures to change her accent, though Gwynna had already decided to remain silent for the entirety of the evening. Her attempt at the upper class tongue was abysmal, no matter how Sophia ensured her it was "perfectly fine."

Yes, they'd planned for everything, even ensuring Gwynna knew where the servants were situated so she might avoid them all the better. Still, she was overcome with worry. "Mr. Rennalls and 'is meddlesome wife be walkin' 'round, and now Mr. Pinnick is out there. I only just saw 'im a few days past. He'll recognize me, to be sure."

And he would not hesitate to involve the constable. Mr. Hawkins had already promised to use his status as a gentleman and intervene, should the constable be implicated, but would that stop Mr. Pinnick from pushing for the harshest punishment for dressing above her station—months for Gwynna in Bodmin Jail and the loss of her work at Favour?

"Mr. Pinnick?" Sophia asked, twisting her lips. "Mr. Hawkins has told me how that man is always causing trouble amidst the investors at Wheal Favour, complaining about one thing to the next. If only he'd pull his investment so Mr. Trevethan might run the mine in peace." She shook her head. "I assure you, Gwynna, with a man that concerned with himself, I'd be shocked if he looked at anyone else beyond his own likeness in the mirrors this evening."

Her words rang true to Gwynna's agitated mind. After all, Mr. Pinnick hadn't even looked at her that morning in the counthouse, unlike Mr. Trevethan and his son.

Jack Trevethan's dark eyes appeared in her mind's eye, but she readily discarded them like she would a piece of ore with no vein of copper in sight. She wouldn't have to worry about the father and son that evening. Mr. Trevethan had already declined the invitation. According to Mr. Hawkins, the mine owner would be occupied this evening with new investors, and his son would no doubt be joining his father.

Sophia squeezed her hands reassuringly. "As I said, if you truly wish to leave now, you have my full support. But allow me to reassure you once again that no one will recognize you. No one will see you for who you really are. This is what you wished for, is it not?"

Gwynna hesitated. That *was* what she'd wanted. But now, with rouge on her lips and cheeks, and white pearls encircling her neck, matching the ones decorating the chignon at the crown of her head, she didn't even recognize herself. Her parents wouldn't have either.

She pulled away from Sophia's hold and wrapped her arms around her middle. She'd turned her back on them, all of them. She'd been at war with herself all evening, but now, dressed as she was and about to make her appearance in such a grand room, she was slowly losing the battle against her conscience.

How ashamed Mama would be of Gwynna's lies. How worthless Papa would feel, thinking he hadn't provided enough for his daughter. For surely, if he had, Gwynna wouldn't be lying to experience a better life for one evening.

"I just feel like I be betrayin' me family," she finally whispered aloud.

Sophia was silent for a moment before she spoke, each word carefully thought out as her expression sobered. "May I speak candidly for a moment?"

Gwynna eyed her warily from the side. Her hope silently scratched at its cage to be let free as she nodded for Sophia to continue.

"Your work at the mine begins tomorrow," Sophia said softly. "Your difficult labor, your real life, will begin anew. You have one night left, one night to be someone else. Please, do not waste a single moment longer on whether you are betraying your family or not. For you are *not*. You are simply allowing yourself to have one night of carefree frivolity."

Gwynna's shoulders straightened as Sophia continued.

"Forget your troubles for one evening, my dear friend. Allow yourself to be free of strife and responsibilities—to be a lady. Everyone deserves a night away from hardships and burdens and trials. And you deserve a night away after what you did to help me." Tears welled in her eyes, though she swiftly blinked them away. "If this is still what you wish to do, then I shall do my very best to ensure you do not regret a single moment of it."

The firm pleading in Sophia's voice slipped past Gwynna's reservations and buoyed her courage. Gwynna *had* been through much, but so had many other maidens. The difference now was that very few of those girls would be so crazed as to risk their livelihood for one night of fun—and not one of them had a friend like Sophia.

Finally, though her nerves remained unsettled, anticipation blossomed within Gwynna like the long-awaited sea thrift after a freezing winter.

She sighed. "Fine. I'll do it. But I be mad, ye know."

Sophia raised her shoulders. "We both are. But we certainly have more fun this way. Now I must leave to announce the first dance. You still do not wish to dance it, I assume?"

Gwynna shook her head. She wasn't quite ready for *that*.

After a quick embrace and the promise to follow soon after, she watched Sophia disappear through the curtains. Finally, Gwynna gathered her courage that had fallen down around her then took her first step into the ballroom.

Outside of the dim alcove, the blazing lights pulsed against her eyes, and she winced. The music and conversation were much louder out here, no longer muted by the thick curtains. The voices around her reverberated in her ears with a gentle hum, like leaves rustling in a summer breeze.

From here, she could better appreciate the setting and the finery of those around her. Mothers stood by as sentinels, closely observing their daughters, who fluttered their fans and eyed gentlemen hungrily from across the room. The men stood a little taller with the attention, their starched collars and bright waistcoats holding their own in the colorful sea of women's dresses.

Smiles abounded as the dancers skipped and turned in the set, all in time with the lively music from the musicians at the front of the room.

As Gwynna stood there, taking it all in, the corners of her lips lifted. Her entire life, she'd wondered what attending a high-society gathering would be like. Now, she was finally experiencing it, and as luck would have it, the sights and sounds were exactly what she'd hoped for, exactly as she'd imagined them.

She ignored her conscience and focused instead on Sophia's words.

"I deserve one evenin' free from strife," she whispered.

And she would allow herself to have it.

With leaden feet, she took her first steps around the ballroom. A couple passed her by not a moment later, and before she could remind herself to be a lady, to play the part, both of them nodded their heads with polite smiles and walked on.

Gwynna stared after them in stunned silence. Never had she been treated with such...respect. She couldn't count how often she was ignored or brushed aside by the upper class. That was just daily life for her.

That evening, she'd half-expected to be discovered the very moment she met eyes with someone, then chased off with a flaming candlestick and polished silverware.

But that couple, they hadn't known she was a miner's daughter. They hadn't known that she wasn't one of *them*.

She continued on, her step a little lighter. Two ladies walked past her arm-in-arm with another kind acknowledgement, and Gwynna reeled. Truthfully, she shouldn't have been surprised, what with the change in her appearance, but this was just too strange to comprehend all at once.

As she neared the top of the room, the crowds parted, and Mr. Pinnick emerged from the masses. Her steps faltered, and she nearly turned around to flee, but she froze when their eyes met.

He narrowed his gaze slightly, clearing his throat to speak. Gwynna's breathing restricted. Was he going to declare her identity? Alert the entire room of her presence?

But he merely smiled and tipped his head with a pleasant, "Good evening, miss," before going on his way.

Gwynna bit her tongue to prevent a smile as broad as the pickaxes they used at the mine. She continued along the outer wall of the room, recalling Mr. Pinnick's words.

"As much as one might attempt, one cannot improve the state of a miner, nor his family. In manner or cleanliness."

Mr. Pinnick had certainly been proven wrong that evening.

Gwynna had planned to merely make one round about the room then slide back into the safety behind the curtains. But then, she'd just deceived that gentleman into believing she was someone she was not. She should have felt remorse for her deception or perhaps slight hesitation. Instead, she felt free.

She glanced around. No one treated her with disdain. No one peered down at her with feigned pity for her lower class life. She was their equal. She was a lady.

With renewed confidence, she raised her chin—"A lady never walks with her head hung low, Gwynna," Sophia had said —and sauntered through the crowds. She passed by older women seated on cushioned chairs and a group of giggling girls sipping drinks from shining glasses.

She wouldn't mind a drink right now, but she couldn't afford her tongue any looseness. Instead, she moved to the refreshment table, dodging behind a young woman's oversized feather to hide from the footmen. After pouring herself a small glass of lemonade, she stepped a short distance away from the servants and took a sip. The cool liquid slid down her throat and spread through her limbs like a frozen fire. She longed to down the entire glass in one swig, but Sophia had warned her against such behavior.

Instead, Gwynna took another miniscule taste and swirled the drink around in her mouth, watching the dancers and wondering how she'd grown so comfortable so quickly.

Perhaps she was born to be a lady.

She eyed her lemonade, the cloudy yellow liquid slightly frosting the glass. She'd better avoid this drink, too. The sugar was going straight to her head.

Instead of putting it aside, however, she happily took another drink. What did it matter if she was carefree and confident?

No one would recognize her that evening anyway.

CHAPTER SIX

*J*ack entered the bustling ballroom with a satisfied smile. The dancing had already begun, and the music was lively. This would be just the sort of thing to distract him.

The weight from his shoulders shifted—it never completely departed—and he removed any lingering thoughts about Father and the new investors' meeting from which he'd excused himself.

"You're leaving?" Father had asked. "But we've hardly begun."

"My apologies, Father, but I believe my cousins are anxious for entertainment this evening."

It hadn't been a lie. Jack's cousins, Hugh and Amy Paxton, whom he'd brought with him from Bath, weren't accustomed to sitting at home often. So when Father's business acquaintance— a Mr. Hawkins, was it?—had invited him to attend a ball that evening, he'd readily agreed.

The Paxton siblings had proven valuable assets in keeping Jack busy and away from Father, for they required entertainment often. Apart from the first day, of course, when they'd chosen to rest at home while Jack was coerced into spending the day at the mine with Father.

It was unfortunate Hugh and Amy's parents were off gallivanting around the Lake District. They could have provided even more of a distraction.

Jack set aside his thoughts and pulled his mind back to the present. He'd never been inside Fynwary Hall, always passing it from the outside with Mama on their occasional carriage ride to St. Just. It was a grand house, from what he'd seen of it, but he'd been witness to more lavish ballrooms in Bath. Either way, he was more interested in admiring the women than the lights or flooring. Ladies were the best sort of distraction, even more so than a drink or gambling, as he'd discovered since kicking the habits.

Women didn't leave him with splitting headaches and regret.

Not usually, anyway. And not with too much regret that he wasn't able to shuffle it to the back of his mind where he could no longer feel the effects of it.

"It certainly is livelier than I imagined it to be." Hugh, standing at Jack's left, eagerly eyed the women around him. "You told us Cornwall was quite lacking in a societal aspect, cousin."

"That is because he does not like Cornwall. Do you, Jack?"

Jack turned to Hugh's sister, Amy, who stood on the other side of Jack. She raised a blonde brow and curved her lip.

"I'm not particularly partial to it, no," he replied.

That wasn't exactly true. He'd once loved living in Cornwall, being near the ocean and enjoying the sights as any Cornishman did. He'd wandered the cliffsides with Mama hundreds of times as she'd point out the jackdaws and seagulls, the pink sea thrift and yellow gorse.

Now, Cornwall was simply tainted with the memory of her death.

"I really am impressed with the quality of females here," Hugh continued. "They are much better than I anticipated."

Two women passed by, smiling behind their flitting fans. Jack tipped his head in greeting.

"Hugh," Amy scolded once they passed, leaning forward past Jack to scowl at her brother. "You mustn't speak such things. We are not livestock to be appraised."

Hugh smirked. "Are you not valued in the same regard? Breeding, beauty, ability to birth?" He paused, raising his brow. "*Weight*. Am I not correct in saying so, Jack?"

Jack didn't understand Hugh's incessant teasing of his poor sister, but he wasn't about to jump in between yet another sibling argument. The carriage ride to Cornwall had been filled with their quarreling.

Amy's lips tightened in a frown. "You will never marry, brother."

"Who says I wish to marry? Jack and I shall remain single forever, *by choice*. Will we not, cousin?"

Jack and Hugh had spent most of their growing up together in Bath, privately tutored at Hugh's home before attending Cambridge. There, they'd decided that they would never marry. Hugh said remaining single was easier, and while Jack agreed, his dislike for marriage ran far deeper than a desire for ease of life. Mama's death had seen to that.

"Yes, I'm afraid marriage is not in my future," he finally agreed.

Abruptly, Amy spun on her heel and stalked away across the ballroom. Jack stared after her in confusion. Typically, she could rebuff Hugh's teasing with her own wit, but since coming to Cornwall, she'd been behaving strangely.

"What's the matter with her?" he asked.

"Womanly troubles. I'd put my money on it, if I were a betting man. Which I am." Hugh grinned. "Speaking of which, shall we agree upon the usual wager this evening?"

Jack waited until Amy disappeared into the masses before he responded. "We may as well do something to make the evening more entertaining."

"Excellent. The prize?"

Jack observed a woman in a deep green gown as she performed the steps to the dance flawlessly. "If you win, I'll buy you a drink. If I win...you must agree to never leave me alone with my father again."

He ignored Hugh's pensive gaze by finding a woman dressed in white to stare at next.

"Jack, you'll have to speak with him at some point. You know that's why he brought you to Cornwall in the first place, to discuss your future here."

"I have no future here."

"You haven't any desire to speak with him? Not even the slightest? He is your father, after all."

Jack bristled. "In word alone. My father is not like yours."

Mr. Paxton, Father's distant cousin and Hugh and Amy's father, was a kind gentleman. He'd attempted to take Jack in as his own, but Jack didn't need another father. Not when his own had disappointed him so greatly.

Instead, he'd kept him at arm's length—the same distance he kept everyone.

Hugh smoothed his fingers along the side of his hair, the nervous tick that signaled his desire to end a conversation. Jack was more than willing to oblige.

"So, have we an agreement?" Jack asked.

"Yes, I will agree to those terms. And you?"

Jack nodded.

"Then let the best blackguard win." Hugh winked, then slipped seamlessly into the crowds.

Jack stared after him, straightening his jacket lapel as he attempted to disregard the guilt that always accompanied the game he played with his cousin—seeing who could end their evening with a kiss from a lady first. The wager was just a little something to make otherwise dull evenings livelier, as Jack was not inclined to the mundanity of social events.

After three years of the game, however, assuaging his conscience was getting more and more difficult. This was not due to his worry over what people might think of him for later evading those women whom he'd kissed. Most of them treated him with the same avoidance anyway. Nor was the guilt due to his deservedly spoiled reputation, as he cared very little for Society's opinions.

Any thought of his mother, though, and he was finished. He could only imagine how appalled she'd be of him using women in such a way—taking their affections to dam his emotions like the annoying, perpetual river that they were.

That was the reason he did not dwell on her for too long. Thoughts of Mama, or any memory of his lost childhood, led only to sorrow, which in turn led to drinking.

The one thing that helped him avoid doing just that?

Women.

But now wasn't the time for such thoughts, not when so much was at stake. He knew Hugh would help him avoid his father if he obtained the first kiss or not, but the man had won the last three times, and Jack was in need of a victory—and a kiss.

He linked his hands behind his back and scoured the room. A woman in yellow laughed heartily nearby, doubling over at whatever her friend had said to her. Drink sloshed from the top of her glass, and she pulled back with a hand to her mouth.

Jack needed someone jolly, someone who wouldn't mind sneaking outside to the rose gardens he'd spotted from the window. This woman dressed like the sunshine was not one to be considered, though, as she could hardly give coherent consent.

Even though he enjoyed kissing women as much as the next man, he wasn't a total blackguard like Hugh had suggested.

He stepped around the room, nearing the refreshment table and spotting another young woman with a large feather nearly shading her head from the light cast by the chandeliers. Her eyes trailed up and down his person with a demure smile.

She would do nicely.

He took a step toward her, but after a quick glance to the left of her, he paused, captured instead by a woman in a soft pink gown, swaying from side to side.

She glanced around her, as if ensuring she was not being watched, then in one swift movement, she swigged the rest of her lemonade.

A silent laugh escaped Jack's lips. He'd never seen a woman do such a thing before.

When the last drop had been swallowed, she lowered the glass to the table, swiped her glove across her mouth, then straightened.

His eyes dropped to her arm. A small red stain of rouge marked the spot on her glove where she'd touched her lips, but she didn't notice, walking through the crowd with a contented smile.

Unwittingly, he took a few steps forward as she weaved her way round the couples. Now that the glass no longer hid half of her face, he could better see her pretty features. He narrowed his eyes. There was something familiar about her.

Every other woman in the room, with their colorful dresses and feather headpieces, fled from his mind as he tried to place the lady in pink.

He'd absolutely seen her before, but where? In Bath? A woman he'd passed by on the street? Or was she someone from his childhood?

She seemed in an entirely different world as she watched

those around her. Her full lips held the hint of a smile, as if she was keeping a secret, and her eyes...

They met his across the room, and suddenly, he knew. Those amber eyes, sparkling in the ballroom—wide, innocent, and suddenly filled with fright—were the same as those he'd taken notice of in the dim light of the counthouse at Wheal Favour.

Now what exactly was a bal maiden doing, attending a ball dressed as a lady?

CHAPTER SEVEN

$\mathcal{G}$ wynna's mouth parted, her eyes rounding as shock usurped her ability to move. The lemonade she'd just gulped down bubbled in her stomach.

He was here. Why was he here?

Mr. Jack Trevethan's eyes honed in on her, a half-smile tugging at his lips. An invisible force latched her feet to the ground, preventing her escape until he advanced toward her.

Finally, his movement jerked her limbs awake.

Whirling around, she fled through the crowds, ignoring the looks of surprise by those she rushed past.

A quick glance over her shoulder affirmed that she'd escaped just in time. The gentleman was no longer in sight, but if *he* was there, would his father be also? Could she remain at the ball a moment longer and risk being discovered by them both?

Her lungs burned as if she'd breathed in powdered ore. What a fool she'd been that evening, thinking she could leave her true life behind. Her deceit of others, her arrogance, had brought her down swiftly. She deserved to be discovered.

She ducked past the footmen by the refreshment table and

skipped past the dancers until she spotted Sophia walking near the edge of the room, arm-in-arm with her husband.

The Hawkinses were a perfect painting of joy, their doting eyes focused on only each other as they made their way through the crowds.

Gwynna and Sophia had agreed to keep some distance between each other to avoid suspicion from others about their closeness, but she had no choice but to break their directive now. She was leaving the ball, that very minute.

As she approached, Sophia's eyes brightened, but her brow soon crumpled with worry. "What has happened?"

"Mr. Trevethan," Gwynna began breathlessly, "he be here, lookin' right at me."

Sophia shook her head, lowering her voice. "No, he said he couldn't attend this evening."

"Mr. *Jack* Trevethan," Gwynna clarified.

"Ah, yes."

Sophia and Gwynna swung their eyes up to meet Mr. Hawkins as he casually piped up.

"You knew of his attendance?" Sophia asked her husband.

Taken aback, he nodded matter-of-factly. "Of course. I invited him to attend only this morning, while I was on business with his father."

Gwynna's hands flew to her cheeks, and Sophia flinched, the only tell of her calm exterior faltering. "My dear, do you not see the problem you've created?"

He glanced between the women before his eyes rounded. "Gwynna, you know Jack Trevethan?"

Gwynna nodded, her hands sliding down her cheeks before dropping to her sides. "I met 'im, not four days past."

Regret sunk in his eyes. "I'm so sorry. I truly hadn't any notion. I thought, what with him arriving only a few days ago, he wouldn't know you. When I met with him, he and his cousins seemed rather desperate for entertainment, so I thought tonight…"

Sophia placed a comforting hand on his upper arm. "All is well, my dear. It was a simple mistake."

"'Tis true," Gwynna agreed, not blind to his suffering. "I don't blame ye for not knowin'. But I'd best leave now, 'fore he has chance to see me closer."

Sophia hesitated. "Are you quite certain? You haven't even had the opportunity to dance yet."

"It be for the best, Sophia."

Sophia wrung her hands together. "Are you certain he established it was you?" She faced her husband. "You hardly recognized her from across the room. Isn't that right, my dear?"

Mr. Hawkins affirmed his wife's words with a nod.

Gwynna glanced over her shoulder for what had to be the hundredth time. What she wouldn't give to move their conversation to the alcove behind the curtains, but the host and hostess couldn't very well disappear from their own ball.

"Per'aps that be the truth, but…" Her words trailed off. The regret in Mr. Hawkins's eyes, and the pleading in Sophia's, made her hesitate. "Ye really believe he didn't recognize me?"

The husband and wife simultaneously nodded. Mr. Hawkins leaned forward. "Even if he did, he might keep quiet on the matter. He seemed a decent fellow, quite like his father."

Gwynna longed to believe his words, hope trickling into the empty chasm of her chest. Perhaps she wouldn't have to leave early. Perhaps she could remain hidden or simply—

"Excuse me?"

Her stomach dropped, the sinking sensation causing her legs to drain of all feeling. It was he. It had to be Mr. Jack Trevethan.

She couldn't stifle her sigh of relief when she turned to see not Mr. Trevethan standing beside her, but another gentleman entirely.

"Pardon me for interrupting," the man continued, "but Mrs.

Hawkins asked for me to find her earlier." He cast a hesitant glance at Sophia.

If Gwynna wasn't scared out of her wits, she'd probably find him very handsome, what with his softened brow and kind countenance. Now, she could hardly appreciate his good looks.

Sophia finally responded, and relief swiped across the gentleman's face. "Oh, yes, of course. I'm so happy you've found us. Allow me to introduce to you my friend and Mr. Hawkins's cousin, Miss Joanna Bell. Miss Bell, this is Mr. Graham Davy."

Gwynna blanched. Mr. Hawkins's cousin? Joanna Bell? She shouldn't have been surprised. Of course Sophia would still expect her to play the part of the lady, to use the false identity they'd chosen for her weeks ago.

She most certainly was no longer in the mood to play these games, but she couldn't very well allow this Mr. Davy to know Sophia was lying.

"Good evenin'," she forced out.

Mr. Davy bowed, and Gwynna returned the gesture with a curtsy, though it felt far less graceful than she'd hoped. At least she'd remembered to move slowly. Sophia had told her it wasn't ladylike to "bounce up like a spring wildflower."

"A pleasure, Miss Bell," Mr. Davy said. "Mrs. Hawkins has spoken of your keen ability to dance, and I am anxious to discover the talent for myself. That is, if you are not yet occupied for the next set."

Her mouth opened and closed in silence, not unlike a beached fish, which, incidentally, she was feeling more like every second—unable to breathe, out of place, an imposter.

How could she be expected to dance, knowing Mr. Trevethan's eyes could find her at any moment? It was hard enough to remember all the steps without the added pressure.

Sophia's laughter broke through the silence. "As you can see, Mr. Davy, our cousin is incorrigibly shy. I'm certain she would love to dance with you, providing you do most of the talking."

Gwynna had a mind to tug on one of Sophia's perfectly curled ringlets, but when she spotted the look of pleading in her friend's eye, she was struck with understanding and shame.

Mr. Davy was just as much Sophia's guest as Gwynna was. If Gwynna refused this gentleman's offer, hurting and offending him, the blame for her rudeness would be placed on the Hawkinses, as Gwynna was supposedly their cousin. How could she do such a thing after all they'd done to make this ball come about?

Another moment passed in silence before Gwynna finally turned to Mr. Davy, replying in her broken accent, "I would be happy to dance with you, sir."

She winced at her slow, thick words, spoken as if sap from the trees near her home had stuck to the roof of her mouth and refused to budge.

Mr. Davy seemed not to notice, simply offering his hand to Gwynna. As she placed her fingers on his, grateful for the gloves that hid her unladylike nails, she moved toward the dance floor.

"Shall we join them, Mr. Hawkins?" Sophia said. She walked past Gwynna with a whisper to her ear. "One dance, then Mr. Hawkins and I shall see to your safe removal from Fynwary."

Gwynna drew a fortifying breath. One dance. She could manage one dance.

Sophia stood a few couples down from her in the set, close enough to offer aid if need be but far enough to avoid suspicion.

As the other dancers lined up behind them, Sophia called out the dance. "Bally Croy!"

A hum of assent rippled through the crowds, and Gwynna sent a grateful glance to her friend. Sophia knew this was the dance with which Gwynna had the least amount of trouble.

"Are you enjoying your stay in Cornwall, Miss Bell?"

Gwynna glanced over her shoulder, scanning the crowds for any sign of Mr. Trevethan. She thought he danced farther down the set, but she couldn't be sure, as the dark jackets blended the gentlemen into one dark mass.

After a moment, she spotted Mr. Pinnick standing near the dance floor. His eyes lingered on her with a slight smile. There was no hint of recognition, purely admiration.

Gwynna curbed a discomfited shiver and shifted to the left to stand out of his sight. He clearly didn't recognize her, but his observation was unsettling. What a spasm he'd have, knowing he was ogling a bal maiden.

She would've felt that same pride at fooling him had she not been humbled by Mr. Trevethan's sudden appearance.

"Miss Bell?"

Miss Bell? Blast. That was her.

She faced Mr. Davy. "Sorry?"

His smile had yet to falter. "I asked if you were enjoying your stay in Cornwall."

"Oh, yes."

"Are you to remain here longer with your cousins?"

Gwynna disliked having to lie to this gentleman. She silently pleaded for Sophia's aid, but Sophia was busy ensuring the other guests were lining up. There was nothing else to do now but pray the guests' conversation drowned out her terrible attempt at speaking properly.

"No, I am stayin' in St. Ives with my friends the Fairmans. They would have come tonight, but they remained home, feelin' too unwell to travel. I return to them this evenin', then back to Bedfordshire soon after. I am looking forward to goin' home."

Good heavens. She sounded like a stilted vicar over the pulpit on Sunday, incessantly droning on in memorized sermons. Sophia had told her to intersperse her pretended history throughout the dance. Now she had nothing left to say.

Mr. Davy responded as if he didn't take notice of her rehearsed words. "I am sorry to have not had the opportunity to spend more time with you."

Despite being stalked by two wolves—Mr. Pinnick's admiring gaze and Mr. Trevethan's potential knowing eyes— warmth enveloped Gwynna. What a gentlemanly thing for Mr. Davy to say. Then again, she shouldn't have been surprised. He was, after all, a gentleman.

A gentleman speaking to a bal maiden.

"Have you ever been to the sea before?" he asked.

She eyed the musicians, tapping her foot on the ground. When was the music going to begin? "Yes."

"Would you like for me to speak about myself now so you might remain silent?"

Her eyes swung back to meet his grin. She gave a little laugh of relief. "Yes."

He nodded understandingly. "Not to worry. I've a little niece who isn't partial to speaking either, which makes me rather adept at carrying on a one-sided conversation."

As he spoke more about his family situation, Gwynna couldn't help but think on his kindness. This was how all men ought to be, kind, unassuming, aware of another person's discomfort—with eyes that weren't eating her up like the miners' sons tended to do after too much drink.

Not long after, the musicians played the first notes of the dance, and the movements began. Thankfully, the quick steps left little room for conversation, and the hops and turns used up any of their remaining energy.

Gwynna was surprised she remembered so much. She miss-stepped fewer times than she could count on one hand, and each mistake was swallowed by another young lady farther down the line.

This woman was dressed in yellow and stood out from the more muted colors around her, but her laughter was what drew most of the attention. She tripped over her part-ner's foot a number of times and cackled before ending unceremoniously with a hiccup. If Gwynna didn't know any better, she'd say the girl had *somehow* already had too much to drink.

In truth, she was grateful for the ruckus the girl had created, for it provided a distraction for Gwynna. She only peeked over her shoulder through the crowds half a dozen times for Mr. Trevethan instead of the thousand she'd wanted to, and Mr. Pinnick had soon lifted his attention off of her and dropped it on the yellow dress, as well.

When the song ended, applause and bright smiles filled the room, and Gwynna received an approving nod from Sophia before Mr. Davy led Gwynna off the floor.

As they walked together, Gwynna glanced back at the woman in yellow, who was now being pulled away by a woman —no doubt her mother—with a fierce scowl. The daughter simply giggled and waved goodbye to her partner, who appeared as if he'd just been attacked by a gaggle of geese, his eyes as wide as teacups and his cravat askew.

Gwynna and Mr. Davy stopped at the edge of the ballroom. Once satisfied Mr. Trevethan and Mr. Pinnick were nowhere to be seen, she faced Mr. Davy.

"I must thank you for an invigorating dance, Miss Bell," he said. "Mrs. Hawkins was quite right about your ability."

Gwynna nodded with silent gratitude.

"I do hope we may dance again before you return home."

"And I," she managed before curtsying. *That* one was much better.

Mr. Davy departed after his bow.

As soon as he left, Gwynna backed up against the outer wall near a window and released an airy sigh—not necessarily due to the gentleman, but because of his manners.

A bow instead of a wink. Smiles instead of ogles. Polite conversation instead of gruff words. She'd never really been mistreated by the young men in her life or at the mine, apart from the occasional gawking or attempted kiss. But she'd certainly never been bowed to before. And that respect was something she could grow used to.

But it wasn't something she *should* grow used to.

Her brow furrowed. This was a dangerous game. She'd done exactly what Papa had feared. She'd compared her life with Sophia's and now longed for something she could never have.

"Miss?"

Gwynna jumped. She spun around, coming face-to-face with the very man she'd been attempting to avoid, the very man she'd allowed herself to forget for a single, neglectful moment.

Mr. Jack Trevethan.

CHAPTER EIGHT

$\mathcal{I}$nstantly, Gwynna ducked her head.

"Are you in distress of some sort, Miss?" Mr. Trevethan asked.

She felt like that wretched fish again, unable to speak, unable to move. But then, why had he spoken so casually? Did he not recognize her? Could she leave before he *did?*

Keeping her eyes averted, she took a step back. Her slippers came in contact with the wall. Blast. Why did she have to slink back to the farthest corner of the room? Now an easy escape would be impossible.

"No, I be—I am well," she finally answered.

She peered around his shoulder. He stood between her and the door. She would no longer wait for Sophia to come to her aid. Gwynna would dart around him and flee to Sophia's room, change back into her clothing, then slip out of the house with the help of Sophia's lady's maid.

All she needed to do was maneuver around this man's tall frame and she'd be free.

"Forgive me, but I don't believe you truly are well."

His voice was deeper than she'd imagined it to be. It came from low in his chest, rumbling like waves during a storm.

"Might I be of service?" he pressed.

Music sounded, and another dance began. Now would be the perfect moment to escape, while all eyes persisted on the dancers.

"I am trying to-to make me way to the refreshment table," she stuttered. "I am parched, see."

"Ah, well, allow me to fetch a glass of lemonade for you. You do like lemonade, do you not?"

Was that a hint of humor in his tone? She couldn't risk looking up at him to see if he smiled.

She nodded in response.

"I will return in just a moment." He took a step back, and the tightness in her neck began to dissipate.

Finally.

She moved forward, intent on making her escape while he left, but he turned back to face her, and she dropped her gaze again.

"Before I leave, I must say...you look rather familiar. Have we met before?"

No, no, no! She longed to shout out the answer, but she knew it would only draw more attention to the fact that she was the very bal maiden his father had just hired, the very bal maiden at whom he'd smirked.

Instead, she settled with a mumbled, "No."

"Are you quite certain?"

Panic clawed at her chest like a maddened creature. She couldn't do this any longer. She needed to escape now. "I think I'll be gettin' the lemonade meself," she said, hardly aware of her faltering accent.

She attempted to step around him, but he blocked her way.

"Don't be silly. Allow me to fetch it for you. My apologies for pressing you on the matter of our possible acquaintance. But I suppose you are correct. I'm certain I would precisely remember a face as lovely as yours."

Gwynna wasn't sure whether to feel flattered, triumphant, or offended. Other miners had offered her flirtatious remarks before, but obviously never a gentleman. Of course, she was no great beauty like Sophia, but she wasn't terribly ugly, either. So what did that say about her forgettable appearance, that Mr. Trevethan clearly noticed her before, and yet had no recollection of her "lovely" face now?

With no response, she stepped to the other side of him. The only thing stopping her from merely running away from the gentleman was the thought of offending one of Sophia's guests, something she wouldn't allow herself to do.

So she attempted to use politeness instead. "Please, excuse me, sir."

"Yes, of course. The lemonade." He didn't move. "Only, might I have your name? I would be indebted to you, if you agree to dance with me this evening."

He dipped his head to meet her gaze, but she pretended to smooth out the length of her glove. When did she obtain that red stain? Could she claim it was blood and feign a cut on her arm as an excuse to leave? No, that would simply draw more attention to herself.

Searching for anything to help her in her escape, she finally recalled more of Sophia's instruction.

"I'd prefer to be properly introduced by the hostess, if ye—if you wouldn't mine."

She curtsied then finally stepped around him. He reached out a hand to stay her, his fingers sliding along her silk glove. Flares of heat rushed through her skin before he released his hold.

"But we do not need an introduction, do we?" he said.

Her voice trembled as she spoke. "Why not?"

Silence followed, unease creeping up her neck as she finally, reluctantly, met his eyes.

Mr. Trevethan was more handsome than she recalled, his half-smile charming, his hair blacker than the night. And his eyes, those dark, penetrating eyes revealed exactly what she feared.

He took a step toward her, causing her to crane her neck to maintain eye contact. "Because we have already been introduced, have we not, Gwynna Merrick?"

Gwynna's heart sunk deeper than the shaft at Wheal Favour. He'd spoken softly enough for no one else to hear, but not one person, not even Mr. Pinnick, mattered in comparison to this man, the son of her employer. Who somehow, for some reason, had remembered her name.

She was done for.

She leaned forward, lowering her voice as her façade disappeared. "Please, sir. I beg ye not to tell. I be sorry I'm here, dressed in such a way. I need me work at the mine. Please, don't tell your father."

His smile faltered, the light in his eyes dimming for a brief moment before he shook his head. "Worry not. I shan't say a word to anyone."

The breath rushed from her lungs, and she placed her hands to her lips. "Oh, thank ye, sir. Bless ye."

Mr. Hawkins had certainly been right. This Mr. Trevethan *was* as kind as his father. She took a step away from him, nodding her head with gratitude once more. She'd made her decision. She was going to leave. This man had just saved her place at the mine, and she wasn't going to risk losing it again by anyone else recognizing her.

She bounced on the tips of her toes and made to turn around, but his voice stopped her once more. "I won't tell a soul…on one condition."

Her smile faded, and her feet flattened. "Condition?"

He took a step toward her. His smile wasn't like Mr. Davy's —kind and welcoming. It was charming, but unnervingly so.

"Yes. I will keep this little secret between us, and you can keep your place at the mine. But you must simply agree to save your next dance for me and then take a small stroll with me in the gardens. Alone."

He motioned over his shoulder to where large glass doors led out to the veranda.

Her eyebrows pulled together. Why in heaven's name would this gentleman wish to dance with a bal maiden and then speak with her in the privacy of the gardens? Would it not harm his reputation? Wouldn't it...

Her eyes found his once more. His brow hovered above his dark eyes in a daring gaze, and the provocative look on his face finally revealed his true intent.

Sophia had told her what the gardens were typically used for—secluded strolls with one's intended, secret kisses to be shared unseen. Most gentlemen would avoid the compromising situation in which one could find oneself in the gardens.

Now she understood. He did not have the same kind eyes as Mr. Davy or Mr. Hawkins, or even the other gentlemen she'd seen that evening, because Mr. Trevethan was no gentleman.

Her eyes hardened as the realization of his request continued to sink in. She was to do as he asked or forfeit her place at the mine, thereby sacrificing her family's livelihood. Did he think her so void of morals, so destitute, that she would accept his offer?

Instead of fear gripping her, or worry over what she would do, a coolness chilled her. She straightened to her full height, though she still stood a half-foot shorter. With eyes she knew perfectly reflected her anger, she began.

"How dare ye suggest such a thing. How dare ye assume I'd *do* such a thing."

His smile remained, unfaltering as she pressed on. A few glances were sent in their direction, but she paid them no heed.

"Ye can tell your father, ye can tell me parents. Tell all of Cornwall if ye wish. I'd gladly lose me work at Wheal Favour if that meant I'd not 'ave to work anywhere near the likes of ye." With a pointed finger she lowered her voice to what she hoped was a menacing level. "Ye ought to be ashamed of yourself."

For a single, fleeting moment, uncertainty flickered in his dark eyes, but it was soon overpowered by his flippant smile.

With a disgusted shake of her head, Gwynna left the man behind, forcing her footsteps to remain calm and calculated across the ballroom. She would not reveal any sign of weakness, just like she wouldn't be intimidated into compromising her values.

She was finished. Finished with Mr. Trevethan, with the ball, and with high society as a whole. Let the upper class keep their entitled, so-called gentlemen.

She, for one, was over them.

CHAPTER NINE

*G*wynna raised the long-handled hammer overhead and plunged it through the August air with all the force she could muster. As the blunt, iron head made contact with the ore, pieces of the rock flew through the air, a number of them pelting her skirts.

She raised the hammer again, ignoring the throbbing muscles in her back and the stinging in her hands.

Crack!

One more piece broke into fragments, clacking as they bounced against each other.

Crack!

Another swing, another direct hit. Gwynna had forgotten how satisfying this was. Not many women were capable of cracking the ore apart in one swift blow, but she'd always had a knack for the task. Even the three months away hadn't lessened her ability in that regard.

What the three months *had* done was prevented her body's remembrance of the fortitude required for such a work. Every inch of her muscles ached, from the small of her back to the blisters burgeoning on her fingers.

She winced, gripping onto the ash handle of her hammer. She eyed the curved markings in the light wood—a mere excuse to give her a moment's respite—then swung the tool once more toward the ground.

The pressure of the blast vibrated up the handle and throughout her hands with each strike, despite the makeshift gloves she wore. The pain would have been unbearable, had she not the sea to distract her.

The waves roared, a constant rumble hundreds of feet below as the water heaved itself at the mercy of the cliff's rugged confines. Seagulls' piercing cries punctuated the air above the water. Now that the mine's midday meal was finished, they'd abandoned their unsuccessful search for food from the miners and moved instead to the sea.

The other surface workers and maidens were positioned behind where the spalling took place, far enough away to avoid being struck by stray shards of rock. From her position, though, near the front of the engine house, the sea stretched out in an endless, watery expanse.

Gwynna stole another moment of reprieve, drawing in a deep breath, focusing on the smell of the sea instead of the pinch in her lungs and the imposing scent of musty ore brought up from the earth below.

Though the day had waned, and five o'clock was nearly upon them, the mine still hummed, alive and hectic—to the outside eye, anyway. To Gwynna, it was organized chaos. Like a swarm of bees producing honey, the workers knew where they needed to be, carrying out their tasks of dumping and crushing and grinding.

Above the ocean, the air was abuzz with clinking metal and dull claps of ore as the male surface laborers and young maidens tipped heavy barrowfuls of the rocks into piles that never really seemed to dwindle.

Gwynna eyed her own heap that needed finishing. She'd best stop dawdling before the mine captain caught her.

She took another swing at the ore. Was he still watching?

Discreetly, her eyes trailed along the purple heather clinging to the cliffside before she reached the man at the top.

She'd been told by the other maidens that Mr. Harvey and the owner often stood there to ensure the work was continuing in a proper manner, but to have him perched on the edge of the cliff like a peregrine falcon, silent and focused, was rather daunting.

Especially because she wasn't exactly sure if he was judging her ability to spall or if he was choosing the right time to tell her she was being released from work at Wheal Favour, on order of the Trevethans.

Anger surged through her as she recalled the night before.

Crack!

She still couldn't believe Mr. Jack Trevethan had suggested such a thing as kissing him in exchange for silence. Of course, he hadn't gone so far as to say he required an actual kiss, but she was not naïve—and his eyes had lied.

To have a gentleman stand there and assume she was void of all morals, she could hardly bear it. Of course, she'd instantly regretted her own behavior. Not that he didn't deserve her scolding, but he was her superior, and she could have simply walked silently away, if only for the sake of her family's livelihood.

She'd been glancing over her shoulder all day, fearing the news that she'd been removed from her position at the mine, but it hadn't come yet.

Were they simply waiting for her to finish her work, or had Mr. Jack Trevethan decided to remain silent on the matter?

She scoffed aloud. That man wasn't capable of doing anything honorable.

Laying her hammer on the ground beside her, she hunched

over to pick up handfuls of the broken ore, now smaller than the palm of her hand. The pieces clicked together as she dropped them into a nearby hand barrow.

When she took up her hammer again, the shrill sound of the working bell soared over the mine, ending the workday.

Maidens' footsteps retreated nearby, and miners spilled out of the shaft, bees fleeing the hive, anxious to be out in the light, though wincing at the brightness of the sun. The horse pulling the whim round in circles was stopped, cutting the creaking of the wooden pully system. The hum of conversation replaced the clatter of toiling tools as the workers washed up in a nearby bucket of water.

Gwynna continued working. She couldn't risk leaving before her pile was depleted. With the toe of her boot, she flicked a few of the rocks from her pile onto the dirt before her, ready to break them apart.

"Are ye not yet finished, Gwynna? Have ye lost your talent then?"

Gwynna greeted Kerensa Hocking with a smile. "Just a little behind, but ye best expect me tomorrow to show ye up."

The girls had been friends since they began working at the mine at nine years of age. Before Gwynna had left, she and Kerensa had been the only two spallers and would often create contests to see who could finish first. Kerensa was of a thicker sort, with broad shoulders and strong arms—far stronger than Gwynna—though she lacked the same finesse.

"I hope so," Kerensa said. "It's good to 'ave ye back. With Mary workin' alongside me, there wasn't much competition."

Mary Hocking, Kerensa's sister, was the spaller whom Gwynna had replaced. She was a short, thin girl of seventeen years who'd despised working at the mine.

"How be your sister?" Gwynna asked. "Is St. Ives and married life suitin' her?"

"I believe it to be. She certainly be happier there than she be here. Ye know she don't feel the same pleasure at Favour as we do."

"No, I 'spect not."

Pleasure was a strong word, but Kerensa was right. The work was backbreaking, and at times, unbearable, but there was a certain satisfaction Gwynna experienced as a bal maiden. Never mind that she preferred it to cleaning fireplaces, cooking endless meals, and being forced to remain indoors and away from the sea all day. Not many women could succeed in the work at a mine, and she was proud to be one of them.

"I can help ye with these," Kerensa said, pointing to the pile of ore.

Gwynna motioned to the upper cliffside. "Thank ye, but I best perform for me audience."

Kerensa sniffed a laugh as she caught sight of Mr. Harvey. "Ah, he be judgin' ye then?"

"'Fraid so." Gwynna stared beyond Kerensa's shoulder to where two girls waited nearby. The youngest, Tamesin, was not more than ten years old. She rubbed her red eyes while her fifteen-year-old sister, Delen, yawned. "I can finish these off fine. Your sisters be waitin' for ye anyway."

Kerensa glanced over her shoulder, holding up a finger to signal them just a moment. The girls' shoulders fell, though they remained silent.

Gwynna rushed on, anxious not to keep them any longer. "How are ye doin'? Your sisters and mother?"

"We be managin' as best we can."

Gwynna's lips pulled down. Kerensa's father had died in the same mining accident that had stolen Jago. Now, with only a mother to raise her four daughters, and a sister wedded, Kerensa had taken on much of the responsibility to care for her two younger siblings, sacrificing what little time she'd had to herself. *Kerensa* would never risk the livelihood of her family by following some selfish whim to dress as a lady.

Gwynna averted her eyes. "Ye go on home now. And tell your mother me family sends our love."

Kerensa took a few steps back. "Ye make sure to get some sleep tonight. I want ye well-rested for tomorrow so ye can 'ave a fair shot at beatin' I."

Gwynna chuckled then assailed the ore once again as soon as Kerensa was a safe distance away. With the early evening sun sliding farther down the sky, she pushed back her loose, cotton bonnet. The breeze slid across her sweat-covered brow and the back of her neck, as if a wet cloth had been wrapped around her head.

The cooling sensation invigorated her enough to crack a few more pieces of ore just as Father approached.

"Are ye doin' well, Gwynna?"

CHAPTER TEN

*G*wynna straightened from her stooped position with a smile—a smile she hoped distracted from the weariness she knew was very well reflected in her eyes. Papa didn't need anything else to worry him more than he already was.

"I be fine, Father. Nearly done, see."

He eyed the pile of ore. Was he purposefully avoiding her gaze? "I'd like to wait for ye, but the Causeys…"

She nodded. The Causeys, a local, landed-gentry couple, had hired Papa and a few other miners to clear the land for a new crop of winter barley to be planted this October.

Gwynna had taken work at the mine to alleviate Papa's need to carry on extra tasks, but as he'd already agreed to the work with Mr. Causey, he wouldn't go back on his word.

"That be all right," she reassured him. "I don't mind walkin' home on me own."

He nodded, bending down to pick up one of the pieces of broken ore from the hand barrow. "Are ye still determined to work here?"

She softened her tone. "Yes, Papa."

"Even after ye been strugglin'?"

She nodded, and he tossed the ore back into the barrow. Had he expected her to change her mind after a single day? Or had he *hoped*?

She closed the distance between them and kissed his soot-covered cheek. That morning, they'd both kept silent instead of joining in with the other miners and maidens singing as they made their way to Wheal Favour.

Gwynna knew Papa was considering the last time they'd made the journey together, when Jago was with them. Now that Gwynna was his only child, he worried over her own safety incessantly, but they couldn't function any longer in such a way.

She tipped her head to the side to soften her words. "I know ye be worryin' about me workin' here, Papa. But I promise. I be sore and tired and dirty, but I be happy. I finally be helpin' me family again."

He raised a hand to her cheek. "Don't ye ever think of your-self, Gwynny?"

She blinked, currents of guilt rushing through her. She'd been about to protest vigorously after her behavior last night, but he continued before she could.

"I know ye want to 'elp. And in truth, knowin' ye be up here, waitin' for I to finish below ground…I suppose it gives me some sort o' comfort knowin' I ain't be alone no more."

With his heavy tone and weary brow, Gwynna's heart crum-pled like the pieces of ore on the dirt before her. Jago's death had been hard on them all, but more Papa than anyone. His only son, the pride of his eye, had gone far too soon. And Gwynna ached all the worse for his sorrow.

Papa must have realized he'd shared too much of his feelings, for he dropped his hand and took a step back. "Did ye enjoy last night then, with Mrs. Hawkins? Your mother said ye came home early."

Gwynna scratched at her nose. "Oh, yes. I-I thought it better to get more sleep."

"That be wise of ye. Ye look tired today, even still."

Gwynna managed a half-smile. Returning home early last night had not aided in receiving a restful evening. In truth, she'd been so occupied with her confrontation with Mr. Trevethan, she hadn't fully prepared herself for sleep or the nightmares.

"So ye be fine walkin' home on your own?" Papa asked.

Gwynna cleared her throat and set the apparition of Jago's screams and his fear-stricken face as he died—one she hadn't seen but could only imagine—from her mind. Dwelling on them would only make the nightmares worse tonight. "'Course, Papa."

Raising a hand in departure, he joined the other workers finding their way from the mine.

Gwynna swiped her sleeve across her brow, grit scratching at her skin. Thank goodness she wasn't wearing Sophia's silk gloves. Although, she'd soiled those last night, too, with what she'd later realized was rouge.

She shook her head. She wasn't going to dwell on the evening any longer. It only produced anxiety in keeping her position at the mine, and contrition, for the fact that she'd heartily enjoyed being a lady.

Until Mr. Trevethan had shown up.

Crack! Crack! Crack!

As her pile finally began to shrink, Mr. Harvey made his way down the incline toward the engine house, toward *her*. Her palms clammed up, despite the heat infusing her body.

She wouldn't get any work done if she had to stop each time for visitors.

As he drew nearer, her chest tensed. Was this it? Was he going to tell her not to return tomorrow? That he was going to report her to authorities and have her locked away at Bodmin Jail until she learned her lesson? Her parents would never forgive her lapse in judgement, nor her vanity.

"Gwynna?"

She glanced up. "Sir?"

"You've done a fine job today."

She attempted to swallow, but dust coated her throat. "Thank ye, sir."

"I must admit, I didn't think you were up to the task. Though, knowing your father, I never should have doubted you."

Hope flickered. "Thank ye, sir," she repeated.

"You'll remember to return your hammer to the tool house?" He raised a small bucking hammer in his hand. "Maidens who leave them out will be spaled."

Gwynna nodded. She was well aware of the many ways maidens could be spaled, or fined—losing a tool, arriving late, cursing, thievery, brawling—but it was a good reminder. She couldn't risk losing any of her hard-earned money now.

"Yes, sir. I'll remember."

"Very good. Until tomorrow." He tipped his head then left without another word.

Tomorrow.

She bit her lip, but her smile could not be stopped. Mr. Trevethan had not told his father or Mr. Harvey of her reckless behavior after all.

She would live to see another day at the mine.

When the final ore had been split and placed into the barrow, she held her hammer on the handle close to its head and trekked across the dirt, nodding at the few workers still chipping away at their piles.

She pressed one hand against her thigh to help propel her up the incline then delivered her hammer to the tool house and moved to the lean-to nearby. There, she unwound the grey, makeshift gloves Mama had generously given her that morning, made from the stockings she'd darned the night before.

She'd expected the blisters forming, but as the angry red

welts and bubbling white skin glared up at her, she sucked in a sharp breath. Somehow, seeing the wounds made them hurt all the worse.

With a wince, she retrieved her clean apron from a nail pounded into the wood, then reached for the small, linen crib-bag that had held her pasty.

Her stomach gurgled. Perhaps tomorrow she'd hide the bag beneath her working apron, like some of the other girls did. Eating wasn't allowed on the dressing floor apart from their one meal, but work was made more difficult when hunger pains accompanied it.

She removed her dirty apron and replaced it with the cleaner one, tucking the dust-filled towser between her knees, along with the crib-bag and her bonnet. Finally, she dunked her hands into the nearby bucket of murky water.

Her breath caught in her throat as she flung the lukewarm moisture over her face. It wasn't what she'd call refreshing, but when the wind caught the water in its grasp, she finally cooled.

With droplets streaming down her face and fingers, she draped her belongings over her left arm then left the mine to meander across the cliffside.

A sense of accomplishment welled within her, something she'd been missing for months. If her back weren't so stiff and her muscles didn't protest with each step, she'd be skipping home.

Today had turned out infinitely better than she'd thought it would. Not only did she still have her position at the mine, but she'd also managed to make it through the rigorous work.

Now, she would reward herself by taking the longer route home. Mama would soon be needing her help for dinner and tomorrow's meals, but the way only added a quarter of an hour.

It also brought her closer to the ocean.

She typically enjoyed walking home with the other miners,

singing songs and laughing together until one by one they left for the cottages speckled across the moors and countryside.

But today, she was glad to be alone with the sea.

These warm summer days wouldn't last much longer. But rather than dwelling on the harsh winter ahead, its wind and rain pelting her face with the same force she blasted the ore with her hammer, she hummed a tune and fought the urge to pull out her hair pins.

They weren't hers, after all, the hairpins. She hadn't had time to take them out before she'd left Fynwary Hall. Sophia's lady's maid, who had been sworn to keep their secret, had helped her remove the pink gown without damaging it, then Gwynna had swiftly replaced the fine clothing with her grey underpinnings and brown dress.

As she'd walked home that night without alerting the Hawkinses, she'd pulled out the pins one-by-one and held them securely in her hands, tying her worn rag around her hair so her parents wouldn't take note of the difference.

Fortunately, the dim light inside her home had hidden her curls from Mama, who hadn't pressured her for information about her evening when Gwynna had clearly wished to keep what had happened silent.

Gwynna didn't need to worry about the ringlets today. Her sweat and bonnet had done a proper job in straightening them out before the morning was spent.

A soft breeze fluttered her skirts and danced with the yellow wildflowers nearby. The sun wouldn't set for a few hours still, but a calmness had already befallen the land. Golden shadows painted the rocks she walked beside, and the waves ambled toward the cliffs below.

The sun would soon fall asleep, pulling the sea's deep, blue blanket over his bright eyes. Then the stars would appear to carry on their secret conversation with the waves that never slept.

Despite her stinging hands and aching back, joy swelled within her. The sea always made everything better.

A horse's whinny carried on the wind as a gentleman approached on a dark brown horse. Gwynna turned away with disinterest, but her eyes whipped straight back to the handsome rider. Her steps faltered, and she gritted her teeth.

"Mr. Trevethan," she muttered under her breath, ready to turn back the other way and sprint home.

She was still upset about his behavior last evening and the unnerving possibility that he could yet spill her secret. But perhaps expressing her gratitude might encourage his discretion to continue.

Grumbling internally, she moved forward. Things would be far better if the two of them never spoke again, but she needed to thank him first. Then they could continue on as strangers, or better yet, master's son and bal maiden.

As their paths finally crossed, he pulled in his horse, reins jingling as the animal shook his head. He remained mounted, peering down at her with gleaming eyes. "Good evening."

Why did he always appear so amused when he saw her? His shining eyes unsettled her.

"Sir." She pursed her lips, fighting off her pride in wishing to snub him completely. "I wish to thank ye for keepin' me secret. I be grateful to ye."

There, she'd said it. With a single nod, she kept to her path and moved forward.

"Is that all?" he asked with a chuckle.

She paused, looking over her shoulder. He pulled the leather reins to the side, moving his horse to stand before her.

"I save your place at the mine, and that is all I receive, a simple thank you?"

CHAPTER ELEVEN

*I*ndignation festered, and Gwynna's brow twitched. "Oh, ye be expectin' another walk in't gardens?"

Why did she have to happen on Mr. Trevethan instead of the gentleman she'd danced with the night before? What was his name again?

Mr. Trevethan threaded the reins through his gloved hands. "Ah, you are still upset about my behavior last night. I suppose I ought to be grateful then that you even condescended to thank me."

She needed to proceed with care, to remember who this man's father was, that he still held her fate in his hands. He'd also admitted to his wrongdoing. Almost.

Unfortunately, she disregarded her warning completely.

"Yes, ye ought to be grateful."

She tipped her nose to the sky then walked along the pathway again. His horse's hooves thumped against the earth, the steed coming up behind her as his broad, brown nose stuck out at her side.

She turned her head the opposite way to view the sea, willing it to share its comfort with her again, but the pain in her hands called out and the aches in her muscles gnawed—and his horse snorted just above her ear.

Her nose wrinkled. Mr. Trevethan really wasn't a gentleman. Of course, there was no need for him to treat her as a lady. Why wouldn't he be riding his horse alongside her, talking down at her like the working class female she was?

"Do ye need somethin' more, sir?" she asked.

"Merely an answer or two, if you would be so kind."

She bit her tongue for as long as she could. "And if I don't, will ye threaten to reveal me secret to others again?"

"Not necessarily. I just feel, in light of our situation, you would be more than willing to divulge certain information."

She folded her arms over her belongings, wincing as her blisters brushed against the rough fabric. "Such as?"

"Such as why you were at the ball in the first place. Where you found the lovely gown you wore." His leather saddle creaked as he leaned forward, his voice lower. "If you've ever tasted lemonade before last evening."

Her feet stopped, and she craned her neck to eye him astride his horse. He raised a knowing brow, and her cheeks over-heated, as if the sun had just doubled its light. He'd seen her gulping down the lemonade then, had he? Blast. Sophia had warned her that impropriety would be the death of Gwynna at the ball.

The scent of leather and musky cologne drifted under her nose as he dismounted. "I also wonder if Mr. and Mrs. Hawkins would be upset knowing a bal maiden had snuck into their ball, sampled their drinks, and shouted at one of their guests."

Gwynna's embarrassment fled at his veiled threat. He thought he could intimidate her by telling Sophia what Gwynna had done? Oh, how she wished he *would* tell her friend. She could only imagine the tongue lashing he'd receive.

A thin smile spread across her lips. If he insisted on playing games with her, she would play right back. "Per'aps ye ought to ask them then."

He blinked. "Very well, I think I will."

She sniffed out a laugh then walked away. What was the matter with her, goading him into action? What if he became angry with her friendship with Sophia then he really did tell his father?

She was mad. Pure and simple.

"I have more questions," he said, walking up behind her. "If you answer them, I promise not to say a word to anyone."

She kept silent. Why was he following her, expressing such interest in her reasonings? Had he not better things to do as a gentleman than pester a fatigued maiden?

"That first day at Wheal Favour," he continued, "I learned you were *returning* to work at the mine. What caused you to leave in the first place?"

She pressed her lips together. Her parents had always taught her to respect others. They'd also encouraged her to have a strong mind and will. In this case, she truly did not feel she was obligated to answer.

"Was it because of someone you worked with perhaps?" he guessed. "A friend, or perhaps someone more?"

The silence was heavy, but Gwynna would not be prodded into saying another word. She eyed the smooth, white sand of Tregalwen Beach, only now just coming into view.

"Or did you leave because of an injury, or perhaps the work-load? I've heard a bal maiden's task is as arduous as a miner's."

She gritted her teeth. She would not turn around. She would *not* turn around.

"Were you not up to the task? I suppose some women prefer being a lady and just aren't capable of doing—"

She spun on the heel of her boot, facing him with nostrils flared. Why did he insist on provoking her? Following her like a fox tracking a rabbit? His smile was innocent, but his eyes glinted playfully.

Gwynna felt anything but playful. "Ye think I can't handle the work of a maiden?" She raised her hands between them, fingers in the air, palms facing him. His smile faltered as he eyed the blisters stippling each crevice in her skin. "I'd like to see your own hands doin' the work I just did with these."

She lowered her palms. "'Tain't your business why I left the mine, or why I chose to do what I did last night. As ye can see by the sweat on me brow and the calluses on me skin, I ain't be no lady. I be a bal maiden, through and through. And that, sir, be enough for I."

His brow rose only a fraction—from being impressed or stunned, she couldn't tell.

Gwynna bobbed up and down in as dignified a curtsy as she could muster then left the man behind.

This time, his footsteps didn't follow.

She reached the top of the next ridge, the green cliffside accented with purple heather opening up in front of her. She clenched her fist in frustration, but the piercing pain of her blisters nearly made her cry out.

She couldn't understand him, mocking her, speaking with her. What did he want?

Before she could fathom an answer, she noted two girls standing at the sandy mouth of the beach.

She narrowed her eyes. Delen, Tamesin? Kerensa's sisters. What were they doing out here alone?

She rushed toward them when they turned worried eyes on her.

"What be the matter, girls?" Gwynna asked at once, leaning forward to better hear them over the sound of the sea.

"It be Kerensa," Delen said, pointing to the beach. "She be gettin' into a scrap and told us to stay up here, but we be fearin' she be gettin' into too much trouble."

Gwynna followed their line of sight to farther down the beach where a group of seven young women joined together on the sand, fists flying and intermittently screaming.

She cursed under her breath. With a dull pounding of her heart, she glanced up the ridge from which she'd come. Mr. Trevethan *had* followed her and was now watching the fight with an intent stare.

If the girls didn't stop their fighting now, they'd be spaled for certain, and none of their families could afford to lose a single pence.

"Stay here," she commanded the girls, then she sprinted down the sandy slope alone.

*a*s Gwynna neared the brawl, she recognized three of the young women from Wheal Favour. The other four hailed from a neighboring mine, Wheal Jenny.

"Aye!" she called out, cursing the sand that jumped into her ankle-high boots and slowed her down.

The girls didn't stop, their shouts mounting as she approached, their fists clenched as they swung pitch after pitch.

"Stop! Kerensa! There be someone watchin' ye!"

A few maidens turned as she called, backing up out of the crowd as their eyes caught sight of Mr. Trevethan above.

"Kerensa!" she tried again, heading straight for her friend.

Kerensa was the largest of them all, hitting girl after girl who pushed toward her, but when she found Gwynna, she paused. Anger pulsed across her red face, veins bulging in her neck. "They be stealin' our goods, Gwynna!"

Gwynna had an inkling as to what she was speaking of, but fighting wouldn't resolve the issue, especially not with a gentleman observing them. "Mr. Trevethan's son! He be watchin'!"

Kerensa easily pushed aside a girl attempting to assail her, then focused on the cliffside. She blinked, taking a step back from the group, though the others continued their fight.

Gwynna jumped right into the middle of them, heading straight for a girl atop another, pulling them apart by their collars. Fabric ripped as she shouted for them to look to the cliffside.

"Do ye want to lose your wages?" she cried out. "Do ye want him to ride for the constable?"

"Aw, get'on outta here!"

Gwynna turned just as a girl she recognized from town, Ruth Ayer, raised a fist and dealt a blow to Gwynna's ribs.

Gwynna growled in pain. Ruth raised another fist, but Gwynna ducked just in time. The girl was considerably larger, but Gwynna used her anger to propel her forward, shoving her shoulder into Ruth's stomach and pushing her with all her might until Ruth stumbled in the sand.

As Ruth lay winded, face-up on the ground, the others finally stopped.

Gwynna turned to the girls from Favour, chest heaving. "What are ye all doin'? Have ye no sense? If that man tells his father, we'll lose half a day's wages!"

"What that be to us?" Ruth had finally managed to stand, shooting a scowl toward Gwynna.

"It matters to ye 'cause he'll tell Mr. Bargus, as well. Ye know how the mine owners speak."

The girls exchanged glances. Tears riddled their dresses, sand carpeting their hair and speckling their faces. The energy between them simmered, like the crest of a wave about to dive headlong into the water.

"Calm down," she commanded, "then tell me what be the cause o' all this."

Everyone spoke at once.

"They stole our belongings!"

"Go on, we found 'em first!"

"They be liars, the whole o' 'em!"

Gwynna raised her hands between the two sides. "If ye start fightin' again, I'll run to that gent and get 'im to alert the constable meself!"

They grumbled again but kept apart.

She faced Kerensa. "Ye tell me what 'appened."

"'Course she be listenin' to her friend first."

Gwynna shot Ruth a look of exasperation then faced Kerensa once more.

Kerensa wiped the blood trailing down her lip and pointed to a small pile of boxes and crates poking out of the sand. "They be stealin' the goods we found, Gwynna. They dug 'em up and was takin' 'em for themselves 'fore we caught 'em."

"Who's to say *ye* buried them?" Ruth returned. "Ye could 'ave claimed they be yours when ye found us diggin' 'em up."

Their voices merged, each shouting their version of the story before Gwynna's rose above the rest.

"I be sorry, friends," she said, addressing the other maidens, "but the goods here belong to Kerensa."

Gwynna had no evidence for the truth, but she knew Kerensa, and she knew her friend wouldn't lie.

"'Tis true," Kerensa said. "We found 'em mornin' last, on our way to the mine. We hadn't time to bring 'em home, so we buried 'em and marked 'em with the twigs ye saw here 'fore."

"Ye 'ave no proof," Ruth protested.

Gwynna motioned to the pile. "Kerensa, can ye name everythin' ye found?"

"'Course I can." She rattled off the small list as the girls inspected the goods. "There be a crate o' wine padded with straw, a few writin' boxes, and one with an officer's name on it."

"Ye could have easily seen all that simply by bein' right here," Ruth muttered.

Kerensa raised her eyebrows daringly. "In the lieutenant's

box be a golden sextant, a compass, and a small purse with coins in it."

The girls glanced to one another as Ruth rifled through the box. With a scowl, she stood, thrusting the box to the ground. Coins jingled, and the compass jumped to the sand. "Fine. They be yours, then. But a word of warnin', next we find any o' your treasures left behind here, we'll be sure to take 'em 'fore ye come back."

She left them with a look of warning, then motioned for the girls to follow her, leading them down the beach.

"Thank ye, Gwynna," Kerensa murmured as soon as they were alone with just the girls from Favour. "We would've been in a world o' hurt had ye not shown up."

"*Would've* been?" Gwynna eyed the red mark on Kerensa's cheekbone and caressed her own ribs.

Kerensa merely grinned as she knelt down in the sand by the goods.

Gwynna glanced up to the sandy ridge. Delen and Tamesin were just beginning to approach, but Mr. Trevethan still stood there, perched and focused, like Mr. Harvey at the mine. Was he waiting for her so he could learn what had caused the ruckus? Well, she wouldn't give anything away if it was going to injure the maidens.

She joined the other girls in the sand, moving to the small officer's box and replacing the compass with the rest of the navigational equipment. She closed the lid and eyed the engraving on the side of the box, smoothing her thumb over the metal to wipe away the sand.

"E-d-m..." She finished with a sigh, frustrated with her poor attempt to read the name. "Can any of ye read this?"

One of the girls examined the letters. "Edmund...Har-Harris?"

Gwynna dropped her gaze to the box. She knew the lieutenant.

He was working at Golowduyn Lighthouse with his previous captain after their ship wrecked nearby. He was a good man who didn't seem to mind very much about classes. They'd carried on conversations themselves at a few gatherings on the beach.

She eyed the goods the girls began to divvy out. "These must be from the HMS *Valour*." The ship once headed by Captain Gavin Kendricks. "They'll fetch a pretty penny if ye choose to sell."

"Exactly." Kerensa paused, looking at the other girls. "I think it be only fair that we share some o' this with Gwynna. After all, she did 'elp us to keep it."

The other maidens instantly agreed, but Gwynna protested. "No, I ain't be takin' what rightfully be yours."

"Not even a bottle?"

Her parents would certainly appreciate the wine, but she couldn't. She hadn't been the one to discover the items. "No, I be all right. Only…"

She eyed the box. She couldn't tell them she wished to give the box and its contents back to the lieutenant. There were far too many valuable things here to improve the lives of these maidens and their families. Besides, it was common practice for locals to keep what they found on the beach.

Still, she couldn't keep the box, knowing who it had belonged to. She could simply tell the lieutenant she'd found it empty. She didn't want to lie, but if it benefited the greater good, she almost needed to.

"Can I keep this? Not what be inside, mind. Just the box."

They agreed, then Gwynna helped fill Kerensa's towser pockets with the navigational equipment.

"I ain't be keepin' all o' this," she said.

Gwynna continued unimpeded. "Ye be needin' this more than any o' we."

"'Tis true," another maiden agreed.

Gwynna motioned over her shoulder to where Kerensa's sisters were almost upon them. "For your family."

Kerensa blinked furiously, hiding the moisture in her eyes. "Thank ye," she mumbled in a broken tone.

Gwynna squeezed her friend's shoulder in response, then wrapped the box in her apron and held it close to her chest. She'd deliver it to the lieutenant when she had a spare minute.

"Ye best get these home quick, girls," she said, motioning to the goods. "Mr. Trevethan still be up there."

The girls worked more swiftly, thanking Gwynna again before she made her way up the beach. She touched her aching side where Ruth had hit her. She didn't believe anything had been broken, but that girl's fist was like the head of a spalling hammer.

A horse's nicker at the top of the beach reminded her of Mr. Trevethan's watchful eyes. She wasn't sure what she could say to the man to avoid his alerting the constable as to what had occurred, or his father. Of course, if she did attempt to do so, he'd probably agree, then ask for something in return. Answers to his questions, a kiss. She wouldn't put anything past the man.

In truth, it would be better if she simply remained silent.

And this time, *really* remained silent.

CHAPTER THIRTEEN

*J*ack stared speechless. What on earth had he just
watched?

Gwynna approached his spot at the mouth of
the beach, flitting her eyes toward him. A squared lump had
formed beneath the apron she held against her chest.

"Are ye still here?" She plopped down on the sandy grass and
removed her boots one by one.

"What was that about?" he asked.

She poured a stream of sand from her footwear. "Life, Mr.
Trevethan."

He fixated on the maidens on the beach as they packed away
items in their own aprons. He'd seen the whole thing, the fists
swinging from girl to girl, Gwynna being hurt and responding
with a tackle of impressive force, especially for one so thin.
Then she'd broken apart the fight and held her hands up, as if
controlling the girls with an invisible force.

Footsteps retreated against the dirt pathway. When had
Gwynna replaced her boots and begun to walk away?

He tugged his horse from the grass to catch up with her.

Gone was his teasing nature from before, set abruptly aside at the sight of women—*women*—fighting.

Now he had even more questions.

"What were you all fighting over?"

"Some o' the maidens took things that didn't belong to 'em."

He reached her side, shocked at her unconcerned state. Was this an everyday occurrence for a maiden, brawling? "So they chose to fight? Couldn't they have simply discussed the matter?"

Gwynna scoffed. "Oh, and ye 'ave never exchanged fists 'fore? Gotten angry o'er a game o' cards or a misplaced bet?"

"Well, of course *I* have. But women tend to—"

"So it be well for ye to defend your rights, but not for we?" She stopped walking, facing him directly. "This be our way o' life, sir. Per'aps ye ought to learn it 'fore ye judge."

His lips parted as he stared down at her. Her cheeks no longer held the red rouge from the night before, replaced instead with dirt from the mine and a healthy ruddiness, no doubt due to her fight. Her hair was twisted back with that same tatty rag from the counthouse, a few stringy strands sliding out from beneath it.

Even still, she had remarkably pretty features. Full lips, though slightly chapped. A petite nose. Amber eyes in the shape of the wide almonds he'd once eaten from the top of a blanc-mange in Bath.

And the way she stood there, proud and sure of herself, even before a gentleman, was appealing. Appealing and intimidating.

He struggled for something to say under her watchful, accusatory eyes. Why was he faltering for words? He'd never done so before.

"I suppose I'm simply unaccustomed to your ways. I found myself imagining the ladies from the ball last night behaving in the same way and found it rather shocking. Can you imagine them, pulling one another's hair pins out because of a misplaced glove?"

Was it just his imagination, or did he truly cause a smile on her pretty lips? It was gone before he could tell.

"Well, as I said 'fore, I be no lady." She walked away. "Good day, sir."

She clearly didn't wish to speak with him any longer, just as she hadn't before. And yet...

"Where did you learn to fight in such a way?" he asked, catching up with her again. "By practice?"

"Me father and brother taught me."

"You have a brother? Does he work at the mine, too?"

She pulled her eyes away so he couldn't see them. "He used to. He died a few months back."

"Oh. I'm sorry."

She didn't respond. Was her brother's death the reason she left Wheal Favour? What made her come back?

One question at a time, Jacky. Mama always said he'd had an inquiring mind. Father had said *too* inquiring.

"To be clear," Gwynna said, drawing his attention back to the present, "we don't be fightin' daily, as I'm sure ye be thinkin'."

He tossed his shoulders up and down in a guilty shrug.

"And I don't take to violence, neither. Father be the best man that I know. He taught that words be better than fists. But when words don't work, a shoulder should do the trick."

He pushed up his lips, impressed. "I'd best stay clear of your father then."

Her humorless eyes didn't flicker. "Yes, ye should."

He pulled back. This woman, this bal maiden, was fascinating.

He'd been stunned when she'd turned him down at the ball. So stunned, in fact, that he'd been unable to devote any real attention to flirting and coaxing other women, resulting in a loss to Hugh, who'd ended the evening with the intoxicated girl in the yellow dress.

Jack didn't mind losing this time. He'd been too preoccupied with thoughts of Gwynna, who had appeared so regal that she'd tricked everyone in the room into believing she was a lady. She couldn't be a complete rascal, though, not with how she stopped the fight rather than egging them on. The other maidens must respect her a great deal to have listened to her.

He glanced over his shoulder, but the girls were no longer visible on the beach as he and Gwynna had moved farther away. "Did all of those maidens work at Wheal Favour?"

Gwynna studied him. "Will they be gettin' into trouble if I answer that?"

"No, I'm merely curious."

She scrutinized him as they walked side-by-side. He couldn't blame her for her hesitance. He hadn't exactly been trustworthy, what with all his threats, even if he had been teasing. For the most part.

Finally, she responded. "Only the girls who stayed back with me work at your father's mine."

"But all of them listened to you when you told them to stop?"

"Yes, sir. 'Cause I told 'em ye would alert the constable and your father."

Ah, there was that elusive smile. Only the corners of her lips tipped up, but it did funny things to his stomach.

"So you used me to inflict fear within them?"

"Be I not right to do so? Why wouldn't ye tell, after threatenin' to reveal me, when I was only havin' a little harmless fun at a ball?"

"So that is what you were doing, simply taking pleasure in a night away?"

She tucked her hair behind her ear. "Be that difficult to believe that a maiden be wantin' an evenin' of pleasure?" Her gaze dropped to the path they walked across. "I only wanted one night to be someone else, but I couldn't even do that 'cause…"

"Because…of me," Jack finished. He winced at the sudden

ache in his chest, as if he'd been the one to be thumped by the stocky bal maiden.

She didn't respond, silence accompanying them as they walked.

Why should Jack feel culpable? This woman was the one who made the silly decision to dress like a lady. If he hadn't discovered her, *someone* would have.

Another path veered off from their own, and Gwynna took a few steps on it. "This be the way to me home. I'd best return now 'fore Mama starts to worry."

He nodded. He wasn't about to follow her, in case her father was at home and really was as good with his fists as Gwynna had suggested.

Not that Jack was doing anything wrong, of course. He was merely talking with her. Never mind that it was strange for a gentleman to be pursuing—not pursuing.

He chuckled tensely to himself, rubbing his hand against the back of his neck. *Pursuing* made it sound like he wished to court the maiden, which he obviously did not. They were from two very different worlds, worlds that could not come together without colliding catastrophically.

He was simply *asking questions* of a maiden.

Still, as she walked away, he felt that same pull to her that he'd had the night before. The same pull that had caused him to ask for a dance, and the one that had been hindered when that dance did not occur.

"Gwynna?" he called out before he could stop himself.

She turned around, the wind blowing her tendrils under her smooth, soot-covered jaw. "Yes, sir?"

"I was never going to tell, you know."

She stared.

"About you at the ball. I had no intention of really telling anyone."

She tipped her head in disbelief.

"Truthfully," Jack pressed, taking a step forward. "I was merely having a bit of fun, but I can see it was not aptly timed."

She narrowed her eyes pointedly. "So ye be teasin' then 'bout bringin' me out to the gardens?"

Discomfited with the seriousness of their conversation, he attempted a joke, spreading a smile across his lips once more. "Well, I'd never say no to a kiss."

She crinkled her nose as she turned away.

What was the matter with her? Women usually fawned over his smiles.

"No, no. Please, wait." What was the matter with *him*? Why did he care so very much to have her know the truth?

He hesitated when she turned around with a passive look. "What do ye want, sir? I be afeared that I can't give me trust to ye."

"You can, actually. If my mother taught me anything, it was to be true to my word."

Which is how he found himself in Cornwall, visiting Father. She'd made Jack promise not to abandon him completely.

"Your father didn't teach ye the same?"

He pulled his attention to the sea. "Father taught me other things."

How to put work before all else. How to forget one's family.

He cleared his throat and faced Gwynna, who watched him expectantly. "You have my word. I will not tell another soul about your evening at the ball, nor about the fight on the beach."

Their eyes met. Jack held his breath, expecting Gwynna to brush him aside and return home.

To his surprise and pleasure, she nodded. "Very well. I believe ye. Thank ye, sir."

He tipped his head in a small bow. When he straightened, she was already walking away.

He followed the sway of her skirts near her calves. A lady

wouldn't be caught dead with such high skirts, but he certainly wasn't going to complain about the sight.

Her words from earlier echoed in his mind. *"I ain't be no lady."*

A smile played on his lips, his eyes lingering on her legs. No, Gwynna certainly wasn't a lady. But if a bal maiden could dress as a proper woman one night—then tackle another to the ground the next—she was undeniably remarkable, lady or not.

CHAPTER FOURTEEN

*J*ack closed his bedroom door behind him and slipped on his riding gloves. He set down the corridor absentmindedly, filtering through the options as to where he ought to ride with his cousins that morning, when he glanced up at the painting of a horse on the wall.

Interesting, he couldn't remember the last time he'd seen that one.

He halted, looking from side to side. He hadn't been down here since he was a child, before he'd been sent away. It was the corridor he avoided almost as much as he avoided his father—the corridor that led to his mother's old room.

Guardedly, he studied the third door on the right, *her* door. The smooth dark wood, the square paneling. His chest tightened uncomfortably. With Mother's weak constitution, they'd spent hours together in that very room. Memories of what had occurred there saturated his mind—reading with Mama in the mornings, slipping in late at night when he'd had night terrors, wiping her brow when she'd taken a turn for the worse and the nurse was resting.

Father was absent during it all.

Anger burned Jack's insides, as it did whenever he considered his own inability to save his mother—and his father's decision not to.

As his scowl grew, so seemed the door until it towered above him, ready to swallow him whole. He blinked, willing the door to return to its regular size before he spun swiftly away.

How had he allowed himself to become so distracted as to walk down that corridor? He shook his head, securing his gloves as he headed for Hugh and Amy, who awaited his arrival in the front hall.

"There you are," Amy said with a broad smile. "Hugh was just about to set forth in search of you."

Jack gave a polite smile, though his nerves were still rattled. "My apologies for the delay. My valet couldn't find my gloves."

"That's all right, isn't it?" Hugh said. "Now tell us, Jack. Where have you decided to take us this morning?"

"Well, I thought—"

The front door opened, interrupting his words as Father stepped inside.

"Ah, good morning to you all." His red cheeks and cheerful countenance grated on Jack's nerves. How could the man be so happy after all that had occurred in this house?

"Going out riding, I see," Father continued. "Whereabouts?"

Father's smile faltered when he caught sight of Jack's glower.

With a deep breath, Jack put out his anger like a candle snuffer to a flame. It wouldn't do to despise the man again. Mama wouldn't have approved. A simple dislike would suffice, but he needed a distraction if he was to ignore Father's many faults.

He raised his brow innocuously. He knew just the thing.

"I was going to lead the way toward Golowduyn Lighthouse, as I've not seen the structure since I was a child."

Father nodded, handing his hat and gloves to a footman. "Ah, marvelous. Mr. and Mrs. Kendricks run the lamps now. I do believe they hold tours for those interested."

Jack brushed aside the information. "Yes, it would be a fine outing. But then I thought…perhaps another tour around the mine would be even better."

Father's brow rose. He was clearly surprised Jack would wish to go back, after his son's less-than-enthusiastic response to it during their last visit. "Oh?"

"I know you've just come from there, but Hugh has expressed a desire to see it, and Amy might find it interesting. Or she could simply keep to tea in the counthouse."

"Oh, yes, I should like that very much," Hugh agreed.

Amy's eyes merely trailed away disinterestedly.

"Perhaps we might even be allowed down the shaft this time," Jack suggested. "And the bal maidens are always fascinating to watch."

There was one maiden in particular he was keen on watching today, one he hadn't seen working, when last he was at the mine. Gwynna would certainly provide the perfect distraction, even if he couldn't speak with her.

Father squinted one eye, hesitating. "I'd be happy to show you around again, but about the shaft…I don't know, son. It's quite dangerous."

"Come now, Father," Jack said with a coaxing smile. "How else am I to learn the ways of our new family business if I can't take part in every aspect of it?"

Instantly, Father's shoulders straightened, his eyes brightening. "Well, I suppose we can do so, if you really wish to."

Jack should have felt worse about moving the strings of his father's will in just the right way to get what he wished, but he didn't.

Once Father had retrieved his gloves and hat from the footman, Jack exchanged excited looks with Hugh and urged a sighing Amy to come along as they moved out into the bright sunshine.

After a rainy day yesterday spent indoors playing chess and whist, Jack relished the feel of the sunshine once more. He was in high spirits, despite his trek down the wrong corridor—and having to spend more time with Father—for Amy and Hugh were there, and they would provide the perfect diversion.

As they rode for Wheal Favour, Hugh moved farther ahead with Father and spoke of the investors of the mine, and Jack held back with Amy. Typically, she would prattle away about some dress she'd just purchased or the latest gossip sailing about Bath.

But today, her mouth was uncharacteristically still, like the night of the ball.

"Are you well, Amy?" he asked.

She glanced up at him, blinking mutely before seeming to come out of a deep thought. "Oh, very well, thank you. Just admiring the beautiful scenery."

Then her eyes dropped back down to the chestnut mane of her horse.

Jack eyed her for a moment before shrugging and *actually* admiring the scenery. Amy was a kind woman and quite intelligent. As a young girl, she'd clearly been interested in him, but he'd only ever considered her a sister, so the fascination soon subsided, and they became friends. But ever since coming to Cornwall...

He shifted in his saddle. No, he was done thinking of his troubles. If Amy wished to remain cryptic, then he'd let her be.

He raised his chin, eying the blue skies above. An occasional cloud would pass by the sun, creating a chill with the brisk wind, but as the clouds passed, the warmth sunk into his dark jacket and rested on his shoulders.

The sea soon appeared on the horizon, sparkling as it carried a vessel across its waters, white sails drawn and billowing. Jack had missed this view, and he would miss it again once he left.

They reached the mine shortly, leaving their horses tied near the counthouse. As Amy situated herself near the small fire with Mrs. Harvey, the mine captain's wife who'd come for a visit, Jack and Hugh were instructed to move to the side room.

An earthy smell permeated the small space as they removed their jackets, waistcoats, and cravats, and replaced them with musty, oversized clothing to protect their white shirts and pressed breeches.

"I wonder who died in these to make them smell so poorly," Hugh joked as he threaded his arm through the sleeve of a black jacket.

Jack's smile broke. Days ago he would've laughed but knowing Gwynna's own brother had died in the mines had stolen all humor from such a comment.

When they were properly covered with caps to protect their heads, they left the counthouse and traipsed down the muddy hill to the lower cliff, following Mr. Harvey and Father, who'd also changed into protective wear.

Jack blended in more naturally with the other miners now that he was dressed as one of them, but a few bal maidens still stopped their work to greet him with broad smiles, some of them saucily winking at him before breaking into fits of giggles.

Amused with the attention, he quickly scanned for any sign of Gwynna. Where were the spallers anyway? Father had said they used long-handled hammers, but the only tools he could see were spades and shorter mallets.

As they approached the engine house and shaft, however, Jack finally caught sight of her. He smiled at first, proud of his discovery, then his pace slowed until he stopped altogether.

CHAPTER FIFTEEN

*J*ack had seen the maidens working before, walking the rounds with his father, on occasion with his mother from afar, but Gwynna…she was so thin, so petite. How was she doing such work?

The other spaller nearby was thicker, smashing into the ground twice before managing to strike the ore with her blunt hammer and obliterating it from her sheer power.

Gwynna, however, placed the ore in the mud with her boot, pulled back, then swung straight toward the rock with finesse.

Crack!

She landed blow after blow without error, directly onto each rock she set her eye on. Her face was red from exertion, her skirts and apron splattered with mud and soot, but she didn't pause in her work, and Jack remained unseen.

How was this sustainable? How could a woman of her size—or any person, really—go on in such a way for so many hours? Of course he'd seen bal maidens before, but only ever as a child, unable to appreciate their tenacity.

These women were incomparable to those in Bath's society, those women who would shrink walking a mere half a mile or swoon after a single dance. What Gwynna was doing was nothing short of incredible.

"Jack? Are you coming?"

Jack plucked his attention away from Gwynna and made for the engine house, where Hugh held the crooked, wooden door open for him.

"Captured in the presence of their filthy beauty?" Hugh chuckled, motioning to the maidens.

His comment, though simple teasing, scratched at Jack's patience. Was everything a joke to his cousin?

They entered the small engine house, water pooling at the bottom of their boots. A large pump worked in the center of the room, spewing water from below ground and out of the engine house.

"This is rather dangerous, gentlemen." Mr. Harvey said, "and I must urge you to proceed with care."

Hugh sniffed in disbelief and nudged Jack with a devil-may-care attitude. But when Mr. Harvey showed them to the dark shaft, Hugh's smile vanished. Jack was sure his cousin's pallid face was not due to the weak sunlight filtering into the room by mere cracks between the wooden walls.

As Jack peered into the darkness, his own stomach turned. A faint candlelight flickered, revealing a wooden landing with another ladder leading down the opposite side.

Jack wiggled his fingers, unsure if he wished to continue, but as Father led the way, and Mr. Harvey quickly followed, Jack took the plunge and stepped down onto the rickety ladder.

Step by step, they descended into the darkness, the small light from the engine house no longer reaching them. Jack drew steady breaths, and Hugh's constant jokes ended.

All was eerily quiet, apart from the clinking of tools against solid ore and a continuous coughing that grew louder the closer they approached.

Jack's legs trembled after a number of stairs, and he gripped the wooden ladders until his knuckles were white. Not that he could see much of them, what with the small candles they carried needing continual relighting as dripping water snuffed them out. When the candles *did* go out, the black was so thick, Jack thought if he just reached out, he could grasp the darkness between his fingertips.

When they finally reached the bottom, he shook out his hands and sloshed across the muddy ground. A few lanterns lined the curved tunnel of the shaft they walked down. Miners with their muddy clothes and blackened faces glanced behind them as the visitors approached.

"It isn't as glorious as one would think, is it?" Father asked, coming up to walk beside Jack.

Jack could only shake his head. The darkness was already wearing on his soul, his eyes straining to see through the dim light. The tunnel smelled of smoke and dense, sodden earth. A chill ran through the air, and a deep rumbling sounded overhead. He eyed the top of the tunnel, a few pebbles tumbling to the ground.

"Boulders moving along the seabed," Father explained, his eyes directed upward.

An uneasiness crept over Jack. They were below the sea?

The darkness, the smell, and the cold pressed on his chest. He wasn't sure what he'd been expecting, but the stark reality of these men's lives was humbling, if not depressing.

"This is where we've found a new vein of copper."

Jack tried to shake his unsettled feeling and pulled his attention to where Mr. Harvey had stopped to run his finger along the wall. "The men are working to extract it, then they'll send it up for the surface workers and maidens to reduce to smaller sizes."

Jack stepped forward, his boots making a sucking sound as he pulled them from the mud. A few of the miners stepped aside to allow them to better see the copper, coughing into their fisted hands. Jack couldn't quite make out the sight of the ore, though he nodded all the same.

"Unbelievable, isn't it?" Hugh whispered. "I don't know how they manage working in such conditions."

Jack followed his gaze to where the nearby workers chiseled away at the walls. He didn't understand it either.

As Hugh spoke with Mr. Harvey, one of the miners stepped back from the wall, doubling over with a cacophony of coughs. His whole body trembled until he stopped, wheezing into a soiled, black handkerchief.

Father moved to the miner's side. "You all right there, Merrick?"

Jack stared. Merrick? Gwynna's father? The soot and mud rendered his face unrecognizable, though Jack now remembered his stringy hair reaching to his chin.

"Yes, sir. I be fine." Mr. Merrick's fingers shook as he jammed his handkerchief into his pocket.

Father removed his hand from Mr. Merrick's shoulder, seemingly aware of the miner's discomfort from the attention he'd received. "How are the timbers managing?"

Mr. Merrick cleared his throat, his eyes trailing up a broad piece of wood pressed against the sides and roof of the tunnel. "They be doin' their task, sir."

"I'm only sorry they weren't up earlier, to prevent other accidents."

Mr. Merrick nodded with a gaunt expression. Father's eyes met Jack's, but Jack pulled his attention to a small stream of water trickling down the sharp angles of the wall. He didn't want to encourage his father any more than he already had that day in regard to Jack's interest in the mine.

Truth be told, there was a small part of Jack that *was* interested. Not only about the workings below, but above grass, as well—and the people who dedicated the whole of their lives to working the mine.

"When are the other timbers scheduled to be up?" Father asked.

"Within the week, sir. It ought to stabilize the rest o' the workings then."

"Excellent."

"We're all grateful, sir, that ye took the time to listen to we. It'll save many lives, to be sure."

Jack stared more intently at the timber, attempting not to scoff. Father listened to these miner's problems. He made their lives better. He saved *them*.

Jack shouldn't be surprised. Father was always focused more on work than anything else.

"Son, you remember Travers Merrick?"

Jack feigned surprise as he approached them. "Yes. How do you do?"

"Fine, sir."

An awkward silence followed, as did Mr. Merrick's scrutinizing stare. Had Gwynna told her parents that she'd dressed above her station? And more importantly, did she tell her father about Jack's proposition the night of the ball?

He shifted in the mud, grateful for the dim light that shadowed the warmth on his cheeks. He hoped to high heaven Gwynna had kept Jack's behavior to herself.

He noted the resemblance between father and daughter, their thin frames and the way they maintained eye contact. Most working class men and women skirted their eyes. Gwynna and her father watched stalwartly until it suited them to look away.

This man really didn't have the strength to barrel someone to the ground as Gwynna had suggested, did he? After what he'd seen Gwynna do, he wasn't going to chance doubting it.

"How long have you been working here, Mr. Merrick?" Jack asked.

"O'er twen'y years, sir. And more 'an that at another mine, 'fore Favour opened."

Jack could hardly fathom spending twenty years of his life in such cold darkness.

"Merrick knows the workings better than anyone," Father said. "He was here when it first opened. Isn't that right?"

Mr. Merrick simply raised a bony shoulder in a shrug then regarded Jack once more with an unreadable expression. Yes, he certainly had a spine of steel like his daughter.

Merrick soon excused himself to get back to work, and Jack pretended to listen indifferently as Father explained the process of the mine below ground, though his interest had piqued drastically.

When Hugh's pale face turned a shade of green, Father suggested they return to the fresh air above. The three of them moved toward the ladders, but Jack paused as Mr. Merrick coughed again, still attempting to work through his hacking.

"It happens every day, with all of them," Father said, motioning with a toss of his head to the miners. "Merrick's is the worst."

Jack fought the urge to care, but as the coughing grew, bouncing down the caverns and reverberating in the silence, he lowered his voice. "Can nothing be done for them?"

"Short of closing the mine and having them work elsewhere?" Father scratched his head with a helpless shrug. "That would destroy their livelihood. I've been discussing the problem with Mr. Harvey. He's suggested bringing Merrick up to do surface work, but it's just a matter of having enough workers below ground now. I know he'd appreciate it, though, as would his daughter."

Considering the way Gwynna had spoken of her father before, Jack knew she'd appreciate it very much.

CHAPTER SIXTEEN

*G*wynna split open another piece of ore, sweat trailing down the bridge of her nose. She swiped the droplets away and swallowed, the inside of her throat dry and coated with dust.

The sun was merciless, but she preferred it to the rain they'd suffered the day before—and the emotions such weather pushed straight to the surface.

The rain had poured down in droves the day Jago died.

She swiped a hand down her face, allowing the soiled glove to gather as much moisture as it could in its already damp fabric, then she railed her hammer into another rock and another. After, she tossed the ores into the shallow, wooden barrow now filled to the brim.

Two barrow girls, Tamesin and another fifteen-year-old, appeared before Gwynna in an instant, depositing an empty barrow nearby her workstation.

"Thank ye, girls," Gwynna said, pressing a hand to her ribs where Ruth Ayer had pelted her. The ache had subsided only slightly.

The girls lifted the full barrow by its long handles on both ends. The weight of the box, handles, and ore was easily more than the combined weight of them both, but they managed to lift the barrow after a few huffs and carted it away to the riddling station nearby.

As she was left alone, Gwynna viewed her empty pile with a great sense of accomplishment. Not a moment passed, though, before a male surface worker approached with his wheelbarrow and tipped a new pile of ore for her to break apart.

She stifled a yawn and nodded her gratitude as the man tipped his cap then pushed his empty wheelbarrow away.

"The work never be done," she muttered to herself.

Instead of thinking about the hours she had yet to complete, Gwynna focused on what an overall pleasant day she'd had.

She was making excellent progress on the amount of ore she was getting through, she'd welcomed back the permanent dull ache in her muscles like an annoying but constant friend, and her blisters had finally scabbed over after two days of bursting open and bloodying her gloves. Best of all, the sun was shining, and the roaring waves were keeping her company once again.

Yes, today was a good day, indeed.

"Gwynna!"

Gwynna paused mid-swing, glancing up as Kerensa approached with a wary eye.

"What are ye doin'?" Gwynna asked, looking to the upper cliff where, thankfully, Mr. Harvey did not stand. "We'll both be in trouble if ye ain't careful."

"I 'ave to ask," Kerensa said in a hushed tone. "Ye spoke with Mr. Jack Trevethan, didn't ye? About keepin' quiet?"

Gwynna nodded. "He gave me 'is word, so long as we promise not to brawl again."

At this point, Gwynna was on a direct path to living eternity beneath fire and brimstone, what with the amount of lying she'd been doing. After the fight on Tregalwen Beach, she'd told Kerensa that Mr. Trevethan had stopped her and warned her to cease fighting. The falsehood was necessary, though, to avoid the maidens thinking she'd had any further conversation with the gentleman beyond a brief word.

Kerensa nodded, still anxious. "I only ask 'cause he be here now."

Gwynna's breathing hitched. He was here, at the mine?

She swept her gaze round the grounds before her. So much for a day of relative ease. She hadn't seen him since that day on the cliffs two days before. What if he spoke with her here and produced rumors about them?

Instantly, she chastised her stupidity. Mr. Trevethan had only spoken with her when she was dressed as a lady or when they were alone on the cliffside. A gentleman wouldn't want to risk the rumors that would form by speaking with a bal maiden in public.

"Where be he now?" she asked.

"He just be comin' up from tourin' the shaft," Kerensa continued. "I'm sure he'll walk the grounds with 'is father again. I be that worried, Gwynna. Per'aps he goes back on 'is word?"

For a fleeting moment, anxiety wrung Gwynna's stomach like a sopping rag. Suppose he *did* go back on his word?

However, as she considered the change in his manner when she'd come up from the fight on the beach, she rejected the feeling.

His provocative smile had all but dissipated, and his words had lost their teasing touch. His eyes weren't as dark as she thought them to be, either. They boasted a warm brown tone, like the color of freshly dug up earth or wet bark on a tree after a spring rain.

His eyes had spoken the truth, and Gwynna had believed him.

She rested a calming hand on Kerensa's shoulder. "There be nothin' to worry about."

"How can ye be so sure?"

"I can't. Not for certain," she answered truthfully. "But I believe he be in earnest."

Kerensa chewed on her lip then glanced beyond Gwynna with a curse. "They be comin' now," she hurriedly whispered.

Gwynna peered over her shoulder. Sure enough, Mr. Jack Trevethan walked toward the engine house. He'd removed his topper and jacket, the sea breeze ruffling his black hair and flapping the fabric of his jacket against his arm.

Her heart trilled against her chest. Purely from nerves, she was sure.

He was accompanied by his father and two others whom Gwynna did not recognize—one, a gentleman with light hair, and the other, a lady who stepped cautiously across the mud, raising her skirts with pinched forefingers and thumbs, little fingers pointed in the air.

Gwynna turned swiftly as they focused on her station, intent on working as if nothing out of the ordinary was occurring. Because nothing out of the ordinary *was* occurring.

The mine had visitors nearly every week—investors, family members, curious passersby, and strangers from other counties. She had no reason to be nervous, even if Mr. Trevethan held a secret about her that could destroy her livelihood. She was certain no more surprise meetings or conversations would occur between them again.

"He be the one with darker hair?" Kerensa asked. Why had she not yet returned to her work?

"Yes," Gwynna replied.

Kerensa arched an appreciative brow. "I ain't seen 'im this close 'fore. He be quite fine to look at."

Gwynna lined up a few rocks in a row at her feet. "I s'pose, if ye like that sort o' thing."

"That sort o' thing?" Kerensa asked incredulously. "What's not to like about 'andsome men in tight fittin' clothes? Do ye think he be the type o' gentleman to stick with 'is own people? Or would he be fine kissin' maidens?"

Gwynna stiffened, heat pricking her cheeks. She needed to relax. Kerensa had no way of knowing Gwynna's personal experience in that regard—that the gentleman was more than willing to kiss a maiden, or at the very least tease about it.

She attempted a flippant shrug. "I've no idea. What I do know is ye better go on 'fore they catch us both not workin'."

"You mean 'fore they catch us both gawkin'."

Kerensa chortled as Gwynna pushed her away, and her friend finally departed.

Gwynna went about her work as ordinarily as she could, though as Mr. Trevethan and the others approached her station, her limbs strangely weakened.

"These are the spallers," the elder Mr. Trevethan explained, keeping a safe distance from the flying ore. "After the ragging is done by the surface men, they send the ore to these maidens."

Gwynna lowered her head. She wouldn't look up at them. She was to pretend they weren't even there. But then, would they think her rude, unappreciative of the chance to work there? Perhaps just a peek wouldn't hurt.

Slowly, she shifted her attention toward them. The elder Mr. Trevethan was pointing out the ore in the pile before Gwynna. The young gentleman and lady's eyes were scaling the engine house, clearly not listening.

And Mr. Jack Trevethan, well, he was staring at Gwynna.

Gwynna swallowed, attempting to push her heart back down to her chest, as it had somehow managed to leap to her throat.

A look passed between them, one that spoke of the secret they shared. Hurriedly, she redirected her attention to the ore. For him, having a secret was probably simple fun. For her, it was too precarious a position.

"After the spalling, the ore is sent to cobbers, then buckers,"

Mr. Peter Trevethan rambled. "Each maiden in turn crushes the ore smaller and smaller. Washing stations are situated between each process to ensure no copper is left behind."

From the corner of her eye, Gwynna noted each young person now focused on her, instead of where the mine owner pointed.

This must be how the animals felt on exhibit in the Royal Menagerie—everyone gawping at some strange creature they'd never seen before. Of course, Gwynna had never seen the menagerie herself, but Sophia had told her of it.

Gwynna would never get any work done with them in her line of sight, so she shifted her body away and continued with her work, refusing to be intimidated by their presence.

As she pelted the ores, snippets of their conversation drifted toward her.

"You see how she hits the ore perfectly to—"

Crack!

"Our finest spaller—"

Crack!

"She's stronger than she appears—"

A few more shattered pieces, and Gwynna brushed them aside to gather more. Her nerves threatened to break, but she would not allow herself to falter, no matter the spectators.

She tossed the ore into the barrow then hammered again.

"Might we proceed, Jack?" a feminine voice spoke behind her. "Watching this work is rather tiresome."

Gwynna huffed out a quiet, disbelieving breath. They should've known better than to bring a sensitive woman to such a harsh place. Ladies were hardly able to bear the sounds and smells—and now apparently the sights—of a copper mine.

As their retreating footsteps moved to the cobbers nearby, Gwynna paused, finally comprehending what the woman had said. She'd called Mr. Trevethan by his given name. Did that mean they were family, or were they attached in another way?

Discomfort wedged between her ribs and her lungs. Mr. Trevethan wouldn't have asked to kiss Gwynna if he was actually engaged, would he? Even if he *had* been teasing?

She held her hammer overhead. Not that she cared if he was engaged or not. The man could do whatever he wished. Just like all gentlemen, she supposed. Never mind the offense they caused.

She whirled the hammer toward the ore, but in a split second, she knew something was off. Her placement of the ore and her hammer weren't lined up properly. Instead of striking the center of the rock, Gwynna hit to the side of it. Pieces of ore flew in every direction, pelting her skirts and arms.

She dropped her hammer and yelped as a stinging pierced the side of her face.

CHAPTER SEVENTEEN

*G*wynna pressed a glove to where the shattered rock had sliced her skin near her left temple. A crimson circle ate across the grey cloth as she pulled her hand down.

She cursed under her breath.

"Are ye hurt, Gwynna?" Kerensa called out from across their stations.

Swiftly, Gwynna tugged her bonnet lower to hide the wound, darting a look toward the visitors—mostly to a certain son—who'd turned toward her at the sound of her cry.

"No, I be well, Kerensa," she said loud enough for them to hear.

She picked up her hammer and set about her task again. Mr. Jack Trevethan's eyes remained on her until he followed his small party toward the bucking area.

Only then did Kerensa inch closer to her. "Ye be bleedin', Gwynna. All the way down your cheek."

Gwynna had thought it was sweat. She swiped it away, only to see Kerensa's concerned brow. "Ye best get it looked at."

"I can't. I'll lose the progress I be makin'."

As the throbbing continued, and Kerensa's stares increased, Gwynna dropped her hammer with a heavy sigh. "Fine. I be goin'. Just to please ye, mind."

She continually wiped away the draining blood with her gloves, making a mental note to apologize to Mama for once again sullying the stockings. Her mother sacrificed so much. Gwynna would hate to be considered ungrateful to her.

After determining that the Trevethans had not yet returned to the counthouse, their horses still tied nearby, Gwynna knocked on the door to alert Mr. Harvey of her wound.

"'Tis be but a scratch, sir," she began as he eyed her cheekbone.

"But better to be safe than sorry. I'll send for the mine surgeon."

As he went out to see his wife home, who'd stood by in silence with a kind smile, Gwynna was instructed to sit on a chair by the table until the surgeon arrived.

She avoided the continuous stares coming from the counthouse woman who hunched forward, cleaning the fireplace. Was the woman still upset about the dirt Gwynna had supposedly tracked through her workstation the week before? Or was she still concerned that Gwynna was hankering for her tasks?

Gwynna nearly laughed at the idea. She far preferred spalling, even if she was injured from time to time.

She hunkered down in the chair, ignoring her pulsing cheek and preparing herself for the inevitably long wait for the arrival of the surgeon. The first time she'd been injured as a young girl on the gears near the engine house, the mine surgeon had taken longer than an hour to arrive, other times she'd had to wait nearly two.

To her surprise, however, a quarter of an hour had hardly passed by before he stepped into the dim light of the counthouse.

"Hmm. Yes, it won't require sutures, but it will need to be cleaned," the surgeon said after eying the gash.

As he removed a few shards of ore from the open wound, Gwynna fisted her hands, welcoming the pain she caused the scabs on her palms as they provided a distraction from the stinging in her cheekbone. Was the man using a butcher's knife instead of his small tweezers to remove the debris?

By the time he was finished, the bleeding had begun anew, so he wrapped a piece of fabric around her head to hold a small bandage in place, sopping up the blood.

"You ought to spend the rest of the day at home," the surgeon suggested as he eyed his various instruments now covered in her blood. "Just to be sure you don't swoon."

Swoon. Gwynna didn't swoon.

"Yes, sir," she agreed vocally, though she'd already concocted a plan on how to hide the enormous bandage that made her look like she'd just undergone extensive surgery.

If Mr. Harvey saw the dressing, even beneath her thin bonnet, he would in no way allow her to continue working. The pain wasn't even terrible, now that the surgeon had stopped mauling it.

She left him in the room cleaning up his supplies, then slowly closed the door behind her. After taking a thorough look around the counthouse, she darted to the side of the structure. With her attention forward, she slowly unwrapped the cloth, catching the smaller bandage pressed against her blood before it could fall to the mud below.

The long piece of cloth wasn't smooth by any means, but it was sturdy. Perhaps she'd use it to supplement her gloves or for better protection for her legs. She stuffed it into her towser pocket then dabbed the small bandage against her cheekbone before examining it.

Just as she suspected, the blood was nearly gone. All she needed to do was place her bonnet slightly to the side. It would hold the bandage in place for a final moment or two, then she'd be perfectly fine to—

"Healed already?"

She started, twirling as she faced a pair of fine, dark brown eyes.

"Mr. Trevethan," she breathed. "Sir, I didn't know ye were there."

"Obviously." He leaned against the side of the counthouse with arms folded.

She glanced over her shoulder, then behind his. "What are ye doin' up here?" she whispered. She hated to think of the counthouse woman or the surgeon overhearing them. "And where be the others ye were with?"

"You needn't worry. They're down near the engine house, listening to my father go on about the circling whim. I made the excuse of checking on our horses, but..." He eyed her up and down. "I found a much better distraction."

So he was back then, the teasing man from before. The blackguard. She'd best leave before someone caught them, or before he found some other way to torment her.

Placing her bonnet back on her head, she took a step back. "Well, ye must excuse me, sir. I've work to do."

"Wait just a moment, if you would be so kind."

She paused, and he took a step toward her.

"You allowed the surgeon to see you?"

"Yes, sir. 'Twas only a scratch."

"That's not what that large bandage in your apron would suggest." He motioned to her towser.

She slipped off her cotton bonnet and pushed back her hair to reveal more of her cheekbone. "See? 'Tis not even bleedin'."

"And the surgeon said you were all right to go back to work?"

Why was this any of his business? It's not like he was the owner of the mine. Yet. "Yes, sir."

His look of amusement increased. "Lying comes quite naturally to you, does it not?"

She raised her chin indignantly. "Fine. If ye must know, he did tell me to go home. But I can't afford to, nor can I afford to be speakin' with ye any longer. Now, I expect ye to keep me wound to yourself. Good day, sir."

Heavens, was she bold around the man. Mother would scold her for not showing more respect to a superior. Father would probably slip her a proud wink.

Gwynna hid her smile and walked away, slipping the bandage between her replaced bonnet and her upper cheekbone.

Mr. Trevethan spoke after her. "Before you go, how many more secrets do you expect me to keep, just so I can prepare myself?"

She paused, peering around the other side of the counthouse to ensure they were still alone. Finally, she moved closer to him with a lowered voice. "What do ye mean?"

"All of your secrets," he repeated. "You dressing as a lady—"

"Hush!"

"—breaking up that brawl. Now you ask me to hide your injury. What is next? Asking me to keep silent about a secret tryst you have with one of the miners?"

She pulled a face. She really shouldn't stoop to his level, especially when she needed to leave before someone caught them together, but blast it, if she didn't have to defend herself. "I be havin' no tryst, sir. And ye wouldn't 'ave to keep all these secrets if ye'd stop your meddlin'."

He opened his mouth, hesitating. "All right, you have me there." He tapped his finger against his chin. "Very well. I'll keep your wound a secret, as well as all the others, if you promise to answer just one question for me."

She huffed a laugh. "No, sir. Ye ain't goin' to trick me again. I know ye won't tell, even if I leave now."

She spun on her heel, taking only one step before her bonnet was plucked from her head, as if a bird had snatched it with his claws.

She whirled around, the bonnet dangling from his fingers.

"What ye be up to now?" she asked, retrieving the small bandage that had fallen to the ground due to his pilfering. Fortunately, the mud hadn't time to cling to it yet.

He held the bonnet out to his side. "I'll give it back if you answer my question."

She tried to snatch it, but he pulled it back out of her grasp. After another attempt, she propped her hands on her waist and pursed her lips. "I haven't time for this, sir. I need to be about me work."

"Then you'd better hurry and answer my question." He raised his brow in a dare.

"Why do ye 'ave so many questions?" she asked, lifting her arms out to the side. "Can't ye just leave me alone in peace?"

"I'm afraid I can't." His eyes were far too bright with glee.

She eyed the bonnet. She wouldn't reach for it again. He was too quick. Perhaps there was another way to retrieve it without giving anything away.

Either way, she needed to make haste. Every moment that ticked by made it more likely that they would be discovered.

"Very well," she said, folding her arms. "What be your question, sir?"

For a moment, he seemed surprised at her willingness, then he recovered with another charming smile. "Where did you get the gown? The pink one you wore to the ball?"

She quirked an eyebrow. "*That* be your question?"

He nodded.

Gwynna contemplated her answer. She really ought to respond truthfully. If she satisfied his curiosity, perhaps he'd finally leave her be.

"I..."

Before she could continue, another thought struck. Did he... did he think she *stole* it? A chilled pride iced throughout her. Of course, what else was he going to think? Certainly not that she'd befriended a lady. No, that was far too above a bal maiden.

Fine, if the gentleman expected such a response, she would allow him to have it.

Leaning forward, she lowered her voice with a sobered expression. "I...I stole it, sir."

"You did?" he questioned. The playfulness drained from his eyes, and his smile faded away, replaced with—to his credit—shock. So he hadn't truly thought her capable of such a thing?

Her eyes flickered towards the bonnet lowering in his hand. "Yes, sir. I be so ashamed, but I can't 'elp meself. Ye see, sir, 'tis a bad habit I've formed, stealin'. Ye won't tell, will ye?"

He blinked. "No, no. I'll keep it to myself. But perhaps you ought to—"

His words ended as she swiped her bonnet from his hands. She pressed the bandage back between her wound and the fabric, then tied the bonnet securely beneath her chin. "Don't believe everythin' ye hear, sir."

He stared open-mouthed. "You mean to say, you didn't steal the dress?"

"We maidens ain't be as bad as ye think, sir."

With a flourished curtsy that would've made Sophia beam with pride, Gwynna left the gentleman behind the counthouse with only his growing smile for company.

CHAPTER EIGHTEEN

$\mathcal{B}$y Saturday afternoon, Gwynna was more than ready for a break from the mine. She'd worked her half-day at Wheal Favour, retrieved her basket and instructions from Mama, then set forth for St. Just.

The streets were filled with maidens and ladies, miners and gentlemen alike, each class anxious to see what new items shops offered or what delectable pastries they could snag from the bakery. Stalls sprung up outside nearly every door, displaying clothing, food, and household items, such as shining cutlery or tin plates.

Gwynna meandered through the masses, purchasing the items for which Mama had sent her—a few apples, a small bag of oats, and nails to fix their buckling floor. She nestled them securely in her small basket then weaved her way past children holding onto the backs of their mother's dresses and around gentlemen who purchased their sweethearts sparkling jewelry.

She stepped past a stall with fluttering ribbons in every color just as someone shouted her name from nearby.

"Gwynna! O'er here!" Kerensa stood outside the Golden

Arms Inn with a few other maidens who waved their arms at Gwynna. "Will ye join we today?"

A few ladies dressed in blue and brown Spencer jackets walked past Kerensa with taut lips, no doubt displeased with her shouting, though they didn't a glance once in her direction.

"I can't. Mama's orders, see." Gwynna raised her basket. "Next time."

"I be holdin' ye to that," Kerensa returned, then she slipped inside the inn with the other girls.

Gwynna stared longingly at the door closing behind them. It had been a long time since she'd joined the maidens there for market day, celebrating their moments away from the mine with a few drinks, perhaps even a hearty bowl of stew.

Not that the Golden Arms had particularly appetizing food. But it was better than barley bread and pillas.

She pressed her fingers against the pocket of her apron, tracing the outline of her faded coin purse. She'd been saving her pocket money for a few weeks now. Certainly a few farthings could be spared for a bit of pleasure.

With a firm shake of her head, Gwynna redirected her attention forward. Perhaps when she was paid for her work at the mine, she would allow herself a reward.

Never mind that the quarterly sale of ore wasn't for another month and she wouldn't see a pence until then. Mama was more important than a glass of ale or a Banbury cake or jam tartlet—and she was in greater need of new stockings than Gwynna was for a drink or pastry at the moment.

She traversed through the crowds and approached the modiste's shop, straightening her shoulders and aligning her courage before entering.

As she stepped over the threshold, Mrs. Follett's eyes instantly fell upon her. The woman's greeting shifted from an open smile to tight lips that put even the counthouse woman's cold scowl to shame.

"Good mornin'," Gwynna greeted, closing the door with a short jingle from the bell above.

"Shirley," Mrs. Follett said in a short tone to her assistant.

Shirley stood at the window display, splaying fans and propping up parasols. Mrs. Follett jerked her head toward Gwynna, signaling for the girl to see to her.

The young assistant nodded, skirting past the display and counter toward Gwynna with quick steps. "How can I help you, miss?" she asked with an easy smile.

At least there was one person in the shop who would deign to see to her. "I be lookin' for some stockings."

"Oh, yes. Right this—"

"Show her the ones in the back," Mrs. Follett interrupted. She didn't look up from the ledger book in which she wrote. "Perhaps she'll be able to afford those."

"Yes, Mrs. Follett," Shirley dutifully responded, though she gave Gwynna an apologetic look.

Gwynna would rather have the counthouse woman than Mrs. Follett as a taskmaster. At least she could still hear the sea from inside the counthouse.

"Right this way, miss."

Gwynna followed Shirley past Mrs. Follett and down the center of the room. Counters lined both sides of the space with stools for ladies to sit as they were shown hats, gloves, or parasols. Sunshine poured in from the front windows, lighting the swaths of fabric hung between the counters. Like a waterfall during a vibrant sunset, the cloth poured to the floor in purples, blues, pinks, and yellows.

Gwynna stopped at the back of the room as Shirley stepped behind the counter. Standing on a stoop, the assistant reached for the small drawers piled high on top of each other, stacked midway against the walls nearly to the ceiling.

She reached for one of the highest drawers and rifled

through the stockings as Gwynna placed her nearly full basket on the counter, yawning behind a fisted hand.

"Long day at the mine?" Shirley asked.

Gwynna nodded. Yes, she'd had a long day at the mine—and a long night with very little sleep, as usual.

Her nightmares always began the same, reliving the day Jago died. The rain, the explosion. Men coming to surface, but not him. Then the dreams shifted beyond reality. Gwynna would enter the shaft to rescue her brother, only able to hear his cries and see his frightened face before the water swelled up to drown her alongside him.

"You'll be happy for your day of rest then tomorrow," Shirley said, pulling Gwynna's attention back to the present.

"Yes, I be lookin' forward to it."

Shirley pulled out three stockings then moved to the counter and laid them out before Gwynna. "Will any of these suit?"

Gwynna eyed the three white stockings and chewed the inside of her lip.

That morning, since she hadn't been able to go back to sleep, Gwynna had helped Mama with the early morning chores before heading to the mine. As they readied the laundry for later today, Mama raised her skirts to step over a pile of clothing, and Gwynna had caught sight of the gaping hole in her mother's stockings, stretching from her ankle to well up her calf.

Gwynna wanted to purchase something fine for Mama—especially after Mama had used her only other pair of stockings for Gwynna's gloves. But if her mother wore white ones, they'd be covered in dirt faster than she could say, well, dirt.

"Have ye any in other colors? Per'aps blue or brown?" she asked.

"Yes, of course."

As Shirley returned the stockings to the drawer and pulled

out another, Gwynna glanced to her left where a few bands of fabric were displayed at her side near the counter.

A lovely red silk stood out among the others with stitched floral designs throughout. She glanced to Mrs. Follett, who still focused on her writing. If the shopkeeper caught her touching the fabric, she'd accuse Gwynna of spoiling it with her unclean, maiden hands.

She'd be smarter for keeping her fingers to herself, but the temptation was too great.

With slow movements, Gwynna reached forward and stroked the smooth cloth that draped all the way to the spotless floor. It felt very much like the dress she'd worn at the ball. Would she ever be able to wear such fine clothing again?

Her brow lowered. She ought to be grateful for what she'd had the opportunity to do. Besides, it's not like she wanted to go through the anxiety of *that* situation again. Although, without Mr. Trevethan's sudden appearance, she had been enjoying herself immensely.

Shirley returned to the counter with more stockings in hand, and Gwynna snatched her fingers away from the fabric.

"How about these, miss?"

As Gwynna examined the brown stockings, the bell above the door jingled, and more customers entered the shop.

"Oh, good morning!" Mrs. Follett's cheerful voice mimicked the ringing bell. "What can I help you both with this lovely day?"

The customers were obviously wealthier than Gwynna. That wouldn't be difficult. Most people in St. Just earned more than miner families.

Instead of eying the fine women in their no-doubt silk dresses, Gwynna focused harder on the stockings. They were all fairly simple, in varying shades of brown with very little decoration.

As she debated between two pairs, the conversation trailed toward the back of the shop.

"We were walking by and couldn't help but notice your lovely window display. I wonder, might we see the parasols a little closer?"

"Why, of course," Mrs. Follett happily agreed.

The patter of their feet crossed the wooden floor.

"These are the latest fashion, as I'm sure your fine eye can see."

Gwynna picked up a simple, brown pair. These would do nicely for Mama.

"Oh, yes," the customer responded. "These are as fine as any I've seen in London or Bath. What do you think, Jack?"

CHAPTER NINETEEN

*G*wynna dropped the stockings onto the counter, her fingers rigid. It was just a coincidence. She was sure of it. Mr. Trevethan wasn't here. There were no doubt a plethora of gentlemen in St. Just with the same name.

But there was no mistaking his deep, buttery tone. "Oh, I'm sure I know nothing of the fashion of parasols."

With a subtle shift of her feet, Gwynna leaned closer to the counter, further hiding herself behind the swaths of fabric. She pressed a hand to her brow. What was the possibility they'd run into each other in town, at the modiste's no less?

There really was no need to hide. He wouldn't be speaking with her, just like at the mine. Until, of course, they'd been safely hidden behind the counthouse.

But here, they were in a public space with three other women present—one of whom was potentially his betrothed. The most he'd do was regard Gwynna with a knowing smile, which she wasn't even obligated to return.

"Of course you do," the female voice—whom Gwynna was now certain was the same woman who'd been at the mine—

responded. "I chose you to join me here for a reason. You have a far greater fashion sense than my brother."

"Miss?"

Gwynna's eyes swung up. Shirley tipped her head with a look of concern. "Are you well?"

Gwynna nodded, leaning closer to the counter and pointing to the stockings she'd just dropped. "'C-'course. I'll take this pair, please."

Shirley gave her an odd look after Gwynna's whisper, then reached for a small brown paper and strand of twine. As she wrapped the stockings for Gwynna, the conversation at the front of the shop continued.

"Well, I may not know if it's the latest fashion," Mr. Trevethan was saying, "but it certainly becomes the blue in your eyes."

"Oh, you are such a charmer, Jack."

A gnawing picked at Gwynna's stomach, as if she hadn't eaten in days. Yes, he certainly *was* a charmer. How would this woman feel, knowing Mr. Trevethan had asked a *maiden* to kiss him?

"Here you are, miss," Shirley said, sliding the package toward her on the counter. "That will be two shillings and six pence."

Gwynna fished out her coin purse and pulled out the correct change, setting them in Shirley's outstretched hand before retrieving the brown package, freshly tied with the twine.

"Come back again, miss," Shirley said with a smile.

Gwynna nodded, grateful for the girl's kindness, despite the unease erupting inside her. As Shirley busied herself returning the stockings to the drawers, Gwynna took an overtly long time situating the stockings in her basket.

With a sidelong glance, she discovered Mr. Trevethan and the woman still facing the window with their backs turned toward her. If she made a run for it right now, she'd be able to sneak past them without notice. Then she didn't have to ignore *or* acknowledge him.

In swift movements, she retrieved her basket from the counter and spun on her heel, darting forward.

She only managed a single step before her boot caught in the red silk. The shredding of fabric split the air as Gwynna tumbled to the ground, landing on her hands and knees. Her basket and its contents scattered across the floor, as did what little vanity she'd had before that moment.

Apples rolled underneath the stools, the stockings hit the bottom of the counter, and nails rattled as they bounced out of their box and across the wood. Worst of all, the sack of oats burst open, splaying the off-white grains in a skewed circle across the floor.

Gwynna's knees and palms stung from her fall, as did her cheeks, burning hotter than Wheal Favour at noonday in June.

Not a split second passed by before the clatter from her tumble was replaced by Mrs. Follett's cries and angry footsteps.

"Oh, oh, my goodness!" she said, pulling the red fabric through her fingertips. "You've ruined it!"

Gwynna scrambled across the floor, praying she might gather her belongings before Mr. Trevethan and his—well, whoever she was—joined them. "I be sorry, Mrs. Follett," she mumbled, scooping the nails up in her palms and dumping them freely into her basket, not bothering about the pricks she received.

Mrs. Follett still hovered above her. "Well, I see no way around this apart from you simply paying for the damage done. At least a yard of it."

Gwynna's chest tensed. She shot a quick glance up, noting a long tear straight up the edge of the fabric. Mrs. Follett would require her to buy a yard, even if the tore stretched only a few inches away from the edge? How could Gwynna afford to do such a thing? "Ma'am, I don't—"

"Is that really necessary?" Mr. Trevethan's voice cut through her own.

What Gwynna wouldn't give just to leave the shop right now. How could she have allowed this to happen? She could only imagine his look of amusement. Although, his tone had sounded void of humor.

His boots stopped before her, and he hunkered on the ground, retrieving the bag of oats carefully to salvage as much of the grain as possible.

"I'm sure no harm was meant by the maiden, Mrs. Follett," he said as he moved next to the nails.

"Oh, do not harm yourself, Jack," the lady warned. "Your leather gloves would provide greater protection."

"That is all right, Miss Paxton," he responded, still grasping his gloves in one hand as he gathered the remaining nails with his other.

Gwynna tried not to notice the pucker in the lady's brow, in Miss Paxton's brow, at being ignored.

"But-but the damage cannot be undone," Mrs. Follett continued.

"Yes, I can see that," Jack said, "but it was an accident. You can salvage the rest of the silk, or if that does not suffice, I will pay for the damage done."

Gwynna's cheeks flamed. Was he defending Gwynna because he knew she couldn't afford such fabric, or simply to be nice? She didn't need him to fight her battles. Though, Mrs. Follett was more likely to listen to a gentleman than a maiden.

The floor creaked as he stood, and Gwynna reached for the stockings and the last apple she could find.

"Just a moment, Jack," Miss Paxton said, moving around to caress the fabric. "This red is quite lovely, and truthfully, I see no point in your purchasing fabric you shall never use. No, I shall buy the fabric and enough to make a new gown. Mrs. Follett, I'm sure that will satisfy the debt?"

Mrs. Follett's expression shifted from lividity to sheer pleasure. "How very generous of you. Indeed, it will, Miss Paxton."

The young woman no doubt missed the modiste's joy, for Miss Paxton's stares belonged solely to Mr. Trevethan.

Gwynna secured the last of the items in her basket, scooping up what was left of the oats and dumping them to the bottom. She pressed a hand to the floor to stand, pausing as Mr. Trevethan's fingers hovered before her.

Was he...offering to help her stand? Had he lost all sense, forgotten she wasn't a lady and could simply rise on her own? She should do just that and flee from the shop as quickly as her legs could carry her.

But then, how could she deny his kind offering, especially after what he and Miss Paxton had just done for her, saving her weeks' worth of wages?

She swallowed, her mouth dry as she placed her callused fingertips into his outstretched palm. His fingers curled around hers, his thumb resting just below her knuckles as he pulled her gently up. Warmth tiptoed from her fingertips to her arms until it enveloped the whole of her chest.

Their eyes met as she stood. His lips parted, his gaze intent. Was he considering how rough her hands were, especially when compared to Miss Paxton's?

He blinked then finally released her, holding his hands behind his back as he cleared his throat. "Are you hurt, after your fall?"

"No, sir," she murmured. "Thank ye, to ye both."

She nodded to Miss Paxton, who handed her an apple Gwynna hadn't seen.

"I ought to be thanking *you*," she said with an easy smile. "Were it not for the mishap, my attention might not have been drawn to this fine silk."

Gwynna couldn't detect a hint of malice in the woman's tone, but her cheeks still stung.

After another ignored apology to Mrs. Follett, Gwynna lowered her head and darted from the room, not bothering to stop for a stray apple she spotted tucked beneath another swath of fabric. The fruit wasn't worth another potentially embarrassing moment before Jack Trevethan.

At least there was one bright spot in all of this mess. She hadn't done anything that would require him to keep a secret.

This time.

CHAPTER TWENTY

"*T*hen I just ran out the door and straight here without stoppin'. I be tellin' ye, Sophia. 'Twas awful."

As she finished her tale, Gwynna buried her face in her hands, rubbing away the dull ache in her temples that had surfaced from reliving the memories of the past week.

She'd just spent the last quarter of an hour sitting on an iron bench at the edge of Fynwary Hall's gardens, reiterating to Sophia all that had occurred between herself and Mr. Trevethan —from the threats at the ball to his helping her that afternoon at the shop. Now all she wanted was to burrow under the ground like the rabbits who'd hidden from her as she passed by their home on her way to the estate.

"I'm so sorry all of this has occurred," Sophia said, placing a comforting hand on Gwynna's shoulder. "Had I any knowledge of it, especially Mr. Trevethan's behavior at the ball, I assure you, Mr. Hawkins and I would have been the first to defend you."

Gwynna plopped her hands into her lap with a heavy sigh. "I know, but don't worry. I ain't be too upset about that. Not anymore, at any rate. I be more horrified at fallin' in front of 'im. I've ne'er been so embarrassed in me whole life."

Sophia stared. "So you aren't offended by his threatening you?"

"I certainly ain't be justifyin' his behavior. But I can't be mad about it, as he's more than made up for it by keepin' me secrets."

Sophia hummed in response as she seemed to consider Gwynna's words. Gwynna shifted against the bench. The small cushion she sat upon did very little to prevent the ironwork from numbing her backside.

A red-breasted robin chirped from a nearby ash tree, the sun peering through its rustling leaves above like a child moving back and forth to see baked goods inside a shop window.

Her stomach rumbled. She should've taken Kerensa up on her offer to go to the inn. Gwynna would've had pocket money left over to still purchase Mama's stockings—and then she would have missed seeing Mr. Trevethan altogether.

"Do you find him an upstanding gentleman?" Sophia asked, breaking through the silence. Her eyes focused on the grass nearby. "Or do you feel discomfited around him?"

Gwynna knew what Sophia was hinting at—did Gwynna feel Mr. Trevethan would ever take advantage of her?

In an instant, she shook her head. "No, I ain't never felt uncomfortable 'round 'im. Not in that way. But I be nervous only 'cause he be botherin' with me. Helpin' at the shop, talkin' and askin' questions. I can't understand why he be so interested in me."

Sophia leaned back against the bench, her eyes taking on a faraway look. "I do wish I knew more about his upbringing. I know very little of him or his family, apart from his mother dying when he was a child."

"I didn't know that." Gwynna frowned. The familiar ache of empathy within her. "Do ye know what 'appened?"

"Only that she was very often ill due to a weak constitution.

After her passing, his father sent Mr. Trevethan to live with family in Bath, as he could no longer care for his son."

Gwynna rubbed the heel of her hand against her chest to dispel the pain in her heart. So not only had Mr. Trevethan lost his mother, but also, in a sense, his father. Losing Jago had been an insurmountable struggle for her, but she didn't know what she'd do without her parents.

"His lack of parental love might explain his behavior. Or perhaps there is another reason." Sophia glanced sidelong at Gwynna.

"What be that then?" she asked.

"He has taken a liking to you."

Gwynna gaped. "Mr. Trevethan, to me? Sophia, ye be mad."

Leaning forward, Sophia's smile grew. "Can you imagine if it were true, though? Would you be opposed to him liking you?"

"Well, 'course not, but I…" She blinked, her mouth opening and closing as she fished for the right answer. "It be nice to 'ave any 'andsome man's attention, but 'tis a ridiculous idea."

Ridiculous though it may be, her spirits brightened, as if a fire had been lit in a dark cove. Still, she turned her back on it. It wouldn't do to dwell on wishful thinking. Especially when Mr. Trevethan could very well be engaged to Miss Paxton.

No, especially because Mr. Trevethan was a gentleman, and Gwynna was still a bal maiden.

Uncomfortable with where the conversation had gone—and with how her stomach now rolled like the apples across the modiste's floor—Gwynna stood, rubbing the ache in the small of her back as she retrieved her basket resting on the bench. "I best be goin', Sophia. I wish to stay, but Mama'll be needin' 'elp with dinner soon."

Sophia stood. "Allow me to walk with you. I had Mrs. Patten bake a few small items for your family. I'd hate to have you return home empty-handed."

Gwynna smiled with gratitude as she followed Sophia

toward the house, where her lady's maid awaited outside with a basket.

Every visit, Sophia sent Gwynna home with freshly baked bread or pie, new needles and thread, or full baskets of potatoes or apples—all on top of another weekly delivery of food for the Merricks.

"Ye don't need to do this every time, Sophia," Gwynna said, her already full basket now overflowing with biscuits and tartlets. "Especially not now that I be workin' again."

The lady's maid curtsied then walked back to the house as Sophia waved a flippant hand. "It is my pleasure. I owe a great deal to you and your parents, as you well know. Besides, food is the only way I am allowed to help you, after you declined all of my other efforts."

She shot a pointed look at Gwynna, though her lips still held a whisper of a smile.

Along with a constant supply of food, Sophia often extended help to Gwynna in other ways, including volunteering to teach her to read and offering to hire her as a maid or companion.

Naturally, Gwynna had declined each offer. Not only did she fail to see the value in learning to read as a lower class female, she also couldn't fathom being in service, especially now that she'd resumed her work at Favour. Servants were beholden to their masters day and night and were required to adhere to strict guidelines. As difficult as spalling was, she wouldn't give up the freedom she tasted as a maiden.

Still, Sophia's offerings had been made from the goodness of her heart, and Gwynna hated to appear ungracious. "I be 'appy at the mine and with me work there, Sophia. But I hope ye know how grateful I be for your 'elp."

Sophia looped her arm through Gwynna's as they traversed to the front of the house, their footsteps brushing against the smooth, catered grass. "I'm truly pleased that you are happy. I do hope you will let me know if there is anything more I might do to help you and your family."

They shared a smile. Gwynna secured her grip on her heavy basket and nudged a playful shoulder against Sophia's. "I'd make the same offer for ye, but there ain't nothin' a maiden could do to 'elp a lady."

Sophia moved her eyes away in silence. Had Gwynna said something to upset her? "What be the matter?"

Sophia's eyes swung to hers. "Pardon? Oh, nothing."

"Clearly it ain't be nothin'."

"It's but a trivial matter, really. Nothing I cannot solve."

Since when had Sophia ever held back her words? Gwynna's intrigue grew. "Can I help ye with it?"

Sophia pulled her arm from Gwynna's, wringing her fingers as they walked side by side. Her uncharacteristic agitation unsettled Gwynna's nerves, like a breeze to a weakened flower, sending petals of her peace to scatter about the wind. What on earth was upsetting her friend?

Finally, Sophia responded. "As I said, it is nothing. But, well, Mr. Hawkins's mother has a very dear friend, Mrs. Parnell, who will be passing through St. Just on her way to visit friends farther south. According to Mr. Hawkins, Mrs. Parnell is rather fussy. She is expecting a small party to entertain her when she comes for dinner at Fynwary, and it would offend both Mrs. Parnell *and* Mr. Hawkins's mother if we did not provide one for her."

Gwynna nodded, attempting to keep up with the particulars of high society. It all seemed rather complicated, unnecessarily so. How different would her own life be if her only concern was planning a dinner party?

"We invited the Causeys to join us," Sophia continued, "but with Mrs. Causey approaching her confinement, they are to remain at home instead. And now I have no guests to come at all."

Frankly, Gwynna would have told her mother-in-law's friend to be happy with what she was given, but clearly, that was not an option.

"So what will ye do? Be there anyone else to 'elp?"

"Well…" Slowly, her eyes slid up to meet Gwynna's.

As realization struck, incredulous laughter bubbled from Gwynna's mouth. "Ye want me to sit in on your dinner party? Ye *are* mad, Sophia."

Sophia pulled in front of her, stopping their progression across the garden. With hands clasped together and raised under her chin as if she were praying, she faced Gwynna. "You must know I would never ask such a thing of you were I not entirely overcome with desperation, especially after hearing what else had occurred the night of the ball. But I've asked three other families, the Kendrickses, the Madderns, even Mr. and Mrs. Rennalls. No one is available to attend at such short notice. A public assembly is occurring that very night, and they've all made plans to attend."

Gwynna shook her head. Sophia couldn't be serious. She couldn't possibly be asking Gwynna to go through such an ordeal again.

Yet, Sophia continued, reaching forward and grasping Gwynna's forearm before Gwynna could say a word in protest. "You know my relationship with Mrs. Hawkins is on tender grounds. We've managed to form a friendship after a tentative beginning, but I should hate to do anything to ruin it now."

"And ye think bringin' a maiden to speak with your mother-in-law's friend will be a way to impress her?" Gwynna released a self-deprecating laugh. "Ye know me fitty way o' talkin' be horrible. The noise of the ballroom muted it enough, but with no other guests 'sides me, she be findin' out that I ain't be a lady in a second."

"But you wouldn't need to say a word. You know I love

speaking and can go on for hours. I promise, you shan't even have to make a single sound if you don't wish to."

Gwynna winced. She felt for Sophia's plight. Really, she did. But how could Gwynna dress as a lady again? Never mind that she desired to wear another silk gown. Never mind that keeping up appearances would be far easier without Mr. Trevethan and half of St. Just in attendance. She couldn't do it. Pretending to be a lady once was mad. Doing the same thing twice was simply asking for trouble.

"I be sorry, Sophia. But I can't risk everythin'. Not again."

Sophia's expression fell. Though a feigned smile stretched her lips, the hope in her eyes swiftly fled. "Oh, that is all right. There really is nothing to apologize over. I should not have asked you to do such a thing." She looked away. "Sometimes I forget what really matters. *Who* really matters."

They continued forward, guilt chewing at Gwynna's conscience, like a rat gnawing persistently in a floorboard to get to food. "What are ye to do then?"

Sophia drew a deep breath. "There is not much I *can* do. Mrs. Parnell must simply learn to be happy with Mr. Hawkins and me for company. If she or my mother-in-law are offended, that will be their fault alone. Besides, my husband's opinion—and my friend's—matter more to me than anyone else's."

Sophia's manner had calmed, and her words conveyed sincerity, but Gwynna was still unsettled as she absentmindedly scratched the scar at the back of her upper arm.

How often had the Hawkinses helped Gwynna? How often had they come to her aid when her family was going hungry, or when they needed help with repairs at their home and Mr. Hawkins was the first to arrive?

Gwynna had wanted to repay their kindness, and now was her chance. But could she really take on her identity as Miss Joanna Bell again?

As the name entered her mind, her heart leapt. To wear another gown, to have her hair done, to actually remain the whole of the evening instead of ending it prematurely—all of it sounded far too appealing. But she couldn't be that lady again...could she?

Gwynna chewed her bottom lip. Sophia had said the party would be small. Gwynna would only need to convince one woman of her status, and even if she didn't, she could leave before any lasting suspicion occurred. She also wouldn't have to convince her parents to allow her to leave, as she would be back long before midnight.

Maybe, just maybe...

With a sigh, she nodded. "Very well, Sophia. I'll do it."

Sophia instantly protested. "No, I'll not have you sacrifice so much simply for the sake of my pride."

"It be me own pride that be convincin' me to do this. I want to finish me night as a lady."

Hope twinkled in Sophia's eyes. "But I was being selfish before. All is well. I can handle my mother-in-law, and Mrs. Parnell can—"

"Hush now, 'fore I change me mind. I be goin', and that be final."

Sophia expelled a great sigh as she shot toward Gwynna with outstretched arms, nearly knocking her basket to the ground. "Oh, Gwynna. Heaven knows I don't deserve a friend as wonderful as you. It certainly is no wonder Mr. Trevethan has fallen for you."

Gwynna groaned, wriggling from her friend's grasp as Sophia laughed at her own words.

After discussing a few plans for the party that would be held the following Wednesday, Gwynna departed from Fynwary Hall with a lighter step than when she'd arrived.

Yes, she may have agreed to do something spectacularly

stupid again, but at least the situation would be more controlled this time.

And at least Mr. Jack Trevethan wouldn't be there to spoil her fun.

CHAPTER TWENTY-ONE

*T*hat was Gwynna. Jack was sure of it. He peered out of the carriage window as the horses pulled to a stop in front of Fynwary Hall. Gwynna was crossing the grass, a basket in the crook of her arm as she walked away from the estate.

What had she been doing here, visiting a servant perhaps? Is *that* how she'd attended the ball?

"Are you going, Jack?"

He glanced to Amy, who awaited him to exit the carriage after Hugh and Father had already departed. "Oh, yes. Forgive me."

He withdrew from the carriage with a brief glance at Fynwary Hall, its three-storied, beige stone reaching far above his head. Father had insisted they call upon the Hawkinses that afternoon, so Jack and his cousins had joined him after their time in town. Jack was certain he was going to be bored out of his wits visiting these people he hardly knew.

His afternoon was shaping up to be far better, now that he'd spotted the bal maiden.

As Hugh helped his sister from the carriage, Jack held his

hands behind his back and seamlessly slipped off his gloves, tucking them into his jacket and smoothing them down without notice.

He brought up the rear of the small group and waited just a moment before halting his progression.

"Oh, I believe I left my gloves on the carriage seat," he said, eying the departing carriage as it turned around the edge of the house.

"Why the devil did you remove your gloves in the carriage?" Hugh asked.

Jack hadn't thought of that. "I-I had a terrible itch."

Hugh and Amy exchanged glances.

"Can you not simply wait to retrieve them until after our visit?" Amy suggested.

Jack's footsteps crunched in the gravel as he backed away from the others. "I wouldn't wish to appear underdressed."

"We'll wait for you, son," Father said, securing his own gloves on his hands.

"Oh, there's no need," Jack said, already heading toward the carriage that was no longer visible. "You go on without me. I'll be but a moment behind."

He moved slowly until his family was shown inside. When the click of the door closing signaled he was alone, Jack veered away from the house and strode out across the grass.

Gwynna had gained much ground as Jack had attempted his escape, but his quickened pace allowed him to catch up with her swiftly.

However, a few steps away, his advance faltered. What on earth was he doing, chasing this woman down? What if someone from the house discovered him? How would he explain his behavior to them, *or* to Gwynna?

He had nearly convinced himself to turn around and slink back to Fynwary Hall, but at that exact moment, Gwynna glanced over her shoulder with a double take. "Mr. Trevethan?" She faced him directly. "What are ye doin' here?"

He shrugged, attempting to gain his bearings. "Merely visiting Mr. and Mrs. Hawkins. Are you doing the same?"

He tossed her a haughty smile, hoping to draw attention away from his erratic behavior.

Really, chasing after a bal maiden. Was he mad?

Gwynna raised her chin indignantly at his comment. "Per'aps I *was* visitin'. Per'aps I be friends with Mrs. Hawkins. What do it matter to ye?"

Jack would have never guessed this woman, standing with straightened shoulders and a stalwart gaze, was the very same who'd scrambled across the floor to gather her belongings at the modiste's shop.

When he didn't respond, she shifted her basket to her other hand with a sigh. "Be ye needin' somethin' from me, sir? Be that why ye chased me down?"

He stiffened. Why *had* he torn across the grass to track her down? That same discomfort from before crept upon him again, a warmth seeping through his skin and overheating his body like a chicken roasting over a fire.

Is this what embarrassment felt like? He wasn't sure he'd ever felt such a thing, always having had the upper hand with, well, everyone. But now, he had the sudden urge to escape in his carriage and leave his family behind to fend for themselves in finding a way home.

"Sir?"

He cleared his throat. "Yes, I was simply coming to ask if you were well after what occurred at the modiste's."

That was a good enough reason. As a gentleman he was required to ask after a woman's health, even if that woman was a bal maiden.

Gwynna crossed her free arm over her stomach. "Yes, I be well."

By her lowered eyes, Jack didn't believe her, nor did he blame her if she was still upset. Mrs. Follett had behaved abysmally, attempting to charge an impoverished maiden for torn fabric, though the fault had been her own for having the silk drape to the floor.

Jack had been unable to stop himself from coming to her defense.

Be a champion to women, Jacky, his mother taught him long ago.

He'd been failing miserably at that very task for years.

"I ought to thank ye again," Gwynna said, "and your...your friend, or whoever she be."

She turned her head after her laden comment, and Jack narrowed his eyes. Why did she wish to know who Amy was?

"Yes, it was good of her to purchase the fabric. But then, my cousin has always been kind."

"Oh, she be your cousin." She was clearly feigning disinterest.

He concealed his smile. "Yes. Growing up together allowed us to form a relationship rather like a brother and sister."

She took a step away without a response. "Well, if there be nothin' further ye need, sir, I'd best be on my way. I've chores, see."

"Of course. My apologies for keeping you."

She nodded, eying him sidelong before turning and leaving him behind.

He stared after her for a moment, opening his mouth to call her back. But without a good enough reason to do so, he walked away himself, deep in thought as he justified his actions.

He was clearly just speaking with her because he was bored —bored of remaining at Father's estate, bored with Hugh's constant need for gaming, bored of Amy's strange behavior.

Gwynna was just an easy distraction. Whenever he was around her, life seemed far more exciting.

The thought was supposed to calm his nerves, but his agitation increased until he joined the others in the sitting room.

"Sorry for the delay," Jack said with a bow.

"Did you find your gloves?" Amy asked.

Blast. He'd forgotten to replace them. He pulled his hands behind his back. "I did, thank you."

"Do come in, Mr. Trevethan," Mr. Hawkins said, motioning him forward. "Your father was just informing us of the happenings at the mine."

Wonderful. Jack moved across the room with a strained smile. The only way he'd want to listen to Father speak of the mine is if he talked of the bal maidens. He glanced toward the window, and a smile raised his lips.

Gwynna still traipsed across the countryside, basket swinging happily in her hand. Was she skipping?

"You seem taken with our grounds, Mr. Trevethan." He turned as Mrs. Hawkins approached his side. "Perhaps you'd like to see them closer?"

She motioned him forward, and they walked to the window together.

"There," Mrs. Hawkins continued, her voice so low, it reached no other ears but his, "now you shall have a better sight of her."

The blood slipped from his face, leaving a cold clammy feeling to his skin. "Sorry, of whom?"

She motioned through the window with an innocent expression. "Gwynna."

He tipped his head to the side, hoping he appeared nonchalant, though his mind was reeling. "Do you know her?"

"Of course. She is my dearest friend."

Jack couldn't quite grasp her words. Gwynna was, in actuality, friends with this fine lady?

"She told me this afternoon you have agreed to keep silent about her time at the ball."

It was true. They *were* friends. He blinked multiple times to rid the shock from his eyes. "So you knew about her attending?"

"Knew? My dear sir, I'm the one who helped her carry it out. All was going splendidly well until a rogue mine owner's son decided to end our fun prematurely."

She raised an accusatory brow. Heavens, was it hot in that room. He stuck a cool finger between his neck and cravat, staring out the window again, but Gwynna was no longer in view.

"Yes, I-I apologized to her already."

Finally he was receiving the answers for which he'd waited so long. No wonder Gwynna hadn't told him herself. Though she'd hinted at her friendship with Mrs. Hawkins only moments before, there was no way he could have believed all of this were he not hearing it directly from Mrs. Hawkins.

Ah, here was his reasoning for pursuing Gwynna. He wished merely for answers. Now that he was receiving them, he was sure to leave the bal maiden alone.

He ignored the barren feeling rising within him at the thought. "Might I be so bold as to ask how the two of you became friends?"

"Certainly. A few months ago, before I married Mr. Hawkins, the Merricks brought me into their home after I had lost everything. They are the best sort of people. Kind, loving, forgiving." Mrs. Hawkins stared out of the window, losing focus before blinking and facing Jack head-on. "I would never allow anyone to hurt my friend. So I shall be the bold one now and ask you this, have you any ill intentions concerning Gwynna?"

Jack would've chuckled at her candor, had her stare not caused his laugh to shrivel back like a dying weed in the heat of the blazing sun.

He considered her question for a moment. For so long, he'd kissed women and set them aside without further contact, intending to do the very same with Gwynna. He'd never entertained any shame for his behavior for long, able to swallow the guilt and his mother's imagined reprimands. But with Gwynna, something was different.

Perhaps it was the state of her hands from working at the mine, or the way she'd stopped the brawl on the beach. Or maybe it was because he'd finally realized that his harmless kissing game wasn't so harmless after all.

He'd gotten to know her, seen the effect his behavior had on her, and now, the thought of hurting her almost hurt *him*.

"No, Mrs. Hawkins," he finally replied. "I do not wish to hurt her."

Mrs. Hawkins studied him for a long, silent moment. "I believe you, Mr. Trevethan. Now, I wonder…might I ask a favor of you?"

CHAPTER TWENTY-TWO

"*Y*ou live here in St. Just, you say, Miss Bell?"

Mrs. Parnell's loud voice echoed through the stillness of Fynwary Hall's drawing room. As she spoke, Gwynna flinched again.

This was the third time she'd started at the woman's words. Mrs. Parnell had clearly suffered hearing loss in her old age and now had to shout to hear her own voice.

"Yes, ma'am. I—"

"What was that?" Mrs. Parnell leaned forward.

"Yes, I have," Gwynna repeated, still in a tone that matched the elegance of the room.

Or so at least she hoped.

She glanced to her right, where Sophia sat beside her on the white-cushioned sofa. She did not receive the reassurance she'd hoped for as her friend's eyes pulled to the door again.

Whom was she expecting? The whole party was already in the room—Gwynna, Sophia, Mr. Hawkins by the marble hearth, and Mrs. Parnell, who sat nearby in a single chair that had clawed legs braced into the carpet like a cat ready to pounce with a mighty hiss.

"And you find it has all the society you require?" Mrs. Parnell shouted out.

"Yes, I do," Gwynna replied.

When she'd first entered the drawing room, she had suffered with the same angst as at the ball. However, knowing she would only have to convince one woman—instead of an entire ball-room—that she was a lady, most of her nerves had scattered as quickly as a flock of curlews near a charging wave.

But now, she was anything but comforted by the woman's direct attention. Despite her hearing loss, Mrs. Parnell was bound to catch Gwynna's terribly false accent, what with the amount of questions she'd assailed at Gwynna. What her family situation looked like, if she'd had a governess, where she preferred spending her holidays. The questions were unending. Why was Sophia not living up to her end of the bargain, speaking so Gwynna wouldn't have to?

Gwynna cleared her throat. "Don't ye—you agree, Mrs. Hawkins, that St. Just be fittin' for entertainment?"

Sophia stared, dazed. "Oh, yes. Yes, I do agree." Then she glanced once more to the door.

Gwynna's perplexed brow wrinkled like her work towser. Sophia had been behaving strangely all evening. She'd barely made an appearance as Gwynna was primped by the lady's maid, rattling off a few things for Gwynna to remember before excusing herself to "take care of a few small matters before dinner." Now, she was hardly saying a word.

Sophia's smooth feathers must simply be twisted by Mrs. Parnell's ruffling presence. After all, what else could be unsettling her?

Mrs. Parnell drew in a breath, clearly winding up to throw another question at Gwynna, but Mr. Hawkins blessedly spoke first.

"Do you have the chance to visit with my mother often, Mrs. Parnell?" he asked.

Mrs. Parnell turned to face him more directly as she answered. "Oh, yes. We live not far from one another, so we see each other nearly every day. In fact, we..."

Her voice faded from Gwynna's ears as Sophia leaned toward her with a discreet whisper lost to Mrs. Parnell.

"Gwynna, I must speak with you for a moment."

Gwynna turned to her friend. She was fairly certain speaking while another guest was talking would be frowned upon, but then, what did Gwynna know about such matters?

"What is it, Sophia?" she whispered in response. "Ye've been so quiet all evenin'."

"I shall explain now." With a quick glance to Mrs. Parnell then back to the door, Sophia continued. "Our guest may be more astute than I had supposed. My Frederick told me that Mrs. Parnell is apparently the sort of woman who would not hesitate to turn you over to the constable, should she expect you to be anything less than a lady."

"What?" Gwynna breathed. She glanced to the door herself. Is that why Sophia was so anxious, because Mrs. Parnell had already somehow alerted the constable? Mr. Hawkins might be able to convince the man not to press for Gwynna's imprisonment, but the constable would no doubt feel constrained to alert Mr. Peter Trevethan of her delinquency. She would lose her place at the mine for certain.

"Why didn't ye tell me?" Gwynna whispered fiercely. "I wouldn't have come!"

Sophia shoulders sunk low. "I'm so sorry, but we didn't know. Frederick only assumed as much after conversing with her briefly, and he only had but a moment to tell me as we arrived in this very room." She grimaced. "Mrs. Parnell had less than favorable things to say about the lower class."

Gwynna pressed a fisted hand to her mouth, the glove smooth against her lips. She'd purposely declined wearing rouge that evening, knowing how often she touched her face. "I know I promised to 'elp ye, Sophia, but how can I stay here if this woman be findin' me out?"

A flash of delight dispelled Sophia's earlier trepidation. "Worry not, my friend. I have enlisted another to help, one who can ease the attention away from you easily."

"What?" Gwynna's voice came out in a high-pitched squeak. Fortunately, too high for Mrs. Parnell to hear. She pressed her hands to her cheeks. "Ye didn't! Who?"

Sophia winced. Or did she smile? "You assured me yourself that he was trustworthy. And he was the only one who knows your secret. He was the obvious choice to help you while Mr. Hawkins and I see to Mrs. Parnell."

Gwynna shook her head, her chest tight, as if her stays had been laced too snugly. "Sophia, ye didn't invite—"

"Ah, Mr. Trevethan," Mr. Hawkins greeted. "Do come in."

CHAPTER TWENTY-THREE

*G*wynna swung her head toward the door, her jaw slack. No, Sophia wouldn't have done such a thing. She would never invite the one man who'd ruined Gwynna's evening the last time she'd pretended to be a lady.

Yet, there he was.

Mr. Trevethan entered the room, commanding attention in his navy blue waistcoat, hair darker than his black jacket. His eyebrows were low, but an easy smile curved his lips. He paused to bow, then his deep brown eyes found Gwynna.

Her heart tripped. Swiftly, she turned in her seat to face Sophia with an accusatory stare, but the time for their private discussion had ended as Sophia stood.

Gwynna instinctively followed suit.

"So lovely to have you here again, Mr. Trevethan," Sophia said.

Gwynna stared at the intricate floral rug beneath her slippers. Mr. Trevethan's shoes appeared in her sight, stopping just at the side of where she stood near the sofa. Would he attempt to speak with her? Tease her for her dressing as a lady once again? He had apologized for his behavior at the ball, but who was to say he wouldn't attempt the same game as before?

"Thank you for the invitation, Mrs. Hawkins. I've been greatly looking forward to this evening." Mr. Trevethan's deep tone rumbled through the silence, like smooth thunder rolling across a summer sky. Only, this thunder rolled directly through her chest.

His shoes shifted slightly closer to Gwynna. Would he say her real name, reveal her identity? Or had he agreed to join the pretense with the Hawkinses?

Would that she could be a small piece of lint and slip into the cracks of the cushions upon which she sat.

Mr. Hawkins took a step forward. "Mr. Trevethan, allow me to introduce to you my mother's dear friend, Mrs. Parnell. Mrs. Parnell, a friend and neighbor, Mr. Jack Trevethan."

A nod from Mrs. Parnell. A bow from Mr. Trevethan. Then Mr. Hawkins continued.

"My wife, you know, of course. And lastly, I'm certain you'll recall Miss Joanna Bell. You met briefly at the ball, I understand?"

"Indeed, we did. Lovely to see you again, Miss Bell."

So he was to play along with them then. How could Sophia not have told her about this?

Silence followed Mr. Trevethan's words. Gwynna knew she ought to say something in return as all eyes weighed heavily on her, but her tongue was bound by bands of uncertainty.

The Hawkinses were under no false illusion as to who Gwynna was. If she made a mistake, revealing her lower class tendencies, they would not—they *had* not—batted an eye.

But Mr. Trevethan was sure to poke fun, and Gwynna couldn't handle such teasing, not while in a vulnerable state. Knowing her pride, she'd scold him again, just like she'd done at the ball.

Her eyes traveled up from the carpet toward the open door.

The easiest solution would be to flee from the room that instant. Sophia would be fine on her own. In truth, she deserved to squirm a bit under Mrs. Parnell's glares after keeping Gwynna in the dark.

As if she'd overheard Gwynna's thoughts, Sophia nudged her discreetly with her elbow. With a look of pleading, she silently begged Gwynna to play along.

Gwynna knew how important this evening was to Sophia. After marrying Mr. Hawkins, Sophia had lost most contact with her parents. If Mrs. Parnell—the dearest friend of Sophia's mother-in-law—complained about any poor treatment, Sophia would lose any chance of having a close, maternal relationship.

Gwynna could not abandon her friend, no matter her own frustrations. With a tight jaw, she nodded her head toward the gentleman. "Mr. Trevethan."

Mrs. Parnell had certainly not heard *that* whispered greeting, but it seemed to satisfy the room enough for the ladies to resume their seats and another conversation to occur.

"When will the others arrive then?" Mrs. Parnell asked loudly, looking about the room.

Mr. Trevethan shifted where he stood. The musky scent of his cologne wafted under Gwynna's nose, swirling about her head until she was dizzy. She parted her lips to breathe through her mouth instead.

"This is our entire party—"

"Please do speak up, Mrs. Hawkins," Mrs. Parnell shouted with a cupped ear.

Sophia repeated her words louder, though her voice slightly shook. "This is our entire party this evening."

Mrs. Parnell blinked in surprise. "Oh, I see."

Sophia immediately defended herself. "We were to have a larger affair, but many of our friends had already planned to attend the public assembly held this evening, and we did not wish to overburden them with another social event."

Mrs. Parnell hummed, still disapproving. Mr. Hawkins placed a comforting hand on his wife's shoulder. "We preferred a more intimate party, anyway. It will allow us the chance to speak with you a little more than if we had a grand number with us."

"I suppose," Mrs. Parnell said. "Though I wonder why others would choose an assembly over a private dinner. I've never had the taste for public gatherings. Too much rabble."

Rabble. If only Mrs. Parnell knew just exactly who sat across from her, hidden under the guise of her lavender gown and silver ribbons.

"I don't recall you saying the party this evening would be quite so small," Mrs. Parnell continued. "This shall be an experience, I daresay."

The door opened, and the butler entered the room. Sophia excused herself from the group, moving with quick steps toward him. Gwynna shifted uncomfortably under his gaze. The butler had been sworn to secrecy about Gwynna's attendance, and Sophia said he was more than trustworthy, but still, it unnerved Gwynna to rely on the man's word alone.

"In London, I enjoy far larger parties," Mrs. Parnell said, smoothing out her deep green gown.

No one responded.

Sophia cleared her throat from across the room. "Dinner is served."

Mrs. Parnell was the first to stand, and Gwynna, the last to rise. She brought up the rear of the migrating party. Mr. Trevethan's shoulders stretched out directly in front of her. They were quite nice in that jacket of his. Very broad.

She blinked, looking beyond him to Mr. Hawkins, who escorted Mrs. Parnell across the room. Gwynna tipped her head to the side. Was this part of the etiquette Sophia had prattled off to her earlier?

She glanced to her friend, who motioned Gwynna forward.

"I cannot help you this evening as much as I should like to," she whispered in quick words. "But worry not. Mr. Trevethan has agreed to assist you where I cannot."

Gwynna scoffed with disbelief. "Mr. Trevethan, lead me to what be proper? Ye do recall our conversation from earlier, do ye not? The gardens? The threats?"

"But you said he apologized." Sophia's eyes shone with innocence, though a small smile curled the ends of her lips.

Sophia wasn't trying to bring Gwynna and Mr. Trevethan closer. She had to have only been teasing the day before...hadn't she?

Sputtering, Gwynna pushed the thought aside. "Well, yes, he apologized, but still, to rely on 'im instead of ye to—"

"Ladies?"

Gwynna forgot to be all things graceful as she whirled around to face Mr. Trevethan. He outstretched his arms toward her and Sophia both.

"Shall we?"

Gwynna avoided his stare. Had he heard her? It didn't matter if he did. She'd only said the truth.

"Oh, thank you, Mr. Trevethan," Sophia said, "but you may escort Miss Bell to the dining room alone. I must speak with my butler for a moment."

So it *was* common practice, being escorted to the dining room. And now Gwynna would have to do such a thing without Sophia—and with Mr. Trevethan.

"Go on, Miss Bell," Sophia said with an encouraging nod.

Before Gwynna could say a word of protest, Sophia turned toward her butler. That didn't stop Gwynna from scowling at Sophia's perfectly coiffed black hair.

"Miss Bell?"

CHAPTER TWENTY-FOUR

Gwynna's shoulders tensed. With Mr. Hawkins and Mrs. Parnell already gone from the room, and with Sophia occupied with the butler, Gwynna was essentially alone with Mr. Trevethan. Again. How did they always manage to do this?

He offered his arm to her, but she hesitated, imagining a thorny branch in place of his smooth jacket sleeve. She'd hate to be pricked by one of those thorns.

"You are aware of what to do with an outstretched arm, are you not, *Miss Bell?*"

He emphasized her name with a wink. No doubt he'd caused many a woman to swoon with such behavior.

Gwynna raised her chin indignantly. "'Course I be aware."

Abruptly, she grasped his arm and pulled him toward her. He teetered off balance for a moment and chuckled. "You are far stronger than you appear, you know."

With his firm arm beneath her fingertips—even with his jacket and her gloves between them—she felt anything but strong. Warm embers sparked in her chest, but she quickly stamped them out.

"Ye'd be wise to remember such a thing." Her threat fell hollow as her voice cracked.

She followed him from the drawing room and down the left corridor, toward the sound of Mrs. Parnell's vociferous voice.

"Are you upset that I am here?" Mr. Trevethan asked, hardly louder than a whisper.

"No," she lied. "Merely surprised to see ye. Will your father be here, too? Or your cousins?"

Fear tightened its grip round her middle. How would she manage to escape *them*?

Mr. Trevethan peered down at her, but she wouldn't meet his eyes. They were far too close for that.

"No. I told them I had a matter of business to attend to and promised to join them after at the assembly tonight. They've no idea where I am."

Well, at least Sophia had managed to not bring along Gwynna's employer.

"But...you were surprised to see me?" he asked.

She nodded in silence.

"Mrs. Hawkins did not tell you I would be here?"

"No, she didn't."

He rubbed his chin with his free hand. "I apologize. I had no notion she would keep this to herself."

Silence followed so thickly, Gwynna was sure not even her spalling hammer could crack through it. Fortunately, her words would do the trick. "So why did ye agree to come tonight?"

"Mrs. Hawkins asked it as a favor of me."

"So ye agreed to lie, to pretend I be a lady, merely to satisfy a woman ye hardly know? I be findin' that hard to believe, sir."

He stared at her again. She turned to the paintings of men with raised chins and women with stoic faces. They gaped at her as she passed them by. *Imposter*, their eyes said.

"Well, that isn't the only reason I agreed to come," Mr. Trevethan responded.

She lifted her fingers from his arm to avoid touching him further. If she wasn't so worried about Mrs. Parnell spotting her, she'd have removed her hand altogether. "I'm sure the greatest pull for ye is bein' able to tease me for another poor decision I be makin'."

"Gwy—" He stopped himself, lowering his voice, though no one was around to hear them. Their footsteps slowed. "Miss Bell, allow me to calm your unease in regard to my intentions. I agreed to come here for one reason alone, and that is to make amends for my behavior at the ball."

Her eyes swung up. They were even closer than she'd thought, but she couldn't look away. She needed to see if he was in earnest.

"It's true," he insisted, his expression as serious as the paint-ings now behind them, though far-less condescending. "I have experienced considerable regret since I've been made aware of the substantial preparations that must have been required for you to attend. I am sorry that I put an end to it, due to my...my ill-timed remarks and distasteful request. I sincerely hope to rectify the situation this evening by behaving as the gentleman I should have always been. I only hope you will allow me to do so."

As he finished, the rigidity dispelled from around Gwynna's chest, replaced with an airy lightness. She redirected her eyes forward as they rounded a corner. The enticing smell of flavored meat, steamed vegetables, and sweet pastries flooded her mouth with moisture.

"Thank ye, sir," she said. She rested her fingers against his arm. Her hand had grown tired from hovering in the air, that was all. "So, I suppose ye know now that I didn't pinch the pink gown after all."

His lip twitched. "Yes, your friend informed me of such. I do apologize for ever doubting you."

"I can forgive ye, sir, so long as ye don't suggest we leave the party to, what was it ye said, 'take a walk in't gardens'?"

She watched him from the corner of her eye, satisfied as a blush crept across his brow.

He cleared his throat. "Well, you needn't worry about that. I have had enough scoldings from you to never wish for one again."

They shared a smile, her eyes lingering a moment too long on the angle of his firm jaw.

As they continued, Gwynna attempted to make sense of everything that was happening. Instead, all she could focus on were the embers in her chest, now glowing orange once again.

Was she dreaming, or was she truly walking down a corridor of a stately home in a fine gown on the arm of a gentleman—a gentleman who wished to make amends for the way he'd treated her?

Was that why he continually sought after her? Or was it because he had feelings for...

She blinked hard to dispel the thought. It had been produced from Sophia's earlier, teasing words. Of course this man was not interested in Gwynna. The idea was preposterous. Laughable. He was merely being the gentleman he said he wished to be.

Besides, she wasn't interested in him either.

Other than being extremely attracted to him, but there was nothing untoward about that.

They rounded another corner just as Mrs. Parnell's white feather from her headpiece disappeared into the dining room.

"Are you ready?" Mr. Trevethan whispered.

"I s'pose."

"Worry not. Mrs. Hawkins has promised to occupy Mrs. Parnell, and I have been charged to help you through any situation that occurs. Simply follow my lead, and I promise you will leave unscathed this evening."

Follow his lead. Follow *Mr. Trevethan's* lead. Because she clearly wasn't a lady who knew what to do on her own.

They entered the dining room, the grand red walls, floral plates, and forest green chair cushions shrinking her spirits. Perhaps she *was* that piece of lint she'd wished to be earlier.

Mrs. Parnell was already situated in her seat. Mr. Hawkins stood at the head of the table and motioned for Mr. Trevethan and Gwynna to take the chairs opposite Mrs. Parnell.

Gwynna moved to the chair directly in front of the woman, pulling it out herself before Mr. Trevethan's hand rested on top of hers.

"Allow me."

She withdrew in an instant and avoided his smile. Muttering a word of gratitude, she sat down and attempted to pull the chair in, but his grip prevented her, allowing only a slight movement forward before he took his place next to her.

Was she supposed to be this far from the table? There had to be a foot between her and her plate. How was she to avoid spilling or maintain her posture while eating?

The perpetual ache in her back moaned in protest as she straightened once more.

"I do apologize for keeping you," Sophia said, rushing into the room with all the grace Gwynna didn't have. "I'm afraid matters of the house never end."

Mr. Hawkins pulled out the chair at the head of the table for his wife, then sat down at her left.

"Are you to sit *there*, Mr. Hawkins?" Mrs. Parnell shouted.

Gwynna eyed the chandelier above. She was sure the crystals trembled from the woman's voice.

"This is not so formal an affair," Sophia said with a smile that wasn't convincing. "And we certainly wouldn't wish for him to be seated alone at the far end of the table."

"I prefer sitting close by my wife anyway," Mr. Hawkins added.

They shared an affectionate smile, then Sophia situated something across her lap, Mrs. Parnell doing the same.

Gwynna raised her chin to see over the table. The napkin! Of course. Gwynna snatched hers and laid it across her dress, waiting to see what came next.

As the footman and butler served bowls of soup to the guests, Gwynna attempted to recall any of the information Sophia had thrown at her earlier, but as she stared at the forks, plates, and glasses, she had no idea which to use first.

Her cheeks pricked with heat. She'd practiced using a knife and fork for a few days alone in her room at night, but she was nowhere near proficient. The Hawkinses would ignore anything unsatisfactory. Mrs. Parnell might not notice, due to the large trays of food between them. But Mr. Trevethan... would he think less of her inability to eat properly and speak properly—to only dress the part, but not *be* the part?

When would she think logically again? The gentleman had witnessed her downing a glass of lemonade at the ball, brawling on a beach, and working through a bleeding wound. The only finesse he would expect from her would be when she wielded her hammer toward the ore at Wheal Favour.

As she'd said to him before, being a bal maiden was enough for her, even surrounded with such finery. Eating properly didn't put food on the table. Well, not her table. She would simply do her best and worry not about impressing him.

Or at the very least she'd try to do so.

"I trust your parents are well, Miss Bell?" Mr. Trevethan asked, breaking into her thoughts.

The footman attending dinner that evening—who had only recently been hired and fortunately would not recognize Gwynna—placed a bowl of green pea soup before her.

She'd never been fond of peas.

"Y-yes, they be fine," she answered distractedly.

She wrinkled her nose at the scent. Heavens, it was pungent.

This was certainly not the smell she'd been enjoying outside the room.

Mr. Trevethan fell silent, and Mr. Hawkins struck up a conversation with Mrs. Parnell about London. Gwynna eyed the contents of her bowl. Was she expected to eat all of it?

At the other end of the table, Sophia slid the soup onto the side of her spoon and soundlessly lifted it to her lips.

With a pursed mouth, Gwynna finally did the same, pausing just before the soup could touch her lips. The scent accosted her nostrils, and she wished for nothing more than to push the bowl aside and ask for the meat she'd been smelling earlier. But she couldn't offend Sophia.

Swiftly, she slipped the spoon into her mouth. The earthy flavor and slimy texture spread across her tongue like an earthworm slinking across overturned dirt. With a cringe, she swallowed the contents in a single gulp.

What a horrid vegetable. She could only pray the rest of the meal was better. She scooped up another bite before Mrs. Parnell fixated on Gwynna's hand.

Gwynna studied her spoon. Was it too full? She hadn't slurped it loudly. That much she remembered from Sophia's instructions. So of what did the lady disapprove?

As Mr. Hawkins continued speaking, Sophia caught Gwynna's attention and mouthed out a word.

Love? Gwynna frowned. Was she teasing about Mr. Trevethan's feelings again? Gwynna looked away in a huff, about to suffer through another spoonful, but Mrs. Parnell's brows arched all the more.

"Your gloves."

Mr. Trevethan's whisper reached only her ears.

Gloves, not love! She'd forgotten to remove her gloves.

She tried to set aside her embarrassment, but her face overheated again. Gwynna had readily accepted Sophia's earlier tutelage, but Mr. Trevethan's guidance was humiliating.

She was a child who could never live up to his proper experience.

She lowered her spoon carefully, then slipped off her gloves, placing them atop her napkin on her lap. She reached for another spoonful and brought it to her lips as if she hadn't made some grave error. Apparently, with the look Mrs. Parnell had given her, she had.

When the attention finally shifted, Gwynna could only manage a quick nod of gratitude to Mr. Trevethan, who simply smiled then returned to his soup.

He hadn't teased her. He'd been speaking the truth then. He was simply there to help her through the evening.

She drew in easier breaths.

"How are your children, Mrs. Parnell?" Sophia asked.

Mrs. Parnell swallowed her bite, flickered a glance at Gwynna, then replied in a loud voice.

"They are well."

As Gwynna flinched, the soup from her spoon dripped back down into the bowl, splashing over the edge with a plop. That was one way to be rid of it. Her eyes darted around her, but no one seemed to notice.

"And what of your grandchildren?" Mr. Hawkins asked next.

"What was that?" Mrs. Parnell questioned.

"Your grandchildren?"

"Oh, they are darling. I do dote on them."

Gwynna gathered another spoonful, then forced it down, hardly allowing it a moment to touch her tongue. Much more of this, and she was sure her face would soon match the color of the soup.

"You don't have to eat all of it, you know."

The spoon hovered above her bowl, and she swiveled to face Mr. Trevethan, who'd spoken for only her to hear.

"What do ye mean?"

He motioned to her serving. "The soup. You don't have to eat all of it if you're not enjoying it. A few spoons will suffice."

The tips of her ears burned. "Oh, I-I be enjoyin' it," she stuttered in a whisper.

To prove her words, she swallowed another mouthful, but it ended with an involuntary shudder.

Mr. Trevethan's shoulders raised in a silent laugh, and the heat from her ears crept down to her cheeks.

She may as well begin by being humble now. She had a feeling she was going to experience many pride-swallowing moments with Mr. Trevethan that evening.

"Very well," she conceded. "I be done now."

"That is for the best. We wouldn't wish for the evening to begin with you ill."

His eyes shone with amusement as he returned to his bowl.

Before long, Gwynna bade a silent, cheerful goodbye to the last of the putrid soup as it was taken away by the footman.

Fortunately, the following food was everything she'd hoped it would be. The moment the lids were raised from the trays and bowls, the delectable scent pervaded the room—beef-steak, stuffed tomatoes, scalloped oysters, venison pie. It was a veritable feast for her eyes and nose.

Mr. Trevethan leaned toward her. "What looks appetizing to you?"

She scanned the trays. "All of it."

He chuckled, and Gwynna laughed tensely in return. She hadn't been joking. Was it impolite for her to sample everything?

"How about we begin with the items closest to us?" he suggested.

She nodded. She was fine with that, just so long as that beef-steak made it into her belly.

Mr. Trevethan worked to fill her plate and his at once. She cringed at his special service, but as Mr. Hawkins helped dish food onto Mrs. Parnell's and Sophia's plates, as well, she breathed a sigh of relief. This was just another way for a gentleman to help a lady.

She could grow accustomed to such aid.

Mr. Trevethan held out a bowl of peas before her. "I assume you wish to pass on these?"

She pulled back with a wrinkled nose. "Ye be right about that, sir."

He set the peas aside, doing a poor job of hiding his smile.

When he finished, Gwynna stared at the food on her plate. The yellow boiled potatoes and bright orange carrots rivaled the colors of wildflowers at sunset, and the beef-steak warmed her stomach just by the sight of its juicy texture.

The soft clinking of dishes and quiet conversation pervaded the room. Everyone was focused on their own servings, which meant Gwynna could eat for a moment without anyone taking notice of her.

She plunged her fork into the meat first, awkwardly slicing into the steak, grateful for its tenderness to make the cut easier.

As she took a bite, the flavors spread through her mouth like a wave sliding up the beach. She loved pasties and stargazey pie as much as the next maiden, but this food was incomparable. What she wouldn't give to have her parents join her, or Kerensa and her family.

Of course, she highly doubted any of them would have gone to the extent Gwynna had to eat at Fynwary Hall that evening, nor taken the risks. But Gwynna had, and by heaven, she was going to enjoy this meal if it was the last thing she did.

Providing she did nothing too embarrassing.

CHAPTER TWENTY-FIVE

*J*ack took another bite of his potato to keep his smile at bay. He'd never been so delighted watching someone else eat. He'd never seen someone so delighted *to* eat.

Gwynna had done her best at playing the part of a lady, just like at the ball. She nearly hid her accent, sat straight in her seat, and walked with slow steps. If Jack didn't know any better, he would have thought she *was* a lady.

But now, as she dug into her plate, sighing quietly with pleasure after each new bite, he knew this was a treat for her, and the sight was endearing—and humbling.

He'd never befriended anyone of the lower class before, and the thought of not having such food readily available, like Gwynna and the other miners, was sobering.

He couldn't solve the problem for all of the lower class, but for Gwynna…

He pulled back, the potato in his mouth turning to mush. He had no idea where that thought had been headed, and he wasn't about to find out.

He forced down his food, reverting his attention away from

Gwynna and how adorable she'd been choking down the pea soup.

That girl was making his mind softer than the curls gracing her temples. Her innate goodness had caused him to feel remorse for the way he'd treated her at the ball, but once his time at Fynwary ended, he was headed straight for the assembly. He needed some distance from her to remember who he really was.

Perhaps he'd even suggest the usual game with Hugh. Spending time with another woman was sure to rid his mind of the bal maiden.

He shuffled his conscience to the bottom of his worries.

"From where did you say you hail, Mr. Trevethan?" Mrs. Parnell blurted out, interrupting his thoughts.

He lowered his fork and knife, grateful for the excuse to stop eating for a moment. The food he'd eaten tossed unsettled in his stomach. Had the potato been rotten? "I lived here in St. Just but spent the majority of my life with family in Bath."

Gwynna continued to eat her food, but he didn't need to notice that. He was only there to help her in case she fell into a spot of trouble.

"Oh, Bath," Mrs. Parnell said. "A lovely city. But have you ever been to London?"

"Yes, I have been fortunate enough to do so."

"What was that?"

He repeated his words, ready to have the conversation shift away from himself so he wouldn't have to shout across the dinner table any longer.

"Ah, yes," the old woman replied. She took a bite of her food then faced Gwynna. "And you, Miss Bell. I assume you've been to both cities. Which do you prefer?"

Gwynna's cheeks blushed the color of cherries. Jack hadn't wished for the attention to move to her, especially as she swallowed the great lump of food in her cheek and straightened in her seat. Mrs. Parnell was sure to have witnessed that.

"Oh...Bath?" came Gwynna's weakened response.

Mrs. Parnell's eyes narrowed just a fraction. "And what do you so enjoy about Bath?"

Gwynna blinked. She might have eventually concocted an answer, but Jack couldn't bear the sight of her struggling any longer. After all, he'd promised to help her when needed. It's certainly what a gentleman would do. Never mind that he hadn't cared to be so very gentlemanly before. Tonight, with Gwynna, he did.

"We were only speaking of this the other day, were we not, Miss Bell?" he began. "I recall you mentioning your particular affinity for the Roman Baths."

Gwynna clearly had no idea to what he was referring, but she pumped her head up and down all the same. "Oh, yes. The Baths."

Mrs. Parnell pursed her lips, ready to pitch another question toward Gwynna, but Mrs. Hawkins jumped right in with words of her own.

"Has my mother-in-law spoken of Mr. Hawkins's dislike for London, Mrs. Parnell?"

With the woman's attention drawn away in defense of her beloved city, Gwynna leaned toward Jack once again. "Thank ye," she murmured, pressing a hand to her cheek.

His eyes lingered a moment on her long fingers that ended with short nails framed in dirt.

She must have caught his stare, for she pulled her hand down, took one look at her fingers, then buried them in her lap. "I scrubbed them," she whispered. "They just be hard to clean out."

Instantly, Jack shook his head. "It matters not. I hardly care."

Fool. What did it matter what *he* cared? She was no doubt more concerned over Mrs. Parnell noticing her hands. "And I'm certain she hasn't noticed from where she is sitting," he finished with a slight toss of his head.

She nodded, still ducking her head in shame.

This wasn't right. Gwynna hadn't done anything wrong. What could he do to withdraw the confidence she so often crowed?

He leaned toward her. "There's nothing to be ashamed about. Your hands merely reveal what you have done for the sake of your family today. Just as Mrs. Hawkins's does. She probably has…thread beneath her fingernails."

Gwynna cracked a smile. As if the sun had just broken forth from heavy clouds and now graced his body, Jack's chest swelled with warmth. He hadn't intentionally helped another in quite some time. The fact that he was helping *Gwynna* only increased the potency of the emotion.

That warmth continued to grow as the meal progressed, and Gwynna's confidence returned. She ate the meal heartily, though Jack noted she learned to chew her bigger mouthfuls when Mrs. Parnell was occupied chattering about the grand-children she was to travel with in the south of the county.

Soon, the dessert was served, and plates filled with cherry tarts, apricot fritters, pear dumplings, and marbled jelly were revealed.

He could practically see Gwynna salivating for each platter, so he served a small helping of each piece onto her plate, doing the same for himself so she'd feel more comfortable. Fortunately, his stomachache had since mysteriously disappeared.

As he ate his pear dumpling, Gwynna dove into her cherry tart as if it might sprout legs and run from the table. Fortunately, Mrs. Parnell was so taken with her own food as to not notice.

However, when the woman suddenly exclaimed over her delight in the choices of dessert, Jack's attention was drawn not to Mrs. Parnell, but straight back to Gwynna.

The poor girl must have been so focused on her cherry tart, she hadn't been expecting the loud voice to call out again, and she jerked to attention. Her fork escaped her hand and clattered to her plate, flinging cherry across the table and toward Jack.

He jerked back, but it was too late. The tart splattered across his forehead and cheek, tumbling down his cravat and lapel of his jacket and ending in his lap.

"Oh!" Gwynna gasped. "I be that sorry, sir!"

Swiftly, she flung her napkin toward him, dabbing at his face and collar as he brushed aside the crumbs across his lap.

"Oh, it be stained," she mumbled, apparently unaware of her reverting accent.

Mrs. Hawkins spoke from the head of the table. "That's all right, Miss Bell. Accidents happen."

"Indeed," Mr. Hawkins agreed. "When I was younger, I spilled white soup all over my mother's tablecloths and dining room floor. She rather enjoys telling the story. Have you heard it before, Mrs. Parnell?"

The couple were clearly trying to draw the old woman's attention away from the struggling bal maiden, but Mrs. Parnell must have detected Gwynna's slip of the tongue. Her lips tightened before she ultimately turned to Mr. Hawkins. "No, I don't believe I have."

As they spoke, Gwynna continued dabbing at Jack's cravat and jawline, the nearby footman cleaning up the cherries across the tablecloth. "I be such a fool," she mumbled to herself.

Jack didn't know how badly his clothing was stained, nor did he care. He was more concerned with why he'd been struggling to draw in a steady breath since the moment Gwynna had touched him.

"Worry not." Why was his voice so hoarse? He cleared his throat. "I'm sure it's nothing that can't be washed out."

Their eyes met, and her hand froze, as if she'd only now realized their proximity. Straightaway, she pulled back, dropping her napkin to her plate and lowering her gaze.

Jack blinked and reached for his glass, needing to wet his suddenly parched throat. It must have been the dumpling. Surely nothing else could have caused the dryness.

CHAPTER TWENTY-SIX

*G*wynna's appetite vanished, as did what little remained of her pride. Red-faced, she sunk low in her seat, longing to hide behind the dining room table. Surely that's where an insignificant piece of lint belonged.

"Well, ladies," Sophia said, standing from her seat, "shall we leave the gentlemen to their port?"

Gwynna darted up from her chair, but she only managed a few steps before Mr. Trevethan called out to her. Or rather, to the woman she could never be. "Miss Bell?"

He bent toward the floor, picking up her gloves splayed out across the rug. They must have fallen in her mad dash to inappropriately swipe her napkin across the gentleman's face.

With a murmur of gratitude, she retrieved the gloves then followed the ladies promptly from the room, pulling the smooth silk up her arms. She was glad to be covering up her filthy nails again, even if Mr. Trevethan's attempt to ease her embarrassment had worked.

That is, until she noted the red marks streaked across the delicate fabric—yet another pair she'd ruined. Now she remembered Sophia's earlier advice.

Place her gloves *beneath* the napkin. Little good the knowledge did her now.

With dragging heels, Gwynna reached the drawing room after the others. Mrs. Parnell situated herself on the same chair nearest the fire, but Sophia stood at the doorway, waiting for Gwynna.

"Are you all right?" she whispered.

Gwynna raised her arm to reveal the cherry stain on the underside of the glove. "I'll replace them for ye."

"Worry not. I have plenty to spare."

Of course she did. Gwynna lowered her arms, then motioned to where Mrs. Parnell sat awaiting them, her beady eyes peering from across the room. "We'd best return to your guest."

Sophia stayed focused on Gwynna. "I must ensure you are well first."

Gwynna strapped a smile on her lips, no longer wishing to be a burden on her friend. She was certain she'd already ruined the evening for her.

"I am well," she blurted out louder than necessary. The proper words sat thickly at the tip of her tongue.

Before Sophia could reassure her again—and Gwynna could disbelieve her again—Gwynna moved across the room with what she hoped was an elegant pace.

Sophia did her best to keep Mrs. Parnell's attention away from Gwynna, but time and time again, the woman's focus shifted toward her, lines encircling her pursed lips like weedy petals on a dying flower.

"Have you any siblings?"

"When did your governess leave you?"

"Do you play any instruments?"

Gwynna was sure Mrs. Parnell suspected her lower status. There was no hiding it, for what lady spoke so brokenly, didn't know how to play the pianoforte, and volleyed a cherry tart across a gentleman's face?

After what had to be the longest half hour of her life, in which Gwynna would far rather be doing anything else, even bucking ore at the mine, the gentlemen finally came through.

Matters did not get any better, however, as her fear of embarrassing herself increased tenfold. Mr. Trevethan stood farther away from her than earlier. She was grateful for the distance, but his eyes continually drifted toward her, no doubt to ensure she hadn't spilt tea across her gown—which she'd somehow managed to avoid, even with Mrs. Parnell's shouting.

As the woman droned on about a small dog she was contemplating purchasing—"I am leaning more so toward pugs. I have a certain affinity for their darling facial expressions"—Sophia stepped across the room to deposit her teacup and saucer on the tea table before returning to her seat.

Could Gwynna do the same without being considered rude? She debated for a moment before ultimately deciding it was better to be rude and leave for a moment than be rude and shout at the woman to terminate her incessant talking.

She retraced Sophia's steps and placed her cup and saucer next to hers. Well, that hadn't taken as long as she'd hoped.

She glanced over her shoulder. All eyes still focused on Mrs. Parnell.

"I do wonder what will be the required maintenance of such an animal, though, and if he will enjoy my grandchildren as I do. I have mentioned my grandchildren to you, have I not? I have four now, and they are delightful angels. I do dote on them."

Gwynna closed her eyes. She couldn't sit through another moment of it. Facing forward, she turned toward a nearby window where the golden haze of the evening sun poured rays of light through the glass.

If she could just look outside for a single moment, she was

sure she could handle another hour of this woman's conversation.

Holding her breath, she tiptoed across the floor, praying to be overlooked as she stepped into the sunlight. Instantly, her nerves slipped around her, like a wave cascading down the sides of a rock, pooling at her feet.

Staring out across the grass, she imagined she was standing before the sea, water speckling her face, wind playing with her hair.

This was what she needed. Time away. A moment to breathe, relax. To realize what was occurring that evening didn't matter. She wasn't a lady, and that was fine. She didn't need to be a lady to earn money for her family. She didn't need to be a lady to be happy in her life.

Her neck lost its rigidity, and her face cooled of the blush she'd feared would soon become a permanent addition to her cheeks.

"May I join your escape?"

Warmth crept up her neck at Mr. Trevethan's whispered tone. Blast. She'd almost been rid of her embarrassment. Would it begin all over again?

"I-I wasn't escapin'."

Fortunately she didn't have to hide her accent, being far enough from the others so Mrs. Parnell might not hear.

Mr. Trevethan stepped to her side, his jacket sleeve brushing against her arm. She traced the trees outlined in the blinding light of the sun, willing her breathing to remain level.

"So using your teacup as an excuse to leave the conversation was simply by accident?" he questioned.

When would she learn to remember his astuteness? "All right, I be escapin'. I just can't take another minute of her shoutin'."

Mrs. Parnell's voice carried across the room at that very moment. "Oh, and I've been to see Dr. Kent. He says my aches and pains are all part of my old age. I do wonder how old he thinks I am. I am not so very aged as to be happy with a permanent aching in my muscles."

At least her and Mr. Trevethan's words would go unheard if the woman continued.

"That is precisely the reason I've come to join you," he said. "To allow my ears a moment of reprieve."

She eyed his stained clothing. She may be better for his ears, but certainly not for his cravat.

"Does that mean I ain't be allowed to speak of me own aches and pains?" she joked.

He stared down at her without a hint of a smile. "Have you many, due to the mine?"

She ignored the ache in her back that pulsed at the mere thought. She hadn't meant to complain. "No more than usual, sir. Other girls 'ave had to stop from shortness o' breath. But I be strong enough."

Two sparrows chased each other across the sky, swooping in circles, wings splayed out to catch the wind. If Gwynna focused hard enough, she could imagine hearing their joyful chirping instead of Mrs. Parnell.

"And what of this? Did you acquire this at the mine?"

"Acquire what, sir?"

He reached over, stroking his forefinger down the back of her arm, from the end of her sleeve to the top of her glove. Her insides surged in surprise. The birds flitted behind a tree. Mrs. Parnell's voice no longer reached her ears. She could see, hear, feel nothing besides the chills of pleasure cascading down her arm.

He withdrew his hand in an instant, staring down at her with focused eyes. Her frenzied thoughts spun round her mind, unable to comprehend his words.

"The scar," he clarified, "on the back of your arm."

CHAPTER TWENTY-SEVEN

*S*car? Scar. Gwynna crossed her arm over her stomach, placing her finger where Mr. Trevethan had just caressed her skin with his smooth glove. Even through her own glove, she could feel the markings of the wound she'd acquired years before. Heat rushed through her body in what she could only assume was a sign of her embarrassment. She was certain her gloves would've hidden the marking. At least her now-scabbed injury she'd received from the wayward rock was hidden by the curls at her temple.

"May I ask how you obtained it?"

She tightened her grip on her arm and turned to fully face the window. "I was eleven, bein' reckless and playin' near the machinery at the mine. The back of me skirt caught onto one of the gears and pulled me in. Lucky me brother be there to pull me out 'fore I died, crushed to death like a girl the year 'fore that."

Mr. Trevethan was silent for a moment. Had she shared too much? Surely he was aware of the deaths that could occur at Favour.

"How old was your brother when he saved you?" he asked, his voice low.

"Only nine at the time, 'fore he started work below ground."

He shook his head. "I can't imagine. What a remarkable boy."

Pain twisted in her chest. He *was* remarkable. Her best friend. He'd saved her life, and yet, she couldn't save his.

Mr. Trevethan's brow drew high with compassion. "The heartache never leaves. But the pain does become easier to bear."

Of course he would know how she felt. His own mother had died. A look of understanding passed between them, and a peace Gwynna hadn't felt in months settled around her shoulders like a blanket dried and warmed by the fire.

He was right. The pain, she knew, would be there forever. But somehow, having someone else to share in her grief eased her burden.

A moment passed. Mrs. Parnell's words barely reached them before Mr. Trevethan spoke again.

"Have you any other siblings?" he asked.

"No, Jago was me only brother. Me mother had four other children, but they all died young 'fore me and Jago were born."

"How terrible that must have been for your parents."

Gwynna nodded. Deaths in mining families, and the lower class in general, was a recurrent nightmare. Papa had lost most of his siblings, as well, including his dearest sister, Meraud, when she was only a young woman.

"Me parents always said they wanted a large family. But now with Jago gone, I be all they 'ave left."

"I see now why your father wished for you to remain away from the mine."

She hummed a response, dropping her hands from her arms, her scar long forgotten. "And what of ye, Mr. Trevethan. Have ye any siblings?"

He drew in a deep breath and responded in a sigh. "No, I was never fortunate enough. My mother did not bear children easily, due to her poor constitution. She always told me I was enough for her. Though I'm fairly certain she meant I was *too* much for her."

Gwynna narrowed her eyes. "Were ye as difficult as ye are now?"

He smiled, looking down to the floor. "Believe it or not, I was perfectly behaved as a boy."

"I don't believe ye, sir."

"No, no. It's true. I never did anything wrong. I ate my vegetables. Wore my coat when I was told. Spoke kindly to my elders."

"Never asked a girl ye just met to kiss?"

He chuckled. "No, never that. I wouldn't dream of that."

"Heavens." She feigned an exaggerated look of surprise. "Now I be wonderin' what 'appened to change ye."

The light in his eyes faded, and realization settled over her. She winced. Of course she knew what had changed him. His mother's death.

She turned away. "Forgive me, sir. I ain't be in me right mind tonight."

He shrugged, his tone sober. "You needn't apologize. My mother's death affected me greatly, as I'm sure you've already surmised. Having the center of my boyish world torn from my arms was trying, to say the least. That is why it is difficult for me to be in Cornwall. The memory of my mother is fresh at every turn. And with my father here, well, he was hardly a comfort before he sent me..." He closed his eyes, giving a quick shake of his head, as if he'd just spoken something he hadn't wished to. "At any rate, it is all in the past now."

Gwynna wasn't so sure that it was. The heartache he spoke of before seemed as fresh as her own, and the burden was clearly resting heavily on his shoulders.

Anxious to ease the tension forming a crease in his brow, she sought for something to say. "I be sorry, sir. I can't imagine losin' me own mother. But it must be some comfort knowin' she'd be proud of ye and the man ye've become."

Rather than the comfort she'd hoped to bestow, his frown increased.

"If only that were true," he mumbled. "But thank you for your words, all the same."

Their eyes met. "Sir, can I ask ye a question?"

"Of course."

She chewed on the inside of her cheek. "Why...Why be ye doin' this? Helpin' me. I know ye said ye wished to make amends, but be there another reason?"

She regretted her words the moment they fell from her lips. What did she expect him to say? What did she *wish* for him to say?

She took a step back, ready to retreat and rescind the question, but his response stopped her.

"Do you recall the moment we shared behind the counthouse at Favour? When I asked you how you came about obtaining the dress?"

She lowered a perplexed brow. What did that have to do with anything? "Yes. I kept the truth from ye. Again."

He peered down at her, a slow smile sneaking across his lips. "Precisely. Which is why I think I shall do the same for you right now."

She blew out a disbelieving breath. "Tain't fair of ye to do that, sir."

He winked, sending her heart flapping like the wings of the sparrows that had chased one another through the sky.

"Ye really ain't be tellin' I?"

He shook his head, staring out the window with a raised chin. "No, I don't believe I..." His words faded, and he leaned closer to the glass, clearly distracted by something. "Is that..."

Gwynna followed his gaze to where an approaching carriage

rolled to a stop in front of Fynwary's doors, and out stepped the last gentleman she expected to see that evening.

"Father," Mr. Trevethan said.

The word sent a chill throughout her person as cold as any winter wind. Mr. Peter Trevethan was at Fynwary Hall.

"Why be he here?" she breathed, recoiling from the window as if it had turned into a venomous adder. "Did ye tell 'im ye was comin' here?"

Mr. Trevethan lowered his brow, as if offended by her accusation. "No, of course I didn't. I told you he has no knowledge of my attendance."

"Then why be he here?" she repeated.

Mr. Trevethan frowned, staring back out the window, but his father was no longer in sight.

Gwynna pressed a hand to her brow. How could this be happening again? She faced Sophia, raising on her toes to catch her attention. Sophia instantly excused herself from her husband and Mrs. Parnell, but halfway across the floor, the door opened, and the butler entered the room.

Thoughts swarmed Gwynna's mind, a swirling eddy of fears and regret. Was Mr. Peter Trevethan going to enter the room now? He would surely recognize her, and she would no longer have her place at the mine. Mrs. Parnell would discover her social status and call for the constable at once.

Her head spun. Her hands clammed. Her vision spotted, and she teetered on her heels.

"Breathe, Gwynna," Mr. Trevethan whispered.

His hand pressed at the small of her back. Warmth spiraled from each of his fingers, jolting life back into her body.

She drew in a deep breath and planted her feet apart, pulling herself from the panic.

Her eyes tore around the room. Mr. Peter Trevethan was nowhere in sight, the butler was gone, and Sophia was headed in her direction.

As soon as she reached their side, Mr. Trevethan withdrew his hand, leaving the fabric of her gown cool against her flesh.

"Mr. Trevethan," Gwynna breathed, but Sophia was already nodding.

"Mr. Page has just alerted me he has arrived," she said calmly. "Worry not. He has been shown to the study. But Gwynna, you and Mr. Trevethan must leave now before either of you are spotted. I fear if he sees his son, too many questions will arise."

"Yes, I agree," Mr. Trevethan said.

Gwynna, still attempting to gather her wits, merely nodded. Her parents expected her by nightfall, otherwise Sophia would've suggested holing up in another room. Gwynna, however, simply wanted to be rid of the house, never to return —at least not while dressed as a lady.

Mr. Trevethan continued. "Calling for a carriage or my horse will take too much time. Perhaps we leave on foot, and I'll return later for my horse?"

"Yes, that will do." Sophia laced her fingers together, her knuckles white from her grip. "The back doors will be nearer the servants, so the two of you must slip through the front door. Mr. Hawkins will only be able to keep your father occupied for a time. Can you manage?"

"Of course," Mr. Trevethan said. "I will ensure the both of us remain unseen."

A heavy pressure planted on Gwynna's chest, as if all the weight of the hand barrow she'd filled with ore that afternoon now pressed down on her. Would their plan work? Or would she be discovered and ruined?

"Sophia, I—"

"What do the three of you speak of over there?" Mrs. Parnell called out.

Gwynna flinched. Curse that woman.

Sophia gave a firm nod to Gwynna then turned to face her guest. "Oh, it is terrible news. Mr. Page has just relayed a message that Miss Bell's mother has taken ill. I fear she must leave straightaway. Mr. Trevethan has agreed to see her home."

Before the woman could protest about the impropriety of a gentleman escorting a single female home—that was another thing Gwynna remembered from Sophia's instruction—Sophia continued. "Mr. Hawkins, my dear, I believe there is a guest awaiting you in your study, the owner of Wheal Favour."

Mr. Hawkins, who had been staring at his wife in confusion since she'd begun speaking, finally nodded with understanding. "Oh, oh. Of course. Do excuse me for a moment, Mrs. Parnell."

The woman's sour expression spoiled further. She was clearly displeased with the whole matter, being left alone at the party given in her honor. Mr. Hawkins departed swiftly with a brief word to his wife as Mr. Trevethan bowed to Mrs. Parnell.

"It was a pleasure to meet you, ma'am. I do hope the rest of your stay in Cornwall exceeds your expectations."

"That will not be difficult," she muttered. "Good evening."

Gwynna curtsied. "Ma'am." Why should she bother saying anything more?

Mrs. Parnell tipped her head then turned to the fire with a weighty sigh. Mr. Trevethan motioned for Gwynna to precede him across the room.

"I will have your dress delivered covertly to your home this evening," Sophia whispered, then she faced Mrs. Parnell alone with a weakened smile.

Before Gwynna could even consider Sophia's plight with being left alone with the old woman, the butler met them outside the door with Gwynna's cloak and Mr. Trevethan's hat. "The study is down the corridor to the right of the entryway," he whispered. "Mr. Hawkins has advised you to take care."

Gwynna ducked her head. "Thank ye, sir."

He gave a silent nod and walked away. He'd obviously never approved of her behavior. He wasn't alone in that regard.

She followed one step behind Mr. Trevethan as they fled

down the corridor, pausing as they approached a corner that led to the entryway. He pressed a finger to his lips as he peered around the wall then motioned Gwynna forward.

She snuck up behind him, careful to situate herself with enough distance from him to avoid any accidental touch.

The murmur of soft voices traipsed toward them down the corridor. She peered past the black and white flooring of the entryway and down the subsequent corridor where a single light seeped out from beneath a closed doorway.

Her breathing grew ragged. How could she have put herself into such trouble again? And now involving Mr. Trevethan? She was inexplicably stupid.

"Are you ready?"

Mr. Trevethan held out his hand to her. The thorny branch she'd imagined before was gone. Instead, his offer was a direct path to safety.

With a deep breath, she placed her fingers in his. Their eyes met, and his grip tightened before he pulled her forward.

CHAPTER TWENTY-EIGHT

*G*wynna and Mr. Trevethan darted across the entryway, their quick footsteps echoing about the open room. One foot after another, they pattered across the marble flooring like jittery mice, hoping to escape the house cat before its claws tore into them.

Halfway there, Gwynna could almost taste the freedom the fresh air would provide her. Then her foot slipped against the smooth floor.

With a yelp, she flew to the side, grasping Mr. Trevethan's arm to avoid falling to the ground. Her feet continued to move, though he tried to pause.

"Are you all right?" he asked.

Her eyes flew to the opposite corridor. The study door remained closed, though they were sure to have heard her yelp.

"Curse these fitty slippers," she hoarsely whispered as they continued across the floor. "I swear I'll ne'er wear 'em again."

She thought she caught a grin flashing across Mr. Trevethan's lips, but it was gone the moment he opened the door and the late evening sun spread its welcoming light over the both of them.

He released his hold of her as they crossed the threshold, closing the door behind them before tearing across the grounds toward the trees on the far side of the property.

With the study on the opposite side of the house, there was no chance of being spotted by Mr. Trevethan's father from any window, but Mrs. Parnell might still find them from her place in the drawing room.

Once they found cover beneath the thicket of trees, however, their footsteps slowed then stopped altogether. Mr. Trevethan bent over, his hands on his knees as he caught his breath. Gwynna stood with a hand to her back, wincing at the pain running had induced. She'd forgotten how difficult everything was made to be with this continuous pain from spalling.

As their breathing slowed and the birds chirping overhead filled the air, Mr. Trevethan straightened.

"We mustn't rest for long. I've no idea when my father will leave. We must take the pathway closer to the cliffs so he cannot happen upon us by the road."

Gwynna pursed her brow, slipping off her gloves. "We, sir?"

"I did promise to see you to safety, did I not?"

"Ye did, sir, already. But I be thinkin'—"

"Jack."

She blinked. "Beggin' your pardon, sir?"

"I am weary of all this 'sir' business. I call you Gwynna. It's only fair for you to call me Jack."

She scoffed, tucking in her chin. "I be callin' ye sir 'cause of your station, sir. I ain't be calling ye...*Jack*."

He took a few steps toward her. His height was intimidating, but she maintained her ground. "What ye be doin', sir?"

In a swift movement, he snatched her cloak and gloves from her hands. "I'm being a gentleman and holding your items while I see you safely home."

She watched him walk out of the cover of the trees, the tails of his jacket flapping up and down against his—

"I thought it ain't proper for a gent to be alone with a woman?" she countered, catching up to him. "Ye be better off leavin' I alone."

He ignored her, shifting her cloak and gloves to his left arm. If someone happened upon the two of them together, rumors were sure to surface. Of course, happening upon someone so late was highly unlikely. Most of the miners she knew would be abed already.

Still, she felt she at least had to try to protest. "And don't ye 'ave a dance tonight, sir? Won't ye be late if ye walk me home?"

"Yes, but that shouldn't be a problem."

He'd set aside *that* issue promptly.

Still, walking her home would be a great inconvenience. "I be sorry if I ruin your evenin' then."

He raised a brow. "If you recall, my father was the one to ruin the evening." He paused. "If you learn anything from tonight, let it be to never invite a Trevethan to a party. We will be sure to end everyone's enjoyment."

Somehow, the mere sight of his easy smile tipped the last of her hesitance away. She couldn't come up with any other reason to keep the man from walking her home. He would just concoct another excuse anyway.

She folded her arms, pretending to be far more upset than she was. "Fine, ye may see me home. So long as ye leave a distance away so me father won't see ye."

"I think I can manage that."

"And," she continued, "I be needin' me cloak back to hide Mrs. Hawkins's dress."

He examined her head to toe. "I think I prefer seeing that gown to this." He raised her faded, brown cloak. "It's far more appealing."

Heat pinched her cheeks. Appealing? Mr. Trevethan thought the gown on her...appealing?

No, the dress, not Gwynna, was what he found appealing.

They continued in silence, creating more distance between themselves and Fynwary Hall. The road lay behind them now, and as far as she could see, the landscape was covered in grassy hills, tan, weathered tors, and stretches of yellow wildflowers, entirely vacant of anyone apart from themselves.

Above them, the sky shone a dark purple, shifting to pinks and orange as the sky spread toward the lilac sea. The air was warm, and soon, the faintest sound of the melodical waves sang in her ears.

This was certainly not how she'd intended the evening to end, walking alone at sunset with Mr. Trevethan as he accompanied her home. And yet, she couldn't complain.

Of course, she was still at risk for being discovered by another, especially in her gown. But for some reason, walking with Mr. Trevethan that evening brushed the rest of her worries away like stalwart broom bristles to vexing cobwebs.

Appealing.

She cleared her throat. "Lest ye be thinkin' I be ungrateful, sir—"

"Jack."

She stared up at him blankly, unable to remember what she'd been about to say. "I ain't be callin' ye by your given name, sir."

"We are friends, are we not?"

How in heaven's name could she respond to such a question? "I-I suppose."

"Then you must call me Jack."

She had absolutely no intention of doing so, but she nodded all the same. How had she found herself friends with both a lady *and* a gentleman? A gentleman whose jawline had more of a solid angle to it than even the most chiseled of stone.

They continued in silence for a moment, nearing the cliff's edge. The sun had already slipped into the water, darkening the sky to shades of blue and pink. The waves rippled softly toward the land, and the wildflowers swayed themselves to sleep.

Mr. Trevethan motioned ahead of them to an engine house in tatters. "What is that mine?"

The tip of the chimney was missing, half walls were chipped at the top, and the windows were void of any covering.

"That be Wheal Penharrow. Well, the ruins of it anyway, as it closed years ago. That be where me father worked 'fore Wheal Favour opened. Mrs. Hawkins's father owned this alongside Wheal Favour 'fore he sold 'em. He ran out o' money to continue 'em both."

She eyed the old stone walls with affection as they stopped nearby. "'Tis a lovely mine, though. Its views rival Favour's. Maybe even better, as ye can see the whole countryside and the sea from the workings."

"It's strange to see one so vacant, especially after the busyness of Wheal Favour. It's almost...frightening."

She eyed him sidelong. "They do say it be haunted."

Mr. Trevethan rubbed his jaw. "Haunted, you say?"

"They be just rumors, 'course."

He raised a daring brow, taking a few steps ahead. "Shall we see if it's true?"

Gwynna hesitated. "Oh, but it ain't be our property."

His shoulders raised flippantly as he progressed toward the engine house.

"Sir, ye can't just—"

"Jack." He didn't turn around to correct her.

She sighed. "Ye can't go there. The shaft be only slightly boarded up. Ye could fall through and get hurt."

"Well you had better join me then, to ensure I stay protected."

She propped her hands on her hips. "I ain't be riskin' me life for ye, sir."

"Jack."

"Fine!" she shouted, having to raise her voice as he continued closer to the mine. "I'll just go home without ye!"

He raised her cloak and gloves still in his arms, calling to her over his shoulder. "I thought you needed these?"

Blast. She'd forgotten he still had her cover.

Mr. Trevethan continued. "You can follow me to the ruins and retrieve it, or if you call me Jack, I'll give it back to you right now."

Curse her pride. She was going to be stuck there all night, torn between what to do, for she was fairly certain Jack—Mr. Trevethan—was as stubborn as she.

He moved around the tall building, no longer in sight. Gwynna remained where she stood, eying the pathway lined with yellow gorse. She couldn't sneak into her house without a cover. She needed that cloak. Really, she *should* follow him, if only to be sure he was safe. He may know more about sitting around a dinner table than she ever would, but a copper mine was *her* territory.

She picked up the side of her skirt and traipsed across the ground. What she wouldn't give to be wearing her boots. Every bump and stone in the ground protruded through her slippers. They were sure to be ruined after this journey.

"Sir?" she called out, stepping lightly as the pathway narrowed. The gorse thickened as she neared the mine, snagging at her dress.

No reply.

"Mr. Trevethan?"

She reached the engine house, peering around both sides of it. Still no reply. Was he playing tricks?

She continued around to the other side, but he wasn't there. "Ye best answer 'fore I think ye be dead."

Nothing.

With a heavy sigh, she finally relented. "Jack!"

"Yes?"

She jumped at his voice directly behind her.

CHAPTER TWENTY-NINE

*M*r. Trevethan chuckled, and delightful irritation scratched at Gwynna. She swatted his arm. "How dare ye? I thought..." Her words trailed off as she realized she'd just struck a gentleman. "Oh, I-I be sorry."

He laughed, rubbing his arm. "No, I deserved that."

She fixed her eyes on him as he walked to the front of the engine house.

The ruins of an old counthouse stood in a skewed square, and old pieces of rotting wood lay abandoned on the ground—evidence of a dressing floor that was no more.

"Have ye seen any ghosts then?" she asked, standing beside him.

"No, unfortunately not." He pushed aside a decaying timber with his shoe. "Seems a terrible waste, doesn't it? To let all of this deteriorate so."

"'Specially with the miners who might benefit from more work."

He studied the wood for a moment then peered about the rest of the mine. "So tell me, where would the spalling take place here?"

She searched the grounds, pointing near the entrance to a shaft only partially boarded. "Nearest to the landin' area."

He drew a blank expression.

"Where the ore be deposited," she clarified.

"Ah, I see. And are you the first to receive the ore when it comes from below ground?"

"No, first the raggin' must be done."

"Ragging. Right."

She quirked a brow. "Ye 'ave no idea what raggin' be, do ye?"

He chuckled. "Would you look down on me if I did not?"

"'Course not. But I thought your father already explained the process to ye?"

"Well he did, but I may or may not have been too distracted by a certain maiden wielding a hammer to listen to a single word."

How did even the faintest hint of a smile from him send her heart fluttering?

"Be ye teasin' I?"

"No. Merely expressing my admiration. I do not know any woman personally who could do what you do, day in and day out."

She rubbed the scar at the back of her arm, unsure of what to do with such attention. "'Tis simply part o' the job, sir."

"Jack."

"Yes, sir."

He cast his eyes around him once more. "Will you show me the process here, so I do not have to ask my father for another lesson?"

"That depends, sir. Will ye listen to I?"

He pressed a hand to his chest. "Upon my honor."

She pretended to scrutinize him for a moment before nodding. "All right. The process be done differently at every mine, dependin' on where it be situated on land, among other things. But I'll do me best to explain what we do at Wheal Favour."

She led the way past a pile of discarded ore, closer to the engine house. "The raggin' be done first by strong men. They break down the biggest pieces 'fore sendin' 'em off to we spallers.

"After we finish, they be barrowed to riddlin', where they clean and separate the ore through a sieve." Mr. Trevethan watched her intently as she held up three fingers. "There be three types o' ore. Prills, deads, and gangue. Prills be the best and can be sent to samplin'. Deads ain't worth a pence. The gangue, or dredge, be what's in between that."

She pointed to where a flat table lay a distance away, one of its legs broken to slant the wooden top. "The gangue be sent there, to the cobbers. They be the ones who use smaller hammers 'til the rocks be 'bout half the size of their palms."

"Ah, yes. I do remember seeing that."

She glanced around for the next stage of the dressing process. Finally, she found a small, stone hut. Half the roof was torn away, but the four walls still stood strong.

"That be where the buckin' takes place, I believe."

"That is one I have heard of before." Mr. Trevethan said, following her into the one-roomed structure. A table stood at the far end with a broken wheelbarrow nearby on its side. "If I recall, you were nearly assigned to that task."

She paused. How had he known such a fact?

"My father mentioned it when I first came to the mine," he explained.

And he'd remembered? Gwynna bit her bottom lip to stop her growing grin.

"Is the task arduous?" he asked.

Speaking of bucking would be just the thing to prevent her glow from increasing. "Yes. The maidens crush the ore into powder with another hammer, usually in a small shelter or room. It be terrible work, hittin' fingers constantly and breathin' in the ore. We hear that some mines be mechanizin' the process, but not yet at Favour."

Jack seemed to contemplate her words, rubbing his jaw with a distant look. Was she boring him with all of her details?

Rushing forward, she ended her explanation. "After the buckin', the ore be sieved durin' the jiggin' process, then buddlin'. All o' that just makes the ore finer 'til it be fit for samplin', when it be sold."

Jack blew out a slow breath, his brow high. She *had* overwhelmed him.

"I never would have thought the process involved such intensity," he said. "When one thinks of a mine, one typically considers only the men below ground."

"That be true. I'd never wish to do what they be doin' down there in the dark all day. It be hard work and dangerous—just like what us maidens do. But it be worth it, for me family to live more comfortably."

He studied her for a moment. Under his unnerving smile, she turned away, exiting the decaying bucking room and retreating past the engine house toward the pathway. "I only be sorry we didn't 'appen on any ghosts while in there."

"It is a pity."

She paused when his voice sounded farther away. He remained by the engine house, viewing the sea over his shoulder.

She really ought to be getting home by now, or at the very least on her way. Her parents would start to worry. But the call of the sea and Mr. Trevethan were too great.

She joined him, and they faced the water together, watching the dark ocean swelling forward. The sun had vanished, leaving a grey world in its wake, but the soothing sounds of the sea warmed the air.

"I take it that smile on your lips is not due to the evening you had." His dark eyes focused on her lips.

She hadn't known she was smiling. "I had a more pleasant evenin' than ye might think."

Despite the mishaps that occurred—flinging food across his jacket, suffering through Mrs. Parnell's questioning, fleeing from his father—all of it seemed so inconsequential in that moment with this man beside her.

"How can that be?" He leaned against the wall of the engine house. He folded his arms, crossing his legs at his ankles. "It ended precisely the same way the ball had ended, and we both know that was far from enjoyable for you."

She shot him a pointed look. "Perhaps 'tis 'cause I didn't experience the same idle threats this evening as I did last."

"I can do so now, if you are missing it. Or perhaps I ought to simply suggest another walk in the gardens?"

She ignored the thoughts that accompanied his words. "I think we both be better off if ye leave that suggestion unspoken, sir."

She turned away from him, wrapping her arms across her chest as a cold wind sailed around her neck.

"Why? Are you concerned you'd be unable to refuse me this time?"

CHAPTER THIRTY

*G*wynna forced a flippant laugh. "I ain't be worried o'er such a thing."

Mr. Trevethan pushed away from the wall and made to stand between her and the sea. "So confident?"

His voice was low, deeper than the roaring ocean that was quickly fading from their view.

"Just as confident as ye are, sir."

He took a deliberate step toward her, removing his gloves finger by finger. "Do you know what I think?"

She raised her chin to maintain his eye contact. "What be that, sir?"

"I think," he began, his words slow and calculated, "that if I asked you to kiss me...you wouldn't be able to refuse."

His eyes flickered to her lips, and her heart pattered against her chest. "I think ye be wrong, sir." Her voice was weaker than she'd hoped it would be.

"Do you?" he asked. He took another step toward her, his smile matching the one he held at the ball—low brow, determined eyes. Enticing lips.

Only this time, she didn't wish to express her frustration with him. This time, she wanted to do something else entirely.

Another cool wind blew past them, and chills sailed across her skin.

He removed his hat, depositing it on a dilapidated half-wall nearby with her gloves on top. Then he pulled her cloak from his arm and draped it around her shoulders, tying it at the base of her neck. His fingertips brushed softly against her skin, and his eyes lingered on hers.

He adjusted the cloak around her shoulders, smoothing it as he slid his hands down her arms.

"What do you say, Gwynna?" he whispered, peering down at her. "Do you think you would wish to say no?"

She took a step away, but her foot hit against the wall of the engine house. When had she backed up so much? She had nowhere else to go as he closed the distance between them.

Her breathing shallowed. "Per'aps." What had his question even been?

He pressed his palm on the wall beside her, tucking in his chin as he leaned closer toward her. He raised his free hand, his fingertips brushing a curl from her brow, and her stomach twisted with sheer delight.

Then her throat tightened. She was afraid. Afraid he was teasing her, afraid she was the only one feeling the stirring in her chest. What did all of this mean? "I think ye don't want it yourself, sir. I think ye be teasin' I, just for the sake o' teasin'."

She was testing him, pushing to see if he felt something in return. She watched him carefully, then fixed her attention to his mouth. His coaxing smile disappeared. She swallowed hard, as if her throat had closed off entirely and she could no longer draw in a breath.

"You don't believe I wish to kiss you?" he whispered.

His hand brushed against her temple once more, then trailed down her cheek, lingering on her jaw. She pressed her hands against the wall, willing the rough feeling of the stone to knock sense back into her.

It didn't.

"I believe ye would wish to kiss any woman," she breathed.

She spoke the words aloud, reminding herself of the truth. She was nothing special to him. He hadn't known her from anyone, and he'd asked to kiss her in the dark at a ball, even knowing she was a bal maiden.

"Perhaps that was true once," he said, moving his thumb along her jaw and resting it at the tip of her chin. Slowly, he urged her head back. His breath tickled her lips. "But now, I only desire it...from you."

Sense screamed that he was lying, that he only desired her in that moment because no other lady was available. But soon, her desire pushed away any lingering apprehension. She wanted his kiss to be hers.

"Do you know how I first recognized you at the ball?" he whispered.

"No, sir."

His eyes flicked between her own. "It was your eyes. Even from across the room, I recognized their warm, rich color. Like honey right before it is poured into tea."

He tipped his head to the side, focusing once more on her lips that had since parted on their own.

"I've never much cared for tea. But honey..." His upper lip touched hers as he spoke. "I crave it."

Any breath, any control she'd hoped to conserve was gone in that moment. Finally, she would have his lips for her own.

"Do you crave me, Gwynna?" he asked, his voice husky. "Do you wish to kiss me now?"

Her eyes struggled to remain open.

Yes, Jack. Wrap me in your arms and kiss me 'til the moon and stars be our only light.

Only, she couldn't admit to such a desire aloud. She would lose the last of her control, and then where would she be?

She drew in a rattled breath. "No, sir?" she stated in more of a question.

Jack blinked, his eyes caressing her lips as he released a slow breath. "No? I suppose you were right then. You *can* deny me."

Gwynna had only lied because she'd been certain he'd still kiss her. After all, what reason had he not to?

But as he stepped away, her breath caught in her chest, ripe with regret. Should she call him back, reach for his jacket lapels and kiss him herself?

"Come along, Miss Bell. We must return you to your parents and leave the mine before the ghosts join us."

Had she imagined his disconsolate tone and his sunken shoulders, or were they a figment of her own disappointed mind?

He moved around the engine house, leaving Gwynna breathless with blinding disappointment.

She'd never regretted her pride so fiercely.

Jack scrubbed his hands down his face as he rounded the corner of the engine house. He had to shake this off now before that tempting maiden walked once more by his side and he pulled her in his arms and kissed her until morning.

He was a total fool. He'd only been teasing her before about kissing her, but when he saw the desire in her eyes, a fire ignited in his chest. His heart hadn't beat in such a way in years. Surely never when he'd kissed any other woman. Those moments had been purely carnal.

He was attracted to Gwynna, of course. Her pink lips, the spatter of freckles across her nose. But there was something more than physical desire. He was *feeling* something more.

And those feelings scared the devil out of him.

Thank heavens her final declaration of "no," though feigned as it was, had finally given him the strength to pull away.

He had promised himself to leave Gwynna once his questions had been answered. Now that his debt was satisfied from his behavior at the ball, he was free to move on. Free to go to the assembly. Free to kiss other women without guilt. Free to continue the life he'd planned for himself—unmarried, alone, and without responsibilities.

So that's what he was going to do because he couldn't risk *feeling* any longer.

CHAPTER THIRTY-ONE

*J*ack didn't go to the assembly. Gwynna's silhouette had disappeared into the small hovel she called a home, then he'd made his way back to Fynwary Hall by moonlight. After ensuring his father had departed, he'd informed the Hawkinses as to the safety of Gwynna and rode his horse for Coffrow Place.

He told himself he was just too exhausted from the evening to attend another societal event. But really, he hadn't been up to mingling with well-versed, practiced women who couldn't brandish a hammer or describe the process of the mine's dressing floors with aplomb.

The next morning, after a restive night, he situated himself in the far corner of the drawing room with a book, hoping to rein in his thoughts that continually tried to gallop recklessly to the evening before—and how badly he'd wanted to kiss Gwynna.

He'd never pulled away from a kiss before. Not from a willing woman, at any rate. And Gwynna had certainly been willing. Those full lips, her eyes on his mouth. His blood had never burned so intensely. Even now, energy coursed through his veins like the boiling water in the Roman pools at Bath.

Apart from the kiss—or rather, lack thereof—something else had been nagging permanently since the night before. Something Gwynna had said to him. His eyes wandered away from the pages of his book, staring at nothing in particular across the room.

"It must be some comfort knowin' she'd be proud of ye and the man ye've become."

If only his mother *could* be proud of him. Yes, he'd finally claimed victory over controlling his gambling and drinking habits. But how could Mama approve of his pursuing countless women until he received what he desired? A few kisses with no binding ropes of commitment or responsibility.

He raised his book, holding it directly before him to focus on Shakespeare's words rather than this contrition that had burrowed its way under his defenses and was now battering him daily.

Footsteps outside the room pulled him away from Hamlet's musing better than even remorse could. His lips pressed in a line. He hadn't planned on anyone being up for hours, what with their late night out at the assembly. If Father was coming to speak with him...

But it wasn't father. Amy walked into the room instead.

Her footsteps faltered. "Oh, good morning."

"Morning." He lowered his book to his lap. "I'm surprised you're up so early. Did you not stay at the assembly for long?"

She reached for her wrap strewn across the sofa. "On the contrary. We stayed later than anyone."

Jack turned to the next page of his book, though he had no recollection of a single word.

"We missed you there."

"Yes, I do apologize for leaving the three of you to yourselves. My business extended longer than I expected." Far longer. And far better. "I trust you enjoyed yourselves still."

"We did." She paused in the doorway. "My brother and I were wondering though, what business a gentleman could have if he does not yet run his own estate and refuses to help his father with the one he will one day possess."

His brow twitched. Was that a slight or a hint at her displeasure? Either way, her words nettled his patience.

"Hugh expects you've found another woman here to keep you company."

Her words painted a blush on his cheeks that he hoped wasn't as red as it felt. He stared hard at the page of his book. "Does he?"

"I'm inclined to agree with him," Amy continued, jarring his nerves. Had his cousins seen Jack's odd fascination with the bal maiden? "I must admit the idea is not so very farfetched, what with the kissing games you and Hugh insist on playing."

So she didn't know about the bal maiden. Finally, he looked up. The clear disappointment dimming her eyes jutted up against his defenses. What right had she to be looking at *Jack* in such a way? Surely Hugh was the greater scoundrel.

Irritated, Jack closed his book and settled further in his chair. "What is your intent, Amy, in bringing up such a topic?"

She studied him with an unreadable expression. "My brother has already made his choice to live without regard for others. I merely ask of you, cousin, to not leave behind a trail of broken women here in Cornwall…as you did in Bath."

His brow furrowed, discomfort festering in his chest.

Before he could respond, she walked away with a shrug, her words fading down the corridor. "But what business is it of mine what you do?"

Clenching his jaw, Jack opened his book and stared down at the random page he'd turned to, willing his eyes to focus on the black words against the cream-colored paper.

What did Amy know, anyway? Jack hadn't kissed a woman since he'd arrived in Cornwall. Hugh, on the other hand, had to have shared affection with at least two or three—possibly more after the assembly last night. If Hugh felt no remorse, why should Jack?

A trail of broken women.

Had he broken them? And was he breaking Gwynna?

"Jack?"

Blast. He closed his book and scrambled to his feet, attempting to appear as casual as possible as he made to leave. "Father. I was just on my way out."

What were they all doing up? Jack should've just stayed hidden away in his room until he was sure Hugh was awake and could help distract Father. Amy was certainly not being of any help.

"Were you not reading?" Father questioned, eying the book in Jack's hands.

Jack lifted it with disinterest. "Yes, but one can only manage Shakespeare for so long."

In truth, he enjoyed Shakespeare. But he'd lie about anything to leave. Besides, Father didn't know what Jack did or did not like to read. He didn't know anything about him, really.

Jack set the book on a table nearby. "I believe Hugh has been hoping for a ride. I ought to be ready for him when he awakens."

"You will be waiting quite a while for him then," Father said, entering the room more fully. "Amy and I rose early out of habit, but Hugh was behaving rather lively last evening."

Jack gave a quick laugh. "That's Hugh for you."

And that explained Amy's comments. She must have been mortified with her brother's inappropriate conduct and decided to take it upon herself to correct Jack before he could embarrass her any more than her brother had.

He progressed toward the door as Father spoke again. "Does he always behave in such a way?"

Jack paused. "In what way?"

Father watched him carefully. "Drinking heartily. Laughing above the sound of even the music. Sneaking off into gardens with women."

Jack raked his fingers through his hair. Was he to suffer through the same taxing conversation with Father that he'd just had with Amy? "He's merely having a little fun, Father."

"I know. And there is nothing wrong with young gentlemen enjoying themselves. But when rumors begin to emerge from all the pleasure, one must be careful."

Jack folded his arms, building even more of a barrier between him and his father. "What are you saying?"

Father hesitated. "Merely that I hope you are better able to avoid rumors than your cousin has been, in your dealings with ladies of your own class...and the working class."

Fear hardened Jack's stomach. Did Father know about last evening, Jack helping Gwynna, Gwynna dressing as a lady?

He noted Father's innocent expression and quickly set the worry aside. Not only had Mrs. Hawkins taken every precaution, no one had seen them after dark across the cliffsides. How *could* his father know?

Annoyance replaced his timidity. Why did Father believe he could offer Jack advice? Had he raised his son, perhaps he was entitled to such guidance, but not now.

"You needn't worry about me, Father. I've taken care of myself since you sent me away. I can take care of myself now."

CHAPTER THIRTY-TWO

*J*ack hadn't meant to speak the words aloud. He grappled with his emotions, struggling to remain detached, to bring back the familiar numbing sensation. He had no problem silently criticizing his inattentive father, but to his face? That would lead to a conversation he wasn't willing to have.

Sure enough, as Jack tried to depart, Father called him back. "Wait a moment, son."

"I must ready for my ride with Hugh."

"Please, wait."

Tapping impatient fingers on the doorframe, Jack faced him again. "What do you need?"

Father paused, his shoulders sinking, eyebrows drawn high. Mama had always said Jack had his father's eyes and brow. Jack had always ignored the resemblance.

"I feel as if we haven't spoken much, Jack, and you've been here a fortnight. Before we know it, summer will be at an end, and you will have returned to Bath."

Jack couldn't wait for that. Although, leaving for Bath meant no longer seeing Gwynna. He blinked away the image of her wispy hair trailing down her neck, having fallen from its pins on their walk home last evening. He didn't need anything keeping him in Cornwall or keeping him closer to his father.

"We've spoken more often than usual," he said.

That wasn't a hard feat. Father was usually locked away in his study. Just like the night Mother died.

"Yes, but only mere conversations about Wheal Favour or your cousins." Father wrung his hands. "I'd like to speak about you. How you've been."

No, it was too late for that, getting to know each other. If Father had really cared, perhaps he should've tried earlier. "I've been more than happy living with the Paxtons, as I'm sure you're aware."

Father twisted round the ring on his little finger. "I'm glad you've found a home with them. And have you any plans for a future home? With Amy, perhaps?"

Jack pulled back. Why the devil would he even say such a thing? "No, Father. I have no plans to marry anyone at the present, least of all my cousin."

He pushed aside the imposing image of Gwynna's honey-colored eyes. What was she doing appearing at such an inopportune time?

Father attempted an easy smile, as if them speaking of matters such as matrimony were the most natural thing in the world. "I wouldn't wait too long before you settle down. You know, I was quite young when I met your mother."

Jack stiffened. He knew Father would bring up Mama eventually. He couldn't help himself.

But Jack couldn't do it.

"Even though I was but nineteen," Father continued, "I knew straightaway she was the woman with whom I wished to spend my life."

A metallic taste flooded Jack's mouth, as if he'd just drunk water from a rusted, tin cup. He pulled his tongue away from his clenched teeth, realizing only then the curious taste had been blood.

Father hadn't spent his life with Mama. He'd spent it chasing one venture after another, always leaving Jack and her behind.

"Yes, we had a pleasant life together. She was the best thing that ever happened to me. And you, of course."

Jack hung his head, fisting his hands. How dare the man speak of such things, as if he wasn't the cause of her death. "You don't have to do this, Father."

"Do what?"

"Speak to me as if you..." He shook his head. Squaring his shoulders, he peered at him impassively, not willing to allow Father's pitiful expression to penetrate his barriers. "We may simply continue as we have been. A few words of greeting. Talk of business and the estate. That is how it has always been, and that is how it ought to remain."

He nodded his head, then left the room.

"I miss you each day you are away from here."

Jack froze, the tendons in his neck as tight as a metal rod. Backtracking, he returned to the room. "You miss me," he repeated. His voice was dry of all emotion, like the parched creek bed near the Paxtons' home. Not *his* home. He didn't have one, thanks to the man standing before him.

"I do," Father replied.

Jack nodded his head, though he had no belief in his words. He ran his tongue along the inside of his cheek. "I see. You miss me so greatly you send a mere letter a year."

Father opened his mouth, but Jack wouldn't allow him to explain. The man had had eleven years to explain. It was Jack's turn to speak.

He took a step forward. A shaken dam had been broken, and the waters were raging forth. "And what do you wish me to say in return, Father? That I missed you, as well? That I have thought of you every day since you shipped me away?"

"No, I don't—"

"That is fortunate for your sake, because I fear I cannot say such things."

Father's lips twitched in a frown, but Jack was past the point of feeling sorry for the man. When had Father ever felt sorry for his own son?

"I did what I thought was best for you, son. After her death—"

"Stop." Jack squeezed his eyes shut, holding the bridge of his nose between his forefinger and thumb, attempting to thwart the anger that pulsed between his eyes from traveling to the rest of his limbs. There was no use. The words rushed forward with the strength of an unstoppable wave.

"That is a lie, Father. You were not doing what was best for me. You were doing what was best for *you*, which is what you have always done. It has always been about you, the business-man, Peter Trevethan, and what reckless scheme can pull him away from his wife and son next."

"Just a moment, I—"

Jack sliced his hand through the air, ending his father's words. "No! For once in your life, be honest with yourself and with me! Mother spent every waking moment with me. She kept me home from Eton, hired a private tutor, just so she could be near me. Yet, after her death, you couldn't bear the obligation of having a son to watch over. Instead of sending me to a boarding school, seeing me four times a year, you simply passed the entire responsibility of raising me to the Paxtons so you would not feel obliged to see me at all."

He stopped, his chest rising and falling. Father stared at him, pain etched into each wrinkle on his brow.

Jack silently gathered his emotions, bottling them up once again. "It hardly matters now, anyway. What's done is done."

He turned to leave, but Father stopped him again. "But we must speak of such things, Jack."

"No, it will do us no good."

"It will, if we—"

"No, it won't!" he shouted, whirling round. "You didn't wish for me to be home, so just admit it! You—"

"I sent for you, Jack!"

Jack froze, and Father checked his tone. "I sent for you, son. After you were gone, I was driven to madness. I buried myself even more into matters of the estate, our tenants, the businesses in which I held shares. But it did nothing. I lost my entire family within days."

Jack scrambled to ward off Father's words. He couldn't believe them. He *wouldn't*. "I don't need to listen to this."

Father stepped forward with a look of pleading. "I am not blind to my neglect of you and your mother, and I regret that every day. But that is why I sent you away. I thought you'd be better off living with someone who wasn't so taken with business and always moving on to the next venture. The Paxtons are good people, they—"

"I didn't know them, Father!" Jack leaned forward, his hands out to his side. "*You* hardly did!"

"I was not in my right mind," Father defended, "clearly! But I assure you, I came to my senses swiftly and wrote to my cousins to send you home."

Shock rippled through Jack's limbs, the blood draining from his head. He stepped back to maintain his balance. "No, you did not."

"I did!" Father walked toward him. "But Mrs. Paxton wrote to me and told me you were better off there, that you had adjusted and settled well. That you were happy."

Jack turned away. Father was lying. He had to be.

"I wanted to be sure," Father continued, his tone softer, "so I visited you that first December you were away. And I...I saw you there with the siblings your mother and I could never provide for you. With two parents who loved you as their own. With a home. You *were* happy."

Jack rubbed his eyes, frantically scooping out the memories pouring into his mind, flooding every thought. He remembered that Christmas. The first day he'd seen his father since Mama's funeral, as Jack had left for Bath with the Paxtons that very night. Jack had feigned joy with his cousins to prove he was better off without Father, but the night Father left, Jack had torn apart his room then sobbed himself to sleep.

"You were finally happy, Jack. How could I take that away from you?"

He should've known. Father should've known deep down that Jack was not happy.

Slowly, Jack met his eyes. "You were not the only one grieving Mother's death. I had to fake my happiness, or I'd have died in my grief." He lowered his voice. "Just like Mother."

Tears filled Father's dark eyes as Jack's pointed stare tore into him. With a disgusted shake of his head, Jack stormed from the room and slammed the door behind him.

CHAPTER THIRTY-THREE

*D*ark clouds stretched their reach across the sky, hovering heavily over sea and land. The green grass across the cliffside was tinted black, and the muted wildflowers shivered against the cold wind.

Gwynna tightened her cloak around her shoulders and flicked a lingering tear from her cheek. The storm was imminent that night, which was why she'd gone out. Jago had always loved storms.

Much to Mama's apprehension, he would stand at the edge of the cliff, the stirring sea a feast for his eyes as waves cut through murky water. In honor of his memory, Gwynna visited his grave during storms whenever possible, then walked along his favorite path, near Tregalwen Beach.

Mr. Trevethan had been right. The pain of her brother's death was still there, but it was becoming easier to bear, if only because she knew what ache to still expect.

Mr. Trevethan. He was a welcome distraction to the continual pain digging into her heart. Although, she couldn't say she particularly enjoyed the regret and shame that accompanied any thought of the man.

She blew out a heavy breath, absentmindedly pulling out the pins in her hair and tucking them one by one into her apron pocket. Her skin warmed, despite the cold wind scraping at her cheeks.

She'd revealed far too much last night. She had wanted to kiss him. Foolishly, she'd thought he'd wanted the same. But the ease with which he'd pulled away, and his keeping a healthy distance from her the rest of their walk to her home, had reaffirmed that there was no way he felt any attraction to her. Either that or he'd finally realized his mistake in nearly kissing a bal maiden.

She stepped hard down the incline that sloped toward the sandy mouth of Tregalwen Beach, the dirt path slowly merging with the sand.

She was certain many gentlemen did a number of things with lower class women, but Jack obviously did not want to be entangled with anything of the sort.

Not that she was complaining. She couldn't be more relieved the kiss hadn't occurred. No matter how badly she'd longed for the touch of his lips on hers, for his fingers to caress her skin forever. Had the kiss occurred, she, and her heart, would have been in grave trouble.

Involving herself any further with the gentleman would be terribly unwise. As such, she was determined to keep her distance from now on.

Yet, as she paused at the mouth of the beach and found the very man of her thoughts standing at the edge of the sand where the water couldn't reach, her determination fled.

He stared out at the sea, his hands holding his jacket behind his back. His feet were braced apart, the bottom of his black boots buried in the sand. As his white sleeves rippled against his arms, the wind blew his short hair behind him.

An invisible rope of longing tugged her toward him, despite her better judgment. Nothing good could come of her drawing closer to the man, especially after blatantly ignoring the deal she'd just made with herself.

But then, had she forgotten to thank him for his help last evening? It would certainly be a disservice if she *didn't* go down to meet him. Just a simple expression of gratitude, then she'd part from him forever.

Before she could think better of her actions, Gwynna stepped off the pathway and traipsed through the sand, the tall grass at her side bent back as the wind pressed its will against the blades. The gusts plastered her skirts to her legs, as well, as if attempting to prevent her progression toward the gentleman.

She ignored its warning.

The wind didn't know what it was talking about anyway.

"Sir?"

The wind whistled in Jack's ears and the waves crashed only a few feet from his boots. But he knew that voice from anyone's. "Gwynna."

She stood beside him, her hair loosed from her pins and blowing behind her shoulders, though the same scant piece of cloth held back most of it from her face. A warm spring flooded his chest, a comfort to the cold that had iced around him since his conversation with his father that morning.

"What are you doing out here?" he questioned. "It will no doubt rain soon."

"I was about to ask ye the same question, sir."

Her eyes lingered on his waistcoat hanging half-open and his loosened cravat drooping slightly down his neck. His angry tears had all but dried, but he was certain his eyes were still red.

"Are ye well, sir?"

He forced a smile. "Of course. Do I not seem well?"

She raised a shoulder. "We've spoken more than a minute

together, and ye still haven't threatened or teased me. Somethin' must be wrong with ye."

Her full lips tipped upward, but he could hardly match her humor. "I suppose that is a valid argument. But perhaps you will excuse me until next we meet. I'm afraid I'm a little tired to threaten you today."

The excuse was pitiful, at best.

She brushed her disbelieving eyes across his features. "If ye insist, sir. I be sorry to impose on ye. I merely came down to thank ye for last evenin'."

He tilted his head to the side. She'd already thanked him profusely for his service the night before. Had she come down for another reason? To simply be with him perhaps? The spring in his chest heated, spreading through his limbs. "I was more than happy to help you, Gwynna."

Their eyes met, and her gaze dropped to his lips before she took a step back. "Well, I best be headin' back. Me parents expect me 'fore the storm hits."

She walked away, and instantly, the warmth vanished, replaced with a lonely, indelible chill, of which he was desperate to be rid. Desperate enough to bring her back. "Yes, I'm certain *they* will be awaiting your return."

She stopped. "And your father? He will be awaitin' ye, too, no doubt."

He turned away, unsure whether to be displeased or relieved his words had managed to keep her. The mist rolled across the sea toward land. Clouds streaked down toward the water, as if great hands had raked their fingers through them, creating tears in the clouds for the rain to pour down to the earth.

"No, I don't believe my father will be expecting me to return until much later."

Her footsteps sifted through the sand as she returned to his side, bringing all the warmth of the sunshine with her, despite the impenetrable clouds above.

"Why be that, sir?"

What was he doing? Now he'd have to answer her questions, now he'd have to make sense of the thoughts swirling in his mind and the feelings swirling in his heart.

"It was nothing. We merely had another disagreement."

There. That was all he would share. He wouldn't think about his father any longer.

"I don't wish to interfere, sir, but if ye wish to speak, I be here to listen. As your friend."

His friend. How strange that word sounded in relation to himself, even when he'd been the one to suggest they *were* friends. He wasn't sure he had any beyond Hugh and Amy, and no one he kept closer than an arm's length away. It was far too risky to bring anyone nearer, not when they could forsake him at a moment's notice.

And yet, with Gwynna's wide, receptive eyes staring up at him, he knew he could find a true friend in her. Might he be able to let his guard down just this once to share the discouragement shrouding his spirits?

"Well, I..." He drew in a deep breath before trying again. "It is silly, really. And nothing I cannot handle. But he—my father —he attempts to befriend me when all I ever...I just feel it is too late."

His words were stilted, choppy, like the waves before them, running into the other before the first had a chance to complete its course. He'd never shared his feelings, always hiding behind flirtatious, flippant behavior, even with the Paxtons. What kind of sorceress was this bal maiden, to bewitch him into speaking his truth?

"I be sorry ye 'ave such a troubled relationship with 'im," she said. "I can't imagine how difficult it must be for ye to come to Cornwall. Not only with the memory of your mother, but also 'cause o' your father."

Jack released a slow breath. He'd never been understood

before, even the slightest amount. Her small insight was the hidden key to the chest he'd locked away so long ago, and soon, the words flowed forth, pouring from his lips before he could stop them.

"It is difficult. He made the decision to send me away. Now he tells me today that he has regretted it, that he has wished to be with me all along. But I wonder, if that were really true, why did he not do more to make it so? He could have just as easily sent me away to school, only seen me when I came home after terms. I just don't understand why he had to ship me away to be raised by someone else entirely." He rubbed his neck. "It is too late. The damage has been done. Yet, he cannot understand that though he wants a relationship with his son...his son does not want a relationship with *him*."

CHAPTER THIRTY-FOUR

Silence followed. Had Jack revealed too much? Would this good, kind-hearted maiden now leave him alone in the storm because she simply could not understand how someone could be so *cold*-hearted?

Instead of the disapproval he'd expected, compassion nestled in the depths of her eyes.

"I can't imagine what ye've been through, sir. First losin' your mother, then your father days after. No child ought to suffer such. No adult either."

The care in her tone, the empathy she shared, enveloped him in a warm embrace.

Suddenly, he felt foolish, vulnerable for revealing his hardships.

"I really have moved on from such feelings. But sometimes, being here, I'm reminded why I enjoy Bath far better."

In silence, her eyes removed to a wave that slid dangerously toward them, mere inches from their feet. He took a step back, unsure if it would reach their boots, but she did not falter a movement.

"Before your father purchased Wheal Favour, we miners and maidens were in a bad spot."

He turned toward her as the wave retreated without a lick at her boots.

"The previous owner, Mr. Rosewall, didn't care about any of we. He never was at the mine, and he hired a captain who assaulted women weekly and turned a blind eye to the other men who did the same."

Anger stirred in his belly. He was aware of the poor conditions of many of the Cornish mines—and the ignored treatment of most of the female workers—but the thought of such things happening to Gwynna made his blood boil.

"I was kept safe by me brother and father," she continued much to his relief, "but many girls weren't so fortunate."

She reached down, grasping a handful of sand and letting it slide from her fingers grain by grain. It cascaded through the air, flying with the wind down the rest of the beach.

"It was a terrible place to work," she said. "There was only one break, and that was to eat. The water was sparse, too. Once, when me and me friend Kerensa were only young, she had come down with a bad cough from all the ore flyin' in the air. She couldn't stop her coughin', so she went for a drink of water. The old mine captain thought she be havin' too much, so he poured what was left in the pitcher atop her head, shoutin', 'Have ye had enough now, maiden?'"

Jack's lips raised in disgust. It didn't matter the class, to treat someone with such disdain was despicable. "What happened to her?"

"Her cough worsened, and she was out o' work for days, which meant her family suffered, too."

He shook his head, unable to comprehend what such a life would be like.

"All that be to say...Wheal Favour has improved a great deal now your father be runnin' it."

He eyed her sidelong. An uneasy feeling creeping up his spine, as if another unanticipated wave was approaching from behind. What was she getting at?

"He makes improvements daily. He be workin' on providin' a shelter for we maidens and reinforcin' the mine for safety. He—"

"I'm sorry," he interrupted. "Gwynna, I-I understand that he has done many good things for all of you. And I'm grateful for that. I am. But I cannot see how that would improve his relationship with me."

She leaned slightly forward. "Don't ye think he be tryin' to make amends for 'is treatment of ye? To make Wheal Favour a better place because ye won't allow 'im to make your relationship better?"

The warmth she'd brought to him dissipated in a flash. His eyes hardened. "I won't allow him to improve our relationship?"

She frowned. "No, sir, I didn't mean...I only meant to say he *must* love ye, and since ye can't—"

"Love me?" He barked out a derisive laugh. Now, instead of feelings he was unable to hold within, it was angry words. "Oh, yes, he must love me because I'm his son. Just like he must have loved his wife, though he pushed her to an early grave."

She pulled back. He'd revealed too much. Turning away, he forced himself to hold his tongue.

"He be tryin' to make amends, sir. Just as ye did with me. And just like ye, he deserves forgiveness, too."

Jack's jaw tightened, anger pulsing through his blood, ridding himself of all patience and logic. He never should have called this woman back to him. What had he been thinking? Of course a bal maiden would have no idea as to the struggles between him and his father.

"I thank you for your help," he said, "but you know nothing about our situation and nothing about forgiveness."

The words were born from irritation and vulnerability, but

the moment he said them, regret secured its tight grip around him. He blinked, his jaw slack as Gwynna's eyes rounded, tears brimming in their depths.

She had not faltered when the wave had approached earlier, and yet with Jack's words, she took a step back.

"Gwynna..." He reached a hand out toward her, anxious to apologize, but she backed away.

"Ye be right, sir." Her voice broke. "I know not what your situation be like, so I don't 'ave a right to say a word."

Fool! He was an absolute fool. What a thing to say to someone who was merely attempting to help him. "Gwynna, wait!"

She continued on her way.

He pressed his palms to his temples, groaning at his stupidity. But in the next moment, she stopped. Slowly, she turned to face him with a raised chin and straightened back—like she did often when wearing a lady's gown.

Only this time, she was far more regal, a portrait of peace and calm control. Her hair blew about her, and her eyes leveled with his.

"I'm sorry," he began.

"You are wrong, sir."

"I know, I—"

"No, ye must let me speak now."

He'd said the same words to Father. He pulled back like a hound in trouble with his master.

"Ye be wrong about me, sir. I do know about forgiveness, as I've experienced it meself and seen it in others. The other mine owner, Mr. Rosewall, was responsible for the death of Jago, as well as five others. That man was Mrs. Hawkins's father."

The air pressed from his lungs, as if squeezed by invisible, unrelenting ropes. Of course. He recalled the Rosewalls owning mines and having a daughter. Even Gwynna herself had mentioned Mrs. Hawkins's father owning Wheal Favour. How could he not have made the connection until now?

She maintained her temper as she continued, something he'd been unable to do.

"I don't know what it'd be like to have me father abandon me, or to lose me mother. But I do know what it be like to forgive a man who could've prevented me brother's death. And I *do* know what it be like to forgive a woman who disregarded his life. Kerensa Hocking forgave Mr. Rosewall after her father died, leavin' her mother to care for four starvin' girls. And Mrs. Yeoman forgave him after startin' work at the mine again as a widow, havin' lost her husband in the same accident."

He longed to plug his ears, unable to bear the sorrow, the shame and regret. But his tongue was bound. He merely bowed his head in contrition.

"I'm sorry I offended ye, sir. But I only be tryin' to 'elp. Forgivin' Mr. Rosewall allowed me to be happier. Forgiveness ain't forgettin' your mother, or forgettin' whatever it was your father did. It be allowin' yourself to no longer be tied down by another's actions, to no longer restrict your happiness. It means risin' above, refusin' to allow bitterness to swallow ye whole. It means ye can live again, sir. And that's worth forgivin' for."

She finished her words, silence pulsing between them until she dipped her head and walked away, leaving Jack just as the rain began to speckle his shoulders and face.

Jack didn't call her back. He didn't deserve to speak with such a woman any longer. Another wave rushed toward him, but he didn't move that time. The water rushed over the tops of his boots.

She was right. He *was* bitter, and he'd allowed it to ruin his chance at living a happy life.

If he'd been able to forgive his father, he wouldn't be so angry. He wouldn't have sought attention as a youth by rebelling. He wouldn't be distracting himself from his pain by his philandering.

But he wasn't good like Gwynna. And he couldn't forgive his father. It was too late to change. He'd already become the person he'd be for the rest of his life—bitter, cynical, and alone.

CHAPTER THIRTY-FIVE

*J*ack leaned back in his chair, scowling fiercely as he swirled the brandy round in his glass. He sat by the window in the Golden Arms Inn, staring at the raindrops chuting down the glass in quick movements.

The rain hadn't stopped for three days, ever since his time on the beach. It had been a wretch getting to the inn that morning. His horse had thrown a shoe and was now with the farrier, but he'd needed an escape from Coffrow Place and his cousins. Hugh and Amy hadn't ceased in their attempts to improve his mood, and he couldn't bear their chipper attitudes any longer.

At least Father had had the sense to keep away from him.

Jack drew in a deep breath, still swirling his glass. The air around him was stale from too many bodies taking shelter from the inclement weather. Loud laughter and conversation bounded in his ears, punctuated by empty glasses thudding against wooden tables and rumbling thunder outside.

He occupied a small corner of the room by himself. Card games and bets were the order of the day at every other table, but he'd already exhausted the coins he'd brought with him.

That was the only way he'd learned to control his bad habit—by gambling only with the money he brought with him.

If only he had that same control with his drinking.

He pulled the glass to his lips but froze once again near his mouth. The floral, alcoholic scent stung his nose. It was familiar. Intoxicating. This had been his drink of choice as a young man, the drink that allowed him to forget all his troubles.

Three years. He hadn't had it in three years. But today... today it called to him. One sip was all it would take. One sip, and all would be forgotten. The pain would finally be numb.

Jack opened his mouth. He wanted to be deadened, to have no recollection of his mother, his argument with Father. His cruel words to Gwynna.

He stared down into the brandy, lingering on the amber liquid, and the blood drained from his face. That color. It too closely resembled a pair of eyes filled with tears—tears brought on by his own ignorance.

He'd avoided every thought of Gwynna for days, but now, as he peered into the glass, thoughts of her filled his mind to the brim.

He couldn't fathom her nobility in pardoning another so fully as she had Mr. Rosewall, nor her strength in instructing Jack in the ways of forgiveness. And now, after everything, he was going to risk falling to the wiles of drinking once again, only to forget his shameless treatment of her?

His mother had raised him better, and she would be ashamed of him.

Realization of what he'd almost done slid into his mind like the draft blowing past his hair from the window beside him.

In a swift movement, he stood from his seat. The chair fell with a clatter behind him, and he slammed the drink to the table. Brandy covered his hand and splashed against the window. He merely flicked the moisture from his fingers with a single shake, then stormed out of the inn and into the cold rain.

Gwynna tightened her grip on the spalling hammer. She couldn't have it slip again, no matter how drenched her gloves were, no matter how slippery the handle. She'd almost broken her foot moments ago, and that wouldn't do her any good.

She cracked open another piece of ore, then straightened, pressing a hand to the small of her back. The pain had intensified the past few days, due to the different way she'd had to grasp her hammer. The rain hadn't been this bad for this long since...since the day Jago had died.

She was doing her best not to dwell on the similarities between today and that day almost four months ago now—the rain, the ache in her muscles, the cries of the cold, wet children —but each new coincidence that arose tightened her already-clenched stomach.

She could only pray for Father's safety below ground.

A faint crying, intermittent between the clanging of iron, flitted to Gwynna's ears. Two young girls clung to each other nearby for warmth by the cobbing table.

Gwynna cast her eyes to the top of the cliff. With Mr. Harvey nowhere in sight, she dropped her tool and made for the girls.

"Ye must continue workin'," she advised them, shouting above the warring sea. "It'll keep ye warmer."

"She can't, miss," the oldest, who was not yet twelve, cried. "She can't feel her 'ands."

The other girl trembled from head to toe. At once, Gwynna dug into her towser pocket and pulled out her crib-bag. She'd already eaten her midday meal, but inside the thick material lay the dry bandage she'd kept from her headwound the week prior. She'd been saving it for later when her own fingers grew numb, but this girl was in far greater need.

"Here, take this." She pulled off the girl's soaking glove, using her body to shield the rain from the new fabric as she wrapped it around her purple fingers. "Keep it warm beneath your arm 'til the feelin' returns. Then switch it to the other hand, alternatin' between the two 'til ye feel better."

The girls nodded, expressing their gratitude through shaking words before Gwynna returned to her post. She picked up her hammer just as Mr. Harvey appeared in his regular spot, Mr. Peter Trevethan beside him.

They peered down at the maidens, dressed in their great coats, scarves, and hats. Had they seen her not working? Surely they wouldn't spale her for helping a young girl out. Either way, she cracked the ore before her with greater force, hoping they would know she hadn't been shirking her duties.

She watched them from the corner of her eye, wondering if a certain son had joined the owner before setting aside the notion. Mr. Jack Trevethan would certainly not have joined his father at the mine. And he was sure to never wish to see *her* again.

She didn't blame him, after the way she'd chastised him. She did not regret standing up for herself and her heartaches, but she feared he did not take it well.

But offending the gentleman was the least of her concerns at the moment. For now, she had to figure out a way to keep her own fingers from freezing, her back from aching, and her stamina from failing hours before work was to end.

As she cracked her way through her pile, rain dripping from the brim of her bonnet and soaking through her cloak and across her neck and shoulders, she wondered how much longer she could handle this.

She felt as if she'd been wet for days. Yesterday, the storm had been so terrible, Gwynna's dress hadn't dried overnight before the fire, and she'd had to wear her damp clothes to the mine. Not that it mattered, of course, as she was soaked in a matter of minutes anyway.

A movement from the side caught her eye as the mine owner and captain disappeared from the ledge. Gwynna imagined them retiring to the counthouse for a cup of tea, nestled near the warm fire. But in the next moment, as the mine's tinny bell sounded out across the dressing floor early, relief flooded her body.

"Tain't be safe anymore, Gwynna," Kerensa said, coming up toward her with her hammer over her shoulder. "That be why they be sendin' us home."

She pointed behind them where the cliffside in the distance began to crumble, mud and rocks tumbling down into the sea hundreds of feet below.

"I'm sure they be afraid of a landslide or somethin' the like," Kerensa added.

"Thank heavens for that," Gwynna mumbled.

She dropped her hammer to the side of her and loaded the rest of the broken ore into the barrow.

"I praise the day Mr. Trevethan purchased this mine," Kerensa said. "He be savin' all of us, ain't he?"

Gwynna nodded. If only he'd been there early enough to save Jago.

"I do wonder, though, if his son be good enough to take over when Mr. Trevethan moves on," Kerensa said.

Gwynna straightened, her brow furrowed. "He's plannin' on takin' over the mine? I thought he was leavin' for Bath?"

Kerensa gave her a funny look. "Bath? How do ye know that?"

Gwynna scrambled for an answer. "Oh, just from his father tellin' Papa."

"Ah," Kerensa said, appearing to believe her. "I suppose it won't matter either way. I be plannin' on marryin' 'fore ownership be transferred anyway."

Gwynna secured her cloak around her shoulders, then narrowed her eyes. "Are ye...engaged?"

"Oh, no." Kerensa's cheeks and nose were already red from the cold, but Gwynna suspected they were a shade darker now. "Though, I 'ave set me eye on a few 'andsome chaps round here." Her eyes sparkled. "'Twill take a good man, though, to 'elp with me sisters and mother."

The two fell in step together, their boots slurping up the mud with each stride they took.

"Gwynna, can I ask ye somethin'?"

"'Course ye can."

They neared the engine house where the miners were just beginning to pour out from the earth. "Do ye still desire to situate your parents first, 'fore ye marry?"

Gwynna contemplated the question for a moment. Her whole life she'd longed to marry and have children of her own, but Jago's death had placed her plans on hold. "Yes, they deserve 'appiness as much as I."

Kerensa fell silent, though her heavy stare remained on Gwynna.

"What?" Gwynna asked.

"Nothin'. Only, I wonder if ye've heard the rumors."

Gwynna shivered from the cold rain sliding down her back. "Rumors? 'Bout what?"

"About ye."

CHAPTER THIRTY-SIX

"*M*e?" Gwynna feigned a look of innocence, but she feared the panic in her eyes shone through. "What sort o' rumors be they?"

"Ridiculous ones, really." Kerensa lowered her voice. "Of ye dressin' up as a lady and fraternizin' with gents. One even said ye be kissin' 'em."

Gwynna tugged at the bonnet string beneath her chin, suddenly feeling as if she couldn't breathe. "Mad. Where 'ave ye heard such things?"

"Oh, ye know how rumors start, Gwynna. Jealous maidens, bored folk. Truth be told, I 'spect Ruth Ayer started most of 'em."

Ruth Ayer. Of course she would start them. She was still upset about being bested by Gwynna on Tregalwen. "How be she justifyin' such gossip?"

"Well, she be seein' one o' the footmen at Fynwary Hall who swore he'd seen ye runnin' from the house wearin' a gown alongside a gent."

Horrified, Gwynna stared at the ground, her bonnet blocking Kerensa's view of her guilt-ridden face. Gwynna was daft to have ever thought her inappropriate conduct would go without consequence. How could she have made such a grave error? Now the truth was out there, marred by exaggerations. Suppose Mr. Trevethan discovered it, or her parents? She couldn't lie to them any longer. If they confronted her, she'd have to tell them the truth.

"Tell me, Kerensa, how far 'ave the rumors spread? Me parents would worry, see."

Kerensa quickly shook her head. "No, ye ain't need to worry about that. Least not yet. They be brushin' it aside as young folk gossip."

The relief was not as potent as she wished.

"I be sorry to worry ye, Gwynna. I wanted ye to be aware if ye hadn't heard them 'fore now."

"No, I be grateful to ye. I know now to keep me head down."

Kerensa hummed, then waved to her sisters farther up the incline. "I be seein' ye."

Gwynna nodded, staring after her departure. She'd longed to tell the truth to Kerensa but involving her in her schemes would only cause trouble for her friend. And she'd already done that to too many people as it was.

Papa exited the shaft then, coughing into his handkerchief. An ounce of pressure fell from her shoulders at the sight of him, sodden clothing and all. He was alive, and that was something for which to be grateful.

"We be havin' to scrimp and save more now, Gwynny, missin' a full day's work." He draped his arm around her as his coughing subsided. "But I be 'appy to be goin' home with ye."

She leaned into him for a moment, breathing in the damp, earthy soot. It was her father's smell—had been since before she could remember. How it soothed her worry.

They joined the other workers walking past the counthouse. Mr. Peter Trevethan bade them farewell as he secured his great coat around his shoulders with Mr. Harvey. "We will be leaving as soon as the mine is emptied. If the rain stops, return tomorrow. If not, you must simply wait until further notice. Rest well, and stay warm, all of you."

"Thank ye, sir," the miners and maidens continually babbled as they filed past him.

No songs marked the air as they walked across the cliffside. Their voices would've trembled had they attempted. The adults and older children helped the younger boys and girls traipse through the mud as they walked through the low clouds blanketing the land and sea.

Father moved ahead to speak with a few of the miners at the front of the group, and Gwynna fell behind to help Kerensa with her straggling sisters and their sodden skirts.

Halfway home, Gwynna's footsteps stopped.

"What be the matter?" Kerensa asked.

Gwynna groaned. "Me hammer. I didn't return it to the tool house." She could see it clearly now, exactly where she'd dropped it in the mud as she'd piled the remaining ore into her barrow. "I 'ave to return it to the house."

"There be no need, Gwynna. No one be goin' out in this weather to pinch it."

Gwynna rubbed her arms. If someone *did* steal it, she would have to pay to replace it. That would be a whole week's, if not month's, worth of wages.

She took a few steps back. "I can't risk it. I'll make haste. Tell me father I'll be home shortly after 'im."

Kerensa's wary eyes followed Gwynna until she returned her attention to the crying child whose hand she held.

"We be almost home now, eh?" Kerensa said.

Gwynna trudged her way from the group and back to the mine, cursing her careless blunder and nodding to the remaining stragglers who'd left Favour after the others.

When she reached the mine, the grounds were emptied. Not even Mr. Peter Trevethan or Mr. Harvey remained behind.

She walked across the mud, the rain rushing in her ears. She approached the engine house, its red chimney disappearing into the sea fog. She glanced to the door, and a memory flashed in her mind. Standing outside, embracing Papa. Waiting together for news as they brought up three bodies—none of which had been Jago's.

She squeezed her eyes, forcing the image away. She needed to focus on her task, then she could leave the mine all the sooner, and wrap up warm by the fire with her parents. Perhaps she might even convince Mama to make stew. Her mother often agreed with Gwynna's suggestions because of the help Gwynna provided for her.

Humming a cheerful tune to rid herself of imposing thoughts, Gwynna sloshed across the ground. The sea was no longer visible due to the misty clouds falling down with the rain. Not even the gulls were calling, all of creation seeming to have taken shelter in this never-ending storm.

Finally, Gwynna reached her position and found the spalling tool exactly where she'd left it. She tried to wipe the mud from the handle, but the dark streaks became even more evident across the length of it.

With her hammer in hand, she walked to the tool house, only to discover the lock had been secured. She paused, sifting through her options. She couldn't return home with the tool. Not if she wished to avoid the appearance of stealing. And she couldn't just leave it out in the open.

But if she hid it…She scanned the grounds, settling on a shanty lean-to built up against the stone of the engine house. The roof of the meager covering bowed in the middle, and water poured down from the center in a constant stream. Large barrels stood propped against the wood, and discarded pieces of unused ore backed up against the wall.

That would work perfectly.

As swiftly as she could, she plodded through the mud and

ducked under the lean-to, taking care not to walk under the pouring water. Kneeling down, she buried the long-handled hammer behind the barrels and underneath the rocks. Her body jerked as a draft of wind blasted rain against her, but she pressed on.

Finally pleased with her hiding place, she positioned the last ore over the iron head of the hammer then pressed her hands against the ground to aid in her standing.

Before she could make it to her feet, the sharp snapping of wood sounded overhead, and a dull thud pounded her back.

Suddenly, she was drowning.

Doubling over on her hands and knees, Gwynna struggled for breath, water pouring directly on her head. Her lungs burned, her eyes unable to open due to the freezing liquid.

This was what she'd dreamt of, drowning, just like her brother had. Only now, this wasn't a nightmare, but reality. Images of her brother's face flashed in her mind. The water had stopped pouring, but the stinging in her lungs continued.

She tried to tell herself she was safe now. She wasn't in the shaft. The lean-to had just broken. But the darkness that accompanied her closed eyes convinced her she was lost.

Her heart hammered harder than she'd ever struck ore. Her breathing was labored, her head spinning. Clasping her hands to her head, she ducked to the ground, willing the images to cease.

"No," she murmured, her voice washed out amidst the rain and sea. "No!"

"Gwynna!"

Jago? She rocked back and forth. This wasn't real. This wasn't real. He wasn't calling out for her help. He was already dead. She could do nothing for him.

"Gwynna!"

"No, no, no," she repeated over and over again.

A hand curled over her shoulder, and panic clasped its

fingers round her throat. With all her force, she tore open her eyes and swung around.

"No, Jago!" Finally, she found her voice to rid the specter from her mind.

But it was no specter. It wasn't even her brother.

Mr. Jack Trevethan's dark eyes bore into hers, filled with concern. He wore no hat, rain sliding down his cheekbones and dripping from his dark hair hanging over his eyes.

"Jack?" she breathed.

When the word left her tongue, the truth of reality rippled through her body, and she fell forward and wept into her hands.

CHAPTER THIRTY-SEVEN

*J*ack caught Gwynna before she could fall completely to the ground. He knelt down in the mud. With his arms wrapped around her, she buried her head into his chest. Her slight frame shook violently against him as he tried to make sense of what he'd just seen.

He'd left St. Just after retrieving his newly shod horse, seeing Wheal Favour in the distance. Hoping to find fodder to throw at Father for forcing the miners to continue their work in such weather, he'd moved toward the mine, finding only one maiden present.

He'd recognized Gwynna instantly, the angles of her high cheekbones, her slight but feminine frame. He'd watched her for only a moment then decided to leave before he could be spotted. However, when the wood and water fell down on her from the broken roof of the lean-to, he'd swiftly tied his horse and run to her rescue.

He still couldn't understand her reaction. The water must have frightened her, and the boards must have hurt falling against her back. But she didn't appear pained—she appeared terrified.

"He be gone," she murmured. "I can't save 'im."

Jack wrapped his arms tighter around her, tears springing to his eyes. She was speaking of her brother. He was sure of it, not only because she'd mentioned Jago's name, but because Jack had experienced the very same heartache. How often had he sobbed himself to sleep, aching for his mother, ruing the fact that he could no longer be with her?

A shiver racked her body. He needed to get her warm before she became ill, but he didn't wish to harm her further, nor to move her if she was incapable of standing.

Finally, her sobs quieted, replaced with haggard breathing.

He leaned down to rest his cheek on the crown of her wet bonnet. "We need to get you someplace warm. Are you injured? Your back?"

She shifted in his arms. "No, I be fine. But I need to get home 'fore me parents worry."

She tried to stand, wiping her face with her sodden sleeve, but she tumbled forward. He caught her before she could fall face-down in the mud. "No, Gwynna. We're getting you warm now."

She didn't protest again. Her breath continually caught in her throat as he led her forward across the grounds, supporting her as they slowly tramped through the mud.

They reached the counthouse on the upper cliff, but as Jack tried the handle, he found it locked. With a swift movement, he kicked the door open. The wood swung back on its hinges and ended with a loud clatter against the back wall.

"Come," he said gently, his arm around her back, his hand fitting perfectly around her waist.

After closing the door as best he could with the broken lock, he pulled out a chair and placed it before the cold hearth. As she sat, he lit the fire, allowing it to grow before settling a few logs on the ever-growing flame. Next, he removed her cloak and bonnet, draping them near the heat.

He eyed her sodden clothes as she gazed straight-faced into the flames. She needed to remove her gown if she was going to feel any semblance of warmth, but they were already sidling the line of propriety by being alone together in that room.

Instead, he settled on finding a few blankets folded on the bed in the spare room.

"Are you warm enough?" he asked, securing one across her shoulders and the other round her legs.

"Yes, sir."

Sir. Only moments ago, she'd called him Jack.

He knelt down before her, his knees protesting against the hard wood floor. Softly, he took her fingers in his, removing the stained, grey fabric wrapped around her hands. It wasn't a glove, as he'd expected, but an old stocking.

Another tear ripped into his chest.

When her hands were free, he held them in his own, rubbing them slowly to bring the warmth back into her purple fingertips. He examined them, dirt surrounding each of her shortened nails.

He brought them near his mouth, blowing warm air onto her skin. She watched him closely. The tendons in her neck stood out, and her chest and shoulders were raised, as if she held her breath.

His heart tripped. It must have forgotten how to beat, distracted with the heat rushing in his limbs.

The fire crackled behind him, and rain pelted the small window nearby as their eyes remained locked. She was beautiful. Water-logged and teary-eyed, she was completely beyond any lady he'd ever seen primped and polished.

"Is that better?"

She nodded. Did that mean he had to stop? With the way he reacted to touching her, perhaps he'd better.

Slowly, he raised to stand. "Are you hungry?"

"No, sir."

Despite her answer, he moved to the kitchen, rummaging through the cupboards before finding a loaf of bread. He tore off a piece and placed it on a plate, then returned to Gwynna and the fire.

He offered her the meager helping, and she thanked him, though the bread remained untouched in her hand.

"Ye must think I be crazy."

He stoked the fire. "Why would I?"

She gave him a wary look. "Ye saw me, sir. Shakin' like a leaf o'er a bit o' water fallin' down on me."

He set aside the iron stoker then pulled a chair to sit beside her, careful not to block the fire's heat.

"That's not why you were shaking, Gwynna," he said softly. "And there is no reason to be ashamed over remembering a beloved family member's death."

Her chin trembled, and she swiped a finger beneath her nose. He pulled out a handkerchief from his waistcoat pocket and extended it toward her.

"I don't want to dirty it, sir."

"You may keep it. I have plenty."

With a hesitant nod, she took it from his hand and wiped it across her eyes and nose.

She was silent for a moment, tugging the blanket more securely around her shoulders. After a moment, she tore a small piece of the bread and chewed it in silence.

"May I ask how your brother died?" Jack asked as she swallowed.

She tore off another piece, pushing it together with her fingers. "A floodin', below ground."

Jack winced. That's why the water had triggered her.

"I 'ave dreams," she continued, her eyebrows slanted upward. "Dreams of 'im callin' out to me. I never saw 'im dyin' in reality, but in me dreams, I enter the shaft filled with water and see him strugglin', hear him callin' out to me for help. But I never can save 'im, and I end up drownin' meself alongside 'im. When the roof cracked and the water prevented me from breathin', I suppose I just thought of him feelin' the same when he died—scared and alone."

Jack listened, compassion overcoming him for the struggles this woman faced. The bravery she had for even working at the same mine where her brother had perished was beyond him.

She stared into the fire, clearly attempting to gain control of her emotions. "I just want the dreams to stop. I don't want to remember me brother for the fear that must've been on his face. I want to remember the fun we had together, but I just..."

She stopped, her face crumpling in a cry. He leaned forward, moving the plate of bread to the floor and grasping her nearest hand in both of his. "They will, Gwynna. The dreams will end. One day."

"How can ye be sure? How can I know I won't be sufferin' with this me whole life?"

He eyed her fingers. "Because I've had them, too."

She sniffed, peering across at him, clearly wishing for him to say more. "About your mother?"

Jack hesitated. Days ago, he'd determined to board up his heart for good. He'd opened up to Gwynna, and he'd been hurt by the truth she'd assailed at him in regard to his father.

Now, things were different. He'd seen Gwynna in a different light. She was broken, just like he was. Perhaps not to so great an extent—he couldn't see her hurting other people to hide her own pain—but broken all the same. Knowing this, how could he not share his own experience, if only to ease her burden?

"I was the one who found her," he whispered, rubbing his thumbs against the back of her fingers to keep his emotions capped. "Face down on the floor in her bedchamber."

The breath rushed from her lips in a sigh. "Oh, I be sorry. Do you know what 'appened to her?"

Her soft tone verified the compassion he'd expected from

her. He was wise to keep his eyes averted. One look at her loving—her *kind* eyes, and he'd be done for.

"She was ill with a fever and worsened overnight. I refused to leave her side, but Father promised to remain with her so I could sleep for a few hours. Before dawn, I swiftly made for her room, hoping to find her rallied. Instead, she was gone, with a broken cup beside her."

"And she was alone?"

He nodded. "Apparently, her maid had left to retrieve more water. When she returned to find me begging my mother to rise, she dropped the bowl she carried, shattering the porcelain and splashing the water across the room."

"And...your father?"

He clenched his jaw, though stroking Gwynna's skin distracted him from getting angrier. "Nowhere to be seen. The maid said he'd left hours before, but no one knew where he'd gone. No one, but me."

He maintained a loose grip on her hands, drawing in a deep breath as he recalled the memories as if they'd occurred yesterday. "I found him in his study, poring over his blessed work ledgers and correspondences instead of caring for his dying wife. Had he been with her, he could've helped her find the drink she so desperately needed."

CHAPTER THIRTY-EIGHT

*G*wynna studied what little she could see of Mr. Trevethan's face with his lowered head. No wonder he'd reacted so angrily to her suggestion to forgive his father. Their relationship was far more complicated than she'd expected. She couldn't imagine the heartache he must have experienced as a twelve-year-old, his whole world in upheaval with only one person to blame.

"It became easier to accuse my father of wrongdoing rather than myself," he continued. "As a child, at times even now, I can't help but wonder, had I not left to sleep, who knows what I might've prevented. Truly, I know Father was not the cause of her death. She was leaving us already due to the fever. But he made her suffer all the greater by leaving."

Sorrow hung heavily on her, weighing her spirits and emotions to the floor. She knew just how he felt—the regret, what she could've done for Jago had she merely been given the chance.

But it wasn't right to wear the blame.

"It ain't be your fault, sir, that she died. Though I understand why ye be thinkin' so. And about your father...What I told ye about forgiveness, I be sorry. I never should 'ave—"

"No. No, you were right. I ought to be the one apologizing. I have held onto my bitterness for long enough. I wish to release its hold on my life. Though, I fear it will take longer for me than it has for you."

Knowing he did not hold her earlier words against her, she had greater strength to lift up her heavy heart. "It be different for everyone, sir. Me father always said that forgiveness be more about a journey rather than an endin' place."

He seemed to consider that for a moment. "The more I learn about your father, the more I am intimidated by the man."

She smiled. "He ain't be willin' to be pushed 'round, that be for certain. But ye won't find a more lovin' soul." She paused for a moment, thinking of the goodness of her father before her mind wandered to their previous topic. "What did ye do, to bear your dreams 'til they stopped?"

He drew a deep breath. He'd since stopped caressing her fingers, though he still held her hand. "I dealt with them as best I could in the beginning. They were the same as yours. Always extending beyond reality, Mother always dying as she called out my name for help. When I grew older, I numbed any memories by gambling and drinking. And by kissing women."

The tips of his ears reddened. "I'm ashamed to admit it, but my cousin and I often made wagers to see who could kiss a lady first at various social parties. I...I was playing that very game at the ball."

Gwynna pulled back, forcing herself to appear unruffled. That was why he'd asked to kiss her, and why he hadn't since. He thought she'd be an easy target to win a wager, then realized a bal maiden wasn't worth the work.

"I'm not proud of my behavior, nor am I justifying it," he said, "but it did well to distract me. One night many years before, while my cousin and I were away at school, he left for a drink with friends. I remained behind with a hidden bottle of brandy, ready to drink my pain away, as I so frequently did.

"My vision blurred as the usual tears came, so I hastily poured myself a glass. When I reached for it, my trembling fingers spilled the brandy across the table. Furious with myself, I threw the full bottle and glass across the room in a rage, realizing too late I'd have nothing left."

He withdrew his hand from hers, rubbing his jawline, where the shadow of his facial hair covered his flesh. His brown eyes reflected the torment of that moment so long ago, and Gwynna forgot his admission of kissing, focusing instead on the pain he still clearly felt.

"Without the alcohol to block my thoughts, the memories entered with full force into my mind. I sifted through every painful moment of the day I had discovered her, until sleep finally relieved me. Instead of the ache I expected to feel in the morning, a weight had been removed from my shoulders. At times, it returns, and I do not think it necessary for me to tell you I still feel anger toward my Father. But somehow, reliving my mother's death allowed me to process it better. It allowed me to live without the constant need for numbing—and for brandy." He lowered his head. "Fortunately, I have not had a drop of it since that night."

Gwynna was quiet for a moment, contemplating all that Mr. Trevethan had said. Could she really be so brave as to live through the emotions of Jago's death all over again, instead of simply setting them aside?

He reached toward her, taking her fingers and cupping his hands around them. Warmth wrapped around her still-chilled skin, roaming up her arm.

"As you said about forgiveness, so is the same with grief," he said. "What worked for me may not work for you, but I do hope you find relief. You might find the process easier if you work through them with someone else present, if the memories become too much. Your mother or father. Or someone else you trust."

Their eyes met. Did he refer to himself? The fire snapped as a log settled deeper into the hearth. She no longer shivered, warmth infusing her limbs, not only from the heat of the fire and blankets, but by the way Mr. Trevethan watched her.

His eyes peered into hers, focused, intent, until he shifted his attention to her lips. His right hand traveled along the length of her fingers, brushing the top of her leg. Her mouth dried, and he leaned closer.

She longed to shrug off the blankets to cool her overheated body, but she didn't move, afraid to break the spell between them.

"Gwynna," he whispered. "I wish…"

His jaw clenched, the muscles working near his ear, then he pulled back. "If you are warm enough now, we'd better get you home. I wouldn't want your parents to worry."

She wondered at his throaty tone.

After dousing the fire and gathering her soaking outerwear, Mr. Trevethan instructed her to keep the blanket about her shoulders, then helped her to his horse tied outside.

He lifted her on the animal in a seamless movement, despite her protests that she could walk well enough.

"I'll not have you stroll home in this rain and risk having you sliding off the cliffside," he said. "Your terrifying father would not thank me for that."

With a pointed smile, he led her home. Mr. Trevethan walked beside her so she might balance on his shoulder if she teetered.

As they crossed the cliffside in silence, Gwynna sought a distraction from the pulsing in her back where the wood had fallen upon her. She merely had to look down at Jack—Mr. Trevethan, his shoulders moving from side to side, the rain sliding down the contours of his neck.

Soon enough, they neared Gwynna's house, and her parents ran out into the rain toward them.

"Gwynna!" Mama cried out.

Mr. Trevethan helped her down from the horse, nodding his head to her mother and father. "I caught sight of her underneath a broken lean-to at the mine," he explained. "She isn't gravely hurt, but a few boards did fall down on her back."

Gwynna didn't miss Papa's uneasy stare at Mr. Trevethan, though he managed a muttered "Thank you" alongside Mama as he wrapped his arm around Gwynna.

"I be fine," Gwynna said to her parents as they fussed over her, directing her toward the house. "Only a little bruised."

As they ushered her away, Mr. Trevethan remained by his horse. She focused over her shoulder, and he tipped his head toward her.

Before she could smile or express a word of her own gratitude, they shifted toward the house, and her image of the man disappeared.

But the feeling of his eyes on her, and the memory of his hands caressing her skin, remained.

CHAPTER THIRTY-NINE

*J*ack drew in a deep breath, his hand hovering above the door handle. He hadn't stepped foot inside his mother's room in over ten years, yet there he was, readying himself to face the demons of his past.

He still didn't know how the devil he'd found himself outside her chambers again, though he figured it was due to his conversation with Gwynna days before. He'd mentioned processing his mother's death, yet there was one thing he hadn't had the courage to do yet, and that was revisiting the last place he'd seen her alive, and the first place he'd seen her gone.

He had no desire to see the room, how Father had altered it, to no longer see her feminine touch present, just like in the rest of the house. But like a moth to the flame, he was drawn to it. He could only pray seeing her old living quarters would give him the final closure he so desired.

Reminding himself of Gwynna's courage to work daily at the very mine her brother had died, he turned the knob and pushed open the door, holding his breath.

He had expected to peer through the darkness, to perhaps cough from the dust he'd unsettled by opening the door. But a bright, clean room with yellow curtains drawn welcomed him instead.

He'd spent half his childhood in this room, due to Mama's consistently declining health. How he missed those times, walking the cliffsides on her good days then playing quietly in here when she needed to rest.

The four-poster bed in which he'd sat with her as a child, singing songs and reading books, still rested in the middle of the room, its gold and teal wall hangings dusted and neatly pressed. A vase of flowers with withering petals remained at her bedside table, where she enjoyed admiring them from her bed.

The table they'd often sat at to play chess was situated in the same place by the large window. One of the glass panes was still cracked from when he'd angrily thrown a marble pawn at it after losing.

Even now, her easy-tempered voice resounded throughout the room.

"Now, Jacky. Such a temper is not becoming of a gentleman."

The large, red rug hadn't moved an inch on the floor. Instead of witnessing flashes of his mother's body as he'd feared, he noted instead the intricate pattern she'd taught him to dance upon, and the tea stain from when he'd spat out the drink he'd so despised.

"I've never liked it either, Jacky. We shall hide it together."

Yes, everything in the room was exactly as he remembered, apart from one thing. He crossed the room toward a small dresser, where hung above it a large portrait he'd never seen. Painted on the canvas larger than his person was his mother—young and healthy and vibrant, with blue eyes and a smile that pricked him with sorrow.

"I wish for eyes like you, Mama," he'd told her often as a boy.

"Oh, no, son. You have lovely eyes, just like your papa. Kind and warm. If you cease your scowling, of course."

As Jack shifted his view to the younger person painted

beside her in the portrait, his breath departed. There was no mistaking his own brown eyes and unruly hair, nor himself as a young boy.

How could this painting be? He'd never seen it before.

A door clicked, and Jack pivoted to face his father, who entered the bedchamber from the room that adjoined Father's to Mama's.

He held a bouquet of fresh flowers, his eyes wide with surprise. "Jack? What are you doing in here?"

Jack stepped back from the portrait. "My apologies. I wasn't meaning to intrude."

Father stopped his departure with a shake of his hand. "No, that's not what I meant. I was only surprised to see you in here. Of course you are not intruding. You will always be welcome in your mother's room."

Jack scooted his eyes about him, anxious. He hadn't spoken with Father since their argument the week before. Normally, he would've muttered some excuse then fled from the room, as he'd just attempted to do. But Gwynna's words sounded in his mind.

Forgiveness is a journey.

He blew out a breath, his cheeks puffing. "What are the flowers for?"

Father stared down at the bouquet in his hands, walking to the bedside table. "I bring them in every week. It brightens up the room and helps me feel a little closer to her."

Jack's strength dangled by a thread. His father brought flowers to Mama's room every week? Not even sending a servant to do so in his place?

Father replaced the aging flowers with the new bouquet then turned to Jack. They stood in silence for a moment before Father motioned to the portrait above the dresser.

"Do you like it?"

Jack perused the smiling faces on himself and his mama. "I

do. Very much. But I'm afraid I don't recognize it. Was it in a different room, perhaps, before you brought it in here?"

Father slowly shook his head. "I had it commissioned after her death and after you…after I sent you away. The painter used two previous paintings to put you together. Your mother had always expressed her desire to have one with the both of you before she passed."

Jack faced the painting, his focus falling on his mama's painted hand holding one of Jack's, as they'd so often done. Tears pricked his eyes.

How he longed for his mother, to have her arms once more around him, to hear her instructive, encouraging words. How could he continue on without her, in that house, in Cornwall, where the memory of her was so excruciatingly painful, it was as if a dagger was digging around in his chest, searching for the heart he'd buried long ago? Would he ever feel that love, that cherished feeling of peace and comfort as he had with Mama? That warmth in his chest of love and the feeling of being home again?

A jolt of shock pushed through his limbs. Warmth. He hadn't felt that warmth in his chest since his mother was alive—until he'd met Gwynna.

She had revived him. Her own goodness had encouraged him to be better, to apologize. She had brought warmth and joy back into his life.

He knew he'd been a disappointment to his family, and he'd lived with it. But being a disappointment to Gwynna had nearly led him back to drinking, to numb the pain that hadn't been so poignant in years.

Did that mean he had feelings beyond friendship for her?

Fear struck him like a bolt of lightning. What on earth would he do if that were true?

"Are you well, son?"

Jack waited for his thoughts to catch up before nodding. "Yes, merely deep in thought."

"I do not wish to pry, but you appear troubled. Is there anything with which I might be able to help you?"

Help him? Jack didn't need help. At least not with anything he was willing to divulge. He had everything he wanted in the world, apart from his mother. But he knew one—many—who *did* need aid.

An excitement simmered deep in his chest, growing rapidly as his thoughts spilled forth. He'd been selfish before, criticizing Father's desire to help those at Wheal Favour instead of himself. Gwynna and so many others suffered far more greatly than he ever had. Now, it was Jack's time to help.

Perhaps helping her would help *him* to finally make sense of his emotions.

"Jack?" Father pressed.

Jack turned to him with directness. He'd harbored resentment and anger for far too long. It was time to let go, or at least, begin the process. "Father, will you be going to the mine today, now the rain has ceased?"

"Of course."

"Would you mind if I joined you? There are a few items I'd like to discuss with you and Mr. Harvey, if you wouldn't mind."

Father blinked swiftly to hide his excitement, his lips pressed tightly to avoid revealing his smile. "Of course, Jack. Regarding what exactly?"

Jack attempted to make light of the situation, though he knew as well as Father just how strange it was for them to be speaking. "I've recently become aware of the many hardships endured by miners and their families. I should like to improve their lots in life by working through a number of things that could be done to improve the mine, including mechanizing the bucking process and creating proper shelter for the maidens."

Father rubbed the back of his head in stunned silence. Jack

was just as stunned. He was speaking with Father, giving him advice on how to run his business. Of course he was only doing so because it was the right thing to do for the miners. Helping Gwynna—*his friend*—was only an added bonus.

Speaking of Gwynna. "A few days ago, I passed by Wheal Favour during the storm. I happened to see Gwynna Merrick being struck by a breaking lean-to up against the engine house."

Father's brow pulled low over his eyes. "I hadn't any idea of the matter. Was she injured?"

Jack had wondered the very same for days, though he'd been unable to see for himself for obvious reasons. "I believe so. I entered the counthouse to help her get warm. I'm certain you noticed the lock of the door was broken. At any rate, I think it time we take measures to make more improvements, additional to the ones you've already made."

"Well I think that is a superb idea. Mr. Harvey will certainly agree."

"Excellent. I will make ready then."

Jack left the room and his bewildered father behind, releasing a heavy breath as soon as he was alone.

He'd done it. He'd had a conversation with his father—a real conversation—and it hadn't ended in an argument. Their words had still centered around business, but this was certainly a leap in the right direction.

He couldn't wait to thank the woman who was responsible for helping him to make such a leap.

He moved through the house with a light step, about to enter his room before Hugh emerged down the hallway. "Someone seems happier today," he said. "I haven't seen you smiling since Bath."

Jack was smiling? He hadn't realized. He pulled back from his room. "Perhaps I have more to smile over now."

"Care to share?"

"Not quite." Jack grinned, entering his room and poking his

head outside. "I'll be joining my father at the mine this morning. I trust you and Amy will be able to entertain yourselves for a few hours."

Hugh's face fell. "Oh, must you? Amy was very much looking forward to spending time with you. She's been unbearably down lately, and I haven't any idea why. You always seem to cheer her up more than I can."

Jack hesitated, scratching the side of his face. He didn't have time today, especially if Amy was just going to condemn him again. He needed to go to the mine. He needed to see Gwynna.

But he had dragged both Hugh and Amy with him to Cornwall. How was he to know he'd find more enjoyment being with someone else?

"Very well. Perhaps we meet up at St. Just this afternoon? We can sample pastries while Amy shops."

"Now that is an idea I can support." Hugh grinned. "It is good to see you more cheerful, cousin."

Jack watched him depart then entered his room with another smile. Hugh was right. It *was* good to see himself more cheerful.

CHAPTER FORTY

*G*wynna tipped her head back, sighing with pleasure as the warmth from the sun graced her cheeks. She'd long since removed her bonnet. How could one wear such a covering when the sun hadn't shone its light in nearly a week?

"It be gorgeous today." She closed her eyes and laid down against the heather on the cliffside, ignoring the pain in her back, still bruised from the fallen lean-to. "Don't ye think, Papa?"

"Yes, daugh'er."

His mouth was full of the pasty Mama had provided for crib, but Gwynna could still detect the distracted nature of his tone as she sat beside him on the cliffside.

She peeked an eye open as he stared toward the counthouse. "What be the matter?"

He faced forward with a skirted glance. "Nothin'. Only Mr. Trevethan and 'is son be headed our way."

Gwynna shot up from the heather, wincing at her protesting muscles. She gaped over her shoulder as the father and son walked toward them. Her eyes met Jack's, and she jerked forward with stifled breaths.

Jack.

In the privacy of her own thoughts, she'd taken to calling the man by his given name. He'd asked her to do so, after all.

Even still, his name sounded foreign to her tongue, like eating the jaune mange Sophia had shared with her and Mama on her visit yesterday. The jelly had lost its shape and spilled over the edge of the bowl due to Sophia's jostling carriage, but the orange zest and smooth sugar strummed against Gwynna's tongue. It was unrecognizable, but sweetly familiar. Just like Jack's name.

She'd longed to see him ever since he'd delivered her into her parents' arms. Now that the moment was here, however, she fiddled anxiously with her crib-bag, running the strings through her fingers over and over again.

Were they coming to tell her the game was over? That Ruth Ayer had told them about her crimes and Gwynna would now be handed over to the constable? Jack would speak in her defense, wouldn't he?

"Merrick, Gwynna," Mr. Peter Trevethan greeted with a smile.

He didn't look angry or concerned. That was a good start.

She rose beside her father. "What can we do for ye?" Father asked, his mistrusting eyes lingering on Jack.

Papa hadn't accepted the delicacy from Sophia on her visit to see how Gwynna fared. "I be happy with me own food," he'd grumbled, leaving the women to themselves.

He'd done his best to forget Sophia's past and her father's actions, but sometimes, Gwynna knew it was hard for him to be around Sophia, if only because of the memories it produced of Jago. Still, he was trying to forgive.

But then, Jack hadn't done anything to require father's

forgiveness. At least nothing that Papa knew about. So why was he so mistrusting of the gentleman?

"I ought to be asking if there is anything we can do for *you*," Mr. Peter Trevethan said, "especially your daughter." He faced her. "My son has told me you suffered an accident here. I'm terribly sorry. If you wish, you may leave today with full-pay."

Gwynna slunk behind Papa, uncomfortable as all three pairs of eyes fell on her. "Oh, 'tis no trouble, sir. I can work."

"If you insist. But rest assured, it will not happen again. My son here is helping me to ensure the safety of the grounds."

Gwynna stole a look at Jack. He watched her beneath his dark eyelashes. Was this true? Was he working with his father to improve the mine?

Mr. Trevethan turned to Papa. "Now, Merrick. I wonder, might I have a word alone for a moment?"

Papa tipped his brow. "I, sir?"

"Yes, I won't keep you for long."

Papa nodded, wringing his cap in his hands. His hair fell over his eyes as he glanced from Gwynna to Jack, then he left to follow Mr. Trevethan a short distance away.

Gwynna shifted her boots uneasily. She and Jack were in no way alone—what with the maidens sitting farther down the cliffside, miners walking up and down the pathway, and children playing along the heather above—but they'd been *left* alone.

All eyes could see them. They shouldn't linger with one another, especially after the rumors Ruth had started.

"How are you, Gwynna?" Jack asked softly, nodding his head to a widow who hobbled down the cliffside on the arm of a young woman.

"I be fine, sir. But we oughtn't be speakin' now. Others will see."

"I know, but I wish to speak with you about something."

His eyes warmed, even danced. He wished to speak with

her? Her chest swelled, like the air caught beneath the sea's waves, producing bubbles at the surface. She wished to speak with him in return—all about how she had spoken with her parents about Jago's death and now felt more hopeful than ever.

But it was too risky. Even now, she caught the two maidens below watching them both with curious glances. "Not here, sir," she whispered. "Not now."

"Then when?"

"I don't know. Me father, he be anxious to keep me safe. And the rumors..."

She cast her eyes around again. Papa was still watching them, despite Mr. Trevethan speaking to him, and the maidens took to whispering to one another.

Jack looked to the ground to feign disinterest. "Then what about this evening? Under the cover of the stars. Near the ruins of Penharrow."

Butterflies took flight in her chest at the idea. Could she go along with Jack's suggestion, float along easily with the wind? Or would she be caught in an uncontrollable draft, careening out of safety's grasp?

It all boiled down to one question—was seeing Jack worth the risk?

"Yes," she declared at once. "I'll meet ye there."

His expression brightened just as Papa returned to her side.

"Excuse me," Jack said, nodding to Papa before sending a covert smile to Gwynna.

Gwynna didn't return it, fearful Papa might see.

As Jack walked away, rejoining his father near the count-house, Papa tossed his head gruffly toward him. "What he be sayin' to ye, Gwynna?" he asked, his suspicion thicker than the shaft's walls below.

"Merely ensurin' I be well after me fall."

He gave her a disbelieving look. Had he spotted the blush rushing to her cheeks?

"What did Mr. Trevethan want ye for?" she asked.

Thankfully, her distraction worked. A whisper of a smile touched his dirty, chapped lips. "He be promotin' I, to work above grass half days."

Gwynna's mouth parted in a look of surprise. "Papa, that be wonderful! Oh, I be that happy for ye. Did he say why?"

"No, simply told me I be doin' a fine job. He also wishes for me to give more advice on matters of the shaft."

"Oh, I be so pleased. Mama'll sure to be so, as well."

Half-days above grass. That meant half the time to worry over his safety below ground. What a blessing this was!

"That not be all, though," Papa continued. "He also be payin' I greater wages. Which means ye won't have to work any longer."

Gwynna's smile faded, disappointment nudging its heavy elbow between her ribs. Stop working at the mine? She had to admit, no longer partaking in the back-breaking work would be far easier. Spalling wasn't ever a leisurely walk. But how would she receive that same sort of accomplishment if she remained indoors, doing all the chores she despised—washing, scrubbing, laundry, cooking?

And if she stopped working at the mines, would she ever see Jack again? Or was he still planning to leave Cornwall?

Papa pressed a hand on her shoulder. "I know ye wish to work here, Gwynna, but ye don't need to worry about it now. We'll speak later, yes?"

"Yes, Papa."

Her obedient response was muted by the bell signaling the end of their break. Gwynna secured her bag around her waist beneath her towser to sneak what remained of her pasty as she continued working. Once finished, she took a step forward, but Papa's hand stopped her.

"One more thing, daugh'er." His voice lowered. "I want ye to be careful with that Jack Trevethan. There be somethin' about him that...that can't be trusted. Understood?"

She longed to protest, to say Jack *could* be trusted, but then how would she explain how she knew that? Instead, she replied with obedience again. "Yes, Papa."

He leaned forward, kissing her on her cheek, then they joined the other miners as they marched down the cliffside.

Just before he entered the engine house, Gwynna called after him. "Papa, 'fore I forget. I be goin' to Sophia's tonight. She be wishin' to show me her new dresses she just purchased."

He pulled a face. "Dresses? Ain't she seen ye enough day 'fore last?"

"She be my friend, Papa."

He replaced his cap with a heavy sigh. "Fine. I'll be at the Causeys tonight, clearin' the remainin' fields. Remember to tell Mama 'fore ye go."

"Yes, Papa."

He tipped his cap then entered the building.

Gwynna stared at the door for a moment, dazing off as she wondered if she really ought to be sneaking out in the dead of the night to meet with the one man Papa had forbidden her from seeing.

Then Jack's dancing eyes appeared in her mind's eye. She needed to go, if only to see what he'd been so excited to speak with her about. Was it that he was remaining in Cornwall? That he'd had a hand in Papa's promotion?

She tried to lessen her anticipation, but as it weeded out the rest of her guilt, she kept her eagerness close to her chest.

Yes, she would go that evening. Just as soon as she stopped by Sophia's house for an unplanned visit so she might prevent herself from completely lying to her parents again.

CHAPTER FORTY-ONE

$\mathcal{G}$wynna firmly closed the inn door behind her, glad to be rid of the dark, stale air that permeated the Golden Arms, though the meeting she'd had at the inn had been more than pleasant. Lieutenant Edmund Harris had been surprisingly grateful to receive his box back.

Knowing naval officers enjoyed their drinks at the inn, Gwynna had first sought the sailor there. Surely a good deed of returning one's property would counteract her decision to lie once again.

She'd found Lieutenant Harris easily enough, speaking at the far side of the inn with Trevik Honeysett, a local fisherman a few years older than Gwynna. His recently turned sixteen-year-old sister, Poppy, sat beside him. Her presence came as no surprise to Gwynna, as the young woman could often be found trailing alongside her brother, all the while fawning up at Lieutenant Harris.

"How be work at the mine, Gwynna?" Trevik had asked when she'd approached.

"Same as usual," Gwynna had responded. "Back-breakin'. Ye

be lucky ye 'ave them pilchards treatin' ye so nicely so ye don't have to work at Favour."

"Don't I know it."

Gwynna had glanced to Poppy then with a smile. "And how are ye, Poppy?"

"Fine, Gwynna," she'd said, pulling her eyes away from Lieutenant Harris first.

Gwynna couldn't blame her. The lieutenant was a handsome man, and his kindness had been exceptional the few times he'd spoken with Gwynna during small, friendly gatherings on the beach.

After a few more words were exchanged with the Honeysetts, Gwynna had pulled the lieutenant aside and delivered the box Kerensa had let her keep. "I found this washed up on Tregalwen Beach, sir. I believe it be yours?"

His eyes had rounded with joy and surprise. "Good heavens. I never thought I'd see this again. Thank you, Gwynna."

"I-I be sorry your belongings be gone. I found it empty, see." She'd have to find a different good deed now for lying. *Again.*

"Oh, worry not. I've already replaced the items." His eyes hadn't left the box, running his hands along the smooth edges. "But this I could never have replaced. It belonged to my father, who shared my name. He passed before I left for the navy."

Not only had Gwynna been filled with considerable delight, she was also overcome with relief for having followed her instinct in keeping the box for the lieutenant.

And now that the task had been complete, she was on to the next—Sophia, then Jack.

With a chipper step and brightened spirit, Gwynna left the inn and set forth down the street. She pulled in her lips to prevent the same smile that had been hungrily attempting to lap at her mouth all day.

She could not wait to see Jack, to learn what he'd wished to speak with her about. Would he express his desire to no longer run back to Bath? Share with her news of some exciting progress at the mine?

The sun shone through the alleyways between the shops, creating long, rectangular shadows, appearing as darkened, dusty rugs across the road. A carriage rolled by, the horses' tack jingling and hooves clopping along the street. With no crowds to maneuver, due to the lateness of the evening, Gwynna strolled down the road with a light step.

That is, until she spotted Jack standing outside of the bakery, his back toward her.

Her grin could not be suppressed. No one else was on the street. Perhaps she wouldn't have to disobey her parents after all. She and Jack could find someplace private nearby to speak, or perhaps outside of town.

She made her way toward him then froze in the middle of the street. He wasn't alone. A woman stood before him, previously hidden by his broad shoulders.

Miss Paxton?

Gwynna rubbed the base of her throat that suddenly constricted.

Neither Miss Paxton nor Jack spoke, though they stared at one another with such intent eyes, Gwynna could only imagine of what they'd been speaking. Especially when Jack snatched Miss Paxton's hand in his, pulling her toward the nearest alleyway, away from Gwynna and the street.

Sense screamed at Gwynna to keep moving, to not interfere with whatever she had just interrupted. But as she watched them flee down the alley and disappear round the corner to the back of the bakery, her feet propelled forward on their own.

Jack had said he and Miss Paxton were cousins, friends, that was all. But the look Miss Paxton had given him, it was far too close to the look Gwynna knew she'd revealed herself after the dinner party—when she had clearly desired Jack's kiss.

Gwynna slunk down the alleyway on the tips of her toes, silent but for the fierce beating of her heart.

Their whispers reached her ears, but she could make out no words. She reached the end of the alleyway and peered around the corner.

Jack stood by the outer wall of the bakery, his hands falling from Miss Paxton's shoulders as she stood on her tiptoes. The woman's eyes closed, and her lips parted as she leaned toward him.

Gwynna jerked back behind the side wall, pressing a hand over her mouth to stifle any gasp that might have escaped before she tore up the alleyway and back to the main road. She didn't stop, continuing her quick pace until she left the town behind.

Miss Paxton was kissing him. Of course he was kissing her back. Why would he say no to her, a beautiful, accomplished lady? He'd admitted before it was all just a game to him, kissing every woman he could.

Every woman but Gwynna, whom he'd apparently grown a special resistance to. Or perhaps it was just bal maidens, in general?

"Fool," she muttered to herself, cradling her side as she stopped to catch her breath.

Why had she expected it to be different with her? He'd said herself they were only friends. She ought to count herself fortunate they were *only* friends. Anything more, and things would get far too complicated.

Birds chirped as they flocked together overhead. A warm breeze swayed the grass back and forth with lazy breaths. A purple haze shrouded the land, but the quiet calm of the countryside merely mocked the torment inside of her.

Clenching her fists together, she tramped across the pathway. It was silly to feel discouraged, betrayed. She and Jack had no understanding between them. He'd made his friendly intentions clear right after the ball, having come to his senses afterward and wishing for nothing but friendship.

After all, what had she expected? That he could love her for *her*? That they could be together, a bal maiden and a gentleman? She really was daft.

Half-tempted to run home, Gwynna hesitated when she came to converging paths. No, she couldn't return to her parents yet. Not when she was in such a state. Sophia would help her. Sophia would speak sense to her mind.

She took the right pathway that led to Fynwary Hall, but Sophia was not there.

"Have ye any idea when she be returnin' from the dinner party?" she asked the butler as she stood at Fynwary's front door.

"Not until late, miss. But I'll inform her of your calling."

She expressed her gratitude then wandered away from Fynwary until she reached the cliffsides. The sun was no longer shining, having ducked behind the layer of clouds that laid straight across the horizon, like a lazy hound sprawled out on his master's pillow.

Now what was she to do? Jack might already be at Penharrow. If he was still planning to meet her, of course. He would probably be loath to leave Miss Paxton and her affections.

Her lip curled in disgust. Perhaps she should return home, ease her guilt, leave Jack—*Mr. Trevethan*—at Penharrow to question where she was. But then, would she not always wonder what he'd wanted to tell her?

With determined steps, she moved in the direction of the ruins. She needed to go. Not to hear what he had to say, but to share what *she* had to say. She would meet with him to tell him they could no longer see each other.

Papa was right. Jack Trevethan was not to be trusted.

CHAPTER FORTY-TWO

*J*ack was glad to have arrived at Penharrow first. He needed a moment to gather his wits after what had occurred in town. He'd always been so careful around Amy. How could he have even allowed such a thing to happen?

He dismounted his horse, tying him to a neglected stump of wood nearby before turning to the engine house. He blew out a heavy breath, the memory of Amy overheating his skin. He removed his hat, jacket, and cravat as they constricted his breathing, placing them on one of the half-standing walls. Still agitated, he unbuttoned his waistcoat halfway, the evening breeze finally cooling his sweating skin as he ruffled his hair, shaking aside any remaining thought of Amy.

He didn't want to think about her any longer, nor how everything between them had just changed in a matter of moments. He wanted to focus instead on—

"Sir?"

Gwynna. Instantly, her smooth voice eased the scowl down the center of his brow.

His heart skipped in anticipation as he turned to greet her.

"There you are. I was…" He stopped, his eagerness slipping as she stood a few paces away from him, the usual sparkle in her eye nowhere to be seen. "Are you unwell?"

Her expression remained stoic, her lips in an unbending line. "No, sir. I be fine."

Jack's brow pursed. She certainly didn't look fine. "Are you quite certain?"

"Yes, sir. What did ye wish to speak with me about?"

Jack frantically grasped for the joy he'd felt earlier—before all that had occurred between him and Amy, before Gwynna's staidness shadowed his happiness—but it slipped away like a retreating wave.

"It can wait until you are feeling more…yourself."

Gwynna shook her head, displaying a strained smile. "No, sir. Please, tell me now."

Clearly, she did not wish to discuss whatever was bothering her, and Jack didn't wish to push her into sharing something she didn't want to. Perhaps if he spoke of his good news, she'd cheer up.

He forced an easy tone. "I've nothing to say that is so very spectacular, but I wanted to share it with you all the same."

She turned to the sea. Was she still listening to him? "Yes, sir?"

She *was* listening. He continued cautiously. "I spoke with my father today. Not for long. But we carried on a conversation without anger or even a semblance of annoyance."

She turned her head so he could no longer see her expression. "That be wonderful, sir."

Her voice hardly sounded above the waves. "It was. We spoke of how we could improve the mine. We've also created a plan…to…"

He stopped as Gwynna swiped her cheek with a flick of her hand. Was she hiding tears?

He was at her side in an instant, a hand on her shoulder. "What is it? Have I said something to upset you?"

She paced back, his arm falling limply to his side. "No, sir."

Jack's stomach tightened. She didn't wish for him to touch her? "May I ask why you call me 'sir' again?"

She wouldn't look at him, no matter how far he leaned to the side. "It be better this way, if this be the last time we be seein' each other, sir."

He gave a mirthless chuckle, hoping she teased. "Is this your way of telling me you are going somewhere?"

"No, sir, but our relationship, our-our speakin' needs to end this evenin.'"

His smile slid away. "You are serious?"

"Yes, sir."

"I...I don't understand. Why now? Is it your parents? Did they find out about..."

His words trailed off as she shook her head. "No, sir. 'Tis me own choice. We ought not have formed a relationship to begin with. We be too different to even have a friendship, so what do it matter if we end things now?"

He shook his head. How had his evening taken such a dreadful turn?

"I don't understand, Gwynna. We—"

"Ye don't need to understand to accept what be happenin', sir. Ye be leavin' anyway, so what do it matter that I be sayin' these things?"

"Why?" He blew out a disbelieving breath. "I was coming here tonight to tell you I—" He broke off himself. Could he share his feelings? Could he be vulnerable again? "I am considering remaining in Cornwall for longer. To help Father and the mine. And to help you."

Her frown faltered, but she quickly turned away. "Why prolong your leavin'? I don't need 'elp. Ye may as well return now to your gamblin', drinkin', and...and women."

Jack flinched at the cruel words. How could she say such things, after he'd expressed how difficult it had been to overcome his vices? "That is hardly fair. You know I've been striving to be better, to leave behind my past and—"

She interrupted with a derisive laugh. "Leave behind?"

He longed to remain unguarded, but her words stung. "Do you not believe in my desire to change, to improve?"

She didn't respond. Gwynna's goodness and confidence in him had been the very thing to spur him on to be better. What was he to do without her faith in him? And what had happened to have produced the cruelty he'd never witnessed in her before?

Was she simply frightened by his past? The things he'd shared with her? Is that why she hadn't wished to speak to him earlier and was avoiding him now?

His voice hardened. "I am not perfect, Gwynna. I have my faults, like we all do. But contrary to your belief, I *have* changed. It was you who helped—"

"I saw ye!"

Confusion creased his brow. "What? What do you—"

"Kissin' Miss Paxton in town."

As her words slowly sunk in, a blush crept across his cheeks.

"Kiss Miss Paxton? I..." He shook his head. "Were you following me?"

Red raced across her own cheeks then. "I saw ye sneakin' down the alleyway." She swiftly blinked away her brimming tears, continuing in a softer tone. "But it don't matter, sir. We have no understandin' 'tween us. Ye can kiss any number o' girls, as ye clearly wish to do."

What a fool Jack was, thinking Gwynna might actually trust in him enough to understand that he was changing. He rubbed his jaw, desperate to relieve the tension that shouldn't even be there.

Because he did not kiss Amy. Yes, she'd admitted her love to him in the middle of town, desperate to do so while her brother was occupied down the street with another woman.

But Jack had pulled her down the alleyway for privacy, to gently inform her he could not return her love. Amy had then attempted to prove her feelings with a kiss, but Jack had refused as kindly as he could with a turn of his head before any contact between them could be made.

He couldn't kiss her, not when Amy was like a sister to him. Not when he wanted…to kiss someone else. But of course Gwynna would expect the worst from him. Why wouldn't she when everyone else did?

"So even after all we've been through together, you still believe that of me? That I wish to drink and gamble? To kiss other women?"

She sniffed. "What do it matter what I think of ye, sir? Ye will do what ye wish and kiss who ye wish. That be the way of a gent, I s'pose."

He gritted his teeth. "Especially *this* gentleman?"

She said nothing in response.

So she did not believe in him. Even after his apologies, his attempts to respect her, to avoid speaking with her at the mine for her sake. Even after he'd not kissed her when they'd both desired it. She still thought him to be the blackguard she'd first met, the man who cared little about anyone but himself.

Any control, any patience he might have had slipped from his fingertips. With deliberate steps, he advanced on her. "Thank heavens you were able to decipher my behavior before we became too attached."

Uncertainty flickered in her eyes, but she maintained a firm footing. "It do be a good thing."

He reached her, grasping onto her arms, anger pulsing through his veins. "Then I suppose I am still the same man in your eyes. A blackguard out for one thing. Once I receive it, I leave one woman for the next. Isn't that right, Gwynna?"

His words had once been true. But now, he hadn't even been given the chance to prove that he was finished with those games, that he was not the same man he was before meeting Gwynna.

"I suppose that be right, sir."

His eyes dropped to her lips. "So do you expect that now? For me to kiss you and leave you, just as I did with Miss Paxton?"

Tears clung to her lashes, but he would not feel remorse for his words when sorrow was the very thing that brought him to this point in his life.

Gwynna didn't respond. He leaned close to her, a mere breath away from her lips.

As angry as he was, as greatly as he desired to prove her words right, to taste her lips once before he left Cornwall forever...he couldn't do it.

He respected her too much.

Abruptly, he dropped his hands and took a step back, leaving her teetering on her feet.

"I did not kiss Miss Paxton," he spat out, "and if you had any faith in me, you'd know that."

With a final shake of his head, he stalked away from the mine. The hollow beating of his heart mimicked his boots that thudded angrily on the pathway, his route barely visible as dusk captured Cornwall in its grip.

He'd return for his horse later, once Gwynna left. He was too angry, too hurt to face her again.

In truth, he didn't blame her for expecting the worst from him, especially with how his behavior with Miss Paxton must have appeared, but her lack of faith in him was excruciating.

"Sir!"

He flinched at her voice but blazed onward. He didn't want to hear the apology she would no doubt share with him. Because afterward, she was sure to tell him all the reasons they couldn't prolong their relationship. He didn't want to hear such reasons. He wanted to hear...

"Jack, please!"

She'd used his name. How could he continue ignoring her? He turned to face her, watching as she stopped a few paces away from him.

She stared up at him, her chest rising and falling with heavy breaths. She swallowed, seeming to hesitate before finally speaking. "I-I believe ye."

His wary frown remained. Was she saying so just to appease him?

"If ye say ye didn't kiss her, then I believe ye."

He could say nothing, the pain still coursing through him. But she believed him. That had to mean something, didn't it?

She shook her head helplessly as she continued, tears streaking down her cheeks, their trails glowing in the growing light of the moon. "I didn't know what to think when I saw ye with her. I'd hoped ye didn't kiss her. But I didn't think it possible for ye to deny a kiss from a beautiful lady, as ye so easily resisted kissin' me."

"Easily?" He blew out a breath of disbelief. Rubbing his fingers to his eyes, he willed away the image of the beautiful woman standing before him. "Gwynna, not kissing you was the hardest thing I've ever had to do."

CHAPTER FORTY-THREE

*C*hills rushed over Gwynna's body, as if a sudden blast of cold wind knocked the life back into her person.

Jack's brow wrinkled with emotion as he approached her, one slow step at a time.

"I didn't kiss you to prove my respect. I kept my distance, to ensure my regard for you was held in the highest of standards."

Her breathing faltered. Could this be true?

"Don't you dare believe for a single moment that I did not wish to kiss you." He stopped in front of her, his voice husky. "For I have thought of little else but your lips on mine since the last time we stood together at Penharrow."

She swallowed, still reeling at his words. "I've done the very same, sir...Jack."

His eyes flashed between hers then settled on her lips. Softly, he caressed her cheek. "Then we are at a crossroads, Gwynna. We are of different classes, different circumstances. We must now decide to end this before it has begun...or to power the fire burning between us."

Gwynna could no longer deny his words. There *was* a fire

between them, but it wasn't simply physical desire. Her whole soul yearned for his.

His thumb smoothed over her lips. "So what will it be? I shall not proceed until I know your desires."

How could she make such a decision when her head was spinning? When his lips were so close to hers, she could only imagine their touch?

"I don't know what to do," she answered honestly.

He pulled back, focusing on her eyes. His throat bobbed up and down as he swallowed.

"But I do know," she continued, "that I ain't be wantin' this to end."

He released a deep, trembling breath at her words. Raising his shoulders, he cupped her face in his hands, hovering just out of reach until finally, her eyelashes fluttered to a close, and their lips met.

Gwynna was overpowered. She could hardly breathe, despite the slow tenderness of Jack's kiss. She wrapped her arms around him, her hands at his back. The muscles worked near his shoulders as he secured her face between his hands.

How often had she dreamt of this moment, wrapped so securely in his affection. It was everything she'd ever hoped it would be. If she knew before what she did now—how utterly intoxicating his lips on hers was—she would have never been able to say no as she had so readily at the ball.

He tipped his head to the side, their kiss deepening as his hands left her face, trailing down her arms, pressing against her back, and pulling her flush against his body. Gwynna readily responded, standing on the tips of her toes to wrap her arms around his neck as his mouth worked alongside hers to share the feelings that had blossomed between them.

The wind toyed the yellow gorse bushes beside them, tapping them against her skirts, and the breeze whistled in her ear. All was silent apart from the rustling foliage and roaring of the waves below. They were alone on the cliffside. They were the only two people left in existence, as far as Gwynna was concerned.

But should someone happen upon them...

"Jack," she mumbled against his lips, pulling back, "s'pose we be seen—"

Her words ended in a surprised yelp as Jack swooped her up in his arms. He strode down the pathway as she giggled. Wrapping her right arm around his neck and placing her left hand against his cheek, she brought his lips toward hers for another kiss.

A deep moan rumbled in his chest, his jaw working against her palm until he pulled away with a chuckle. "We had better stop before I fall to the ground."

She smiled. As he carried her swiftly toward the ruins, she rested her head against his, breathing in his musky cologne until they reached the engine house. Jack stepped over the threshold of the old bucking room then lowered her feet to the ground.

Gwynna had only a moment to situate herself before Jack took her lips to his once more. He slowly urged her across the room, pressing her against the wall. His fingers trailed down her neck, brushing against her collar bones, though never straying past propriety.

Their lips moved as one in perfect harmony, just as their lives had somehow done since they'd met those few weeks before. How could so much have happened in so short a time?

And how had she allowed herself to fall in love with the mine owner's son?

Gwynna didn't know how long their kiss lasted, but when Jack's lips slowly parted from hers, the sun had fully disappeared, and darkness surrounded them. She could only detect a few features of Jack's face as he stared down at her.

He brushed back her hair from her brow, resting his forehead on hers. "I have never felt such a way before, as I have just now, kissing you."

Gwynna closed her eyes, willing herself to remember the feeling of his touch, his proximity, her love for him. "Nor 'ave I."

But then, what did that mean coming from Jack? Could he possibly love her in return? And if he did…then what?

She tried to maintain hold of the perfect euphoria around them, but it faded away like the setting sun, and the darkness of reality began to settle around them.

They had kissed. They'd both felt something for each other, she knew that. So what did that mean for their relationship?

She sighed, shaking her head against his. There shouldn't even be a relationship between them. She was a bal maiden, for heaven's sake. What was she doing kissing this gentleman? Did she expect him to fall in love with her in return? To drop to his knees and beg for her hand?

Even if such a ridiculous thing occurred, they would never be able to make a marriage work between them.

"Jack, what…what are we to do now?"

He was silent for a moment. "I do not know. But what I *do* know is that…Is that there is something between us. Something that can no longer be ignored."

He pulled back, their eyes catching in the darkness. What was he suggesting? Not marriage, surely. How would that work between their two vastly different worlds?

"Then what do ye suggest, Jack?"

He slipped his arms around her, pulling her up against him and eyeing her lips. "I suggest we allow our troubles to melt away for a moment more."

She licked her upper lip in anticipation. She couldn't refuse his suggestion, especially when their lips met again and Gwynna's worries slipped from her grasp as her heart swirled with love.

"Trevethan!"

CHAPTER FORTY-FOUR

*G*wynna tore away from Jack's embrace with a gasp. Father stood in the doorway, feet planted apart, eyes flaming brighter than the lantern he held aloft.

"Papa?" Shock usurped the feeling in her limbs.

Papa placed his lantern on the ground, his gaze unyielding at Jack. "Ye get away from me daugh'er!"

His command reached every inch of the hut, dust falling from the rafters in a grimy shower.

He progressed toward them with a roar.

"Papa, no!"

It was too late. With a cocked fist, he reared back and delivered a blow to Jack's jaw.

"No!" Gwynna screamed.

Jack stumbled back a few paces, ultimately falling to the ground.

"Papa, stop!"

She ran to her father, holding his arm to prevent him from distributing another sound strike. "Ye can't do this to 'im!"

"I 'ave every right!" Papa growled, still glowering at Jack. "Ye slock me own daugh'er to come here in the dead o' night. I'll get ye!"

Jack rose to his feet, shoulders raised, hands fisted. Blood trailed from the side of his mouth, dripping from his chin to his waistcoat.

Father took an abrupt step toward him, but Jack didn't flinch.

"No, I chose to come of me own accord, Father!"

Gwynna stood between the two of them, pressing a hand to Papa's chest, praying Jack would have the sense to not fan the flames of fury within her father.

"You must believe me, sir," Jack said. "I had no ill intentions where your—"

"Giss on!" Father said through clenched teeth. "Ye be lathered to 'igh 'eaven and dafter than mud if ye think I believe the likes of ye!"

"Father, stop!" she pleaded, looking over her shoulder as Jack's scowl increased. The red on his cheekbone from Papa's strike screamed pain.

Desperate to end the situation before another, worser blow could be dealt, Gwynna fully faced Papa with a soft tone. "I'll go home with ye now, Papa. We can speak o' this on the morrow when—"

"Have ye no honor?" Papa continued, ignoring Gwynna's begging. "Have ye no respect? Do ye not know what this might do to her? Ye'd sully her without a second thought and tear we, her family, apart. Your father—your *mother*—would be ashamed!"

Gwynna winced, turning a pained look to Jack. Fury flashed in his eyes as he swiped the blood from his mouth, angry red streaks now on his sleeve.

"Papa, no more," she whispered, pressing against his chest. She couldn't bear another unkind word spoken to the man she loved. "Please, let us be leavin' now."

Papa's voice dropped to a dangerous level, his finger pointing directly at Jack. "Ye don't deserve me daugh'er. If I see ye anywhere near her again, I ain't stoppin' at a single blow."

A chill slid down Gwynna's spine. Never had Father spewed such threats, never had his eyes burned with such fury. Had she truly upset him so greatly?

"Please, Father," she attempted one more time, grasping his hand to pull him away and reaching for the lantern with the other.

Finally, he dropped his pointed finger then left hand-in-hand with Gwynna, snatching the lantern from her grasp and leading the way from the hut.

Gwynna peered over her shoulder, anxious to apologize to Jack. She only managed a single glance at the ghostly shadows dancing beneath his eyes before Father's departure abandoned him to the darkness.

Papa released Gwynna's hand as they tore across the countryside. She had to jog to keep up with his furious pace.

"Papa, wait. I can explain—"

"No, Gwynna."

His words were final, and Gwynna tucked in her chin. She'd never seen her father so upset with her. Try as she might, she could not blame him. She'd betrayed him and Mama both. She deserved all the anger he leveled at her.

What had she been thinking? Sneaking away, risking so much—her safety, her parents' respect, their livelihood—for what? A kiss from Jack? She knew better. She should have behaved better.

Eventually, Papa's pace slowed, though he still did not speak a word.

With each step that brought her farther away from Penharrow, farther away from Jack, her spirits were only pulled closer to the ground until she could bear the weight no longer.

"I be sorry, Papa," she whispered.

He was silent for a moment. Had he heard her, or was he still unable to speak because of his anger?

"Gwynna, I can't..." He broke off with a groan of frustration. "I can't understand what ye be thinkin'."

She stared down at the grass they walked across, unable to face his disappointed expression.

"I didn't want to believe ye could lie to me in such a way," he said. "I saw Mrs. Hawkins at the Causey's this evenin', instead of meetin' with ye. That be when I knew the rumors travelin' round the mine be true."

Gwynna winced. The betrayal in his tone cut her conscience. Of course he'd heard the rumors. She wouldn't be surprised if Jack's father had, as well.

He continued. "Now I wonder what else be the truth? Have ye been dressin' as a lady, too?"

Gwynna sighed, every breath that left her body impossible to draw in again without acute pain. "Yes, sir."

He ran his hand over his mouth. "How could ye do it? Did we not do enough for ye to be happy with what ye have? Do ye not understand the risk involved?"

She couldn't bear the guilt. "I be more than happy with me life, Papa. And I be more than aware o' the risks, but Sophia and I—"

He groaned. "I should've known she'd be involved. I curse the day I encouraged ye to become friends."

Humbly, Gwynna shook her head. "No, Father. Ye mustn't blame her. She be the sole reason I wasn't caught."

He eyed her warily, shaking his head in dismay. He deserved an explanation, but what could she say? "I...I just wanted one night o' fun. One night to be free, to feel what it be like to be a lady. To dance and dress up and be flattered. Had I known what it would do, had I known how it would affect ye and Mama both, I...I wouldn't have done any of it."

She winced at her own words, but they were true. Had she known her actions would have led to such heartache, would have led to her falling in love with Jack, she never would have done it. Now she had to suffer with ashamed parents, an aching soul, and unreciprocated love.

Papa sighed, his thin shoulders falling forward. "We be more worried o'er how it be affectin' ye, Gwynny."

She eyed him with confusion. If that were the case, why had he reacted so violently? "I assure ye, Papa, no harm has come to me."

"Except givin' your heart away."

She knew he couldn't see her blush, but she ducked her head all the same. "It be nothin' I can't bear."

He winced. "Has he expressed his love to ye?"

The memory of his kiss still pressed on her mouth. "No, least not aloud."

Papa sighed heavily, looking out into the darkness. The lantern's light cast black shadows across his face. "I don't wish to break your heart, daugh'er, but I must, if only to avoid it bein' broken by another."

Worry greedily ate what was left of her hope. "What do ye mean?"

He began carefully, as if every last drop of his energy was used to speak. "Do ye remember me speakin' o' Meraud?"

She attempted to shift conversations. "A little."

Meraud, Papa's youngest sister, had lived with the Merricks before Gwynna was born, as well as two of his other adult sisters who worked full-time at the mine.

One by one, his sisters had moved away, except for Meraud. Though she died before Gwynna ever met her, she knew her aunt and Papa were the closest of their siblings.

"Then ye must remember that she died while givin' birth," Father continued.

"And the child."

"Yes. And…do ye recall any mention of a father?"

Gwynna paused. "I assumed he died, too."

Papa huffed a mirthless laugh. "In a way, I s'pose he did. He left her 'fore she even had the baby." He stopped walking, eying Gwynna squarely. "Gwynna, the father was an agent at the mine."

Gwynna recoiled. She'd heard stories of such things happening, but she had no idea her own aunt had been so closely entangled in the issue.

"I would've told ye sooner, but I don't like speakin' much of it." Papa's tone was gruff, as if to hide his emotion. "The man had claimed to love her, had even gone so far as to say he wished to marry her. 'Course he left her just after he received what he wanted. And then she died 'cause of 'im."

Tears gathered in the center of her eyes. Papa's earlier aggression made sense now. He was afraid of losing Gwynna. But he didn't need to be. Jack had never truly disrespected her. He hadn't even expressed his love for her, nor declared his desire to marry her.

He hadn't done anything but kiss her.

"I know why ye be tellin' me this, Papa, but ye needn't worry about Mr. Trevethan and me. We-we only kissed. But I ain't be seein' 'im again."

Papa's expression remained unchanged. "Are ye certain? 'Cause men like him…they be after only one thing."

She didn't believe Jack was like the man who'd injured Meraud. He'd only ever treated Gwynna with respect. Still, saying so wouldn't help her father's worries.

Instead, she nodded. "Yes, Papa. I understand."

But as she made her way home with him, uncertainty spun about her mind. Jack had been hinting for something more between him and Gwynna. But such a thing didn't matter now.

A marriage between them would never work. Neither would a friendship.

She'd meant what she'd said to Papa.

She would never see Jack again, never mind how sick her stomach was at the thought.

CHAPTER FORTY-FIVE

*L*eather cracked as Jack shifted in his saddle, hoping to alleviate the discomfort of the hard seat against his backside. The warm sun burned into his shoulders, contrasting from the cold letter he'd tucked between his shirt and waistcoat—now pressing icily against his chest.

If only he could tear it to pieces and let it fly away with the wind and out to the sea.

But he couldn't. He needed to deliver it to Gwynna. She deserved an explanation.

He rolled his jaw, the muscles still protesting from Mr. Merrick's fist two days past. A purple bruise had stretched across his cheekbone, but most of the swelling had dissipated near his lip and eye.

Gwynna had been right all those days ago. Jack would've been wise to avoid her father. Mr. Merrick was far stronger than he appeared, just like his daughter. But it wasn't the physical strike that had injured Jack the most.

Ye'd tear her family apart.

Your mother would be ashamed.

Ye don't deserve me daugh'er.

Jack winced. He'd been a fool that night, wrapped up in Gwynna's smile and amber eyes, her warm embrace. He'd somehow convinced himself that he could kiss her with no consequences, like every other woman.

Though the guilt was more poignant than usual, it was what the affection had done to his soul that had the worst affect.

But he wouldn't dwell on how his chest now pinched tightly together, as if his lungs no longer inflated at the mere thought of not being with Gwynna.

He never should have allowed himself to form an attachment to her, to kiss her sweet lips. The physical pull he had for Gwynna was always stirring. But to have his heart involved in a kiss for the first time in his life...

Although, he shouldn't dwell on those thoughts. Their lives were too separate. Their personalities too different. Their desires too conflicting. He'd planned to never marry so he might live a life of leisure. Remaining in Cornwall, making amends with Father...falling in love with a remarkable woman —they'd all been fanciful dreams.

And fanciful dreams were never reality.

Gwynna stepped about the room with her broom, gathering dirt and dust and spare pieces of food from the floor. Silence filled the air, apart from the straw scraping against the wood.

The sound barely reached her ears. Thoughts of what had occurred between her and Jack two days before left little room for any other musings.

She'd tried to remain unaffected by the fact that she would never be with him. She'd tried to convince herself that she didn't love him.

But it was no use. She needed to accept the facts. She loved him, but she could not be with him. And it was her own foolish choices that brought her to this anguish. Now she would have to suffer through it alone.

She swept the dust toward the entrance, opening the door to expel the dirt outside, but she paused mid-sweep when she discovered a folded piece of parchment at the foot of the door.

"Be ye leavin', Gwynna?" Mama called from her bedroom where she folded the laundry that had finally dried that day in the afternoon sun.

"No. Just sweepin' out the dust."

Gwynna bent down to retrieve the paper, only to realize it was a letter. She swung her eyes back and forth outside the door, but whoever had delivered the note was already gone.

She rested the broom against her shoulder and turned the letter back to front, closing the door, the dust pile long forgotten. Eying the writing scrawled across the top of it, she recognized her name.

Could this be from Jack? Did he not know she couldn't read?

With concentrated eyes, she broke open the red waxed seal and unfolded the letter. Anxiously, she scoured the words for any she recognized, but it was no use. She should've taken Sophia's offer to teach Gwynna how to read.

Mama entered the room with a pile of grey, folded sheets. "What be that then?"

Gwynna's first instinct was to hide the letter, play it off as a spare piece of waste, but hadn't lying started this mess?

Mama hadn't scolded Gwynna when she'd returned from Penharrow. Though she'd been upset with Gwynna's lies, she'd understood the ache of her daughter's heart.

If she *hadn't* been so understanding, Gwynna would have felt far more disconcerted with revealing the note. And with Papa working at the Causeys that evening…

"I-I believe it be a letter from Ja—from Mr. Jack Trevethan."

Mama's expression grew solemn. "If your father knew…"

"I know, Mama, but I didn't ask 'im to send it. And I don't know what he be sayin'."

"Don't he know ye can't read?" Mama asked, settling the sheets on a nearby chair and moving to stand beside her. "Ye really ought to throw it in the fire straightaway."

The thought of burning his words—whatever they said—wounded Gwynna to the core. She held it against her chest. "Please, Mama, don't make me be rid of it. Least not 'til I know what he be sayin'."

"Are ye goin' to ask your father to read it for ye then?" Mama asked with a dubious expression.

"No, but Sophia might."

"Be ye think it wise to go to her, after what 'appened?"

Gwynna sighed. The words on the page begged to be read. She turned to Mama with a look of pleading. "Please. I must know, just this once. To see if he be well after Papa hurt 'im."

Mama pursed her lips, then reached for the letter herself. "Fine. Let me be seein' if I can read any o' these words first."

Gwynna clasped the broom handle, anxiously waiting as Mama concentrated on the letters.

She continued, squinting as if she couldn't see the words clearly. "Town," she murmured. "No...Bath...Lon...Lond..."

Urgency rang in Gwynna's ears. Bath. London.

Jack was leaving.

Mama ended with a sigh. "I be sorry, daugh'er. I can't make any more of it out."

Gwynna tried to maintain a level-head, but she tapped her fingers to her thigh. "Mama...I must go to Sophia. I must know what be in the note."

Mama gave her a look of warning. "Gwynna..."

"I know Papa doesn't want me round her, but he can't keep me away forever. And I 'ave to know what it says."

To her relief, Mama sighed. "Very well, but ye make sure ye be home 'fore your Papa be, or he'll come lookin' for ye again."

"Thank ye, Mama!" She swiftly untied her apron and set the broom aside. "I'll be home soon, I promise."

She pressed a kiss to Mama's cheek then sprinted out the door, skirts held high with the letter between her fingers. She left the small homes behind then forced her pace to slow.

It was still early evening. She would have time enough to see Sophia and return before Papa did.

She crossed the countryside toward Fynwary, poring over the letter again to see if she could glean more information before she arrived. She tripped over a divot in the ground. Perhaps it was safer to see where she was walking.

Her steps faltered again, however, when she spotted a gentleman on a horse directly ahead of her at a slow pace, his broad shoulders sunken, but unmistakable.

"Jack," she breathed.

Father would be livid if he discovered them together again. But then, was it not smarter to go straight to the source for the content of the letter?

She ran toward him, calling out for him.

"Jack!"

He didn't stop. Two more shouts, then he finally turned in his saddle. She waved to him, but he didn't respond, merely reining in his horse and turning to face her as he dismounted.

"Jack," she said as she reached him. "I…"

His wary look stopped her. "What are you doing here?"

She eyed his purple cheekbone and the small, dried cut near his lip. She'd caused that injury by her reckless behavior. "I need to speak with ye."

He shook his head. "I can't explain more than what is in the letter, Gwynna."

With an embarrassed, hopeless laugh, she raised the letter in her hands. "I can't read, Jack."

CHAPTER FORTY-SIX

a dull ache spread through Jack's chest. How could he have done something so exceptionally stupid? How could he not have realized she couldn't read?

"I be sorry," she said in a timid voice, clearly reading his silence as disapproval.

He tugged at his cravat. "Do not apologize. I'm the one who made the mistake."

"It be all right," she said with a reassuring smile, though her cheeks were shaded in pink. Just like the color of her lips.

He closed his eyes. "No, it isn't all right. This is precisely the reason we cannot..." He broke off in a sigh. "It is precisely why I'm leaving Cornwall."

"Because I can't read?" Her voice broke.

"No, no." Could he say nothing right? "No, it has nothing to do with your inability to read. That is the least of my concerns."

"Has somethin' 'appened then with your father? Or...or be it about what occurred between us? I can leave ye alone, Jack. We don't even 'ave to be friends anymore, if ye still wish to stay."

Her willingness to help, to sacrifice so much for him, twisted his insides. He dipped his chin, how could he explain his reasoning? That he could no longer reside in Cornwall because being near Gwynna and not being *with* Gwynna would be too torturous.

"Does this say why ye be leavin'?" She raised the letter.

That blasted letter. Why had he even written it? "Yes, it merely explains that I shall be leaving Cornwall to no longer disrupt your life."

"But ye haven't disrupted me life."

"How can you say that, Gwynna? I have threatened you, caused rumors to assail you, encouraged you to disobey your parents. Kissed you in the darkness like the despicable man I am. I *have* disrupted your life."

"Ye haven't, Jack. Ye've only made it better. I know *we* could never be. No gent could ever marry a maiden."

He longed to cry out how wrong she was, how he would give anything to marry her, to disrupt the plans for his future and spend the rest of his life with her, but he clenched his jaw to remain silent.

Gwynna took a step toward him. "When we were at Penharrow, I felt somethin' for ye." Gwynna wrung her hands, the paper crumpling in her grip. "And I think ye felt somethin' for I, too…Didn't ye?"

With ragged breaths, Jack bore into Gwynna's eyes. All he wanted was before him, right within his reach. Peace. Joy. Gwynna. He never thought he'd be happy again after his mother's death, and she—this bal maiden with dirt strewn across her cheek, her hair tied back in that awful, scanty rag—had changed that.

But this was why he needed to leave Cornwall. Gwynna would be giving him everything if they married. Jack would undeniably improve her circumstances, as well, giving her endless love and a vast home with whatever food and finery she wished. He'd longed to offer all of that and more the moment they'd kissed, but reality settled in soon after. As did Mr. Merrick's fist.

Both of their classes would ridicule her for rising above her station, no matter what Jack said in her defense. How could he agree to put her through such torment? She would be giving up too much. Her peace, her way of life, her freedom. Even her family.

"Ye'd tear we, her family, apart," her father had said.

It had been a clear warning to them both that should Gwynna marry Jack, she would no longer be welcome in her own family.

How could Jack ask her to sacrifice so much for him, a man hardly worthy of everything she could give him?

"No, Gwynna." He tightened his grip on his horse's reins and turned away. He wouldn't look at her amber eyes now shining like gold with her precious tears—tears he'd once more caused by his cruelty. "You deserve someone who makes you happy, someone who does not ask you to give up so much. I am sorry, but I cannot be that man for you."

Gwynna's quiet sob caught in her throat, sounding as a muted gasp. It was the final twist to fully tear apart Jack's heart. He bit hard on his lip, mounting his horse and galloping away before he could convince himself to return.

This was for the better. He was making Gwynna happier this way.

So why did it feel like he was doing the opposite?

CHAPTER FORTY-SEVEN

*T*he days were getting harder to work through. Not even the clear skies, cool breeze, or sea was comfort enough for Gwynna. The blue water sparkled like the sapphires Sophia liked to wear—a wedding gift from her husband. Gwynna used to imagine what that would be like, to have wealth, to be gifted finery from a loved one. Now she realized how silly that was of her. She didn't want jewelry or dresses or rouge.

She wanted Jack.

Crack!

She kicked the broken ore to the side, drawing in more rocks with the head of her hammer, avoiding any sight of the upper cliff. She hadn't expected to see Jack again after he'd delivered his letter the day before, yet there he was, standing next to his father and Mr. Harvey.

He'd no doubt been persuaded by his father to have one last walk around Favour before he left. To Bath or to London, Gwynna still wasn't sure, nor should she care.

She'd spent hours convincing herself that Jack's departure was a good thing. They couldn't have made a marriage work between them anyway. Gwynna was willing to sacrifice all she was comfortable with—her home near the sea, her place at the mine, her freedom to brawl and curse and run with her skirts at her knees. She even could have dealt with the criticism she'd inevitably face from both classes.

But she couldn't give up her family. And since Papa would never approve, marrying Jack would never work.

Not that Jack had wanted to marry a bal maiden anyway.

She turned her back on Jack and the other gentlemen, averting her gaze from Kerensa, as well. Kerensa had asked after Gwynna's lowered spirits, but Gwynna had brushed aside any questions with a strained smile and an assurance that all was well. She hadn't patched up her broken heart enough to speak readily about it yet.

Gwynna had cried herself to sleep last night in her room in Mama's arms, just like she'd done the day Jago had died. Her mother hugged her and whispered comforting words as she combed her fingers through Gwynna's hair.

"Ye be fine to cry now, Gwynna," she'd whispered. "But on the morrow, ye must be strong and accept what's 'appened. The pain'll subside. One day, ye be fine again."

But Gwynna wasn't sure if she would be. Jack loved her. She was certain of it. The day before, he'd tried to sidestep his reasoning for leaving, but she'd read between his words. He loved her, just not enough to disgrace himself by marrying a bal maiden.

The fact that she was not good enough for him made the blow of his rejection all the more painful.

A surface worker dumped a new pile of ore at her feet and walked away without a glance. Gwynna sighed, the knee-high pile of rocks as insurmountable as a mountain.

Was this her future, one pile of ore after another? One swing, one crack, one aching muscle at a time?

She swung the hammer again overhead and railed against

another piece of ore. The crack cut through the air like a clap of thunder. Where once the sound had been satisfying to hear, now it snapped annoyingly in her ears.

Perhaps Papa was right. Perhaps she should leave the mine and help Mama at home now. Her parents deserved *some* obedience from their daughter after all Gwynna had put them through.

She'd spotted her father standing in her doorway the night before as she'd cried. Though he'd kept his distance and his words to himself, his eyebrows were drawn with compassion before he'd slunk from her room.

That morning, he'd embraced Gwynna longer than usual. "Bein' away from the mine'll allow ye to forget your heartache, Gwynny," he'd whispered, then he'd departed for the shaft, his last day below ground before his promotion to surface worker began tomorrow.

Gwynna tossed a few pieces of the ore into the hand barrow, sighing with exasperation as a rock bounced out and tumbled across the dirt. She stomped toward the rock and threw it into the barrow like a petulant child asked to tidy her toys.

She *was* behaving like a child. She needed to stop wallowing in her misery and focus instead on her blessings. She lived by the sea, she had friends in both classes, her belly would soon be full of the pasty Mama had made for her, and she had parents who would do anything to keep her safe and happy.

Her parents deserved their only daughter to appreciate the life they'd given her, so she would be happy, no matter what the future held.

Then the ground rumbled at her feet.

Confusion slipped its muddling fingers over Gwynna's eyes. She stood in a stagnant daze, trying to decipher what was occurring as the older women screamed. Surface workers and young maidens dropped their tools with shattered expressions.

The whole mine seemed to merge as one, each worker converging toward the shaft.

When the tin bell pierced through the air like an errant bullet, Gwynna finally understood.

The shaft had suffered a collapse.

"Father," she breathed.

She took off toward the opposite side of the engine house with the others. Shouts of alarm and whimpering cries from children rippled through the crowds. A few men disappeared into the engine house, heading below ground to help the survivors and the injured…and to count the dead.

Gwynna drew in haggard breaths as she stopped, waiting with the others. Fear threatened to loosen her hold of reality, just as it had done when the lean-to had broken on top of her in the storm. Instead of Jago's fear-stricken face haunting her thoughts, Father's worry-etched brow took to the forefront of her mind.

Was he suffering? Wounded? Or had he…

She closed her eyes off to the image of his ashen face. No, she wouldn't believe it. She couldn't. Papa couldn't die. She and Mama wouldn't be able to live without him.

She opened her eyes, glancing around at the tears being shed. Kerensa stood back from the others, her arms draped around her sisters' quivering shoulders. The three of them cried. They had no family below ground, but the memory of their father's death in the last mining accident was no doubt fresh in their minds.

She and Kerensa shared a wary look.

"He be all right," Kerensa shouted with an encouraging nod.

Gwynna swallowed. Would he be?

"Please, make room!"

All eyes shifted from the engine house door to the approaching gentlemen making ripples through the crowds as they cut their way toward the shaft.

Gwynna charted Jack's progression behind Mr. Harvey and his father. Just before he followed them into the engine house, his eyes caught hers.

Time stood still for a moment. He gave her a firm, reassuring nod, then he disappeared through the door, taking the last of Gwynna's hope alongside him.

CHAPTER FORTY-EIGHT

*J*ack folded his arms, fighting the urge to tap his boot impatiently on the floor of the engine house.

"If the whole shaft has collapsed, they'll be gone already," Mr. Harvey said.

Father shook his head. "But the timber we purchased, would that not have prevented an entire collapse?"

"You know, sir, there are no guarantees in this business."

Jack peered down the shaft. The surface workers who had descended to help the others were nowhere in sight. Why were Father and Mr. Harvey moseying along? Every moment that passed in conversation was another moment that could be spent saving Gwynna's father.

Jack hadn't been certain the man was even below ground until Gwynna's fearful eyes had confirmed his suspicion. Now he knew he had to do everything in his power to ensure tragedy did not strike her family again.

And if that meant taking control into his own hands, then so be it.

"We can only hope for the best, sir," Mr. Harvey said.

"I just don't see—"

Jack growled in frustration, interrupting his father's words as he tore off his jacket and untied his cravat. "Well speaking about it isn't going to save them."

"Son, what are you doing?"

Jack ignored Father's anxious tone and retrieved a candle.

"No, Jack. You cannot go down there. It is too dangerous now."

Jack shot him a pointed look. "So you'll leave them all to fend for themselves?"

Mr. Harvey frowned. "We've sent men to survey the damage. Until then, we must wait until they deem it safe."

Jack scoffed. "You're allowing them to risk their lives to save yours."

Father looked away. "They've experience in—"

"I care not." Jack took his first step on the ladder down the shaft. "I do not deem my life greater than any of theirs."

"I highly advise against this," Mr. Harvey called down from above. "There are rules we must adhere to!"

Jack ignored him and plunged into the darkness. He knew it was dangerous, but he had to do this. For Gwynna.

Just like before underground, the same apprehension crept into his lungs, preventing a steady breath. But what did it matter? He was already panting from exertion and fear—fear that Mr. Merrick was not alive. Fear that he'd have to tell Gwynna that another member of her family perished in yet *another* mining accident.

The ladder shivered beneath Jack's fingers, and he glanced up to find Father following closely after him.

"Mr. Harvey *highly advises against this*, Father," Jack said, mimicking the man's words.

"It is fortunate, then, that I am the owner and he is not."

Jack would have grinned under different circumstances. Who would have guessed he had inherited his rebellious nature from Father?

They moved together, soon joining the other miners as they moved from ladder to ladder, tramping through standing water, shrouded in darkness. The shouts and moans from the injured men replaced the usual clanking of tools, hauntingly echoing up the shaft.

Soot permeated the air as Jack neared the bottom of the shaft. He coughed into his sleeve as he ran alongside the other miners down the tunnels.

"How many are injured?" Father asked as they reached the area Jack had first been shown with Hugh.

A few miners exchanged surprised glances to find the owner and his son joining them. "Eleven, sir."

Jack couldn't draw in a deep breath as he visually sifted through the wreckage. He'd expected to see the cave-in closing off access to the tunnels, but only a few boulders piled up against the rock walls.

"Casualties?" Father asked next.

"None, sir."

None. Relief rushed over Jack. Gwynna's father was safe. But then, where was he?

He cast his eyes to the others as Father continued his conversation.

"I'm so pleased to hear that," he said, relief apparent in his tone.

"The timbers be doin' their job, sir," the miner said.

Timbers. Gwynna had mentioned them long ago—Father paying the extra expense to ensure the safety of his miners—and they'd worked.

Sudden emotion overcame Jack. He looked away, furiously blinking away the tears in his eyes. How wrong he had been about his father. He had far more goodness than Jack could have ever guessed.

"We must bring 'em to grass to be treated," a miner called out. "There be broken bones and the like."

Jack pulled out of his thoughts, clearing his throat. Now was not the time to be sentimental.

He slogged through the mud, shining his light down on the men who laid against the walls and on the ground. Finally, he found Mr. Merrick propped up against a large boulder. The man grimaced with closed eyes, his long hair snaking out from his filthy cap.

Jack knelt down beside him. "Mr. Merrick, where are you injured?"

His eyes pulled open, instant fire in their depths. "I be fine."

"His arm be broken," a miner next to him declared. "And he sprained 'is foot."

Mr. Merrick scowled, still facing Jack. "The other men be worse off. See to 'em first."

Jack noted Mr. Merrick's right arm limp at his side. "I'm afraid I cannot do that, sir."

He reached forward, grasping Mr. Merrick's left arm and helping him to stand with a huff.

"This doesn't take back what ye did to me Gwynna," Mr. Merrick whispered, favoring his arm as Jack escorted him to the ladders.

"I did nothing to her, sir," Jack said, glancing around to ensure no one could hear their conversation.

He shuddered to think what Mr. Merrick thought Jack could do to Gwynna.

But Mr. Merrick's glare chilled him straight through, like a frozen saber. "Ye broke her heart."

Jack stammered, a crushing weight falling on his shoulders, as if the shaft had collapsed upon him. "I-I didn't mean to. I was doing what was best for her."

Mr. Merrick scoffed, pushing Jack away and hobbling through the tunnels and to the ladder himself. The man was stubborn and independent. Just like Gwynna.

And Jack had broken her.

Mr. Merrick attempted to clamber up the ladder with only one arm and a smarting ankle, but after multiple grunts of pain, Jack couldn't let him carry on any longer.

He reached forward, holding Mr. Merrick upright with an outstretched hand as the man used his one good arm to climb to the top at a slow pace.

The only thing that spurred Jack forward was the sweet relief Gwynna was sure to experience once she saw her father alive.

Gwynna clasped her hands to her chest, fixing her eyes on the engine house. Only minutes before, the first injured young man had been brought forth from the shaft, and word had spread that not a single miner had been killed in the accident.

She was still afraid to believe such incredible news, but when Father—alive and walking—exited the engine house with Jack supporting him, a sob escaped her lips.

"Papa!" she shouted, running toward him as tears wet her cheeks.

She wrapped her arms around him and cried into his neck.

"I be well, Gwynny," he whispered into her hair. "I be all right."

She smiled through her tears, relief and gratitude rushing through her limbs.

"The surgeon be arrivin' just now," a miner nearby called out.

She pulled back just as two others approached her father. "We be helpin' ye up now, Merrick."

Gwynna took a step back as they helped her father forward. She eyed his limp foot and arm as they walked away. Things could have been far, far worse. Thank heavens for the timbers. Thank heavens for the Trevethans.

Thank heavens for Jack.

She turned to express her gratitude, but he no longer stood nearby. She glanced from side to side, spotting him in the doorway of the engine house.

Their gazes met, his brown eyes framed in red.

"Thank ye, Jack." she said, backing away to follow her father up the incline. "Thank ye."

He gave a singular nod, keeping his eyes on hers until she turned around and made for the counthouse.

Gwynna knew he would return down the shaft to help the other miners still hurting at the bottom.

Because that was just the sort of gentleman he was.

CHAPTER FORTY-NINE

*W*ith the last of the miners brought up from below ground, Jack wiped the mud and soot off his face and hands with the murky water near the tool house. Most maidens had already resumed working through their piles of ore on the lower cliffside, but a few miners continued to celebrate with happy smiles and proud claps to each other's backs.

Their laughter drifted toward Jack as he shook his hands dry. How different the mood would have been at Favour had Father not reinforced the shaft. Gwynna had been right. His father *was* a good man.

With his jacket draped over his arm and cravat retied—despite his now filthy waistcoat—Jack made for the counthouse. He hadn't seen Gwynna since he'd brought up Mr. Merrick. There was no sight of her spalling, so Jack figured she was within the counthouse, tending to her father.

He hesitated outside the door. He didn't want to face her again, nor hear anymore gratitude he didn't deserve, but he needed to speak with Father.

With a deep breath, he stepped inside. The main room had been turned into a makeshift infirmary, cots set up across the floor and into the spare bedroom to accommodate the injured miners. The surgeon fitted a splint on a young man while a few others groaned in pain.

Jack tried to keep his eyes focused straight ahead, but he veered to Gwynna, who sat beside her father. Sorrow peeked through her eyes, though she smiled up at him.

He tipped his head toward her, an action befitting the coward that he was, then took a quick search of the room. Father was nowhere in sight.

Jack sidled past the cots and miners toward Mr. Harvey, who pored over his ledger book behind the desk.

"Do you happen to know where my father is?" he whispered, not wishing to disturb the few miners who were finally able to rest.

Mr. Harvey didn't look up from his scribblings. "He went to the engine house with a few investors but should return shortly."

The engine house. That should take Jack far enough away from Gwynna.

He inched toward the door again, avoiding the penetrating eyes of both Gwynna and Mr. Merrick. But his progress halted halfway as Father entered the counthouse, followed shortly by two other gentlemen.

"Jack, my apologies for keeping you waiting," Father said in hushed tones. "You remember Mr. Farnsworth and Mr. Pinnick?"

Jack nodded to them both, recognizing them from his first few days in Cornwall.

"Pleasure to—"

His words were lost to the clatter that sounded near the door. Gwynna scrambled forward, gathering the empty bowl and spoon she'd dropped to the floor near her father's cot.

"Pleasure to see you both again," Jack tried again, though rather distractedly.

Gwynna ducked her head behind her raised shoulders. Was she hiding from someone?

"And you, Mr. Trevethan," Mr. Farnsworth said with a jolly smile.

Mr. Pinnick simply mumbled an intelligible comment then shuffled his boots noisily toward the snapping fire.

A few miners stirred. Gwynna, however, shifted her entire body in the opposite direction so her back was facing Mr. Pinnick.

Jack narrowed his eyes. She *was* hiding.

"I was told I'd never have to come here again," Mr. Pinnick grumbled as he warmed his hands by the fire. "Now it's even filthier. Filled to the brim with rubbish."

Jack remembered Mr. Pinnick from his first day at the mine. The gentleman had been in a remarkably bad mood then, same as today. Why in heaven's name did Mr. Pinnick invest in a business of which he clearly did not approve?

Father took a step forward, drawing Jack's attention toward him. "Mr. Farnsworth here provided much of the funds to help with the timbers," he whispered, placing a hand on the gentleman's shoulder. "We are all so grateful for them, especially now."

Jack tore his eyes from Gwynna. "Indeed, we are grateful."

Mr. Farnsworth humbly tipped his head. "I was more than happy to do so. Our miners must be protected."

"They *are* indispensable," Father agreed.

"Indispensable?" Mr. Pinnick's voice boomed throughout the room, though he appeared to be speaking to himself again. "They are *expendable*."

Father and Mr. Farnsworth exchanged wary glances, as if they'd expected such an outburst. But Jack stared at Mr. Pinnick with a disbelieving scowl. How dare the man say such a thing before the very men who'd risked their lives for his investment?

Gwynna leaned toward her father, whispering something in

323

his ear. Jack honed in as Mr. Merrick's brow contorted with worry.

Jack's insides twisted. What had Gwynna told her father?

Mr. Merrick jerked his head toward the door, and Gwynna nodded, placing the wooden bowl and spoon on his cot before sailing toward the door.

"Wait just a moment."

Mr. Pinnick's voice pierced the silence in the room. A few miners fluttered their eyes open. Gwynna's hand froze on the handle of the door, though she kept her eyes down.

"You..." Mr. Pinnick pointed at her, moving his finger up and down as if to place where he'd seen her. "I know you."

Gwynna looked away. "Yes, sir. I be a maiden here."

"No, not from here." He narrowed his dark eyes, his tone dangerously low. "You were at the ball...at Fynwary."

Jack's lips parted, the breath rushing from his lungs.

Gwynna had been discovered.

Horror sunk so deep in Gwynna's chest, she could hardly breathe. Would she never be able to leave behind the mistake she'd made in attending that ball?

"Ball, sir? I ain't be at no ball." Her voice trembled. She needed to buoy her courage.

Mr. Pinnick's brow drew together as he took a step toward her. "No, I know you were there. Dressed in a pink gown. Dancing with Mr. Davy."

"Me daugh'er ain't done nothin' o' the sort," Papa grumbled, wincing as he shifted on his cot.

Mr. Pinnick's eyes didn't waver from Gwynna.

She swallowed hard. The gentleman would readily turn her over to the constable if given the opportunity. Would he rally a group of upper class men and women who took exception to her actions? Put her in Bodmin to make an example of her? She'd heard awful tales about the jail—sharing rooms with multiple women, having no food, no light, no exercise for days.

Even if the Hawkinses helped her to avoid being sent away, Gwynna would still lose her work if she was discovered. Now Papa had been promoted, her family could afford such a thing, but suppose her father was also removed from Favour for having such a daughter? Her whole family would be shunned, ridiculed for her selfish actions.

Anything Papa said in her defense would not be believed, and Jack...Jack was no longer obliged to shield her. Without Sophia and Mr. Hawkins present to help, Gwynna needed to defend herself.

Though she longed to square her shoulders and boldly declare her candor, playing the submissive maiden would serve her better, and the less confidence she had, the less recognizable she'd be as the self-assured lady she'd played before.

She breathed slowly. "I ain't be knowin' no Mr. Davy, sir. And I own nothin' but this and a dress for church." She stretched out her brown skirts for added affect. "How could I be affordin' a pink gown fitty for a ball?"

Each set of eyes shifted from Gwynna to Mr. Pinnick and back, the air stilted in the room. She kept her attention from Jack, though, unable to bear the regret he must feel for intertwining his life with hers.

Mr. Pinnick sneered. "There are other ways for you to have obtained a gown."

The blood sunk from her face. Thievery was a much greater crime than dressing above one's station. She could hang for such a thing. She'd teased Jack once that she'd stolen the dress, but Mr. Pinnick was serious.

"I ain't be pinchin' nothin', sir." At least in that regard, she was telling the truth.

Mr. Peter Trevethan stepped across the room toward them,

lowering his voice, though there was no need. Every word resounded about the small counthouse. "Mr. Pinnick, you must be mistaken. The Merricks are a fine family. What you are accusing this young woman of is—"

"I know of what I'm accusing her!" Mr. Pinnick snapped. "She stole a gown, dressed well above her station, and slipped into a ball she was not invited to." He shot angry eyes back at Gwynna. "Did you, or did you not, maiden?"

The miners and surgeon awaited with bated breath. Even the counthouse woman had ducked her head outside of the kitchen to hear Gwynna's answer, the signature scowl missing as she eagerly watched the commotion.

"No, sir." Gwynna's voice shook. "That ain't true."

How she regretted ever attending that cursed ball. How she regretted her pride in wishing for such an evening of frivolity.

Mr. Pinnick shook his head with disgust. "Thank goodness it is the word of a gentleman over a miner's daughter. I will see justice is served. Anyone else who attended the ball will surely side with me."

Gwynna swallowed. She was finished.

"I most assuredly will *not* side with you."

The deep voice from across the room drifted toward her, cradling her fears and sending comforting ribbons of warmth throughout her body.

Jack.

He stepped past his gaping father and gawking miners to stand directly before Mr. Pinnick. "I was at the ball, but I will not side with you."

Mr. Pinnick scowled. "And why is that?"

"Because she was not the woman in attendance." He studied Gwynna. "I remember the lady in pink you described, dancing with Mr. Davy. How could a man forget her beauty?"

Would her face ever resume its normal color?

Mr. Pinnick pumped his head up and down. "Then you must see that this woman is her."

Jack motioned to Gwynna. "As lovely as this maiden is, she does not hold herself as regally as the woman did at the ball."

Lovely. The word was meant to assuage the necessary harshness of his words, Gwynna was sure of it. She lowered her shoulders further, forgetting everything Sophia had ever taught her about proper posture. Doing so now was sure to save her life.

Mr. Pinnick studied her, his upper lip curled in disgust. "Lovely? Her pose *is* severely lacking, but I disagree. A bal maiden could never be *lovely*."

Jack tipped his head with feigned confusion. "Then forgive me, Mr. Pinnick, but I cannot understand how you can confuse her with the incomparable beauty of the lady at the ball?"

Mr. Pinnick fiddled with his hat in his hands, shifting his eyes from Jack to Gwynna, then to the others around the room. A blush crawled up his cheeks. "I-I suppose you must be right, Mr. Trevethan. I don't know what I was thinking. How could this—" he gestured to Gwynna "—ever pass as a true lady?"

Gwynna's pride picked up its head, but she could do nothing but squelch her desire to defend herself. When Jack took a step forward, fists clenched, anger twitching his jaw, she knew she didn't need to. Jack's reaction was more than enough for her.

Before he could say something and lose his cover, as well as Gwynna's, she delivered an off-centered curtsy.

"Ye be right, sir. I could ne'er be a lady."

With a fleeting glance at Jack's focused gaze, she fled from the counthouse, leaving the dangers behind her—Mr. Pinnick and his threats, the curious eyes of the miners...and Jack's protection, which made her love him all the more.

CHAPTER FIFTY

*M*r. Pinnick left the counthouse shortly after Gwynna, mumbling something about having another business matter to attend to. Jack wouldn't be surprised if Mr. Pinnick withdrew his investment from the mine. The man was sure to be humiliated for having nearly been caught calling a bal maiden attractive.

"What in heaven's name was that about?" Father asked in a whisper, stepping up beside Jack.

Jack shrugged. He wasn't about to explain what he knew. "Perhaps he has had more port than he ought to have."

Father laughed a mirthless chuckle before turning to Mr. Merrick. "I'm terribly sorry for his accusation."

Mr. Merrick glanced warily to Jack then placed a hand over his head with a wince. "It be well, sir."

Jack knew Mr. Merrick wasn't feigning a headache, what with the pulsing in his own brow. He never wished to go through such an ordeal again.

Father turned to Jack then, lowering his voice. "Did you truly see the woman in pink at the ball? Or were you simply defending the maiden?"

Even though father's tone was barely above a whisper, the miners around them watched Jack with focused gazes—especially Mr. Merrick.

Knowing he could say very little without placing Gwynna in harm's way, he nodded, responding loud enough for all of them to hear. "I did see the woman in pink, Father. And she was stunning."

Father looked at Jack expectantly, clearly searching for the next clarification—that the lady in pink was not Gwynna. But Jack could say nothing further. "I'm afraid I must leave for Coffrow Place now. I've delayed my departure as long as possible."

Father placed his hand on Jack's shoulder and motioned to the door. "I will walk you out, son."

Jack resisted the urge to wiggle away from Father's touch. He knew what was coming—more questions, then certainly unwanted advice. Jack would do whatever he could to end the conversation before it could reach that point.

Sure enough, the moment they stepped foot outside the counthouse, Father pulled Jack to the side of the small structure, where Jack had once teased Gwynna by snatching her bonnet. How long ago that now seemed. How much had happened since then.

Once they were alone, Father faced him with a hesitant whisper. "Jack, tell me you do not know more about what has just occurred between Merrick's girl and Mr. Pinnick."

Jack averted his gaze. "Very well. I know nothing more."

Father's tensed expression did not ease. "Why do I not believe you?"

"Perhaps because you are not as thick as Mr. Pinnick?"

Father did not appear amused, raking his hands through his hair. "So you do know more. Tell me then, was what Mr. Pinnick said about the girl true?"

Jack stuck his tongue in his cheek, trying to buy more time before he had to answer the question. But he soon realized, the longer he waited to respond, the more the truth slipped out from his hesitance. "I suppose, a fraction of what he said held the truth."

Father's mouth parted in shock. "The girl stole the gown and—"

"No, no." Jack shook his head at once. "No, she would never stoop to such a thing, Father. She borrowed the dress from a friend and attended..." His words trailed off at Father's narrowed eyes. Blast. Jack had revealed too much of what he knew about Gwynna. "I mean, I assume as much..."

His weakened correction did nothing to throw Father off his scent. "Jack, do you...Have you and that girl—"

"She has a name, Father," Jack interrupted with a pointed gaze. "It is Gwynna. And she is certainly not a girl."

Silence pulsed between them, and Father's eyes widened. Now Jack had done it. There was no escaping the truth now.

"The rumors are true then?" Father asked.

Jack blew out a breath between pursed lips. "Rumors?" he questioned, a last-ditch effort to feign innocence. He knew about the rumors. It was impossible to work at a mine, to live in Society, even to walk down the street and avoid hearing rumors about oneself and others.

"They've been spreading around the mine for weeks." Father leaned forward, his words barely audible. "You have fallen in love with a bal maiden."

Jack raised a hand to his brow, shielding his eyes. Hearing the words aloud solidified his feelings for Gwynna even more. How he longed to be with her. How he longed to share his life with her, even with the world's disapproval. But he and Gwynna could not be together. There was too much for her to lose.

Father's next words muffled as he rubbed his fingers against his lips. "I thought you were in love with Amy. Not the girl—Gwynna," he corrected.

Jack blew out a heavy sigh. "No, I do not love Amy." That was merely another relationship he'd effectually ruined.

A few days before, he'd caught Hugh and Amy leaving in their carriage. Amy had avoided him like an illness ever since her declaration of love, and Hugh had told Jack they were to leave straight for Bath.

"I do not blame you, Jack," Hugh had said, uncharacteristically solemn as they stood away a good distance from the carriage holding Amy. "My sister has always had fanciful ideas. She thought you inviting her to Cornwall was a significant sign of your love for her."

Jack had leaned forward, speaking in an earnest whisper. "I am sorry to have hurt her so terribly. That was never my intention."

"I know. But I think it best if you do not return with us to Bath. At least not for a fortnight or more."

Jack had accepted at once, but as the carriage pulled away, Jack had finally understood the significance of Hugh's request. Jack could no longer return to Bath. And he could not remain in Cornwall, being so near to Gwynna.

"I never meant to encourage Amy along with her feelings," he said, coming back to the present as he spoke with Father. "But that is precisely the reason she and Hugh left early."

"So…will you be joining them in Bath?" Father asked.

"No, I will go to London instead," he responded. After all, it was his only option. London, where he had no home, no family, and no friends. It was still the better alternative, for at least he knew in London, he would not happen upon Gwynna.

With Jack's words, Father looked away, but not before Jack witnessed the disappointment flashing in his eyes. He clearly did not wish for his son to leave, and truth be told, Jack was loath to depart, as well. But what choice did he have now?

"I take it that fine shade of purple on your face is from Hugh then?" Father asked next.

Jack softly touched the tender bruise on his cheek. "No. This was courtesy of Travers Merrick."

Father sniffed out a mirthless chuckle. "Trust you to fall in love with a woman whose father's strength surpasses your own."

Jack nearly smiled despite himself. It *was* his fault. Gwynna had warned him her father was not to be crossed.

A moment passed by in silence, then Jack looked up as Father shook his head in astonishment again. "How on earth could this have happened, Jack? A bal maiden, of all women."

His critical words and the culmination of the last few weeks threatened to shove the last of Jack's patience over the edge of the cliff it was perched upon. But he couldn't allow his own frustrations to bruise the tentative relationship he'd finally formed with his father.

He raised a steadying hand and spoke with measured breaths. "Can you really be so surprised, Father? You have seen the strength of these miners and maidens, alike. One cannot help but admire them. And Gwynna, she's simply..." He trailed off, shaking his head. What could he say to describe the woman? She was...perfect.

"I see your point, son, but admire and love are two very different emotions."

Jack let out a quiet groan. "I am not in the mood to be lectured today. Heaven knows I've berated myself enough these past few weeks to last a lifetime."

"But, I...How did you...I don't..."

"I cannot answer your questions with any more logic than you could summon now, Father. I don't know how it happened."

That was a lie. Jack knew full well how it happened. He'd been witness to this remarkable woman's strength, positivity, and goodness, and without Society to judge him, he'd fallen in love with her. Her stamina at the mine, her ability to end the ferocious fight between maidens, her defense and protection of herself and her loved ones—all of this simply poured nourishing water on his already flourishing feelings. She was *everything* to him.

And he'd given her up.

The realization of what he'd done—what he was willingly living without—weighed down upon his shoulders, lowering his defenses. He stared at the walls of the counthouse, its brown, cracked wood as splintered as his heart. "I do not know how I fell for her," he whispered. "But I do know that I am completely lost without her."

Father didn't respond.

"You needn't worry, though," Jack said, predicting the reasoning behind his silence. "I will not marry her and taint the Trevethan name." He spoke the words with derision. How anyone could even think Gwynna—Gwynna, of all people—could taint a name was beyond him.

"Actually, I was not concerned over that matter."

Jack's gaze darted up to meet Father's.

"I was merely wondering if you would remain in Cornwall if you *did* marry her."

"If I married…" Jack blinked. What was Father even doing asking such a question? Marriage between Jack and Gwynna was out of the question. Father would never approve. Mr. Merrick would never approve. *Society* would never approve. Gwynna would be giving up her family—not by Jack's choice—and would be put in the forefront of a judgmental Society. How could Jack do that to her?

And yet, Father's question echoed incessantly in his mind until he answered. "I would not leave Cornwall, no. We would make a home, a life here together." He forced away visions of the two of them waking up together, having children together, growing old together. Those images would only make his heartache all the greater.

Father appeared thoughtful for a moment. "And you care not about her class?"

Jack's brow furrowed. "Of course not. She is a better woman than most ladies of the upper class."

Father rubbed his chin thoughtfully, and Jack paused. "Why do you ask such questions? Do you wish for me to marry her?"

His own question was meant out of jest. And yet, a smile tugged at one side of Father's mouth. "If this woman will get you to stay in Cornwall…who am I to stand in the way?"

CHAPTER FIFTY-ONE

*J*ack gaped. He'd expected words of warning, even a harsh reprimand. But support? Encouragement, even?

Father must have noted his confusion, for he took a step forward, his eyebrows raised high. "I have not been blind to the change that has come over you these last few weeks, son. Your desires to improve the mine. You...you speaking with me more. I assume that I have Gwynna to thank for all of this and more."

Jack looked away, but he could not deny the truth. Gwynna had changed him, and only for the better.

Father continued. "At any rate, I am the last person on earth who has any right to instruct you on any matter, least of all whom you choose to wed. Had I raised you or been the father I ought to have been, perhaps I'd have more of a right to do so."

Humbled by the statement, Jack lowered his eyes. How often had he thought Father was attempting to control his life? How often had he longed for an acknowledgement of the man's neglect? The ever-present tension across his shoulders eased to a barely discernible nudge.

"I am certain I needn't tell you how difficult your life would be if you attempted to mend the gap between gentleman and bal maiden," Father continued. "Society would spurn you. Gossip would abound. Old friends would turn." Father paused, focusing intently on Jack. "But if that is the only reason that is stopping you from marrying her, know that there is one place you will always be welcome—one place that will always be yours. And that is Coffrow Place."

Jack swallowed the emotion rising within him, unsure of how to respond to such acceptance. "Thank you, Father" he said with a nod.

They shared an uncomfortable look, then Father cleared his throat. "At any rate, based on the bruise Mr. Merrick has given you, I assume my approval is not what is stopping you from requesting Gwynna's hand in marriage at this very moment."

The thought of proposing to Gwynna lifted Jack's heart, but he quelled his rising hope. "No, indeed. Mr. Merrick has told me that I would tear their family apart if I pursued her further. Her parents could quite possibly refuse to see her any longer, and I cannot ask her to do that simply to marry me."

"Has she said she is unwilling to make such a sacrifice?"

Jack kicked away a stone with his boot. "No. But what person would willingly do so?"

Father reached forward with a look of amusement, placing a hand on Jack's shoulder. "Son, if there is one thing I learned from growing older, it is that when a man assumes what a woman is thinking, more often than not, he's wrong." He smiled. "Either way, it seems to me that you ought to allow Gwynna the choice to decide her own future."

Jack pulled his eyes to the sea shining in the afternoon sun. From his viewpoint at the upper cliff, only the top half of the engine house was visible. Smoke puffed out from the red chimney and disappeared into the blue skies. He tried to distract himself with the sight, but Father's words dug deep into his mind. *Allow Gwynna the choice.*

Jack knew she loved him. But was it enough to upend her life and marry him? Or had she been relieved to learn that he was leaving Cornwall, for she would no longer be beholden to the gentleman who'd wrapped up his life so keenly next to hers? His chest tightened at the thought.

"Just remember one thing, son," Father said, releasing his hand from Jack's shoulder and walking past him. "You *both* have every right to be happy."

His footsteps retreated, and the counthouse door closed behind him, but Jack hardly noticed. He was too preoccupied with the memory produced from Father's words.

Be happy, Jacky. You have no reason not to be.

Mother would say that to Jack every time she saw him scowling. For years, he'd pushed the words aside, for he had every reason *not* to be happy. He had neither of his parents. He'd been sent to live with distant relatives. He'd numbed his pain with multiple vices. His life was in shambles with no joy or love to patch it up.

Until he met Gwynna. With her, he had the chance to begin again. He could be happy, more so than he ever had been before. Was he truly so foolish as to risk losing her now, after all they'd been through, after the love they'd found with each other?

He would never ask for her to choose between him and her family. But if Mr. Merrick changed his mind, if he accepted Jack's love for Gwynna, perhaps the next obstacle could be eradicated? The very thought of meeting with Mr. Merrick again caused more fear in Jack than he cared to admit, but then, he'd never forgive himself if he didn't try. Besides, Gwynna was worth the risk.

With a determined step, he stormed around the corner and toward the counthouse door. He reached for the handle, but it swung away from his grasp. Mr. Merrick's fierce glower greeted him.

"Mr. Merrick," Jack said, taking a few steps back. He eyed the man's pale face, his courage fleeing. "Should you be walking around with your wound?"

Mr. Merrick didn't respond. He hobbled over the threshold and closed the door behind him with his good arm, all without removing his eyes from Jack.

Jack, however, could not maintain such a stare. He glanced to the heather swaying in the soft breeze. It's carefree dancing mocked Jack as he veritably trembled in his boots.

"I'd like to have a word with ye, Mr. Trevethan, if ye wouldn't mind."

Jack swallowed. "Yes, sir." He fought the urge to shift his body away. He was fairly certain Mr. Merrick wouldn't hesitate to injure his other arm by putting Jack in his proper place—away from Gwynna.

"Me daugh'er tells me ye 'elped the other miners after ye brought me up," Mr. Merrick said, his scowl remaining. He stood at the same height as Jack, so why did Jack feel so much smaller?

"Yes, sir. I did."

"I supposed ye were down there simply to ease me dislike of ye."

A horse's whinny from the rotating whim sounded behind Jack. He longed to turn around, if only to ease the pressure he felt under Mr. Merrick's gaze. But he wouldn't cower any longer. If Mr. Merrick was to see Jack as the honorable gentleman he was attempting to be—the man who loved Gwynna more than his own life—then Jack needed to prove as much, firstly by being honest.

"I went down there first for the sake of your daughter," he said. "I know your family has suffered a great loss with the death of your son. I could not live if she suffered even more with your own passing."

Mr. Merrick shifted his wounded foot with a barely discernible flinch. "I suppose I ought to thank ye then. As well as for your 'elp with that cakey Mr. Pinnick and his gawky fizzog."

Jack nodded, his lips pulled in with humility. Mr. Merrick had expressed his gratitude. That had to be a step in the right direction, hadn't it?

But Mr. Merrick's eyes hardened again. "Ye know my opinion of ye, Trevethan. That ain't changin'. But I must ask ye this. Did ye take advantage of me daugh'er?"

Jack straightened, responding without hesitation. "No, sir. I did not, nor would I ever. Nothing occurred that night beyond a shared kiss."

Mr. Merrick's expression remained unchanged. Did he not believe Jack? "Sir, I—"

"Gwynna was up all night cryin' after what ye said to 'er," Mr. Merrick interrupted.

Jack's chest burned with regret. He'd behaved so foolishly, so selfishly. How could he have hurt her again? "I did not intend to harm her, sir. I sincerely wish only for her happiness, and I knew that could not be possible if I asked her to sacrifice her relationship with her family for my sake."

Mr. Merrick blinked, the deep crease between his brow running into his dirt-covered cap. "Ye be tellin' I that that be the reason ye left 'er?"

Jack nodded. "Yes, sir."

"Not 'cause she be a maiden?"

"No, sir," Jack answered firmly. "I care not about her status. All I care about is her. I...I love her, sir. And I wish to marry her." He paused, bracing for another blow from Mr. Merrick. This one would be sure to render Jack utterly lifeless on the ground.

And yet, Mr. Merrick remained still. "Ye know what marriage will bring to ye both—most 'specially to me daugh'er. Your kind won't take to 'er."

"Perhaps some of them will not. But I know others who will

accept her for the remarkable woman that she is—most importantly myself."

Mr. Merrick hardly seemed convinced. Afraid of losing the
man to disbelief, Jack rushed on. "I know our life together will
not be easy, sir. But I know my love for her is true. I will devote
my life to her, to make her happy and to keep her safe. You have
my word."

The miner drew in a deep breath, his lip twitching. "And...
and do I 'ave your word that I'll still be able to see me Gwynny
once ye be married to 'er?"

Jack's chest overflowed with hope and understanding as a
vulnerability flashed in the man's eyes. "That, sir, I can
guarantee."

Mr. Merrick's jaw twitched, and he looked away as he
nodded. "Then I will leave the decision up to 'er." His eyes
flicked back up to Jack's, and he pointed a menacing finger at
him. "Don't ye be a disappointment to 'er." Then he walked back
to the counthouse without another word.

Jack remained still for a moment, overcome with a rush of
emotions. Father approved. Mr. Merrick agreed. Now what
would Gwynna say?

He approached the edge of the cliff, catching sight of her as
she spalled below. Her cheeks were ruddy, her bonnet dangling
down her back and tied at her neck. Sweat tinged her brow, and
the scanty rag around her head held all but a few stringy strands
of hair down the side of her face. She looked tired, exhausted
from the emotions and strain of the day. But her freckles spoke
of the enjoyment she received in having the sunshine blanket
her cheeks. Her focused, amber eyes were witness to her determination and resolve to see through all of life's hardships. And
her lips held the promise of the words he so longed to hear her
say— needed to hear her say.

His heart flooded with love. He'd never seen her so beautiful.
And he couldn't wait a moment longer to speak with her.

CHAPTER FIFTY-TWO

*G*wynna's spirits sank as Jack walked resolutely toward her. Was Mr. Pinnick back, this time with the constable? Or had something happened with Papa? Her worries swiftly turned to uncertainty, however, as she took in Jack's determined steps, his eyes focused unwaveringly, unmistakably, on her.

"Be somethin' wrong?" she breathed as he stopped directly before her.

"That depends." He glanced around them. Kerensa and a few other maidens had stopped to stare, so he lowered his voice. "May I speak with you for a moment?"

His brow pursed with concern, and Gwynna's heart stirred with worry as to what had happened. "Is it me father?"

"No, I just...I would like to speak with you."

Gwynna stared. If nothing was wrong with Father, then why did Jack speak with her at all? With each moment that passed, more maidens stopped to gawk at the man who really had no business conversing with a bal maiden. "If your father catches ye, sir. If *my* father catches ye..."

His eyes caressed her face. "We needn't worry about them any longer."

What was he going on about? Had Jack spoken with them? Had her father...

Hope crept toward her like the remains of an approaching wave, just enough to wet the sand around her dried heart, but not to make any lasting impression. She couldn't put herself through this anguish again. She couldn't risk hoping for a marriage with the man she loved, only to have it ripped from her hands. Father would never approve, and Jack did not wish to be shackled with a bal maiden.

The eyes around them bore into Gwynna's nerves. Kerensa looked on in confusion, the younger girls near the cobbing table paused to watch them with curious tilts to their heads, and two elderly maidens whispered disapprovingly in their direction. They all knew. They'd all heard the rumors—that Gwynna had had a secret tryst with the mine owner's son.

Perhaps that part was true—but she'd also fallen in love with the mine owner's son. And yet, that love had been destined to fail from the start.

"Gwynna..." Jack began.

But Gwynna could not listen to what he had to say, nor could she bear the heartache of speaking with him any longer. Tears pricked her eyes, and she backed away, dropping her hammer to the ground. "I can't," she whispered. "I can't be doin' this again, sir."

"But, I—"

She ignored his words, spinning on the heel of her boot and taking a running leap over the hand barrow, bolting in the opposite direction of the engine house, of the mine, and of Jack.

"Gwynna, wait!"

He followed after her, his boots scuffling against the hard dirt, but she didn't stop. She needed to escape the invasive eyes and judgments, but mostly, she needed to escape the fruitless love she had for Jack. She rounded the ridge of the cliffside, fleeing down the pathway as the intrusive noise of the mine began to fade from her ears, replaced with the loyal waves rushing below.

"Gwynna?"

Jack's voice sounded right behind her. Why did he pursue her if he did not wish to be with her? Did he come to apologize? To defend his choices once again? Gwynna didn't halt until his hand wrapped around her wrist, holding her back.

She spun around, wrenching her arm from his grasp. "No, Jack! I cannot do this any longer." She wiped the moisture trailing down her cheeks. Curse these tears. She'd promised herself she wouldn't cry anymore over the man.

Wheal Favour was no longer in sight, but Jack's pleading brown eyes remained. "I will leave then," he said, his voice soft with no sign of a threat. "If you truly wish for me to, I will turn around and leave Cornwall this moment."

Sorrow pressed the remaining joy from within Gwynna at his promise. His eyes did not sway from hers, but she could no longer maintain his stare. With sunken shoulders, she faced the sea, unraveling her gloves from her hands. She attempted to gather strength from the clear waves, the water nearly green in the sunshine, but her will weakened. To live a life without Jack would be to live but half a life.

"Gwynna, do you wish for me to leave?" he asked again.

"How could you ever think that I wish for ye to leave?" she asked, her voice breaking. "Ye know I wished for a life with ye. But I ain't be enough for ye."

His brows pulled together, and he took a step forward, stopping when she shook her head and backed away.

"That couldn't be further from the truth, Gwynna. You are more than enough for me. You always have been."

She refused to believe his words. They were too wonderful to be true. "If that be so, then why did ye just…give me up?"

"Because I…" He broke off with a sigh, his shoulders falling forward. "Because I feared I would be asking you to give up too much to be my wife."

She listened with a guarded heart, rebuffing any rising hope as he continued.

"I would be asking you to accept the rumors and criticism that would surely assail us if we married. And I thought, if we were together, that your father would no longer wish to see you. But now I see how I erred. I was deciding our future for us both instead of taking your own opinion into account." He lowered his chin. "But I am finished behaving so selfishly. Thanks to our fathers, I've come to realize something I should have realized long ago—that you have the right to choose your own path in life."

Gwynna held her breath, waiting for what he said next. Then she paused. "Our fathers?"

A half-smile raised his lips. "I spoke with them both, only moments ago."

Her mind raced. "And what did they say?"

"Well, my father told me he would approve of any woman who managed to keep me in Cornwall, and your father…he gave his permission for us to wed."

Gwynna frowned. "This ain't no time to be teasin', sir."

He raised his hands. "I swear to you, I do not jest. He gave us his blessing." He paused, his eyes staring off. "Well, it wasn't so much of a blessing as it was an outright threat to treat you well, but it was his permission all the same."

Gwynna listened in disbelief, questions swirling about her mind. "But what could ye 'ave said to 'ave 'im change 'is mind 'bout ye?"

Jack gave a soft laugh. "Oh, I don't believe his opinion of me has changed in the smallest degree. He is certain to still despise me. But his approval does not have to do with anything I said. It has everything to do with how much he loves his daughter. He wants you to be happy, just like I do."

She looked up at him, fear still holding her back. Father approved then, *and* Mr. Peter Trevethan—a fact that she would believe when she saw it with her own eyes. But if Jack was speaking to them about marriage, did that mean that he...

"Jack, why were ye talkin' to 'em 'bout marriage?"

He took a step toward her. This time, she did not retreat in response. "I believe you already know why, Gwynna." He drew in a deep breath. "I've been a coward. Afraid of loving another person because I did not love myself. But you taught me how to move past my childhood wounds, how to hold on to the things I love the most." His features softened. "And the thing I shall hold tighter to more than ever, the thing I will never let go again, is my love for you."

The breath rushed from Gwynna's lungs. He loved her? He *loved* her?

"I care not about our differences in classes," he said. "I care not what the future holds, so long as we can face it together." He paused, swallowing. "But I will not make the decision for you. You know how I feel, and what I desire. So tell me, do you still wish for me to leave Cornwall?"

He looked away, wincing as he clearly braced for a rejection. But that was the last thing Gwynna wished to do. With a heart near to bursting, she reached forward, dropping her makeshift gloves to the ground and bringing her hand to rest against his cheek. "No, Jack. I don't wish for ye to leave Cornwall. I wish for ye to be with me."

A smile broke out on his lips. "Then...will you marry me, my love?"

Through tears, she nodded. "Yes, Jack. I will."

In an instant, his arms wrapped around her. "I love ye," she whispered in his ear, and he held her all the tighter. She returned his embrace, willing herself to remember the curves of the muscles in his back, the feel of his nose burrowing into her hair, the musky scent of his cologne infiltrating her senses.

After a moment, he pulled back just enough to look into her eyes, brushing her disheveled strands of hair from her brow. "The road before us will not be easy, Gwynna. But I can assure you that I will do everything within my power and beyond to ensure you have all the happiness you deserve."

"I know ye will," she said, and she *did* know.

"And if you are so very concerned with Society accepting you, you needn't worry," he said. "Even if we are shunned, I'm certain the Hawkinses will accept us."

Gwynna smiled. She could only imagine Sophia's elation at no longer having to sneak Gwynna into balls and parties.

"Furthermore," he continued before she could say a word, "I am certain others will come around to the idea of our marriage eventually, too. But until then, we needn't attend any social gatherings unless you wish to. And as for you being a maiden, I know you shall have to leave the mine once you are married, but there are other ways to be of use there. Father will surely be willing to listen to any ideas for improvement that you may have."

He barely took a breath as he began again, his eyes bright, his words becoming more animated. Gwynna listened in a delirious dream as he painted the picture of their future together, each word more glorious than the next. "And even if you cannot spall at the mine, I'll purchase a hammer and a barrow of ore for you. You can practice any time you wish in the gardens of Coffrow Place." She rested her hand on his chest, laughing again at his excitement. "But we do not have to live there if you do not wish it. We could purchase a little cottage by the sea or build a house near your parents. And you must banish the idea of altering anything about you. You will keep your Cornish tongue, your strength of a maiden, even your dress if you wish." He eyed the tattered, faded brown fabric with a strained smile. "After all, it-it is lovely." Her laughter drifted out to the sea at his teasing, and he smiled in response. "And living in our little cottage, I could then become a miner. And we could—"

"Jack." She pressed a soft hand to his mouth. A tremor ran through her at the feel of his firm lips against her skin. "Ye needn't convince me further. I already said I'd marry ye. 'Sides, ye'd be a terrible miner."

Laughter erupted deep in his chest. "You are right about that."

"Awful," she said with an amused shake of her head. "But worry not. I don't need ye to be a miner. And I don't need ye to change for I. So long as ye won't be embarrassed when I use the wrong fork at dinner and spill cherry tart on your fine clothes."

He pulled her closer, his hands at the small of her back. "I could never be embarrassed by you."

"Even if I ne'er be a fine lady, just a bal maiden?"

"*Just* a bal maiden?" Jack instantly sobered. "Gwynna, you are fierce when facing adversity. You forgive and encourage and love better than anyone I've ever known. And you are a loyal and devoted daughter and sister. My mother..." His voice broke, and he cleared his throat. "My mother would have loved you." They shared an emotion-filled smile before he continued, cupping one side of her face with his hand. "I do not need you to be a fine lady. I do not even need you to be Miss Joanna Bell." He winked, wiping a trailing tear from her cheek. "I need *you*, Gwynna Merrick. And if you are *just* a bal maiden, then that is more than enough for me."

Gwynna's chest swelled with love. Slowly, she slid her right hand up his waistcoat and along the side of his neck. He closed his eyes, drawing in a deep breath as she weaved her fingers through his hair. Finally, she raised on the tips of her toes, and their lips met in a kiss that spoke measures to the love they felt for each other, and the hope they shared for the future.

Jack pulled her in closer, lifting her feet off the ground and swinging her around in circles until she broke from his lips with a laugh. "Jack! Ye be goin' to toss us off the side o' the cliff!"

He laughed in return, stopping as he settled her feet on the pathway. He leaned down, placing another firm, stirring kiss on her lips. "May I request one thing from you," he asked mumbling against her mouth, "now that you've agreed to marry me?"

She pulled back, lacing her fingers behind his neck. "What be that then? Learn to read?"

"No—although I would be more than happy to help in that regard, should you desire it. I merely ask that you never attempt an upper-class accent again. Yours is abysmal."

Her mouth dropped open with feigned dismay. "I ain't be that bad at cuttin' it up, sir. 'Sides, I'd wager ye'd be just as awful doin' a fitty Cornish accent."

"Oh, no. That be more 'an easy, ye know." He spoke as if each word was too long to fit in his mouth.

She laughed, shaking her head. "That be awful."

He chuckled. "Then we shall work on both of them together, yes?"

She sighed, perusing every inch of his face with eyes she knew reflected the love in his own. "Together. I do like the sound o' that."

And when their lips met again, the word was sealed between them with love and abiding happiness. For when they were together, life didn't seem so difficult after all.

EPILOGUE

$\mathcal{G}$wynna stretched her arms out over her head with a deep, contented sigh. She couldn't remember having ever had a more peaceful night's rest. Her pillow was far more comfortable than she recalled. And the mattress.

Her eyes fluttered open, welcomed by the sight of cream and green colored bed hangings draped above her and light peeking in from a large window nearby.

This wasn't her room.

With a gasp, she sat upright. The bed bounced up and down as she eyed the marble hearth, oak wardrobe, and floral tapestry along the smooth, wooden flooring.

"What is it?" mumbled a voice from beside her.

Gwynna whirled around, facing Jack as he blinked dazedly, still lying on the bed.

Jack. They were in his house. *Their* house. Her heart thumped for a different reason as she eyed his bare torso. His physique flexed as he ran his fingers through his ruffled hair.

"Are you well?" he asked, rubbing the sleep from his eyes.

"Yes. I didn't mean to wake ye. I just...forgot where I be."

He smiled, propping his hand beneath his head. "Well I hope you aren't too disappointed."

She followed the curve of his smile with her eyes. "I be anythin' but disappointed to be with ye, Jack."

He stretched his arms toward her, and she responded to his beckon in an instant. Resting on his shoulder, she nuzzled her nose into his neck with a contented sigh.

"Did you sleep well?" Jack asked, kissing the top of her head.

"Lyin' in bed with me new husband? How could I not?"

He hummed in approval to her response.

She rested her hand on his chest, holding still as his heart tapped against her palm.

Her new husband.

She never thought the day would come. After the bans had finally been read, Gwynna and Jack were brought together under the bonds of matrimony only the day before at a wedding that far exceeded their expectations.

She and Jack had predicted a small affair with very little support, but the church had been filled to its capacity with both classes. Mama was there with cheerful smiles, and even Papa had managed a congratulatory nod toward Jack, a promise of an improved future between them.

The others in attendance had cast lingering, curious glances toward the bride and groom, but most of them ended the ceremony with well-wishes for the couple. Sophia had continually wiped away her never-ending stream of tears—"I am just so pleased for you both!"—and even Kerensa, whom Gwynna had told everything to a few days before, was there to share in Gwynna's joy.

"So, now that ye be a lady," Kerensa had said with a teasing smile, "will ye be dressin' *I* up in fitty gowns to find me a gent?"

They'd shared a laugh, and Gwynna had promised to do her best in that regard. Though she didn't think another gentleman existed like Jack. He was an anomaly. A wonderful, charming, devilishly attractive anomaly.

She traced her finger down the contours of his chest, smiling to herself at the blessing she had to call Jack her own.

"What would you like to do today, my love?" Jack asked.

She moved her head back along his arm, studying the shadow of facial hair that had grown overnight across his chin and jawline. "Have ye any suggestions?"

He thought for a moment. "We could visit the mine with Father. I believe he will be overseeing the construction of the shelters you've suggested."

Excitement fluttered in her stomach. Mr. Trevethan had listened to every word she'd said about what was needed at the mine and saw to their fruition almost instantly.

She still couldn't fathom the kindness he'd continually shown her.

"I will forever be indebted to you for bringing my son back home, Gwynna," he'd said, pulling her aside after the wedding. "You are a remarkable woman. Now you keep giving me those improvements for the mine, and I'll make you my top advisor."

He'd finished with a wink, but Gwynna had seen the truth in his eyes. She *would* continue to suggest improvements. Her parents and friends at the mine had helped her their whole lives. Now it was time she returned the favor in a way they'd be happy to accept.

"Or," Jack said, drawing her attention back to him, "if you'd rather not consider working at all today, we could take a walk by the sea. Go into town. Call upon the Hawkinses or your parents, as your father is still home with his injury. Whatever pleases you."

Gwynna smiled. "I say we do all of it...Although, I'd be quite content sittin' in bed all day and doin' absolutely nothin'."

"That does sound tempting." Jack slipped his arm out from behind her, propping his fist under his head as he rested on his elbow. "Although…not as tempting as something else I had in mind."

A sly smile slipped across his lips. Gwynna's breathing hitched as he leaned toward her, placing his free hand along her jaw and pressing a warm kiss to her lips. A deep, contented sigh escaped her, and she wrapped her arms around his neck, pulling him closer so his affection might never end.

Jack had never experienced such joy than he had the last few weeks he'd spent in Gwynna's company. He never knew such happiness, such a love could exist. How grateful he was to have her in his life.

After pulling themselves out of bed and away from Coffrow Place, they spent the day together, making calls, visiting family, and simply enjoying each other's company.

But Jack's favorite moment of the day was now, as they stood on the cliffside overlooking the sea, enjoying the last of the summer sunsets. From their viewpoint, Penharrow stood far in the north, and Wheal Favour, a distant shadow in the south.

The early autumn wind trailed its long fingers across the sky, creating wispy clouds above the horizon that was tinted a soft orange. A long stretch of gray clouds settled just above the sea, hiding half the sun as it took its final dip into the tranquil waves.

Gwynna sighed beside him, a soft smile on her lips. Gone was her brown, tattered dress, replaced instead with a light blue that flowed softly in the wind. A navy blue ribbon—a simple gift he'd given her before their wedding—weaved throughout her curls at the crown of her head. He was happy to see her without that rag holding her hair back, though he smiled at the memory of it.

He moved behind her, wrapping his arms around her middle and resting his chin on her shoulder. "Are you happy, my love?"

She leaned into his embrace, resting her head against his. "Yes. More so than ever before."

"Is that because you didn't have to spall today?"

Her cheek moved against his as she smiled. "Per'aps." She twisted around in his arms, sliding her hands around him and encircling his waist. "Or per'aps it be due to the love I 'ave with ye."

The sun lit the golden flecks in her amber eyes, glinting like copper. "Then that is well with me," he whispered, pressing a soft kiss to her brow. "For there is nothing more I wish for than to make you happy."

"Ye do, Jack. Ye do make me 'appy."

He held her tighter. "And you will stay just as happy? You will be able to withstand the world before us, no matter the trials that come?"

She grinned. "Ye know me, Jack. I can handle anythin'. As me father says, ain't nobody stronger than a miner's daugh'er."

Jack tucked a stray curl behind her ear. "Or a bal maiden."

"Just so," she said, resting against his chest. "And with ye, I can do anythin'."

They held each other in a soft embrace, the shadows of Penharrow and Wheal Favour standing as faraway sentinels for them both, keeping watch over the outside world as Jack and Gwynna faced the setting sun together, no longer afraid of what the future held.

Thank heavens the bal maiden had fallen in love with the mine owner's son.

THE END

AUTHOR'S NOTE

While there is not a great deal of information on bal maidens during the early 1800s, I did my best to accurately research their fascinating lives. I really could fill the next hundred pages or so with the inspiring stories I've learned about these remarkable women, but I promise to keep it short. (Short for me, at least.)

First, allow me to say that while I have tried to be accurate, this book is a work of fiction, and a hundred percent precision is fairly impossible to achieve. Even so, I relied heavily on my research to ensure my representation of bal maidens was as truthful as possible. Below, I've included a few fascinating details about bal maidens and their incredible work at the mines —mines that would not have been profitable without them.

To begin, it's important to know the meaning behind their name. *Bal* is the Old Cornish word for 'mining place.' The earliest known reference to the name *bal maiden* was recorded in 1819. As this book takes place in 1815, I was a few years short. For clarity's sake, I did use the full name *bal maiden*, though I did my best to use simply 'maiden' whenever possible.

Next, I want to make it clear that while some women

despised their work at the mine and the hardships they suffered there (like the minor character, Kerensa's sister, Mary Hocking), there *were* maidens who took great pride in their work, like Gwynna and Kerensa. These were a special sort of women—resilient and independent.

Alongside the older maidens, the children were also an integral part to any working mine. Often, I toyed with the idea of saving them at the fictional Wheal Favour, or not including them at all. However, their hard labor was commonplace and used to benefit their families as a whole. I didn't feel it accurate to champion them too greatly, and I felt it would be an injustice to them to exclude them completely, but I like to imagine Gwynna and Jack doing their best to ease the burdens these children suffered.

Another fact I feel is important to point out is that each mine had its own unique way of processing ore. The dressing floor—where the maidens saw to the ore—as well as where the shafts were located were both mainly dependent on the mine's proximity to running water. I based the exterior of Wheal Favour off of Towanroath Engine House from Wheal Coates. However, my shaft is located inside the engine house, while the Towanroath shaft is located just outside of its engine house.

The state of the actual tunnels also varies from mine to mine. Some mines may have, indeed, been boiling hot, dry, and rocky belowground, but my mine—based on others around Cornwall—was cold, damp, and muddy. Alongside that fact, some maidens were provided with shelters, while other were not. The decision depended greatly on the funds available, the year and progress of mining, and the decisions of the owners, agents, and captains.

Now, one of my favorite things about writing this book was being able to pull actual events from history and tweak them into fitting with my story. One of these events was the brawl that took place on the beach between the two opposing mines' maidens. This actually did occur, although the fight was over a shipwrecked box of figs instead of wine and navigational tools. The scuffle also lasted over two hours—which just proves the stamina of these women, to be able to fight for so long after a full day's work at the mine!

The other truths I pulled upon were far less charming and reveal just how harsh their lives really were. The story Gwynna told of the mine captain tipping a pitcher of water over a girl's head was also accurate, as well as the sobering truth of a young woman being crushed to death by the working gears—just like how Gwynna obtained the scar at the back of her arm. The tragic story of Gwynna's aunt was also based on facts. Many women were assaulted by gentlemen though they were often not believed and were subsequently punished because they were thought to be lying. The last horrifying fact: most of the maidens' deaths at the mines were not even recorded by the captains.

Finally, to end on a slightly lighter note, I want to share a few more quick facts. Some mine surgeons *did* take a ridiculously long time to arrive and help injured miners, spallers *were* considerably skilled to be able to break the ore down in a single blow, and stockings *were* used to fashion makeshift gloves. I also read accounts that did say they could hear the boulders on the seabed above the tunnels in the mine, and while some maidens were fine working in service, others greatly resisted the idea early on. There were so many other things I wished to add, like the nightly shifts held at the mine and the protective legwear and armwear worn by the maidens to avoid injury, but alas, my page count did not permit it.

Is it just me, or are all of these little details incredible? The lives these women must have led...I can't even imagine it. Thank you for making it through this author's note with me and taking the time to humor my passion for these inspiring women. I hope to one day in the future write a whole series based on them! Until now, I'll just stay busy by reading more about their extraordinary lives.

If you enjoyed "Near the Ruins of Penharrow," please consider leaving a review. And if you'd like to receive the latest news about my future novels, sign up for my newsletter. I always share newly released and discounted clean romance novels, as well as fun polls, quotes, and giveaways. My newsletter subscribers are also the first to see sneak peeks and cover reveals!

Curious about a certain aspect you read in Near the Ruins of Penharrow that I didn't mention? Contact me! I'd love to answer any questions you might have regarding the book, bal maidens, Cornwall, or my writing.

Make sure to follow me on Facebook (for more clean romance deals) and Instagram (for photos of my travels to the UK and more).

I hope to connect with you soon!

Deborah

ACKNOWLEDGMENTS

I always think that each new book will be easier than the last. Unfortunately, this has never been the case. *Near the Ruins of Penharrow* has been a constant mental battle for me from the start, one that I couldn't have won without the help of so many of the people I love and admire!

I first need to thank the many writer friends I have made who opened their hearts—and homes—and invited me along to their writing retreats this year. Mindy, Arlem, Anneka, and Shaela— because of your generosity, I was able to find the encouragement and stamina to push through my doubts and finally finish this book. Plus, the retreats were just amazing. So. Thanks for that, too.

As always, I need to thank my editor, Jenny. Even with the world going crazy, you still managed to make my story shine. Thank you for your help!

I'm also insanely grateful for my author friends who have helped so much with this book. Kasey Stockton, Joanna Barker,

Esther Hatch, Arlem Hawks, Martha Keyes, and Ashtyn Newbold—whether you helped in the beginning brainstorms or by beta reading this book, I couldn't have done it without you!

A special thanks goes to my sisters and mother for always reading my books. Thanks also for letting me go MIA from all family gatherings during my deadlines. Heh.

Last, I want to thank my husband for humoring me with all our late night chats and brainstorms about my books and painting my office. You're the best. Even when you correct my Americanisms…

ABOUT THE AUTHOR

 Deborah M. Hathaway graduated from Utah State University with a BA in English, Creative Writing. As a young girl, she devoured Jane Austen's novels while watching and re-watching every adaptation of Pride & Prejudice she could, entirely captured by all things Regency and romance.

Throughout her early life, she wrote many short stories, poems, and essays, but it was not until after her marriage that she was finally able to complete her first romance novel, attributing the completion to her courtship with, and love of, her charming, English husband. Deborah finds her inspiration for her novels in her everyday experiences with her husband and children and during her travels to the United Kingdom, where she draws on the beauty of the country in such places as Ireland, Yorkshire, and her beloved Cornwall.